HOOSIER DADDY
a heartland romance

Ann McMan and Salem West

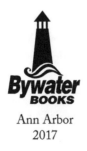

Bywater BOOKS

Ann Arbor
2017

Print ISBN: 978-1-61294-099-1

Bywater Books First Edition: January 2017

Printed in the United States of America on acid-free paper.

Hoosier Daddy was originally published
by Beddazzled Ink, LLC
Fairfield, CA in 2013

E-Book ISBN: 978-1-61294-100-4

Cover designer: TreeHouse Studio, Winston-Salem, NC

Bywater Books
PO Box 3671
Ann Arbor MI 48106-3671
www.bywaterbooks.com

*This book is lovingly dedicated to the memory
of our late fathers, Jimmie and Eddie—
and to our mothers, Wanda and Rebecca.
Thank you for the lessons you taught us.*

"For now we see through a glass, darkly;
but then face to face:
now I know in part;
but then shall I know
even as also I am known."

— I Corinthians 13:12

Chapter 1

This is the city: Princeton, Indiana.

I live here. I'm a Hoosier.

This small prairie town is the heartbeat of America. It's populated by wholesome, corn-fed men and women: folks who work all week from sunup until sundown, then clean up and go to church on Sunday.

Hoosiers are hearty types. They listen to country music, eat fried catfish at the VFW, and never apologize for buying cars that can pass anything but a gas station.

I work for Krylon Motors—now Ogata Torakku of Indiana. We make trucks. I'm a line supervisor, and I carry a clipboard.

I am from here, but not of here. I fit, and I don't fit. I'm a riddle in three syllables.

My name is Jill Fryman.

My friends call me Friday.

Ogata, or OTI, as we call it, is new to the landscape of southern Indiana. The manufacturing plant had formerly been one of the flagship production facilities in the stalwart Krylon Motors family. The Princeton plant produced Krylon's top-selling Outlaw pickup—the lauded "Workhorse of the American Farm." But when the economic tsunami hit back in 2008, Krylon became one of its biggest, Midwest casualties. The undercapitalized, debt-ridden mainstay of the American automotive industry bravely soldiered on for a few more years before collapsing like a rusted-out Yugo. Unlike GM, Krylon wasn't too big to fail; it was just the right size.

Fortunately for me and the other 4,499 employees who had grown up and grown old walking its production lines, Ogata Torakku swept in at the eleventh hour and acquired the Princeton plant lock, stock, and impact wrenches. It wasn't so much the people of Krylon that Ogata wanted: it was the Outlaw—a gas guzzling, monster pickup that managed to lead the pack in domestic sales for six years running. Outlaws were only built at the Princeton plant, and when Krylon went under, we were the pick of the litter in its corporate selloff.

None of us really knew how much our lives would change once the Ogata transition team arrived. We had heard rumblings that they planned to implement the same "lean manufacturing" techniques that were common in other Japanese transplants—and even that they might move production of their all-new Mastodon monster truck to Indiana. Beyond rumor and innuendo, we knew next to nothing else, and the transition was probably still weeks away. Most of us were just grateful to still be getting a paycheck, and we took things one day at a time. That pretty much summarized life in a small, Midwest manufacturing town.

Wednesday started out like any other hot, summer hump day. People were already cranky because of the record heat and humidity, and that made them even more inclined to fuss about all the overtime hours and extra shifts that kept getting tacked on after the sellout. I did notice, however, that the loudest complainers had little to say when they picked up their fat paychecks.

I'd already been on the line for nearly six hours without a break, and my bladder was about ready to burst. I knew it had been a bad idea to drink that whole Bigg Swigg of Diet Dr. Pepper I picked up at Huck's on my way in that morning, but hindsight is always 20/20. I waved my clipboard at Buzz Sheets, the shift foreman with a bad comb-over, and pointed in the direction of the bathrooms. He made a face at me, but I walked off the floor anyway. Enough was enough. I'd been on my feet since seven, and I needed a break.

When I came out of the stall, I heard a familiar voice.

"Hey, Friday? You get a new watch?"

My best friend, T-Bomb, was pointing at my wrist with a crinkle cut French fry.

I looked down at my watch. I'd lost my Ironman at Grammy's a few weeks ago when I took it off outside to give my dog, Fritz, his biannual bath. When he broke loose and hightailed it for the cornfield

2

across the blacktop, his leash snagged the stack of towels—and my watch—and drug them halfway across the front yard. I didn't see Fritz for about three hours, and I never found my watch again, either. And I'd been working so much that I hadn't had time to get to Walmart to pick up a new one.

"Nope." I held up my arm. "It's Grammy Mann's vintage Seiko."

T-Bomb bit off half of the drooping fry. "Thought so, that one's awful girlie."

Terri Jennings had a way of boiling things down to what Grammy Mann called brass tacks. She'd been that way since grade school. And she never eased herself into any situation. She just sort of exploded in the middle of it. That's how she got the nickname "T-Bomb." She was one of only a handful of people at Krylon who officially knew I was gay. But that was not really saying a lot. Around here, it was kind of hard to tell the difference.

I tore off a sheet of paper towel and dried my hands.

"Why do you always eat in the bathroom? It's gross."

"It ain't that bad unless one of them corn crackers drops a bomb." She snagged another fry out of her red-and-white gingham boat. "Besides, if these dip wads gave us more than ten minutes to pee and eat our lunch, I wouldn't have to bring my food in here." She dipped this one in ketchup before shoving it into her mouth. "Ain't this what you managers like to call multitasking?"

A stall door banged open. Luanne Keortge squeezed out, struggling to hike her drawers up over her mountainous backside. She was already chewing on the end of a Viceroy. You couldn't smoke inside the building, so Luanne was multitasking, too. Every time I saw her with a cigarette, I worried that her hair might go up. Luanne tended to use a lot of product.

"You got that shit right," she rasped. "I have to decide whether I want to use my breaks to eat or smoke. Ain't got time for both—the wait in the cafeteria is always too damn long." She glanced at T-Bomb. "How the hell do you always get Pauline to make those? She won't do 'em for nobody else."

Pauline Grubb ran the company cafeteria, and you pretty much got whatever she felt like serving. Ten minutes to load your tray and wolf down your meal didn't leave a lot of time for discussion or argument.

T-Bomb paused in mid-chew. "Hell, I don't know. It's probably because I didn't marry her idiot son."

It was hard to argue with that. Pauline's boy, Earl Junior, was thirty-eight years old and still lived at home in his mother's doublewide out on Peach Bottom Road. There had never been an Earl Senior, as far as anyone knew. So there was pretty wide speculation about how Pauline actually ended up with her big, dim-witted son. There were lots of theories, however, and I had my money on Buzz Sheets. Earl Junior's hair was already starting to recede, and his comb over was beginning to look eerily familiar. Earl Junior worked for Krylon as a stock chaser. He pretty much sucked at it, and I'd had to follow behind him more than once to move skids loaded with lug nuts out of harm's way. Most of us just learned to shrug things like that off, and accept that Earl Junior was "special." That was generally the safest way to ensure that you'd get something other than creamed corn for lunch if you ate in the cafeteria.

Luanne headed toward the door. "See you back on the line, T-Bomb."

I felt like an underachiever, since I was only in there to take care of one kind of business.

"You goin' out after work?" T-Bomb asked. "Bobby Roy's band is playing tonight at Hoosier Daddy."

Hoosier Daddy was our local bar. Most of the people who worked at Krylon stopped in there after their shifts for codfish hoagies and five-dollar pitchers of Old Style. Bars in Princeton pretty much fell out along company lines. That meant if you worked at Krylon, you went to Hoosier Daddy. If you worked at Millennium Steel, you went to Pood's. If you weren't sure where you belonged, you just looked at the types of trucks that filled up the parking lots. Outlaws meant it was a Krylon hangout. F-150s meant Millennium.

"I don't think so."

"Why not? You got some PBS telethon you can't miss?" T-Bomb tended to get louder when she didn't get her way. "Come on. You gotta quit hiding."

"I'm not hiding."

"Well, what do you call it, then? Nobody's seen hide-nor-hair of you outside this place for the last month. All you do is sit at home with your dern nose buried in some old book that nobody's ever heard of."

"I've just been busy."

"Busy my butt. You ain't done nothin' since you caught Misty Ann hittin' it with Jerry behind that stack of Duelers in the warehouse."

I looked around the bathroom to be sure nobody else was there. "Would you mind lowering your voice?" I ducked down and took a quick peek beneath the stall doors.

T-Bomb was still eating her fries. "Relax . . . there ain't nobody else in here."

"Well, hold your voice down, anyway. I don't want everybody knowing intimate details of my business."

"Girlfriend, nobody in three counties gives a twat about your business—including you. And if you don't start using it, it's gonna dry up and drop off." She wiped some ketchup off her fingertips. "I told you that Misty Ann was trash. She's nothin' but a steamin' pile of hot mess. You know she was just using you to get back at her husband for knocking up that Turpin girl again."

I hated it when T-Bomb was right. Misty Ann Marks and I had only been "seeing each other" for a few weeks when I caught her with Jerry. I felt ridiculous for allowing myself to get involved with a straight woman. I always knew it wasn't going to go anyplace. Still, I was amazed by how much it unsettled me when I discovered that she had just been using me, too.

"It was never serious," I said. I knew how lame it sounded as soon as the words left my mouth.

"Yeah? And if a frog had wings it wouldn't bust its ass hoppin' around." She ate her last French fry and tossed the empty paper boat into the trash can. "Donnie has the twins tonight, and I want to go out. It would do you good to go, too."

"Look, I'm just busy, okay? Don't bug me."

"I think you're a lying chicken shit. You need to get back out there."

"Why? So I can humiliate myself all over again?"

T-Bomb picked at something lodged between two of her front teeth. "Nith twy. Ith not nobody'th fault that thu make bath thoithes."

"What on earth did you just say?" I asked. I glanced down at my watch again. "Never mind. If I don't get back out there, I'll have to let Buzz grab my ass again so I won't get docked for being late."

She'd finished picking her teeth, and was examining whatever it was that she'd removed. I headed toward the door.

"I'll wait for you in the parking lot after work," she called after me. "You can go for just *one* drink. It won't kill you."

"Whatever," I said. I headed back out to the line.

The rest of the shift was pretty uneventful. Five minutes before I was ready to hit the time clock to punch out, Buzz caught up with me.

"Got a second?" he asked.

I sighed. Buzz's "got a second" questions always meant I was in for at least another hour of work.

"Not today, Buzz. Okay?" I tried my best to look stern. "I'm dead on my feet and I really need to get out of here on time for a change."

Buzz ducked his head closer to me. That always made my skin crawl—and not just because he was a letch and thought that every woman in the plant wanted to get horizontal with him. Actually, vertical would be more accurate. Buzz seemed to prefer upright hookups—usually back in the warehouse, where I saw Misty Ann with Jerry Sneddin. He also wore too much cheap cologne. The smell of it, mixed in with the ambient odors of axle grease and polymer, was probably giving us all some kind of nasty lung disease that would someday get Krylon nailed in a class action lawsuit.

I took a step back. He didn't take the hint, and moved in closer again.

"There's a film crew here from Channel 14. They need to shoot some footage for a piece they're doing about OTI maybe bringing the Mastodon here."

If OTI decided to ramp up the Princeton plant to produce the Mastodon—a quad-cab, full-size pickup with thirty-two inch Sidewinder radial tires and a twin six engine—it would mean adding four-hundred-and-fifty jobs, and four hundred million to the local economy. This would be a real boon to the tri-state area. It made sense that a TV station from Evansville would come here to get the story.

"Oh, come on, Buzz. Where's Jerry?" Jerry Sneddin was supposed to be our plant's public affairs rep. But the only thing public about Jerry's job was the affairs part. The rest of the time, he was pretty much M.I.A. "I've covered his butt the last three times we've had reporters in here. I'm beat, and I wanna go home."

"Jerry cracked a molar on a pistachio nut, and he's out getting a crown."

"A pistachio?" I waved a hand toward the line. "Who in the world around here has time to eat pistachios? Most of us don't get long enough breaks to use the restroom."

Buzz was losing patience with me. "This won't kill you, Fryman. You're always mouthing off with that high and mighty women's lib crap about not getting promotions, then when we ask you do step up and do something, you complain about it."

"That's a load of b.s., and you know it. When have I not done anything you've asked me to?"

"You mean besides today?" he asked.

What a first class dick Chiclet, I thought. "Okay. Fine. But this time, I expect to get paid for the overtime."

"Management don't get overtime pay. You know that."

"Oh, really? Last time I checked, I still punched a time clock."

He shrugged. "You wanna dance to the music, then you gotta know when to fold 'em."

"What is that supposed to mean?"

"It means you play the cards you're dealt, without biting the hand that feeds you."

I sighed. This was going no place fast. "Whatever." I looked around. "Where are they?"

He gave me a crooked smile that was more like a leer.

"They're setting up on the catwalk." He jerked a thumb toward the rafters. "Just give 'em the standard spiel. You know the drill."

I ought to. I'd pretty much been doing this ever since the OTI buyout got announced.

"Okay. I'm on it."

Buzz reached a stubby hand down to his crotch and adjusted his package. "From your mouth to god's little acre."

I rolled my eyes. "You're a sick man, you know that?"

"Come on, Fryman . . . anybody who hits it with Misty Ann Marks can't be all that picky."

"Screw you, Buzz."

"Any time. Any place."

I gave up and turned away from him. He wasn't worth the effort it would take to convey my contempt.

"You know where to find me when you change your mind," he called after me.

I knew all right. Behind a dumpster, where he belonged.

I headed for the maze of catwalks that ran along the rafters above all the production lines. They crisscrossed the plant in complex patterns that reminded me of Grammy Mann's tatted lace dresser scarves. The Channel 14 film crew was already in place. It wasn't hard to identify the talent. She looked like she'd just walked out of a display window at Ann Taylor. I had no idea how she'd managed to climb up here in those shoes, or where they found a hardhat big enough to cover her hair. She smiled when she saw me and held out her hand.

"Are you Jill? I'm Mona Simms. Mr. Sheets said you'd be giving us the tour. I can't thank you enough for doing this. I promise we won't take too much of your time—we just need some background footage."

I nodded. "No problem. What would you like to see?"

Mona waved a handful of sculptured nail enhancements toward the assembly line below. "This looks pretty good . . . lots of bright color and big action. How about we set up right here?"

We were standing over the part of the line where a massive orange hoist lowered an Outlaw cab and bed onto a preassembled chassis. For people unfamiliar with the process, this was the most exciting part of production because it's where the actual truck came together.

"Okay," I agreed. "How can I be helpful?"

"If you don't mind, I'll just ask you some general questions while Mitch, here, films what's happening."

I nodded.

Mona signaled the cameraman to start recording. "So can you describe what we're seeing below?" she asked me, in a perfectly modulated, prime time voice.

"Sure," I said. "This is the part of the manufacturing process where three major assemblies converge. The cab and bed are lowered onto a preassembled chassis by robotic arms. This particular unit is called the marriage machine, because it's where the body meets the chassis."

"Amazing," Mona added.

Behind Mona and Mitch, Luanne Keortge was ambling toward us on the catwalk. Luanne was a quality control inspector, and part of her job was to walk the line. I signaled to her to wait up for a few minutes. I was pretty sure we'd be moving along to another area soon.

"If you look closely," I continued, "you can see how precisely the cabs and beds align with the vertical chassis bolts. This machine is actually the most sophisticated piece of equipment in the plant."

"The colors are just sensational," Mona cooed. "How many different trucks do you make here?"

"That's a good question. With all of the possible combinations of options—engines, transmissions, tires, colors, interior appointments—I suppose you could say that we make more than sixty thousand different kinds of trucks."

"Incredible." Mona actually sounded impressed.

Below us, another cab and bed were seamlessly lowered onto the next chassis rolling forward on the line.

"What the hell?" Mitch blurted. "Get a load of this!" He leaned over the railing, trying to get a better angle on something.

I looked over at him. "Hey. Don't do that . . . it's dangerous!"

Mona pressed a hand to her mouth. She looked at me, then back toward the marriage machine. I had a sinking feeling. It would be just my luck to have a six million dollar robot pick this precise moment to drop one of the cabs.

"Oh, sweet Jesus." Luanne had plainly seen whatever went wrong, too. "That sure as hell ain't on my checklist." She hit an emergency stop switch on a pillar. The production line below us ground to an immediate, seven-thousand-dollar-a-minute halt. The momentary silence was deafening. Then I could hear laughter drifting up from someplace.

I looked down. Two naked figures were writhing around in the bright yellow bed of an Outlaw Super Duty 450. I was stunned. From the tattoos, I could tell that the woman was Misty Ann, and the man on top of her was none other than our company public affairs rep, Jerry Sneddin.

Mitch laughed. "I suppose this is one of the sixty thousand options?" he asked between snorts. "I could make a fortune with this shit on YouTube."

Luanne huffed her way over to stand next to him. "It sure is, honey." She pulled a pack of Viceroys from her shirt pocket and tapped one out. "But I can't say as I agree with puttin' the stick shift in the back door."

I sighed and took another look at Misty Ann. T-Bomb was right. I'd been hiding long enough.

Tonight, I was heading for Hoosier Daddy.

Chapter 2

Bobby Roy's band wasn't playing until nine o'clock, so the crowd was getting warmed up at the Karaoke machine. Normally, this was just too painful to endure for long. Nothing could make the Belgian beer in my belly turn sour faster than listening to a bunch of drunken auto workers croak their way through a cover of "Friends in Low Places" on open mike night.

I sat at a table in the back with T-Bomb and Luanne, trying to ignore the obnoxious music—and everything else. When I first walked into the bar a little bit after six, it was clear that everyone there had already heard the story about Jerry and Misty Ann. A chorus of "Sixty-Thousand Options!" roared out above the music. I tried to just roll with it and not show how much it annoyed me. That was generally the best way to get people to drop it and shift their attention to somebody else's misfortune.

I was well into my second beer when I caught a whiff of something nasty and took a look around.

"What's that smell?" I raised a hand to my face.

T-Bomb pushed her chair back and took a look beneath our table. "Oh, hell. It's that damn Lucille."

Lucille was an ancient and morbidly obese Jack Russell Terrier. *He* was a fixture at Hoosier Daddy. Nobody really understood why Aunt Jackie, the owner and bartender, had named her unneutered male dog Lucille. Lucille was famous for his bad disposition and his righteous gas. The crankiness probably came from two decades of being called by a girl's name. The epic flatulence was the likely result of being fed a steady diet of fried codfish.

"Sweet Jesus." Luanne fired up another Viceroy and blew a plume of smoke across the table to try and mask the odor. "That damn dog is a menace. Shoo him outta here, T-Bomb."

T-Bomb looked beneath the table again. "Too late. He's already settled-in. Now he's lickin' his business."

"Oh god." I finished my bottle of Stella. I didn't go much for the beers Aunt Jackie kept on tap. "That's an image I didn't need."

"Why?" T-Bomb nudged me on the arm. "Remind you too much of Jerry and Misty Ann?"

Luanne snorted. "Hell. From what I saw, Lucille is hung a lot better than Jerry Sneddin."

T-Bomb shook her head. "Cheap bastard couldn't even spring for a motel."

"Hey? A bed's a bed, right?" They laughed and clinked mugs.

I'd had just about enough of this. "You two aren't helping, you know that?" I looked around the bar. Aunt Jackie was nowhere in sight. I pushed back my chair. "Want another round?"

T-Bomb held up their empty pitcher. "You don't have to ask me twice."

I got to my feet and noticed that someone else had taken the stage—a woman I'd never seen there before. She was petite, with short dark hair and a dusky-looking complexion. She did not look like a local. There was a small round of whoops and hollers when she picked up the microphone.

"Hey, everybody," she said. Her voice was low and kind of husky sounding. "I'm kind of new at this, so don't be too hard on me."

A man who appeared to be there with her was setting up the Karaoke machine. When he had it ready, he gave her a thumbs-up and returned to his seat. The slow, sexy music started. After all the country caterwauling, it turned just about every head in the place.

"*Come to me, my melancholy baby,*" she crooned. "*Cuddle up and don't be blue. All your fears are foolish fancies, maybe. You know, honey, I'm in love with you.*"

You could have heard a pin drop in that joint.

I'd heard that old Ella Fitzgerald song about ten thousand times in my life, but never before had it affected me the way it did right then. It was like her voice had reached right down inside me and wrapped itself around all of my internal organs.

12

And I noticed that my external organs were acting pretty impressed, too.

"Every cloud must have a silver lining. Just wait until the sun shines through. Smile, my honey dear, while I kiss away each tear. Or else I shall be melancholy too."

"Who in the hell is *that?*" Even T-Bomb seemed impressed.

"Her name's El-somethin'," Luanne said.

"L?" T-Bomb asked. "What the hell kind of name is L?"

"E-L," Luanne said. "Like El DeBarge."

"Oh." That seemed to make more sense to her.

"She and that good lookin' fella, Tony, are from New York," Luanne added.

I looked down at her. "New York?"

Luanne nodded and made a face. "UAW."

Oh, man . . . It figured. She was a union rep. And she'd have to be hot, too. And straight. I needed to get out of this damn town.

The crowd in Hoosier Daddy was having no problem with her performance.

El kept on right on crooning. She noticed me as I stood against the back wall, and I about dropped the empty pitcher and my Stella bottle. Her voice actually faltered for a moment, but she caught up to the machine pretty quickly.

"Come to me," she sang. I thought I might slide right down the wall and join Lucille on the floor beneath our table.

"All your fears are foolish fancies . . . you know, honey, I'm in love with you."

What was happening to me? I sank back down onto my chair.

T-Bomb was staring at me. "What the hell is the matter with you? You look white as a sheet."

I tried to shrug it off. "I think I just need something to eat."

"Well, here." She shoved a plastic bowl full of redskin peanuts toward me. "Eat some of these, and we'll order some fries."

I looked down into the bowl. It was mostly salt and skins.

"I think I need some air," I said.

Luanne was staring at me. "Honey, what you need is better sense. You stay away from them agitators."

"What are you talking about?" I was mortified that she might have noticed my reaction to the woman singing.

"I saw the way you were staring at her. It was like somebody looking at their first Eldorado."

T-Bomb slapped her on the arm. "Good one, Luanne. Eldorado. Just like El DeBarge."

I'd had just about enough of these two.

"Excuse me?" a husky voice asked. "I saw that you ladies were dry. I took the liberty of asking Aunt Jackie what you were drinking. May I join you?"

El was standing next to our table, and she was holding a fresh pitcher of Old Style and a frosty bottle of Stella Artois. I looked up at her. She had smoky gray eyes. I opened my mouth to say something, but no sound came out. Up close, she looked like a slightly older version of that dark-haired actress from those *Northern Exposure* reruns that used to be on A&E in the mornings. What was her name? Janine . . . something.

El continued to stare at me, and I realized that she was waiting for me to say something.

Thankfully, T-Bomb was enough like Mother Nature to hate a vacuum.

"Hell, yes, honey. You put that pitcher right down here in front of me and pull up a chair."

Luanne ground out her cigarette and shook her head. Her blood-shot eyes were fixed on mine. "Don't say I didn't warn you." She held up her empty mug. "One more, then I gotta head back over the river."

T-Bomb punched me in the ribs. "What's the matter with you? Get her a chair."

"I'm sorry," I stammered. "Let me get you a seat."

El finished pouring Luanne's beer. "Thanks." She looked at me. "My name's El."

Turner. The actress's name was Janine Turner. El looked enough like her to be her older sister.

I stood up and grabbed hold of the table to steady myself. "I'm Friday . . . Jill."

"Friday Jill?" she asked. "That's unusual."

"No. Just Friday. Jill."

"Friday? Jill?" she asked again.

I sighed. "Jill. But my friends call me Friday."

She smiled. I thought I might pass out. "I'm Eleanor. But my friends call me El."

"Like DeBarge," T-Bomb cackled.

El looked at her. "Just like DeBarge. Although I never understood why Janet Jackson married into that family."

"Me neither," T-Bomb was holding up her mug. El filled it.

"I always liked her on *Good Times*," Luanne chimed in.

"She was a sweet girl before she started acting so slutty." T-Bomb sucked the foam off the top of her beer.

Luanne nodded. "Wardrobe malfunction my ass."

"Hey? I say, if you got 'em, flaunt 'em."

"You sound just like Jailissa."

Jailissa was Luanne's teenage daughter.

"What's your last name?" T-Bomb asked El.

El shrugged and sat down on the chair I pulled up for her. "It's complicated."

"Complicated? How?"

"It's just hard to pronounce, so I don't use it much."

"Hell." T-Bomb scoffed. "That don't make you unique around here."

El smiled at her. It was like somebody turned all the lights on. "Wanna bet?"

"Sure." T-Bomb took the bait. "Let's hear it."

"It's spelled R-Z-C-P-C-Z-I-N-S-K-A."

T-Bomb and Luanne exchanged blank looks.

"How the hell do you say that?" they asked in unison.

"Zhep-sin-ska," El replied.

"Zhep-what?" T-Bomb asked.

"Zhep-sin-ska," El repeated.

"I see why your friends call you El," I added.

El looked at me. "Be my friend, Friday Jill?"

Luanne cleared her throat. It sounded more like she was hacking up a hubcap. "How the hell many points do you get for a name like that in Scrabble?"

El laughed. "About two hundred and eighty—if you had two Z's and were lucky enough to hit a triple word score."

"You sound like you done that a time or two," Luanne observed.

"I do all right," El replied. She was looking at me again.

Maybe I was wrong about that straight part . . .

"We were just gonna order some fries," T-Bomb blurted out. "You hungry, El?"

El smiled again. "As a matter of fact, I think I am."

"Working a room will do that to you," Luanne said.

El looked right back at her. "I guess I don't have to tell you that I'm here with the UAW?"

Luanne shook her head.

"News travels pretty fast around here."

"Well, singing Karaoke ain't the best way to keep a low profile, now is it?"

El laughed. "Touché." She held out her hand. "Nice to meet you, Miss . . ."

Luanne sighed and shook her hand. "K-E-O-R-T-G-E. *Kerr-chee.*"

"Her name's complicated, too," T-Bomb added. She was getting pretty toasted. It was looking like I was going to have to call Donnie to come and pick her up. "I'm Terri Jennings. But my friends all call me T-Bomb."

"Why?" El asked. She shook hands with T-Bomb, too.

Luanne tapped out another Viceroy. "Hang around long enough and you'll figure it out."

El looked at me again. "Sounds like a plan to me."

I stared back at her without saying anything. Then I realized that saying nothing was like saying everything. I dropped my gaze to the table. "So . . . are we going to order some food, or not?"

"Not for me." Luanne took a long drag off her cigarette. "I gotta head back across the river. Bessie Greathouse is comin' by to let out the seams in Jailissa's dress. I swear . . . that girl had to get them boobs from her daddy's people."

T-Bomb looked Luanne over. "Her daddy's people must a had good legs, too."

16

"Kiss my ass. I got these damn cankles from thirty years of standing up for ten hours a day."

T-Bomb held out her left palm and drew the fingers of her right hand back and forth over it in small arcs. "Know what this is?"

Luanne just glared at her.

"It's the world's smallest violin playing 'Who's Sorry Now?'"

I looked at Luanne. "Is Jailissa in the competition again this year?"

Luanne nodded. "That crown had better be hers this time. Jay's gonna go postal if another one of them Hortons walks away with the title."

"What competition?" El asked.

"Pork Day, USA," T-Bomb explained in a reverent tone. "Being crowned Miss Pork Queen is the biggest honor of the year over in Albion." She took a big swig of her beer. "Them pork chop sandwiches are mighty good, too—as long as you don't bite into a bone."

"Really?" El asked. Then she looked at me again. Her eyes weren't just gray. They had little flecks of green and gold in them. "Guess it's a good thing I gave up bones a long time ago."

Ever had beer shoot out your nose? Yeah . . . well, that's what happened to me, and it was mortifying. I sat there coughing and trying to sop it up off the front of my shirt. This was going from bad to worse in a hay wagon. My face felt hot. I hastily got to my feet and nearly stepped on Lucille, who expressed his displeasure by growling and breaking off another ripe one.

"I need to go to the restroom. Excuse me." I hurried away from the table before anyone could notice that I was blushing.

What the hell was my problem? I was acting like a teenager with her first crush. No . . . it wasn't a crush. I was reacting to El like a sow in heat. It had to be some kind of extreme response to seeing Misty Ann in the back of that truck with Jerry. I needed to get out of there before someone else noticed and doused me with a bucket of cold water. I was just lucky that T-Bomb was feeling no pain. I'd never hear the end of it if she got a clue.

The bathroom at Hoosier Daddy left a lot to be desired. One of its two stalls was permanently out of order, and only one light bulb in the ceiling fixture ever worked. Still, for all that, it was clean and

17

didn't reek as badly of smoke and spilled beer as the rest of the place. Unfortunately, I couldn't say the same thing about my t-shirt. It was sticking to me like a pile of last night's mashed potatoes. All I wanted to do was try and rinse it out so I wouldn't smell like a brewery on the way home.

I walked to the sink and took a good look at myself in the cracked mirror. There I stood—Wayne and Sissy's little girl. Even in the half-light, you could tell that I had my father's reddish hair, and the same cowlick on the left side. But in every other way, I took after my mother's people—tall, square featured—with what Grammy Mann called an ample bosom. And as the condition of my t-shirt now suggested, I had the same unfortunate propensity for ending up in colossal messes. That was pretty typical of the women in my family, too. My mom was fond of telling people that my nickname actually came from Friday the thirteenth, because I had so much bad luck.

I sighed and turned the water on. I reached over to pull a couple of paper towels out of the wall dispenser and realized that it was empty . . . as usual. Aunt Jackie stored the extra towels on a shelf behind the only working toilet. I went into the stall to retrieve some more, and snagged the end of my shirt on the changing station. I stood there wondering for the thousandth time why Aunt Jackie even had a changing station in here. I couldn't remember a single time I ever even saw a baby in this joint. Lucille had to be the bar's closest thing to a child, and nobody would ever try to lift his fat butt up.

I tried to tug my shirt free, but only succeeded in getting it more stuck. The cartoon Koala bear kept smiling up at me from the trap door of the changing station, seeming to suggest that being stuck there was something I should be enjoying. I was about ready to give up and tear myself loose when I heard the restroom door open and close.

"What are you doing?" a voice behind me asked.

It was El. I knew it without turning around.

"I'm stuck," I explained. I hoped she'd decide to leave me alone and go back out into the bar. Why had she followed me in here?

I thought of a hundred reasons why she was here, and none of them felt safe. I gave my t-shirt another frustrated tug. Still no dice.

It wasn't budging, and, apparently, neither was El. She stood behind me in the stall. The tiny space filled up with the scent of cucumber and melon. Even though it was a nice change from the omnipresent odors of smoke and stale beer, it was making it impossible for me to think straight. I felt like all the hairs were standing up on the back of my neck.

"Can I help?" El asked. Her voice came from right behind me. I thought I could feel her breath.

"No!" I erupted. "Sorry. I'm a little on edge tonight."

She laughed. "I noticed." She leaned against the open door of the stall. "Do I make you uncomfortable, Friday Jill?"

What do you think? I wanted to ask. "Well, right now, I'm kind of at a disadvantage." I tugged at the hem of my shirt again. "It's hard to put your best foot forward when you're being held captive by a Koala Kare changing table."

"I'll have to take your word for that one."

"I'm sorry about this . . . did you need to use the bathroom?"

"Not really," El drawled. "I followed you."

Oh, god. This was going from worse to catastrophic. "You did? Why?" Oh, that was good . . . now I sounded as dim-witted as I felt.

El sighed. "Why don't you let me help you get unhitched from that contraption so we can talk?"

She wanted to talk? "Talk about what?" I tried to shift my body around so I could at least see her face.

"Well, for starters, I suppose we could talk about whether you're as interested in me as I seem to be in you."

I slammed my knee into the toilet paper dispenser. "Jumpin' Jehosophat!" I was seeing stars—and not just from the pain in my kneecap.

El grabbed the backs of my arms to help support me. "Are you okay?"

I was doubled over in pain. "Do I *look* okay?"

"Hang on a minute." She maneuvered herself around so she could close the stall door and give us more room. "Oh, this is *ridiculous*. Why don't you just take that thing off?"

I was incredulous. "My shirt?"

"No . . . your *pants*." I heard her sigh. "Of course your shirt. Then we can get it out of that damn thing."

"I am *not* taking my shirt off." Although I had to admit that the idea of doing so was already shooting excited little text messages out along my . . . extremities.

"Well then stand still and let me try to loosen it."

"I've been trying to loosen it. It's not budging."

"Move over so I can reach it."

I rolled my eyes. "Move over where? On top of the toilet?"

"We need to open the damn thing."

"I agree—but there isn't room in here."

El was pretty much pressed up against me by this point, and there was no way I was going to ask her to leave.

"Desperate times call for desperate measures." She moved in even closer and reached around me with both arms. "I'll hold onto this, while you pull the tray down."

I was seeing stars. "Um. El?" I managed to croak.

"Yes?" Her voice was coming from someplace right beside my ear.

"That's not my shirt."

"It isn't?"

I shook my head.

"Oh," she said. "My bad."

I noticed that her hands didn't move right away. I turned my head to look at her. In the dim light of the stall, her eyes looked . . . scared.

Scared?

"What are we doing?" I asked. I had no idea where my coherence was coming from.

She gave me a shy-looking smile. "Trying to get you unstuck?"

I thought about Misty Ann and Jerry. Getting unstuck was exactly what I needed. But getting involved with a stranger who also happened to be an organizer for the UAW was not the way to do it. What I was on the verge of doing with El was exactly the opposite of getting unstuck. Grammy Mann would say it was like jumping from the pot into the fire.

I opened my mouth to say as much, but El decided that maybe words weren't really what we needed right then. She was moving in to present a different kind of argument. Just when her lips connected with mine the walls of the stall started shaking. It took me a few seconds to realize that it wasn't an earthquake—it was someone yanking on the door.

"Will you two hurry the hell up," a gravelly voice demanded. "I have to tap off."

Luanne. *Of course.*

El and I leapt apart like we'd been caught . . . making out in a bathroom stall.

"Oh, damn . . ." she whispered.

"Oh, Judas . . ." I replied.

We pushed and jostled against each other in the tiny space trying to right ourselves, alternately banging into the changing station, the toilet paper holder, the shelf loaded with paper towels, and each other. We were slamming into each other like bumper cars at the county fair.

"Oh, sweet Jesus." Luanne had had enough. "Just open the damn door and get out here. This ain't my first rodeo."

El sighed and finally managed to turn herself around. I looked down and noticed that at some point during our tussle, I had managed to yank my shirt loose from its prison. The bad news was that it was now ripped nearly in half. Great. Like I didn't have enough problems.

We managed to pry the door open and squeeze ourselves out of the tiny stall.

Luanne stood there like Judge Judy, chewing on one side of her lower lip.

"There were no paper towels," I started to explain.

Luanne didn't say anything. I could tell that she was staring at my shirt. I was doing a bad job trying to hold it closed—it was torn open about halfway up to my armpit.

She looked at El. "In a hurry, were you?"

El looked confused. Then she glanced down at my shirt. Her face turned bright red. For some reason, that made me feel a little bit better.

"Not that it would make any never mind to you," Luanne continued. "But your partner out there has a couple of live ones cornered by the Keno machine." She jerked a thumb toward the bar. "He asked me to send you back out there."

El looked at me. "I've got a jacket you can use. I'll go and get it."

Before I could say anything, she pushed past Luanne and hurried out of the bathroom. I stared at the door for a minute before I had the courage to look back at Luanne.

"Go ahead and get it over with," I said.

Luanne was already unfastening the front of her pants. "I got nothin' to say, so I'll just say this. If you want to be the next Misty Ann Marks, there's a bar full of candidates out there who would be happy to accommodate you, and none of them are workin' for the UAW."

"That's not fair, Luanne." She squeezed her way into the stall, so I was talking to her broad back. "I am not like Misty Ann."

Luanne didn't say anything right away. I stood there, stupidly, listening to the sound of her peeing. It went on and on. She must've had a lot more Old Style to drink than I realized. Finally, the toilet flushed.

"Like I said. I got nothin' to say about it. A smart girl like you should have better sense. Here . . ." One of her hands shot out around the half-open door. It was holding a stack of folded paper towels. I took them from her. "Put those up in that dispenser."

I caught another look at myself in the mirror. My hair was a mess. When the hell did that happen? Luanne was right. I should have better sense.

The door to the restroom opened again, and T-Bomb burst in. "What the heck is going on in here?" She handed me a lightweight, tan linen jacket. "El DeBarge said I should bring this in to you."

I took it from her. "Where is she?"

"Hell . . . she laid a patch gettin' outta here. She said you could get the jacket back to her some other time." T-Bomb grabbed hold of the hem of my t-shirt. "What the hell happened to your shirt?"

I sighed. "It's a long story."

Luanne managed to extricate herself from the stall. "Hurry up and pee, T-Bomb. I gotta head back across the river."

"Well if you'd get your fat ass outta there, I might could," T-Bomb replied.

"Are you both leaving?" I asked. This evening had sure not ended up the way I thought it would.

Luanne washed her hands. "I called Donnie and told him I'd drop her off on my way home. He said they'd pick up her van tomorrow morning."

"I told you I was okay to drive," T-Bomb bellowed. "I don't need no damn limo service."

Luanne rolled her eyes and grabbed a paper towel. "Just tap it off and be quick about it." She looked at my reflection in the mirror. "Same advice goes for you, missy."

I gave up trying to defend myself and pulled on El's jacket. It smelled just like her . . . sweet and fresh. Like summertime.

I had a sinking feeling that this one was going to be a tough row to hoe.

"I'll try," I said to Luanne.

She snorted.

"What?" I asked.

"That's what Jay told me twenty years ago when we were sprawled out across the back seat of his daddy's Buick. Nine months later, we got ourselves Jay Jr."

"Well, he ended up being a good provider," T-Bomb pointed out.

Luanne nodded. "And now his baby sister is a true contender for that crown."

Jailissa. Edwards County's best hope for this year's Miss Pork Queen title.

I supposed my odds could always be worse.

Chapter 3

"Why can't I just tie these loose strands off in little knots? It'll be a lot faster."

A couple of months ago, I bought six old oak dining chairs at the antique mall in Haubstadt, and Grammy Mann was teaching me how to re-cane their seats. I was just going to take them to Mrs. Greubel, who used to work at the old Haub House restaurant before it changed hands, but Grammy Mann had a fit about that. She said that Betty Greubel didn't know the first thing about how to cane a chair, evidenced by the fact that when my father accidentally knocked one over at the restaurant, the underside of it looked like a flicker's nest. Apparently, the bottom of the chair was supposed to look as neat and tidy as the top. This philosophy of Grammy's pretty much extended to everything else in her life, too.

"I told you." Grammy shook her head. "You don't do it that way. You weave those loose strands into the next hole and clip off the short one." She was sitting on a low, slat-back chair, holding a dinged-up granite roaster on her lap. She was snapping beans, and this was her shelling chair. Years ago, Grampa had cut the legs off so the back was lower than the front, and the whole thing sat close to the floor.

We were outside on the front porch, since it was so warm inside the house. The box fan Grammy had set up on the dining room table wasn't doing much but blowing hot air around. She said that was a lot like still having Grampa there.

I was really starting to lose patience with this whole enterprise. By the time I had one of these chair seats fixed to her satisfaction, I'd be too old to sit on them.

My dog, Fritz, was sprawled out on his favorite spot at the top of the porch steps, catching some rays of afternoon sun. We spent most of our Sundays with Grammy, doing chores or just sitting on the porch, drinking iced tea and watching the comings and goings at the house across the road. Doc Baker and his not quite wife, Ermaline, lived there and scandalized the neighborhood with their alternative lifestyle. Grammy steadfastly refused to gossip about Doc and his common-law wife, but I noticed that she was always ready to correct you if you got any details wrong when you shared snippets about them with anybody else.

Most people in town were inclined to forgive Ermaline for moving in with Doc, who drove an El Camino and ran a lawnmower repair service. She had once been married to Kenny Purvis, before he found Jesus and started preaching at The House of Praise. There were rumors that Kenny never really bothered to divorce Ermaline, claiming that god's law held sway over the laws of mammon. Nobody was ever really sure what that was supposed to mean, but apparently, it gave Kenny permission to take up with a sixteen-year-old girl from Samsville named Desdemona Jones. Kenny had a knack for attracting impressionable young women, and his flock was mostly comprised of starry-eyed waifs who were known as hoppers, because of their tendency to jump and dance around during services at his church. Frankly, I was surprised that any of them had the stamina to hop. At last count, that congregation had about fifteen children under the age of three, and a suspicious number of them looked a lot like Kenny.

I jammed a piece of reed under my thumbnail and jumped about a foot into the air.

"Damn it!"

Grammy looked at me. "What happened?"

I shoved the chair away and sucked on the tip of my thumb. "I can't do this, Grammy. I can't do anything right."

Grammy snapped another bean and dropped it into her pan. "What do you mean? You do lots of things right. This is just something you can't rush through. It's not like playing with that fancy phone of yours. You have to take your time and be patient."

I didn't reply.

Grammy set her pan down on the porch floor. She smelled a rat.

She knew me pretty well. She ought to . . . I'd practically grown up with her. My mother had TB when I was born, so I lived with Grammy for the first few years of my life, and we'd been best friends ever since.

"What's the matter?" She gave me that look . . . the one that meant I might as well fess up, because she wasn't going to drop it until I did.

I shrugged.

"Jillian?"

I knew I was in for it. Grammy never called me Jillian unless it was really serious. Nobody did.

I had a hard time looking at her. "I met somebody." It sounded lame. Even to me.

That perked Grammy up right away. "Who is she?"

Grammy knew I was gay. It always amazed me that this smart, sassy, eighty-year-old woman could be so tolerant—even curious. She never even raised an eyebrow at my twelfth birthday party, when she caught me experimenting with Donna Steptoe out behind the rhubarb patch. She was totally unlike my parents in that way. Ma and Pop, aka Sissy and Wayne, ran a convenience store across the river in Illinois and were a lot more Midwestern in their approach to my sexual orientation. That meant they just didn't mention it. Ever.

"She's not from around here," I explained. "I met her at Hoosier Daddy the other night."

Grammy looked intrigued by that. "Where are her people from?"

"Some place in New York. I don't really know for sure."

"New York?"

I nodded.

"What's she doing in Princeton?"

I knew it was all going to be downhill from here. "She's with the UAW."

"Oh, honey lamb." Grammy closed her eyes and shook her head.

"I know, I know," I said, before she could tell me I was crazy. "But I only met her the one time, and nothing really happened."

Grammy opened her eyes. "Then what are you all in a swivet about?"

"I'm not in a swivet."

26

"No?" She narrowed her eyes. "Honey, are you fighting in the Scarlet Crusade?"

I sighed. "No, Grammy . . . I'm not having my period."

"Well then, I don't know what has you all het up. If you only met her once and nothing happened, then what's the problem?"

I shrugged.

"Jillian?"

She was doing the name thing again. I gave up. "Okay. Maybe something did happen. Something little . . . and it probably didn't mean anything to her."

Grammy folded her arms. "What was it?"

"We were in the bathroom together, and we kind of . . . nearly . . . sort of . . . almost . . . kissed. *Maybe*."

"Maybe?"

I nodded.

"You're not sure?"

I shrugged again.

Grammy sighed. "Honey, do you remember when you were five, and you saw the sheep in the south meadow making baby lambs?"

"Oh, god." I raised a hand to my eyes.

"There wasn't any 'maybe' or 'almost,' or 'nearly' in that . . . now, was there?"

"Grammy . . ."

"I don't know much about what did or didn't happen in that bathroom, but I can tell by your reaction to it that there wasn't any 'maybe' involved."

In frustration, I picked up a coil of chair cane and lobbed it across the porch. It landed near Fritz and skidded to a stop near the end of his nose. He bolted to his feet and took a desperate look around, as if the long-anticipated alien invasion had finally occurred, and he'd managed to sleep through it.

"Sorry, buddy," I apologized.

"Now tell me more about this agitator, and what on earth possessed you to consort with her." Grammy picked up her roasting pan and resumed snapping beans.

"I didn't consort with anybody."

27

"You said that you only just met her at that bar."

I nodded.

"And you said you were with her in the bathroom."

I nodded. Grammy could have clerked for Matlock.

"And that you kissed her?"

"Well . . ."

"Well?"

"Well . . . technically . . . she kissed me."

"Honey lamb, when a buildin's in flames, people jumpin' out the windows don't stop on the way down to ask who started the fire."

I didn't say anything.

"Well." She snapped another bean in two. It sounded like the crack of a rifle. "I don't much like the idea of you gettin' involved with a union rep. But anybody who can get you to look away from that Marks girl is A-OK in my book." She pointed at me with the end of a cooked string bean. "When are you gonna bring her over here so I can lay eyes on her?"

"Grammy . . ." I was horrified—and panicked. "That's *not* going to happen. I told you . . . it was just the one time and I'll probably never even see her again."

Grammy gave me that look of hers . . . that same one she gave a half-rotted tomato before she tossed it onto the composting pile.

"She's a union agitator, isn't she?" she asked.

I nodded.

She slowly shook her head. "You'll see her again."

I had a sinking feeling. I knew she was right. And, as much as I didn't want to admit it, I was sure this was the only reason El was flirting with me. It was all about gaining access to people inside our plant.

"I can't get involved with her," I said. I was pretty sure I sounded as morose as I felt.

Grammy was still shaking her head. "Didn't you say that a month ago about that Marks girl?"

"That was different."

"Different how?"

"Misty Ann didn't work for the UAW."

"That's true," Grammy agreed. "But she was just as dangerous."

"Not really . . . Misty Ann couldn't get me fired."

"Maybe not. But she sure could get you fired up." Grammy chuckled.

"Okay, okay. I made a mistake with her. I admit it. But it's not like there are a lot of available women around here with good, family values."

Across the road, a car engine roared to life. Doc's bright blue El Camino rolled over the scraggly patches of grass that passed for a lawn and turned out onto the county road. Ermaline waved at us from the driver's side window. She was holding a lighted smoke. There were three mower handles sticking up out of its bed. Business must be good.

We both watched the car grow smaller until it disappeared around the bend near the crossroads.

Grammy sighed and looked at me. "Well." She snapped another bean in half. "My mama always said that if you snuggle up with dogs, you're gonna get fleas."

I resisted a sudden impulse to scratch. My half-finished chair sat there mocking me. It was like the rest of my life . . . not quite right. I needed to make some changes, starting with my job. I'd been working at Krylon ever since college, and it was going no place. I was still punching a time clock and getting passed over for promotions. Working on my MBA was probably a big waste of time. It was clear that all I had to look forward to was another twenty-five years of smacking Buzz's hands off my ass. Maybe it *was* time to look elsewhere—someplace with more opportunity and fewer . . . dogs.

Fritz looked up at me with his soulful eyes, almost like he knew what I was thinking. I felt bad for the slight of comparing him to Buzz and Misty Ann.

I got to my feet. "C'mon, buddy. We need to get going or we'll be late."

"You workin' at the store today?" Grammy asked.

I nodded. My parents ran the S&W Fast Mart that was across the state line in Allendale, and today was the busiest day of the week. Their store was the only place over there where people could go to buy adult beverages on Sunday. Everybody thought my father was a genius when he took over that business.

29

"Ma asked if I'd cover for her today. They have that funeral over in Mount Carmel."

"Buster Collins?"

"Yeah. Pretty sad."

Buster worked at Quick Stop Tires, and had a massive heart attack while he was restocking the Motorcraft filters in the oil change pit. Nobody even noticed he was missing until Mike Scoggins went down there to lube the u-joint linkage on a Ram 2500. It pretty much rocked the whole town. Buster had a pretty young wife and four kids; and he was a volunteer fireman and a deacon at the Wabash Valley Church of Christ.

Even though Ma and Pop had retired to Allendale when they bought the Fast Mart, they stayed pretty involved in the life of the Mount Carmel and Princeton area communities. Pop said it was good for business. I was pretty sure that commerce would be brisk after the service . . . funerals made people pretty thirsty.

"Well, you get along then. Don't worry about putting the chair up. I'll tend to it later on."

"Don't you get any ideas, now, Grammy. I want to do this myself."

"You should know by now that I let you clean up your own messes."

I laughed. "Thanks for the vote of confidence."

"You know what I mean."

I did. I walked over to her and kissed her on the forehead. "Thanks for listening. Like always."

She looked up at me as I towered over her on her low chair. "Tuesday's good."

"Good for what?" I was confused.

"For bringing that union agitator over here for dinner. I'll make a pot roast."

"Grammy . . ."

She shooed me away. "You can bring some of that fancy beer you like. I don't think them New Yorkers care much for tea."

It was pointless to try to argue with her. Besides, if I didn't shake a leg, I'd be late for work.

"We'll see." I whistled for Fritz, who lumbered to his feet and followed me down off the porch. Just as we reached my pickup, I saw a flash of blue. Ermaline was tearing back around the bend, headed for home. She must've forgotten something . . . probably her cigarettes.

Yeah.

I needed to find a better place to snuggle.

⁊ ⁊ ⁊

It was one forty-five—almost the witching hour. I went to turn the lights on inside the beer and wine coolers. We could start selling alcohol at the crack of two, and people were already pulling into the parking spaces out front. Some of them were still wearing their church clothes, which meant they probably wanted to stock up before heading out for Buster's funeral at three-thirty.

So far, there had only been a smattering of customers—people buying gas and cigarettes, or coming inside for Jumbo Cups of Mountain Dew and Dr. Pepper. But I knew that would change soon enough. I heard the electronic door tone chime, telling me that someone had just come inside.

"Hello," I called out. "I'll be right there."

I headed back up toward the register and about dropped dead in my tracks when I saw who was standing there in front of the potato chip kiosk.

El.

And she was looking great, too. She had on a short-sleeved t-shirt and pair of khaki-colored cargo shorts, and her legs were pure works of art. Just like the rest of her.

I was mortified. There I stood, practically drooling, in my mother's red, oversized S&W polo shirt, with her name badge sagging off my right boob.

El was staring at me. She looked confused, but I could see a little smile forming around the corners of her beautiful mouth.

"Sissy?" she asked, in that sexy voice of hers.

"Oh." I glanced down at the name badge. "No. This is my mother's shirt."

"You wear your mother's clothes?" she asked. She sounded amused.

"No . . . I mean. She works here. I'm just filling in for her today."

"In Illinois?" she asked.

"They live here. This is their store."

El nodded toward the beer and wine coolers at the back. "I bet it's pretty lucrative for them."

"It is on Sundays," I agreed.

"So I've heard." El smiled. I felt weak at the knees. "I'm actually here to have my own adult needs met. Think you can help me out?"

Okay . . . this was just getting ridiculous. I needed to buck up and stop acting like a complete imbecile. Two could play at this game.

"Maybe," I said. "What are you in the mood for?"

El looked surprised. "Are we talking about the same thing?"

"You tell me." I tried to act nonchalant and rested an elbow on a shelf containing rows of tiny cans of Beefaroni and Vienna sausages. It probably didn't do much to atone for how hot I was certain I *didn't* look in my mother's provocative polo shirt, but it was the best I could do right then.

El just stared back at me for a moment. I thought I saw something flicker in her gray eyes.

"I need beer," she finally said. "Lots of it. And maybe some wine, too."

I straightened up, proud of myself for making her fold her hand. "You've come to the right place for that. I turned around and headed back toward the coolers. "What kind, and how much?"

El followed me. "I don't know . . . what kinds do most people around here like to drink?"

"Well, there's what people *like*, and there's what they can afford. Which kind do you want?"

"Both," she said with another smile.

"I'd get a mixture of Heineken and Old Style. And you might want to throw in a few bottles of our finest, cheap white zinfandel. Folks around here aren't known for being real wine connoisseurs."

"Sounds perfect." She smiled. "We're hosting a little open house at our motel suite later, and I need to stock up."

"And you came to Illinois? Why didn't you go to Evansville?"

She shrugged. "There was some kind of monster wreck on Highway 41. The motel clerk told me that Allendale was the next best place."

"How many people are you expecting?" I was as much curious as I was interested in helping her figure out how much to buy.

This was pretty much standard operating procedure for how these union invasions played out. The big shots rolled into town and got everybody liquored up so their tongues would loosen. Expressions of grievance and wrongdoing would start up and begin to feed off collective umbrage until the whole thing reached critical mass. That's when the labor board would swoop in and call for the vote to organize. I'd already been through this at Krylon twice before. It's not that I thought things were perfect in our plant—there were plenty of abuses to clean up. Even my own situation was beginning to feel pretty pathetic. I just wasn't sure about which approach was best for life in Princeton. Plus, siding with the union forces was always the best way to ensure that you never got off the time clock.

"For tonight? Maybe ten or twelve—if we're lucky. Tony thinks things will pick up after this first gathering."

We stood in front of the coolers. El's reflection in the tall glass doors was nearly as enticing as she was. I forced myself to look back at her.

"Tony?" I asked.

"Tony Gemelli," she said. She held up a hand to about chest height. "The short, Italian man who was with me the other night at the bar."

"He your partner?"

"In a manner of speaking."

"What manner might that be?"

She raised an eyebrow. "The manner where we work together, but he goes home at night to his wife, Rosa, and their three kids."

"Ah," I said. "I think I like this Tony."

"I was fairly certain you would."

"Really?" I leaned against the cooler. I had no idea where my bravado was coming from, but I decided to just go with it. For one thing, I didn't see any fleas buzzing around El. "What makes you so certain?"

"Do you really need to ask me that, Friday Jill?"

There was that sinking feeling again.

I retaliated by looking her up and down. She noticed. I saw a tinge of red creep its way up her neck. *Deuce.*

The electronic door chime went off again. *Great.*

I sighed. "Sorry. I need to check that out. I'll be right back."

"No worries." She sounded relieved. "I need to use the restroom anyway." She looked around. "Where is it?"

"Outside."

She looked at me with amazement. "Did you say *outside?*"

I nodded.

"You're kidding."

"Not so much."

She rolled her eyes. "Where are we? Dogpatch?"

"Welcome to America's heartland." I smiled at her.

She shook her head. "Point me in the right direction?"

"Follow me." I headed back toward the front of the store. Two teenagers stood near the register, probably wanting to buy cigarettes and a forty-dog. *It begins*, I thought.

"Let me give you the key," I said to El, as I threaded my way behind the counter. I lifted the vintage Outlaw hubcap down from its hook and handed it across the counter to her. The key attached to it by a short chain clattered against the metal. "Here you go." I pointed outside. "It's back around the building on the left, next to the ice machine."

El was staring at the hubcap. "What the hell is that?"

"The restroom key," I replied.

She took hold of it. Her eyes met mine. "Don't you have something a bit larger—like maybe a trailer hitch?"

One of the teenagers snickered. The other one was too busy checking out El's ass.

"Be careful with the door latch," I said to her retreating back. "It sticks." I faced the teens. "Okay. Which one of you guys has the fake I.D.?"

They groaned in tandem.

"Come on, lady . . ." the taller of the two complained. "Give us a break."

"And spend the next six months in jail? I don't think so."

"I'm eighteen," he whined.

"Sure you are," I said. "And right after I finish my shift, I'm going to suit-up and run in the Paris Marathon."

Both boys looked back at me with blank expressions.

I sighed. "Unless you guys want some beef jerky or a pack of Nerds, I suggest you clear out of here."

The shorter one, the one who had been staring at El's derriere, poked his companion in the ribs. "Come on, Roy . . . let's go." He headed toward the door.

"Thanks for being a bitch, lady," Roy said over his shoulder. He reached the door and yanked it open just as a woman started to enter.

"Come back real soon, Roy," I called after him.

He muttered something unintelligible and stood back so the woman could get past him. I was surprised to see T-Bomb come strolling in.

"Hey, Roy?" she said to the tall teen. "Your daddy know you're over here?"

Roy and his friend ducked their heads and hurried out past her without saying anything. She cackled and joined me at the register. "Remember how we used to pull that same shit at the Liquor Barn in Grayville?"

I nodded. "Did you really know him?"

"Hell no. I heard you call him 'Roy' when I was walking in." She laughed. "I just love messin' with them kids."

"What brings you over here on a Sunday? You going to the funeral?"

T-Bomb snagged a mini York Peppermint Patty from a box on the counter and unwrapped it. "Nah. I don't really know them Collinses— even though Donnie went to school with Buster's cousin, Bert. You know . . . the one with the gimpy leg?"

"No." I had no idea who she was talking about.

She handed me the candy wrapper. "Yes you do. He dated that Turpin girl . . . the sister of the one Misty Ann's husband keeps banging."

"You mean *Albert* Parks?"

She nodded.

"He's got a gimpy leg? I never noticed that."

"That's 'cause he wears them corrective shoes and baggy pants." T-Bomb shook her dark head. "We always called him Bert Parks . . . remember that?" She chuckled. "Imagine him running a beauty pageant."

"That's kinda mean."

"Why?" she asked. "We weren't makin' fun of his leg."

"I know. I meant it was mean to compare him to Bert Parks."

She laughed. "Yeah, he was sort of a human creep show."

"So if you aren't here for Buster's funeral, I guess you need beer?"

"Yeah. I thought I'd get in here before the crowds showed up."

The phone rang. I waved my hand toward the coolers. "Help yourself." I picked up the receiver. "Fast Mart, how can I help you?"

"For starters," the low voice on the other end of the line said, "you can come out here and open this damn door."

It was El.

"El?" I asked.

Big mistake. T-Bomb, who hadn't yet made tracks for the adult beverage section, was still standing there. Her ears perked right up.

I turned away from her and faced the cigarette display. "How'd you get this number?" I asked El.

"Yelp," she said.

"Excuse me?" I wasn't sure I'd heard her right.

"Yelp," she repeated. "Y-E-L-P. On my phone."

"Oh. Sorry. Um . . . sure. Lemme come right out there. Sit tight." I smiled into the phone. "No pun intended."

"Very funny," she drawled. The line went dead.

I turned around to face an extremely curious T-Bomb. I jerked a thumb in the general direction of the restrooms. "El's here, and she's stuck in the bathroom."

"El DeBarge is out there?" she asked. "Why were you keeping that a secret?"

I opened the cash register and lifted up the change drawer to retrieve the extra bathroom key. "I wasn't keeping anything a secret. She came by to get some beer."

"Here?"

I stared at her. "Yes. *Here.* What's wrong with that?"

"How'd she know you work here?"

I walked around the counter. "She didn't know I worked here . . . it was a coincidence."

"Oh, hell. Coincidence my butt."

"T-Bomb . . . just do me a favor and watch the store for a minute while I go unlock the door for her. You know how it sticks."

She sighed and snagged another Peppermint Patty. "Okay, but when you get back, we're gonna have a talk about this self-destructive behavior of yours."

"Whatever." I walked out.

It only took me a minute to reach the bathroom. I didn't see the hubcap, so I tapped on the door.

"El?" I asked. "Are you still in there?"

"No . . . I folded space and am now mining for spice on the planet Dune," El said from inside.

I heard a truck horn and turned around to see Buzz Sheets pulling in. *Great.* That was all I needed. It was turning into old home day at S&W. I quickly unlocked the door, stepped inside, and closed it behind me.

El was leaning against the sink with her arms crossed and staring at me with an amazed look on her face.

"Isn't the idea for us to be on the *other* side of the door?" she asked.

I sighed. "Just go with me on this . . . there's someone out there I need to avoid."

She raised an eyebrow. "So you're hiding in the bathroom?"

I nodded. "He'll be gone in a minute."

"Good plan, Einstein. Care to explain to me how we get out of here once he leaves, since I'm assuming that's the spare key in your hand?"

I looked down at the key. *Shit.* I tried to open the door. It wasn't budging. This bathroom was built like Fort Knox.

"Um . . ."

El sighed and fished her phone out of her pocket.

"What are you doing?" I asked.

"Calling the fire department." She looked at me. "I assume there *is* one in this town?"

"Of course there is, but you can't call them."

"Why not?"

"They'll all be getting ready for Buster's funeral."

"Who the hell is Buster?"

I rubbed a hand across my forehead. This wasn't turning out at all the way I thought it would.

"It's a long story," I said.

"I begin to suspect that there are no other kinds around here."

"Just give me a minute, okay? I'll think of something."

El glanced up over my head at the transom window. "Does that thing open?"

I followed her gaze. It had a latch at the top. "Maybe. Think you could stand on that trash can?"

El looked at it. "Why me? You're a lot taller."

"I'm also heavier, and the thing's plastic."

"I don't like heights."

"It's barely three feet tall."

She shrugged.

I sighed and looked around the dingy interior. There were some old Cordplast signs that fit the poster frames stationed out front, next to the gas pumps. They were stacked against the wall beside the sink.

"Hand me some of those signs, and I'll stack them on top of the trash can. Maybe they'll distribute my weight better so I can stand on it."

El dutifully handed me four of the larger signs. I stacked them at overlapping angles across the opening of the big, Rubbermaid bin. I slid it over next to the door.

"Here goes nothing," I said as I raised a foot up and rested it on top of the signs. I put a hand on El's shoulder and tried to grab the bottom of the ledge below the transom window as I pushed myself up. For a minute, I thought it just might work. I actually felt my fingers connect with the ledge before I heard a crack, and all the signs collapsed beneath me. I went down like a ton of bricks and ended up half in and half out of the toppling trash can. El tried to break my fall, but it was no use. I went over hard, and smacked the back of my head on the cracked tile floor.

I lay there in a daze, staring up at the flickering fluorescent ceiling light. Then I saw El's face at very close range as she knelt over me.

"Oh, my god. Oh, my god," she was muttering. "Friday Jill? Are you okay?" She tentatively touched my face. "Oh, my god. I'm so sorry. I'm such a wuss . . . I should've done it. I'm so sorry . . ."

I couldn't find my tongue or clear my head enough to reply. But only part of that was due to having the wind knocked out of my sails. El was really close to me, holding my face between both of her hands, and that was making me dizzier than the fall.

"Friday?" She kept saying. "Friday Jill? Can you hear me? Are you okay?" She bent even closer.

I opened my mouth to tell her I was okay. "You're so beautiful," I said instead. *Where the hell did that come from?* Clearly, I had scrambled my brain in the fall.

El didn't draw back. She didn't let go of my face, either. That felt really nice.

"So are you," she said. Her voice sounded funny . . . kind of husky. Maybe my hearing got messed up, too?

"I can't do this, El." Was it getting darker in there? Or had El somehow managed to block out all the light. Her eyes were boring into mine like laser beams.

"Can't do what?" she whispered.

"Get involved with you," I answered.

"Are we getting involved?" she asked. Her lips were nearly touching mine.

I ran my hands up her back and pulled her the rest of the way down. "Oh, god, I hope so . . ."

We stayed there on the floor like that, kissing, for what felt like an hour. How much further we would have gone is anybody's guess, but we never got the chance to find out. Just as I started to work my hands up under her t-shirt, there was a huge commotion outside. We heard alarms going off and the sound of voices shouting. Well . . . *one* voice shouting: T-Bomb's.

El drew back. She was breathing hard. Her lips looked wet and puffy and positively edible. "What the hell was that?"

I was out of breath, too. "The drive-off alarm . . . somebody took off without paying."

She sighed and dropped her head to my chest.

There was a loud banging at the door.

"Friday? You still in there?" It was T-Bomb. The doorknob rattled. "That damn Buzz Sheets took off with the nozzle still stuck in his gas tank. *Asshole.* It's pandemonium out here." The knob shook again. "This dern thing is stuck. Lemme get something to force it open." More rattling. "Friday?"

"Yeah," I called out. "We're still in here. Go get help."

There was no response right away.

"Is El DeBarge in there with you?" T-Bomb asked in a low voice.

El gave me a hopeless look. "Yes. We're *both* stuck."

I could hear T-Bomb snort. "You got that part right, sister. You two just hang on, and I'll go get a pry bar."

El sat up and tugged her t-shirt down. I followed suit.

"I'm sorry about this," she said. It sounded sincere.

"You are? Why?"

I was feeling a lot of things right then, but sorry wasn't one of them.

She looked at me. "You'll just have to believe me when I tell you that this isn't part of my job."

"What makes you think I thought it was?"

She shrugged. "I know what people say about us."

"What people?"

She nodded toward the door. "T-Bomb. Luanne." She lowered her eyes. "Everybody."

I didn't know how to respond to that. Especially since it was true.

"It's okay. We're not doing anything wrong."

"Aren't we?"

I smiled at her. "Not yet."

She leaned into me. "It's not going to be good for you to be seen with me."

"I know."

"I have to do my job, Friday Jill."

"I know that, too."

"So where does that leave us?"

I put my arm around her. "You mean besides stuck in the bathroom at Fast Mart?"

She pinched me on the thigh. "Smart ass."

"What I do outside of work is my own business, El. Nobody else's."

"Uh huh. And you really think that won't change if people find out you're involved with a labor organizer?"

"Are we involved?"

"I thought we settled that."

"In that case, are you busy on Tuesday night?"

She gave me an uncertain look. "I don't think so . . ."

"Good." I tugged her closer. "I hope you like pot roast."

Before El could ask me what in the hell I was talking about, T-Bomb returned with her pry bar, and our conversation was at an end.

41

Chapter 4

Things were crazy at work on Monday. There was word that some of the Ogata people were coming in at the end of the month to meet with senior management about laying the groundwork for the transition. The rumors were spreading like wildfire. Buzz was all over the line supervisors to get things cleaned up and squared away—like any of us ever left things like that undone. We didn't. The only problems we ever had came from him, and others of his ilk who thought they could slough off their responsibilities and ignore the serious safety violations that kept cropping up because they insisted on hiring and protecting guys like Earl Junior. Already, I'd had to move two skids of oil filters out of the way after Earl Junior decided to park them in front of the fire extinguishers next to the axle welding station.

I'd had enough of this negligence. If management wouldn't do anything about Earl Junior, I'd just have to take it up with Pauline. So what if I got creamed corn for the rest of my life? Things needed to change before somebody got seriously hurt.

Buzz saw me heading for the cafeteria on my break and rushed over to cut me off the pass.

"Just where in the hell do you think you're going?" He was out of breath. But that wasn't unusual. Even standing up from a chair winded him.

I held up my arm to show him Grammy's watch. "Lunch, Buzz. Heard of it?"

"Not on my time."

"Oh. Sorry. I didn't realize my break was classified as *your* time."

"It is when the Japs are coming to town. Nobody gets a break until everything is in tip-top shape."

Japs? Oh, yeah. Buzz was going to fare really well with the new owners.

"Buzz . . . everything in my area is in perfect order. So go annoy somebody else."

I started to walk away from him but he grabbed hold of me.

"Let go of me, Buzz." I jerked my arm free.

"Look, Fryman. Gettin' your axle greased by that union bitch don't give you any right to act all high and mighty in here. I'm still in charge."

I bit back my first response, which was to tell him to fuck off. I knew Buzz well enough to know that sinking to his level would just escalate his rude behavior.

"I'm glad you mentioned axles," I said. "Because your protégée left about two tons of stock parked in front of the extinguishers at the welding station."

Buzz waved a hand. "So what? We have backups for that. They're called redundancies. Ever heard of those, Fryman?"

"The only thing redundant around here is *you.* You're worthless, Buzz."

"We'll see how worthless I am when I write your ass up for insubordination." Buzz was really getting pissed off at me. I could see that little vein in his forehead starting to pop out. It looked like a piece of angry clothesline.

"Fine." I'd had enough of his empty threats. I was his best line supervisor, and he knew it. "Then I might as well take twice as long on my break. I mean . . . if you're writing me up, you can just add that to my list of offenses, too." I walked away from him.

"I'm not finished with you yet, Fryman!" he called after me.

I waved a hand over my head. "Buzz off, Buzz."

He yelled something else, but by then, I was far enough away for the ambient noise of the machinery to drown out what he said.

Asshole. I pushed open the door that led to the company cafeteria. Luanne was in there, seated at one of the blue-topped Formica tables, wolfing down a plate of . . . something. She saw me and waved me over.

I looked down at her mostly empty plate. Tannish-yellow chunks of something unrecognizable were floating in a pool of thick-looking gravy.

"What on earth is that?" I asked.

She rolled her eyes. "I blasted Pauline about Earl Junior parking his damn Pinto across three spaces in the lot this morning." She lifted another spoonful of the gelatinous muck. "She didn't much care for it."

"So I see."

Luanne glanced up at the big wall clock. "It ain't like you to take a lunch break. What's going on?"

"Buzz is getting on my last nerve." I pulled out a chair and sat down. "Now I'm not even hungry."

"Well," Luanne ran the crust of a slice of white bread around the edge of her plate, "I wish you could've gone outside and had a smoke for me, then. I don't know as I can make it another two hours 'til my next break."

"Why don't you invest in one of those nicotine patches?"

Luanne snorted. "Hell. I'd have to daisy chain about twenty of those damn things together to cover enough real estate to do my cravings any good."

"I don't think they work that way, Lu. It's more a timed-release kind of thing."

"The only damned timed-release I give two flips about is the one that's gonna spring my son early from Branchville."

I nodded. Luanne's son was serving a ten-month stretch for non-payment of child support. The penalty was so stiff because it was his third offense. Luanne and Jay maintained that Jay Jr. was right not to pay off his scheming Jezebel wife because her kids didn't even look like their son.

"Jay Jr. doing okay?"

"He was the last time I seen him." She shook her head. "He's just sick about missing Pork Day, what with Jailissa being such a contender and all."

"I bet."

Luanne sighed. "Well. It don't pay no never mind to get all het up about things we can't control." She looked at me. "Just like you and that union agitator."

I blinked. "What's that supposed to mean?"

She rolled her eyes. "Oh, hell. Like you don't know that everybody in six counties is talkin' about you and that El DeBarge gettin' locked up in the bathroom at Fast Mart yesterday."

I sighed. "How did you hear about that?"

Luanne threw her head back and damn near bayed herself right off her seat. "You gotta be kiddin' me? You don't think that asshole Buzz Sheets burned rubber getting' back to Hoosier Daddy trailin' this tasty little tale, along with that gas nozzle?"

I rested my head in my hands. "Oh, god . . ."

Buzz blabbing about what happened was nothing compared to the way my parents reacted when they heard that their regular unleaded pump was going to be out of service for half the week.

Luanne wasn't finished. "And that was *after* he told everybody at Buster Collins's funeral about it."

"Oh, god . . ."

"I told you to stay away from her, didn't I?"

"Luanne . . ."

"But you had to go and get yourself all hot and bothered."

"Luanne . . ."

"And now you'll be lucky if you don't find your truck packed in cow shit every night when you leave this joint."

"Judas Priest, Luanne!" I raised my voice, and two-dozen other heads bent over plates of creamed corn pivoted to look over at us. "Will you just shut up about it, already?" I hissed.

She was shaking her over-permed head. "I got nothin' else to say about this, so I'll just say that you need to watch yourself, missy. You might think these assholes around here are just dumb farmers, but they're smart enough to know the signs of a fox rootin' around in the henhouse. You don't straighten up and fly right, you'll be picking buckshot outta your backside." She lowered her voice. "El DeBarge, too." She pushed her chair back and struggled to her feet. "I got nothin' else to say about it."

I sighed. "She's really not like that, Lu. Really."

Luanne collected her plate and silverware. "Not like what?"

"Not like people think. She's not using me."

Luanne looked at me like I'd just said I was the first person in the plant to carry on with Misty Ann Marks.

"You just keep tellin' yourself them fairy stories. I gotta get back to the line."

I got up, too.

"See you later at Hoosier Daddy?" I asked.

"You know it," Luanne said. She dropped her plate and silverware into one of the big dish bins near the exit. Then she disappeared out into the plant.

I still had a few minutes to spare, so I thought I'd go ahead and grab something to eat and try to talk with Pauline. I was sincerely worried about Earl Junior's lapses. They seemed to be increasing in number. Whatever people thought about Pauline in general, it was clear that she loved her son. I knew she wouldn't want anything bad to happen to him, or, hopefully, to anyone else because of him. I decided that compromising the health of my digestive tract was worth the risk.

I walked over to the steam table and picked up a tray.

Pauline was back there, resplendent in her stained white apron and hair net.

"Hey, Pauline," I called out. "What's good today?"

She rapped the edge of a big aluminum cistern with a spoon. "Got some fresh S.O.S." She jerked her platinum blond head toward a small side table covered with platters of white bread. "Got some sourdough for it, too."

"I think I'll pass on that . . . I don't do too well with gravy. Anything I can eat on the fly?" I held up my arm and showed her my watch. "I'm just about outta time."

"How about one of them potato empanadas, over there? They just come outta the deep fryer."

God . . . in for a penny, in for a pound. "Great. Nobody makes those as good as you."

She smiled and walked over to slap one on a plate. It nearly slid off, and left a shiny trail of grease in its wake.

I figured I could always feed it to Fritz later on . . . he loved Pauline's leftovers.

"Anything with it?" she asked. "Tartar sauce or salsa?"

"Um. No. That'll do me." I reached out to take the plate from her. "Pauline . . . I did want to mention something to you about Earl Junior. I'm kinda worried about him."

Pauline pulled the plate back out of my reach. "What do you mean?" Her voice had taken on that suspicious edge it got whenever she felt threatened—like she'd just swallowed a pack of razor blades. I knew I only had a few seconds to turn things around.

"I've been noticing that he seems a little . . . preoccupied lately. I worry that something might be . . . bothering him."

"Nothin's botherin' him. He's *fine*," she snapped. "That Luanne Keortge just has it in for him because she had to walk her fat ass in three feet further than usual this morning."

"No, Pauline . . . that's not what I meant—"

"I'm sick and tired of the damn conspiracy against Earl Junior around here." Pauline clutched my plate. "Everybody is just jealous because he's likely to get that promotion to warehouse manager."

"Promotion?" This was the first I'd heard about any promotion, or about any managerial slots opening up. "What promotion?"

Pauline was glaring at me with her beady eyes. "Don't think I don't know what your little game is. You just want to tar his reputation so you can ruin his chances at this job. But I got news for you. Everybody here knows what you been up to with that UAW spy . . . carryin' on like a harlot."

"Pauline . . . that's not what I . . ."

"Save it. Your break is over." She dug her big spoon down deep into the steaming vat of goo and slopped a heaping mess of it on top of my empanada.

"Here's your lunch." She thrust the plate toward me. "Now git outta here before Buzz comes lookin' for you."

I was stupefied, and stared down at the gummy mass spreading out across my plate. Then I gave up and beat a hasty retreat to pay for my eclectic plate of inedible S.O.S.

One thing was for sure. Luanne wasn't the only one who was going to have a tough time making it until the next ten-minute break.

The mood at Hoosier Daddy that night was pretty morose. I wasn't the only one slinking in there with a backside burned raw from all the bitching it had taken from managers who were scared to death about what might happen when the first wave of Ogata's transition team showed up. People were grumbling and going on at every table. It was clear there wasn't going to be any karaoke tonight . . . nobody was much in the mood for singing.

I did notice that there was a lot of lively activity over at Tony Gemelli's table. Things must be good in the agitator business. A few more days like today, and the UAW might have to move its base of operation to a bigger bar.

I didn't see El anyplace. That was probably a good thing. I didn't need anybody else razzing me or giving me flack about what had happened on Sunday. I didn't know what in the world I had been thinking when I let myself go like that. I knew that El was going to be here, then gone, and I'd be left alone again—this time with a ruined reputation and, probably, a truck bed full of manure.

It was depressing. No matter how hard I tried, I always seemed to make bad relationship choices. It was like clockwork. If somebody plopped me down in front of a cosmic police lineup of potential girl-friends, I could be counted on to point my finger at the one suspect who would be guaranteed to bring me the most misery and heartache. I thought for the zillionth time about quitting my job and moving someplace else. Maybe St. Louis? One of my college roommates was now working in management at Boeing, and she kept bugging me to come out there and work. Maybe she was right . . . it was going to take me the rest of my natural life to get anyplace here.

Just like it would probably take the rest of my natural life for me to meet someone who wouldn't end up using my heart as a doormat.

Aunt Jackie slapped a second bottle of cold Stella down in front of me. I hadn't even realized that my first one was nearly empty.

"You look like you need this," she said. "Must a been some kind of day at that plant. I never seen so many long faces in here."

Lucille was tottering along behind her. He turned around a couple of times, then plopped his fat body down near the leg of my table and grunted. He was staring at the door that led to the parking lot. Even he looked depressed.

"Thanks, Aunt Jackie." I tried to shake myself out of my mood. "Is something wrong with Lucille? He looks off tonight."

"Oh, hell. He's just lookin' for that union woman."

I was shocked. "Who?"

"That other agitator . . . El somebody."

"El?" I asked.

"DeBarge, ain't it? El DeBarge."

"Why is he looking for her?"

Aunt Jackie rolled her eyes. "He's just in love with her." She looked down at her obese companion. "Ain't that just the damndest thing? This dog don't give nobody the time of day. But all that union woman has to do is wag her fanny at him, and he'll about give himself a hernia doin' tricks. *Tricks*. He ain't never done tricks—not unless you count holdin' the world record for the most consecutive farts."

I didn't really know how to respond. I was pretty sure that if El wagged her fanny at me, I'd be making a fool of myself, too—doing cartwheels and handstands, or anything else that would capture her attention. Beneath the table, Lucille grunted again.

I know exactly how you feel, buddy.

"I ain't never seen this dog so hot to trot over somebody. Not unless you count that damn candy-ass Affenpinscher that Jerry Sneddin used to bring in here. Lucille was the same way about her."

I remembered Jerry's fussy little dog. He used to bring it to the plant all the time, and it barked constantly. They were pretty inseparable.

"What happened to Jerry's dog? Nobody's seen it in a while."

Aunt Jackie snorted. "She's at home with her litter of nine puppies."

I looked down at Lucille, who was sniffing his business. "Uh oh."

"You don't know the half of it. Now that ass-wipe is trying to hold me up for support payments . . . for a damn *dog*. And he says I have to take the whole kit and caboodle of mongrels, too. Now just what in the hell am I gonna do with nine of the ugliest dogs in god's creation?"

"Nine?" Nine dogs that looked like toy versions of Lucille?

Suddenly, my problems felt pretty small.

Aunt Jackie shook her head. *"Jack-Affs.* That's what he calls them . . . Jack-Affs. Hell. Who knows? Maybe I can start some kind of boutique trend and sell 'em each for a king's ransom."

I nodded. "Then again . . . maybe you can get Lucille," I lowered my voice so he wouldn't hear and made cutting motions with my fingers, "fixed."

"Shit." Aunt Jackie was watching my delicate pantomime. "They'd have to use hedge clippers on this boy. He's got a bigger pair than most of the men who come into this joint."

Against my will, I looked down at Lucille, who was wholly engrossed with his nether bits now. Aunt Jackie was right. He was pretty . . . endowed.

"You might be right."

Aunt Jackie sighed. "So that union woman better just keep watchin' her p's and q's."

"Where is El?" I tried my best to sound nonchalant.

Aunt Jackie wasn't buying it. "She ain't here, and you don't need to go lookin' for her, neither." She lowered her voice. "If them agitators wasn't so good for business, I'd tell 'em to clear on outta here. I don't need nobody sowing discord in my place. But ever since the filter plant closed, I've had a hard time making ends meet." Her eyes looked dreamy. "Those second shift boys sure could sock it away."

"Hey? Friday?" a voice bellowed. It was T-Bomb. She was making her way across the bar with Luanne huffing along behind her. I heard Lucille emit a half-hearted growl.

"Oh, lord." Aunt Jackie sighed. "Talk about people who can sock it away." She looked down at me. "You heed my warnin' about them agitators, honey. No good can come outta that for you. Now I better go tap off a couple more pitchers. That keg is almost empty, and I need to change it out before the rest of your pals roll in."

I nodded. "Thanks, Aunt Jackie."

She walked off in a blaze of blue polyester.

"How long you been here?" T-Bomb demanded.

Luanne dropped her suitcase-sized purse down on a chair. "I gotta hit the loo . . . that S.O.S. has been cramping me all afternoon." She eyed me. "How'd your chat go with Pauline?"

I shrugged. "I've been pretty cramped up, too. Tell you anything?"

Luanne snorted. "That woman is a menace to public health." She adjusted the waistband of her pants through her oversized blouse. This one had enormous tiger lilies all over it. "Get us a pitcher, T-Bomb. I need something to wash that taste outta my mouth."

"I'm all over it," T-Bomb said.

Luanne was already heading toward the bathroom. "And ask Aunt Jackie for some toothpicks. I got a corn husk stuck in a molar . . ."

"Dang, that woman is high maintenance." T-Bomb turned around on her chair and waved a hand toward the bar. When she caught Aunt Jackie's eye, she made a pouring motion with one hand, and held up two fingers on the other.

"What about the toothpicks?" I asked.

"Hell . . . I got some of them in my purse, left over from last week, when I pissed Pauline off." She started rummaging around in her cavernous shoulder bag. She had an enormous, lime green colored one today. It perfectly matched her Capri pants, which was shocking and disturbing all at the same time. "Hey? You goin' to the fish fry on Thursday night?"

The V.F.W. fish fry was one of the biggest social events of the season in Princeton. Everybody kind of considered it the Indiana equivalent of Pork Day.

"I suppose so."

"Well, don't sound so excited. It should be fun this year. I hear the women's group at Owensville U.M.C. is makin' all the fruit pies. That'll be a nice change from that nasty banana pudding them band boosters brought last time."

"I know. I thought I'd see if Grammy wants to go. She missed it last year."

"That gout of hers was acting up, wasn't it?"

I nodded.

"Well." T-Bomb pulled a bundle of cellophane wrapped toothpicks out of her purse and slapped them down on the table in front of Luanne's chair. "Tell her to eat cherries. That's what the doctor told Donnie. But between you and me, I think his problem comes from spending too much time on his duff, punching a calculator."

T-Bomb's husband ran his own accounting business.

A burst of loud laughter came from Tony Gemelli's table. Several guys were giving each other high-fives.

Aunt Jackie showed up with the pitcher of Old Style and two glasses.

"What's that about?" T-Bomb asked, pointing across the room.

Aunt Jackie shrugged. "Them agitators is just doin' what they do . . . workin' the crowd, gettin' everybody all liquored up and sympathetic to their cause. I seen it happen about fifty-eleven times, now. It don't pay no never-mind, neither. Once that vote happens, they're gone—no matter which way things pan out."

T-Bomb was staring right at me the whole time Aunt Jackie was talking. If her eyes had been lasers, I'd have had two holes burned into my forehead.

"I gotta get back over there. As much as I hate to see them union types show up, they're damn good for business." Aunt Jackie tugged at the straps of her bra to reseat her ample set of assets, then turned around and lumbered back toward the bar.

"What?" I asked T-Bomb. She was staring at me with a raised eyebrow.

"Don't sit there and act like you don't know what you're doing, Missy."

"I haven't *done* anything."

"Oh, yeah?" T-Bomb poured out two glasses of beer. "What do you call that little tango number the two of you was doin' yesterday in the bathroom?"

"That was an accident, and you know it."

"Accident my derriere. You must think I was born yesterday."

"No," I muttered. "It takes most of a lifetime to develop your unique fashion sense."

T-Bomb lowered her glass of beer. "What'd you say?"

"Nothing."

Luanne made her way back to the table and dropped into her chair. The thing groaned and swayed beneath her weight, but she stayed on top of it with all the grace of a champion bronco buster.

"How was that corn report?" T-Bomb asked.

Luanne rolled her eyes. "About as productive as that patch Jay planted out behind the shed."

T-Bomb laughed. "Well maybe he'd have better luck if he moved some of them rusted Oldsmobiles outta there."

"You try telling him that. He swears they're gonna make a come-back, and he wants to have the market cornered when they do."

"Hell," T-Bomb took a big drink from her frothy glass of beer, "if they do, he'll need a ton of them see-through seat covers and a butt load of Bondo."

Luanne was looking around the bar. "I see that business is good at the union table."

T-Bomb nodded. "It always is until the credit card runs out."

"You can't really blame them," I added. "At least it livens things up for a while."

They both looked at me like I had lost my last marble.

I waved a hand. "Come on . . . tell me it's not true. It gives every-body something new to think about, instead of obsessing over things they can't change."

"You been hanging out at the House of Praise again?" T-Bomb asked.

"Of course not."

"Well, you might as well just dye your hair blond and start line dancin' with them hoppers, if you're gonna keep talkin' mess like that."

I looked at her. "You know it's true. There *are* things at the plant that need to be changed."

"I guess you heard about Earl Junior's promotion, then?" Luanne asked.

"You mean he got it?" I was incredulous. "I thought that was just a rumor started by Pauline."

Luanne shook her head. "Nope. Looks like we got ourselves a new warehouse manager."

"What the hell was wrong with the last one?" T-Bomb asked.

"That Davis girl? She couldn't find her own ass with two hands and a flashlight, much less keep up with a pallet full of brake shoes."

"So they replaced her with Earl Junior?" I asked.

Luanne shrugged.

"That's all we need." T-Bomb was shaking her head. "Drool all over the stock. Hey? Maybe they can start calling them Outlaw 450 tires *Droolers*?" She laughed.

I sighed and glanced over at Tony's table. There was still no sign of El. I wondered where she was. Beneath our table, Lucille grunted. Pathetic. I'm a lodge sister with a lovesick Jack Russell.

I finished my Stella and pushed back my chair. "I gotta hit the road." I dropped a ten-dollar bill on the table to cover my tab.

"Why?" T-Bomb looked disappointed. "We just got here."

"I know. But I still have to stop by Grammy's and pick up Fritz."

"Well, don't forget to ask her about the fish fry."

"I won't."

"Why don't you just get her a dog of her own, instead of leaving Fritz over there all the time?" Luanne asked.

"She likes Fritz." I shrugged. "They watch her stories together."

"Hey!" T-Bomb interrupted. "You can give her one of them Jack-Aff puppies. I saw them last week and they're kinda cute . . . once you get past all the wiry hair and under bite."

"I don't think so."

"They're kinda like Jerry," T-Bomb cackled. "Only better looking."

"Yeah," I said. "There's a mental image I didn't need. See you both tomorrow."

I waved goodbye and headed for the exit. About a dozen people were clustered around Tony Gemelli's table now. It looked like half of the first shift maintenance techs were there, plus a smattering of guys I recognized from the pipe fitting area. I figured that once the word got out about Earl Junior, Tony would probably need to move his base of operations to the VFW hall—Hoosier Daddy wouldn't be big enough to accommodate everybody.

∽ ∽ ∽

It was pretty quiet outside in the parking lot. The moon was nearly full, and everything looked brighter and cleaner than usual. Of course, this also meant that all the night critters would be active, so Fritz would be up and down off the bed about a hundred times. I wondered if maybe I should just leave him at Grammy's?

I was nearly to my truck when I noticed that something about it seemed off. It was listing to the left slightly. *What the hell?* I walked around to the passenger side and saw that it had a flat tire. *Great.* This was just what I needed . . . to have to change a damn tire at eight o'clock at night.

I looked around for options—like an unattended vehicle with the keys still in the ignition. There were none, of course. I was going to have to deal with this on my own.

I stood there for a minute and toyed with the idea of heading back inside to see if one of the guys would come out and help me, but I let go of that fantasy pretty quickly. If I asked for help, I'd never live it down back at work. I sighed and unlocked the passenger door so I could retrieve the jack kit from beneath the rear seat.

I unloaded the spare and loosened the lug nuts on the flat.

"Need a hand?" a voice from behind me asked.

I about jumped out of my skin and dropped the torque wrench. It hit me on the ankle. "Shit!"

"Sorry," the voice apologized. It was El.

I angled my body around so I could see her. Even in the semi-darkness of the parking lot, I could tell that she looked fabulous. She had a skirt on tonight, and from my vantage point, her legs looked like they were about nine miles long, which was odd, since she was about a foot shorter than me.

El followed my gaze. "Something wrong with my legs?"

"No, they look just fine." Shit. Where did that come from?

She raised her eyes to my face and half-smiled. I felt like an idiot.

"I'm not used to seeing you in a skirt," I explained. "You look . . . different."

"I do?" She dropped her voice about six octaves. It wasn't helping. "Different, how?"

"I don't know. Fussier. More girlie." *Great.* Now I was channeling T-Bomb.

"Girlie?" She laughed. "I hope I look girlie. I mean, after all, I *am* a girl."

There was no doubt about that. Plopped right down next to the word *girl* in anyone's dictionary would be a big ol' photo of El looking fabulous and sexy as hell.

I tried to regain control. "Why are you so dressed up? This ensemble is a bit . . . haute . . . for Hoosier Daddy."

"Haute?"

I shrugged.

El folded her arms. "I forget what a scholar you are."

"I'm hardly a scholar."

"You certainly aren't typical . . ." She let her sentence trail off.

"Typical of what?" I was curious now.

"Never mind."

"No. You started it." I wasn't letting her off the hook that easily. "Typical of what?"

El looked uncomfortable.

I jerked a thumb toward the bar. "Typical of the other schmoes inside who can be bought off with a few beers and a couple of propaganda film strips?"

El stared at me for a moment. "We don't use film strips any more. We have iPads."

Okay. Now I felt like a real heel.

"I'm sorry. That was pretty rude."

"No. It was pretty honest." She shook her head. "You aren't typical of the average Krylon worker. In fact, you're not like anyone I've met since I got here."

"What do you mean?"

El shrugged. "You're like a chameleon."

"You mean I disappear?"

"No. I mean you fit."

That was odd. I always felt more like a misfit than a fit.

I got tired of squatting and decided to plop back and sit on my butt. I was wearing jeans, so I didn't really care about getting dirty. Besides, I was feeling pretty low, and thought my posture should match my mood. El continued to stand over me with her arms crossed.

"I'm still sorry," I said.

"And I'm still a labor organizer," she replied.

"I guess that makes us strange bedfellows."

"Not yet."

I was glad to be sitting down.

"Are you always this direct?"

She shrugged. "It saves time."

"Are you in a hurry?"

"That depends."

"On?"

"On whatever is chasing me."

"Whatever or whoever?"

"That depends, too."

I looked down at the torque wrench I had been turning over and over in my hands. "Am I chasing you?"

"I hope so."

I looked up at her.

"I promise to let you catch me," she added.

I nearly dropped the wrench again.

El squatted down and somehow managed to fold herself into a textbook, seated posture on the ground beside me. She looked perfect and poised—just like one of the glamorous starlets who adorned the covers of those musty old *Photoplay* magazines I used to flip through out in Grammy's garage. She smelled great. Like night-blooming Jasmine.

"How'd you end up with a flat?" she asked.

I was beginning to learn that this method of verbal bait-and-switch was part of her style. Since she was letting both of us off the hook, I decided to roll with it.

"I have no idea. I just came out here and noticed that the thing wasn't sitting right."

"But it was okay when you left work?"

I nodded.

She shook her head.

"What?" I asked.

"Don't you think this is kind of a coincidence?"

I wasn't sure what she was getting at. "My flat?"

She nodded again.

"Not really. I probably picked up a nail or something in the parking lot."

El raised an eyebrow. "There are lots of loose nails lying about in your parking lot?"

"No. But there are a lot of trucks that double as farm vehicles in our parking lot. It's not beyond the pale that something fell out of one of them."

"I hope you're right."

"What do you mean?"

"Nothing. I just hope you're right."

I looked at my tire, then back at her. "You think somebody did this on purpose, don't you?"

"I think it's possible, yes."

I didn't want to accept that explanation. "I don't know why anyone would bother . . . I haven't done anything to make myself a target."

El didn't say anything.

"You disagree?" I asked.

"Let me ask you a question. Have you ever been involved with any attempt to organize this plant in the past?"

"No. But . . ." I didn't finish.

"But what?"

I looked at her. "I'm not involved with it now, either."

El looked surprised and disappointed by my response. I wished I could take it back.

She shifted her position. The neon light from the bar sign made colorful highlights on her dark hair. She really was just about the most gorgeous woman I'd ever seen, and I was acting like an imbecile. She had to think I was some kind of psycho yo-yo. Only yesterday, I'd been the one minimizing the obstacles that were bound to trip us up like cheap throw rugs. Now I was acting like what had happened in the bathroom at Fast Mart meant nothing to me.

"I didn't mean it like that," I said. It sounded pretty flimsy . . . even to me.

El sighed. "Forget about it."

"I don't want to forget about it."

She stared at me for so long that I began to feel even more uncomfortable. "I don't think you have the first idea about what you want, Friday Jill."

Touché. "That's always been true."

"Maybe you should figure it out, then, before you put yourself in harm's way."

"I'm not in harm's way, El."

She waved a hand in frustration. "Well, what in the hell do you call this, then?"

"I told you . . . I probably picked up a nail."

"Take a look around this parking lot. There are probably at least a dozen, half-drunk Krylon workers inside, swilling beer at Tony's table."

"So?"

She rolled her eyes. "So . . . that means there are at least *three* dozen, half-drunk Krylon workers inside watching them, and getting more pissed off with each pitcher full of beer. Any one of them could have oozed out here and let the air out of your tire."

"Oh, come on, El . . . that's just plain ridiculous. They'd be likelier to key my paint job or piss on my rims. Letting the air out of my tires would take too long." I shook my head in disbelief. "Besides, there's no reason for them to target me. I'm not the one sitting at your comrade's table talking treason."

"Maybe not. But you *were* the one locked up with me in the bathroom yesterday."

"They didn't see that."

She raised an eyebrow. "That doesn't mean they don't know about it."

I had no response to that.

El glanced down at her watch. "This is getting us nowhere, and I need to get inside. Tony probably thinks I got abducted by aliens."

That got my curiosity up. "What have you been doing?"

"Talking with the boys at Solidarity House."

"Detroit?"

She nodded.

"You need reinforcements?"

She looked amused. "No. I think this one might be a lost cause."

"You do?" I wasn't expecting that response. "Does that mean you'll be leaving?"

"Probably, unless something shakes loose soon. We only had a finite window to try and close this before the transition team got spooled up."

"I guess you heard that they're coming in at the end of the month?" She nodded.

I suddenly felt like someone had let the air out of all of my tires— including the metaphorical ones. "Where will you be off to next?"

"I honestly don't know. Texas? Or maybe home?" She rested a hand on my shoulder, slowly got to her feet, and removed her hand.

I wanted to pull it back, but I didn't.

"Sure you don't want my help?" she asked.

"Nope." I held up my torque wrench. "I've got everything I need."

We stared at each other for a few moments. I was pretty certain that El knew I wasn't talking about the tire. I was also pretty sure she knew I was lying through my teeth.

"I guess I'll see you around," she said.

She turned away and headed toward the bar. I watched her straight back dissolve into the darkness as she walked off—fading away like misplaced hope. Then something occurred to me. I quickly scrambled to my feet.

"Hey, El?" I called out.

She stopped and turned around.

"You're still coming to dinner at Grammy's tomorrow night, aren't you?"

She seemed to think about that. "You still want me to?"

"Yes." I knew with certainty that I wanted it more than anything. She seemed to hesitate.

"Please, El. I want you." I paused. "I mean . . . I want you to come." Oh Judas. "I mean . . . to Grammy's. I want you to come to Grammy's."

Though the semidarkness, I thought I could see her smile. She raised a hand and pointed toward my truck.

"Right now, it looks like you have bigger fish to fry."

"What are you talking about?"

I felt something brush against my pant leg. What the hell? I looked down. Lucille.

"Oh, no!" I reached toward him, but it was too late. He'd already raised his fat leg and pissed all over my tire. I had to hand it to him, he had pretty good aim. He managed to hit every single one of the lug nuts.

"Oh, man." I lowered my torque wrench. This all just went from bad to worse at Mach ten.

Lucille finished the job and hightailed his fat ass toward El . . . of course.

Just my luck . . . I get stuck with a urine-soaked flat tire, and Lucille walks off with the girl.

I hated my life right then.

"I'll be there."

I looked at El. She was smiling at me and reaching down to pat Lucille, who was dancing around her feet like a marionette.

Maybe my life wasn't so bad after all.

Chapter 5

The next morning, I called El and gave her directions to Grammy Mann's house. I thought it made a lot more sense for us to arrive for dinner separately, and not just because I was beginning to grow wary about too many wagging tongues if we were seen riding around together. I wanted El to have the wherewithal to leave early if she felt too uncomfortable being there.

In hindsight, it did seem that maybe I had jumped the gun a little by asking her to come by and meet the most important member of my family. But then, Grammy had pretty much steamrolled her way into the middle of everything, and there was no way I could back out now. Besides, I was more than a little curious to see how well El would hold up after spending an hour or two in Grammy's crosshairs. *That* was like getting grilled by Montel Williams, one of Grammy's favorite afternoon TV stars.

I showed up early to help get things ready, which meant making the iced tea and plumping up the cushions on the porch furniture. It was hot outside, but not intolerable. There actually was a nice breeze blowing in from the west. A couple of times, I thought the heavy, summer air smelled like the Wabash River. On a trellis at the end of the porch, a thick maze of Wooly Dutchman's Pipe provided a wall of cool, deep shade for Grammy's rocking chairs. It was still blooming, and if you looked closely, you could see tiny purple flowers.

Fritz took up his customary post at the top of the porch steps. He seemed more alert than usual. He kept scanning the county road that ran past the front of Grammy's house. Probably, he sensed my agitation. That wouldn't be hard . . . I'd pretty much been an emotional basket case since running into El last night in the parking lot at

Hoosier Daddy. I knew that I was just digging myself in deeper by letting Grammy pressure me into inviting El over here. And that was especially true now that it looked like she and Tony would be pulling up stakes and clearing out sooner than anyone expected. It was clear that I was on another fast track to emotional disaster, and instead of easing my foot off the pedal; I was jamming it into the floorboards.

Fritz started up and climbed to his feet. It always amazed me how he could hear a car coming a full minute before I could. Down the road, I could see a red SUV coming around the bend. El. I glanced down at my watch. Right on time, too. I remembered what Luanne told me the other night. "Honey, one thing about them agitators is how they always show up, pronto."

I waved a hand at El to let her know she'd found the right place. Fritz flew down off the porch like he'd been shot from a cannon and raced out to the driveway to meet her. What was it with El and dogs? I followed a little more slowly, and tried to calm myself so I could act nonchalant . . . like having a labor organizer over to eat pot roast with my grandmother was the most normal thing in the world.

El turned off her engine and hopped out. She was wearing a sleeveless, tangerine-colored cotton dress with a scoop neck. She looked fantastic . . . as usual. One thing was for certain: if El ever got tired of being a union agitator, she could make a fortune modeling for J. Jill.

Fritz was dancing around her like a lunatic. She bent over to ruffle his ears and kiss him on the top of his blond head.

"Well, hello there," she cooed. "Aren't you just about the best looking thing I've ever seen?"

I had a hard time not repeating exactly the same words to her.

"I see you made it," I said instead.

She smiled up at me. It was incredible how even a hardscrabble backdrop like Doc Baker's front yard could resemble a rolling vineyard in Tuscany with El posed in front of it.

"I would have been hard pressed *not* to find this place," she said. "It seems that any place of note in this county is either one right- or one left-turn off this road."

I had never thought about it that way. "I guess that's true. We tend to lead simpler lives out here in the Crossroads of America."

She laughed. "Don't I wish that were the truth?"

"You think it isn't?"

"Not where you're concerned."

Apparently, Fritz decided that this was going to be a longer conversation. He sat down at El's feet and rested his head against her knee. Fritz was a leaner.

"I'm not that complex."

El raised an eyebrow. "I don't share that assessment."

I thought about the conversation we'd had last night while I was changing my tire, and the ways my demeanor toward her bounced around. "I guess I have been acting like an idiot."

"I think *idiot* might be a bit strong, but you have expressed a fair amount of ambivalence."

"It's really not ambivalence. It's more like . . ." I searched for the right word. "Confusion."

She was still petting Fritz, who probably would've consented to sit there, plastered up against her leg, until the next millennium. It was hard to blame him.

"What can we do to un-confuse you?" she asked.

"Is that a word?"

El shrugged. "It's more of a concept."

"Jill?" Grammy's voice rolled out from inside the house. "Are you ever gonna bring that girl inside so I can get a look at her?"

I sighed and looked at El apologetically. "It's not too late to lay a patch out of here and head for Pizza Hut."

"I think I'll take my chances." She brushed at the side of her dress to remove some strands of Fritz's hair. He'd already bolted for the steps when he heard Grammy's voice.

"Don't say I didn't warn you."

We walked together to the porch. The screen door opened and Grammy came outside to greet us. She was drying her hands on a faded dish towel. El and I walked up the steps.

"Grammy, this is Eleanor Rzcpczinska."

Grammy's eyes grew wide. "Zhep-*what?*"

64

"Sin-ska," I replied. "Zhep-*sin*-ska."

El stepped forward and held out her hand. "Just call me El, or The Agitator."

Grammy stared at her for a moment, then smiled and took hold of her arm. "We're gonna get along just fine." She led El inside. I could hear their heels clacking along the floorboards as they headed back toward the kitchen.

Fritz stood there beside me, watching them go. Then he raised his brown eyes to my face.

"I got nothin'," I said to him.

He sighed and ambled off to reclaim his perch beside the steps.

"Jill?" Grammy's voice rang out again. "Are you going to join us?"

I looked out across the landscape. Nope. There were no talking animals or caterpillars out smoking behind the barn. It still looked like Indiana. I hadn't somehow fallen down a rabbit hole and ended up in Neverland.

"Jill!"

"Coming, Grammy."

I shook my head and went inside to join them.

૭ ૭ ૭

"So, tell me about your people." Grammy loaded El up with enough pot roast to start her own Oxfam chapter.

El watched as Grammy ladled spoonful after spoonful of the thick, pot liquor onto her plate. Her expression grew more panicked as the mound of food grew larger.

I intervened.

"Grammy, she can't possibly eat all of that."

Grammy paused, mid-ladle, and locked El in her cross hairs. "You look like you could use a bit of fattening up. I don't imagine you get much decent food living out of hotels." She passed the plate across to her.

El gave her one of those smiles that looked like a million dollars before taxes. "Thanks. I do get tired of eating out of vending machines."

Grammy clucked her tongue. "Ain't nothin' in a Zagnut bar that can feed a body."

I didn't bother to tell Grammy that the last known vending machine to dispense a Zagnut bar was probably collecting rust in some abandoned Kentucky rest stop.

"Grammy . . ." I tried again.

She ignored me. "Have some of this cornbread, honey." She plopped a brick-sized hunk of it on the corner of El's plate. "It'll soak up some of that gravy."

I gave up and held out my plate. "Could I have some, too?"

Grammy handed me a slab of the yellow cake without even looking in my direction.

El lifted a forkful of the thick stew to her mouth and tasted it. I thought her eyes were going to roll back into her head.

"Oh my god . . . this is wonderful."

Grammy beamed.

I stared down at my plank of cornbread. It sat naked on my white, Corelle dinner plate, surrounded by a ring of tiny blue cornflowers.

"Could I have some, too?" I asked again.

Grammy glanced at me this time.

"Pot roast. I'd like some pot roast." I pointed at the center of my plate. "To soften up this two-by-four."

Grammy gave me one of those "people in hell want ice water" looks, and shifted the handle of the ladle so it was pointed in my direction.

"Right. *Thanks.*" I got to my feet. "I'll help myself. You two just forget I'm here."

El gave me a look filled with so much affection and amusement that I nearly dropped the ladle.

"So," Grammy said. "Your people?"

El shifted her attention back to Grammy. "Buffalo. I grew up in Buffalo."

I could see Grammy trying to mentally plot that location on a map. "Is that where they make those tiny chicken wings in the hot sauce?"

El smiled and nodded at her. "Yes, ma'am. Chicken wings and lots of car parts." She looked at me. "Not necessarily in that order."

"Brothers and sisters?" Grammy asked.

66

"Lots of those, too," El replied. "I come from a big, loud, blue-collar, Roman Catholic family. I'm the youngest of six—three brothers, two sisters, and one bathroom." She smiled. "On school days, my mother woke us up in five-minute intervals. We had to learn how to work fast."

"That has to be a benefit in your profession," I added.

"It does pay dividends sometimes." She raised an eyebrow. "I have been known to do some of my best work in bathrooms."

I cleared my throat. "Anybody want more tea?" I got up and went to the kitchen to retrieve the pitcher.

Grammy ignored me and stayed on task. "Are any of your brothers and sisters married?"

"All of them." El explained. "At last count, there were eight grand-children and at least two more on the way." She glanced at me. "I appear to be the family's only stalwart when it comes to zero popula-tion growth."

"That's a shame," Grammy said. "You'd make beautiful babies."

I choked on my tea.

Grammy was unfazed. "Where do they all live?"

"Mostly in and around Buffalo."

"That must be very nice for your folks."

El nodded. "My mom never misses an opportunity to let me know that my rolling-stone lifestyle is an annoying departure from the family norm. She really wants me to settle someplace and put down some roots."

"Don't you like Buffalo?"

El smiled. "Have you ever *been* to Buffalo, Mrs. Mann?"

Grammy shook her head. "No, honey. I don't tend to travel much outside the Tri-State. I never did see the reason to go gallivanting all over when everything I need is right here within a stone's throw. Besides, I can get every place I need to go without ever having to make any left turns. Things are just a whole lot simpler that way." She looked at me. "Now, Jill, here, seems to get all antsy from time to time. I think it was going away to school did that. And now all that time she spends workin' on that fancy MBA degree. It puts all kinds of ideas in her head."

"What ideas?" I asked.

Grammy waved a hand at me but kept her attention focused on El.

I looked down at my plate of food. "What ideas?" I asked the medley of beef, potatoes, and carrots that stared back at me. I knew that I was about as likely to get a response from it as I was from Grammy.

"Your mama is right," Grammy said to El. "It would do both of you girls good to put down some roots."

"I have roots," I tried again. "*Lots* of them. It's my roots that get in the way, not my lack of them."

El seemed interested in that. "Don't you like living here?"

"I like it okay," I replied. "Mostly. But I get tired of how . . . unvarying . . . the social aspects of my life can be."

"Unvarying?" Grammy asked. "What in the world does that mean? If that's just a highfalutin way to talk about Misty Ann Marks, then I have to agree with you."

"Grammy . . ."

"Misty Ann Marks?" El asked. I wanted to slide beneath the table. "Who is she?"

"Nobody." I glared at Grammy.

Grammy clucked her tongue.

"Really?" El looked at me and raised an eyebrow. "Do tell."

I drummed my fingers against the side of my iced tea glass.

"See?" Grammy chimed in. "Antsy."

I sighed and pushed my glass away. "How about we change the subject?"

El was chewing on the inside of her cheek.

I tried again. "Tell us about your parents, El. What do they do?"

She made me wait for what felt like an eternity, but finally, took pity on me. "My mother is a retired school teacher. My dad died when I was seventeen—in an accident at work."

"Bless your heart." In an instant, Grammy forgot all about Misty Ann and my antsy demeanor. "You poor baby."

I was shocked. "What happened, El?"

El shrugged. "It was a classic breach of Lockout/Tagout protocol—

one hundred percent preventable. Dad was a machinist, doing repairs on a metal stamping machine. The foreman had refused to allow him to properly lock and tagout the unit before he went to work on it. Apparently, that same foreman walked off to tend to something else, and a line supervisor passed by and turned the machine back on without knowing that dad was still servicing it." She slowly shook her head. "They say he died instantly, but we won't ever really know what he understood or felt. What we *do* know is that management in this plant had consistently failed to enforce LoTo procedures." She looked at me. "And that's the short version of how I became an agitator."

"Lord have mercy." Grammy patted El's hand. "And there was your poor mama with six children to care for."

"Well, most of us were already out of the home—working or in college."

"That doesn't change the fact that she was left alone with nothing but her memories to keep her warm at night."

"I'm really sorry, El."

She looked at me. "It was a long time ago."

"I know. But I'm still sorry."

We sat there staring at each other over our half-eaten piles of pot roast and corn bread.

Grammy cleared her throat. "As soon as you girls are finished making cow eyes at each other, we can go out on the porch and have dessert."

El's cow eyes quickly filled up with panic. "Dessert?"

"It's pie. Rhubarb," Grammy said with pride. "From my own patch out behind the garage. I canned it last spring."

"Maybe we can share a slice?" I suggested.

Grammy got to her feet and started collecting plates. "Why don't you two go out for a stroll while I clear these things away? It should've cooled off some, and maybe you can work up an appetite."

I saw Fritz's ears twitch when he heard the telltale sound of dishes being stacked, a sure fire sign that leftovers were on their way to his food bowl. He lumbered into the dining room with his tail wagging and an expectant look on his face.

"Won't you let us help you clean up?" El asked.

Grammy was already halfway to the kitchen with Fritz trotting along behind her.

"I'll holler for you when the coffee's ready," she said over her shoulder.

El looked at me. "Cooled off? She is aware that it's still about ninety-five degrees out there, isn't she?"

I glanced over at Grammy's ancient box fan whirring away from its perch atop an even more ancient console stereo. It had been blowing hot air past us for the last hour.

"Welcome to the Midwest—where winters get colder and summers get hotter."

"Hotter than what?" El asked.

"I dunno. What's the hottest thing you can think of?"

"Right now, I'd have to say that it's probably the way your face looked when Grammy mentioned Misty Ann Marks."

I rolled my eyes. "Hotter than that."

"Why on earth would people choose to live in a place where they freeze in the winter and fry in the summer?"

"I don't know. Maybe it reminds them of their disappointed hopes."

"Are you talking about them, or about yourself?"

"Yes."

El laughed and stood up. "Want to show me this famous rhubarb patch?"

I'd been down that road before, but I decided it was in my best interest not to mention it.

"Sure."

El came around the table and took hold of my arm. We walked back through the house and out onto the front porch. It was already well past nine, but the moon was full, and everything outside looked like it had been dabbed with silver paint.

The fall bugs were kicking up a ruckus. The noise they made slammed into us like a tidal wave as soon as we stepped outside the door. It was pretty impressive. Imagine the sound a couple thousand insects could make if they ran a chorus of tiny power tools at full-tilt boogie. Then multiply that by ten.

El turned toward me. In the silver light, her face was like an etching—

one of those really good ones that came on commemorative coins from the Franklin Mint.

"What the hell is *that?*" she asked

"Fall bugs."

"What on earth are fall bugs?"

"I think you call them cicadas."

"Really?" She seemed incredulous. "In Indiana? I thought they generally conducted their high-octane sex romps in the southern states."

"Nope. We get 'em every year, but usually not this early, and almost never this loud."

"Hmmm. Isn't this supposed to be one of the seven plagues of the apocalypse?"

"No." I shook my head. "I think that's locusts."

El smiled at me. "You say tomato . . ."

I became aware of a scuffling noise behind us. Fritz had apparently finished his plate of leftovers and was eager to join us outside. I opened the door, and he pushed past me, gaining momentum as he headed for the steps. He vaulted off the porch in a flash of silver light and bounded across the side yard toward the back of the house.

I nudged El. "Still wanna see the rhubarb patch?"

"Try and stop me."

We left the porch and followed Fritz, with greater deliberation and less speed.

El looked around. I felt proud of how tidy Grammy kept things. It was a far cry from Doc Baker's compound across the road. His front yard looked like a cross between a junkyard and a drag strip. Sadly, that approach was more the norm than the exception in these parts.

"I've never really thought much about Indiana," El said. "It always seemed more like a punch line than a place—as if the entire state was an unhappy suburb of Dan Quayle."

"Dan Quayle? Isn't he a little before your time?"

"I've always been precocious and well-informed."

"Apparently."

El was still holding on to my arm, and she gave it a little squeeze. "I'll be sad to leave here—for more reasons than one."

Her words siphoned the luster right off the silver night. Rolling farmland that had been looking lush and romantic now just looked lumpy and gray.

"When are you leaving?" I asked. I tried to sound casual, but I knew I wasn't fooling El. Or myself.

She shrugged. "By the end of next week, probably. Tony says this game is a lot like playing the slots in Vegas. You don't stay with a cold machine."

I didn't know what to feel. In all honesty, I didn't give two flips about whether or not our plant got a union. But I did care about not seeing El any more. I cared about that a lot.

"I wish you could stay," I said. I knew it sounded vague and non-committal. Even now, I was afraid of saying too much. Hell . . . *especially* now.

We reached the garage and Grammy's garden. Corn, tomatoes, and peppers spread out before us in tidy rows. Next to the garage wall were several clusters of big, leafy plants. Their thick, woody stalks looked like polished mahogany in the moonlight. I pointed toward them.

"Voila. Behold the fabled rhubarb . . . coming soon to a dessert plate near you."

"My god. Those things look like shillelaghs."

"Well. They're a bit smaller and more tender when you harvest them in the spring."

"I sure as hell hope so." El looked back at me. "Did you mean what you said?"

I was confused. "About the rhubarb? Yeah. It's a lot less tough when you pick it early on."

El rolled her eyes. "No . . . not the rhubarb. Did you mean what you said about not wanting me to leave?"

"Oh. That."

"Yes. That."

I nodded. "I meant it."

She sighed. "It's odd. Normally, I can't wait to see the back end of a small town like this. But Princeton seems like a place I could actually get used to."

I was surprised. "You like it here?"

"Strange, isn't it? It surprises the hell out of me, too."

"Why not stay, then?" I said it like it was the most natural thing in the world. And as soon as the words were out of my mouth, the idea fell into place right alongside those perfect rows of tasseled corn—like it had always been part of this landscape.

"Are you serious?"

I nodded. "Why not?"

El waved a hand. "Well, for one thing, there's not a lot of demand around here for unemployed agitators."

That was true. "I suppose there are other things you could do?" I asked, hopefully.

"Like what?"

"I don't know. What did you do in Buffalo before you signed up with the UAW?"

"*Signed up?* You make it sound like I joined the Army."

"You say tomato . . ." I quoted.

"Okay, wiseass. How about you guess?"

"Guess?"

"Yeah." El seemed to be warming to this idea. "Guess what I did before I *signed up* with the union."

I knew she was goading me, but I didn't care. I was determined to get it right. I stepped back and pretended to study her carefully, which was totally unnecessary. I could already draw every part of her perfectly from memory.

"You ran a hookah bar?" I suggested.

She smacked me on the arm. "Be serious."

I rubbed my arm. "I *was* being serious."

"Try again."

"Okay. Okay." I thought about it some more. "I think you were a teacher."

I saw the flicker of surprise cross her face and knew I was right.

"That's it, isn't it?" I boasted. "You were a teacher."

El wagged her finger in front of me—just like every teacher I'd ever had. "Not so fast, Einstein. You're close, but not close enough to fire up a cigar."

73

"Whattaya mean? I guessed it . . . you just don't want to admit it."

"Nuh uh. What *kind* of teacher?"

"Oh, jeez . . . come on, El."

She stood her ground. "Nope. You started it."

"I started it? You're the one who told me I had to guess."

"Well," she shrugged, "you're the one who wants to know."

This was getting us no place. "Okay. Um . . . you taught . . . Driver's Ed."

"Drivers Ed?"

I nodded.

"This is your guess? Seriously?"

"Well . . . I *have* seen you parallel park."

"It's true that I have unsung talents. However, that skill would not be among them."

"How about you just tell me?"

"Tell you? What fun would there be in that?"

"El?"

"No. You have to guess."

"I don't want to guess. We've already established that I suck at guessing."

"You mean you give up?"

"El . . ."

"No. First you have to say, I give up. Then, I'll tell you."

"Are you kidding me?"

She sighed. "It's easy to see that you didn't grow up with three brothers."

"Is everything with you a contest of wills?"

She thought about that. "More or less."

"Okay, then. I give up."

El cupped a hand around her ear and leaned toward me. "Excuse me?"

I took a deep breath. "*Uncle.* I give up. You *win.* I *surrender.* If I had a white flag, I'd *wave* it. If I had a sword, I'd *fall* on it. If I had milk money, I'd *give* it to you. Okay?"

She looked unconvinced. "You have to say it like you mean it."

"You're killing me here." I stood there absently tapping my fingertips against my pant leg. El noticed.

74

"Feeling antsy?" she asked, sweetly.

I looked up at the night sky. The stars were especially bright tonight, and it was worth noting that none of them were aligned in patterns that seemed to be favoring me.

"I give up," I muttered to any god who might be up there paying attention to my plight.

"See?" El was beaming at me. "That wasn't so hard, was it?"

"You know," I glowered at her, "if you taught anything other than showing people how to annoy the piss out of each other, I'd be amazed."

"Bingo!" El proclaimed. "Ladies and gentlemen, we have a winner."

"What are you talking about?"

"What I taught. You just guessed it."

I was confused again. "You taught people how to annoy the piss out of each other?"

She nodded. "In a manner of speaking. I taught Industrial and Labor Relations to pimply-faced undergraduates."

I blinked. "You were a college professor?"

"Hard to believe, isn't it?"

"Holy shit." I was stunned. "Where?"

She shrugged. "In New York."

"State or city?"

"State."

"Where?" I held up a hand. "And please don't say 'guess.'"

She smiled. "Cornell."

"Good god."

"Don't act so shocked. It wasn't that big of a deal."

"Why'd you quit?"

"Teaching?"

I nodded.

"After my father's death, I wanted to do something that I thought would really make things better for factory workers. You may not realize that the UAW has a pretty robust scholarship program for children of union members."

I shook my head.

"I got lots of help and financial support from our Region 9 local, and that enabled me to go on to grad school right after college." El gave a wry-sounding laugh. "But I still had to borrow tons of money, and I'll be working to pay off all those loans for a very long time."

I was still trying to make sense of everything she'd just shared with me. "So you were a college professor? At *Cornell?*"

El frowned at me. "Why is that so hard to believe? Do I drool or something?"

"No," I added quickly. "It's not that. It's just . . ."

"Just what?"

"I don't know." I shrugged. "I just don't understand why you would leave a dream job like that to become . . ."

"An agitator?" she asked.

"Well." I shrugged again. "Yeah."

"I hate to destroy the romanticized view you obviously have of my sojourn in academe, but trust me . . . life in Ithaca was far from idyllic."

"What happened?"

"Lots of things." She seemed to consider them all for a moment or two. "Failed aspirations. Failed relationships. Take your pick."

"So you ran away?"

"I prefer to think that I moved on toward something better."

I felt like a jerk for making such a stupid comment. "I'm sorry. I didn't mean to sound so judgmental."

"It's okay."

"No." I laid a hand on her forearm. "It's not. I'm sorry."

She didn't reply. We stood there in silence, with my hand still resting on her arm. I could hear Fritz off in the distance, barking at something. It sounded like he was running—probably chasing one of Ermaline's stray cats. She had about a dozen of them at last count, all living beneath a rusted-out, Leer commercial truck cap that reposed proudly on the scrap heap they called a front lawn.

El heard it, too. "Is that Fritz?"

I nodded.

"Do you need to check it out?" she asked.

"No. I just need to be ready with the Neosporin if he comes back with cat scratches on his nose."

She smiled. "I wish all of our problems could be solved that easily."

"Well, maybe you can be a golden retriever in the next life?"

"It's an idea with some merit."

I smiled but didn't say anything. El noticed me staring at her. "What?" she asked.

"It's nothing," I replied.

She rolled her eyes. "I haven't known you all that long, but I think I can tell when you've got something on your mind."

I shrugged.

"Come on," she said. "Give it up."

"It's stupid."

"Stupid?"

I nodded.

"Friday Jill, I feel pretty confident that whatever it is you're reluctant to share won't rise to the level of stupid, as I define it."

I was intrigued by that idea. "You have a stupid scale?"

"Of course. Doesn't everyone?"

"Um. *No.* What kinds of things make your list?"

"Oh, that's easy. I'll give you the short version." She started to tick things off. "Skinny jeans; Zeppo Marx; peanut butter and jelly in the same jar; Justin Bieber with or without his shirt; people who say OMG; any cable show about bass fishing; three-fifths of the nation's factory workers who believe that labor unions are unnecessary—and the other two-fifths who think they *are*; any woman who exchanges text messages with Anthony Weiner, including Huma Abedin; the on-air talent at the Fox News Channel, except Sally Kohn; and the entire North Carolina legislature—no exceptions."

"That's your *short* list?"

She nodded.

I was amazed. "Mine is nowhere near that long."

El seemed amused. "So what were you not going to say to me because it was stupid?"

"It was just an impulse."

"Sometimes impulses can be good things."

"You think so?"

"Yeah, I do."

Right then, about a dozen impulses roared to the surface. I wondered if I should give in to a few of them and see if El would think they were good ideas. I decided just to come clean instead.

"I was going to say that I hate for you to leave when we're just starting to get to know each other."

El looked out across the silver rows of corn that were starting to fade into the disappearing landscape. The night seemed to be getting brighter and darker all at the same time.

"I don't think that's stupid at all," she said. Her voice sounded different. Smaller. Like it was vanishing, too.

"You don't?" I asked.

She shook her head.

"I wish we had more time," I added.

"Me, too."

"I wish we'd met sooner. In another place and time. Before I made so many wrong turns."

"Why do you sound like you don't like your life?"

"Because right now, I don't."

"But, Friday Jill," El moved a step closer to me, "right now is all we have."

I looked down at her. It wasn't fair. I wanted a thousand—a million—right nows. I wanted enough right nows to last until I was too old or too crazy to care that there were no more to be had. I opened my mouth to try and explain that to El, but she quickly found a way to prevent me from saying anything. She felt sweet and safe, and I knew that I would never want to let go of her. We stood together in the dying light, surrounded by the chattering of the fall bugs and Fritz's distant bark. The roaring in my ears grew louder and, soon, I couldn't hear anything but the thump of my own beating heart.

El pulled away. I reached for her, but she laid a hand against my chest. She said something, but I couldn't understand her. The noise in my head was too great.

"Someone's coming," she repeated. Her voice was like a whisper.

"Oh." I dropped my hands. They were shaking.

I gradually became aware of a dull, pounding noise and turned around to see Fritz loping toward us. A moment later, Grammy materialized from the darkness behind him. She stood illuminated by a sea of tiny, yellow flashes. Lightning bugs . . . hundreds of them. When had they come out?

"Are you two out here waiting on next year's batch?" she called out.

I had no idea how long we'd been gone. I looked at El, then back at Grammy. "Is the pie ready?"

"Been ready. Come on. It's a lot cooler on the porch." She turned around and receded back into the night.

"She's lying," I said.

El looked at me.

"It's not cooler there," I explained.

She smiled and took my hand. "Let's go try it, anyway."

I didn't argue with her. We slowly walked back toward the house with Fritz in tow.

Nothing had been settled between us, but even the gloomiest outcome seemed brighter when it got served up with a fresh, hot slice of Grammy's rhubarb pie.

Chapter 6

"You better get back to the warehouse quick." T-Bomb was out of breath from running halfway across the plant to find me. "Luanne is hoppin' mad about some missing air filters—even though I told her they'd been backordered from that plant in Litchfield for two weeks now, cause of all the flooding and power outages up that way after them tornadoes last month. But she went stormin' back there anyway, and now she's about to get unhinged all over Earl Junior."

She was talking so fast that I was having a hard time keeping up.

"Slow down." I put a hand on her shoulder. Her t-shirt was damp and sticking to her skin. T-Bomb worked in a section of the plant where the AC had been on the blink for most of the month. And today was already one for the record books—ninety-two degrees in the shade, and it was barely ten a.m. "Take a deep breath. Why's Luanne going after Earl Junior?"

"I told you. It's them damn air filters. She went back there to tell Earl Junior that he needed to figure something out pronto, and damn if she didn't find half a truckload of the dern things stashed behind some scrap carburetors. They wasn't tagged or nothin'. And when she showed them to Earl Junior, he just stood there, scratching his bits, saying he didn't know nothing about 'em." She wiped some sweat off her forehead. "I never seen her this mad. You gotta get back there before she takes a box cutter to him."

I sighed. "Where's Buzz?"

It wasn't that I didn't want to get involved, but management had made it clear to me on more than one occasion that jumping into the middle of disputes like this one was above my pay grade.

T-Bomb threw up a hand in frustration. "I ain't seen so much as his shadow since I walked into this damn blast furnace three hours ago." She narrowed her eyes as she continued to stare at me. "What's the matter with you? Has that El DeBarge still got your panties all twisted-up in a wad?"

"What are you talking about?" I fought an impulse to shake out my pant leg.

"Normally, you'd already be halfway to the warehouse instead of standing here arguing with me."

"I am not arguing with you, T-Bomb.

"Well if this ain't an argument, then I don't know what the heck it is."

I was trying hard not to lose patience with her. "I told you. I can't keep getting involved in this stuff. It's not my job. Besides, you know I can't leave the line without backup."

"Well, it sure as hell needs to be somebody's job." She pulled a blue bandana handkerchief out of her back pocket and wiped off her neck. "Fine. When we all have to eat creamed corn for the next month, you can just keep telling yourself that you did right not getting involved."

I sighed. "Isn't your break about over?"

"Damn." She glanced down at her watch, and then looked back at me. "Ain't telling me to get back on the line somebody else's job, too?"

"Come on. Don't be this way."

Behind her, I could see Luanne huffing her way toward us. She looked like an angry bolt of paisley.

"Here comes Luanne," I said.

T-Bomb turned around to watch her approach.

Luanne's face and neck were bright red. It was clear that she was still seething.

"Well?" T-Bomb asked. "What happened?"

"Somebody needs to take a tire iron to that boy." Luanne looked at me. "He's nothin' but a half-wit, and I'm tired of workin' around his mistakes."

"I know, I know." I tried to get Luanne to stand still for a minute and calm down. She was breathing unevenly, and I didn't like her pallor. "Why don't you go sit down in the break room for a few minutes? I'll cover for you."

T-Bomb looked at me. "Who in the hell will cover for you?"

"I'm about due for my break, too."

"Oh . . . so *now* you can walk away?" She waved her soggy bandana toward the production line behind me. "But five minutes ago, it was none of your business."

I sighed. "Don't be like this, okay? You both know I can't keep getting involved in this management stuff."

Luanne snorted. "Management, my derriere. We ain't got no management around here, and that's the problem."

I didn't have any response to that. I could hardly tell them both that maybe they needed to be having this conversation with El and Tony.

T-Bomb agreed. "If solvin' our problems is gonna be left up to the likes of Buzz Sheets and Earl Junior, we might as well walk outta here and get jobs passin' out shoppin' carts at Walmart."

Luanne had moved on. "I got nothin' more to say about it, so I'll just say this." She wagged a stubby finger at me. "You mark my words. If them Ogata people come in here and let these stupid, selfish assholes keep runnin' things, they're gonna end up in a world full of hurtin' with a shitload of lawsuits." She pulled a pack of Viceroys out of her shirt pocket and smacked it against her palm to force one out. "I'm goin' outside for a smoke. If Buzz Sheets comes lookin' for me, you can tell him I said he can kiss me where the sun don't shine."

She turned away and stormed off toward the nearest exit.

"Well if that don't beat all." T-Bomb looked at me. "I hope you're happy."

"Me? What does this have to do with me?"

She waved a hand. "Nothin'. Nothin' has *anything* to do with you. You just stay there all locked up in your own little world, safe from everybody and everything."

"That's not fair—" I began.

"I don't want to hear it. You used to be somebody who cared about other people. Now you're just so damn afraid of making mistakes that you sit there like a hunk of scrap metal."

"I care about other people."

"Oh, yeah? The Friday I used to know would never just sit back on the sidelines while half the damn plant worked back-to-back shifts with no air conditioning during the hottest days of the summer. The Friday I used to know would never keep her mouth shut when a primo idiot like Earl Junior got promoted ahead of five women who deserved it more—especially when she was one of the five women. The Friday I used to know would never take up with trash like Misty Ann Marks, then run scared from somebody decent like El DeBarge."

I was shocked. "What?"

"You heard me."

"T-Bomb . . ."

"Forget it." She looked down at her watch. "I got no time for this. I still need this job."

She stormed off.

I watched her go with my mouth hanging open. We'd been best friends for a lot of years, and T-Bomb had always told me the truth. But I'd never seen her as angry or disappointed in me as she seemed to be today. And what was that comment about El supposed to mean? I thought T-Bomb agreed with everybody else that getting involved with El spelled disaster for me.

All the lights in the plant started blinking. An ear-splitting siren went off and quickly drowned out the ambient rush and rattle of machinery.

Now what?

People were yelling at each other and shutting down the lines. Red lights were flashing overhead. I looked toward the emergency exit in time to see a swath of paisley disappear into the sunlight before the big door slammed shut behind it.

෨ ෨ ෨

"I need to talk with you."

I'd caught up with Joe Sykes in the hallway that led to the front offices.

He looked down at me. His thinning brown hair was damp and

plastered across his forehead like wet pieces of yarn. He did not look happy to see me.

"Stow it, Fryman." He held up the palm of his hand. "I know why you're here, and it's not going to change anything. She's fired. End of story."

"Look, Joe." I tried my best to appear calm. "What she did was stupid. But you have to know that she was just angry about those air filters. She was trying to do the right thing—to keep up production and prevent lost time."

"Oh, really?" Joe crossed his arms. They looked like ham shanks. "If she cared so much about lost fucking time, why'd she set off the goddamn fire alarm?"

"I know. It was a mistake, Joe. She made a bad decision. We all do that. But she cares about her work here . . . you know that. She was just mad about Earl Junior misplacing those air filters. You've been there. We all have."

Joe stood there, glaring at me and breathing through his mouth. I hated that about him. I could see little beads of moisture hanging on the stray hairs that sprouted from the dimple beneath his nose. I forced myself not to look away.

"She's trouble. She's always mouthing off and I'm sick of it."

"Then make her cool her heels at home for a week without pay. But don't fire her, Joe." I lowered my voice to a whisper. "Not with the competition coming up on Saturday."

Joe was a big letch, and he'd had the hots for Luanne's daughter ever since he first laid eyes on her at last year's Pork Day celebration. Everybody knew it.

I could see him waver, so I went in for the kill. "Jailissa's been working so hard, and she's got her heart set on winning this year. Luanne's been working on her costume for weeks."

"Her costume?" he asked. "What's she wearing?" He was practically drooling. It made my skin crawl, but I pressed on.

"It's a sight to behold, Joe. White stretch pants with gold tassels and a matching gold tank top. She's doing her flaming baton routine." I shook my head. "But this news about her mama will likely take the wind right out of her sails." I gingerly reached out and touched his hairy forearm. "You can prevent that, Joe. You can give Jailissa this shot at that crown."

He sighed. "She's a good kid. I guess it's not her fault that her mama's got a wild hair up her ass."

"That's true, Joe."

He let out a long, slow breath. "She'd make a beautiful Pork Queen." His tone was reverential.

"She would. It's her time, Joe."

"All right." He pointed a crooked finger at me. "You tell that big-mouth fat ass that I don't want to see hide nor hair of her in this plant for the next *two* weeks."

I bit back an expletive. Two weeks without pay was ridiculous, but it was better than no job at all.

"And if she ever pulls a stunt like this again, there won't be no discussion." He leaned toward me. "She'll be gone. *Capisce?*"

I nodded. "You're a good man, Joe." I fought an impulse to knee him in the balls. "I'll make sure she gets the message."

I turned away from him and started to head back toward the plant.

"Hold up, Fryman," he said.

I looked back at him.

"Don K.'s been looking for you."

Don K. was Don Krylon—great-grandson of the founder of Krylon Motors. He still kept an office here, although he hadn't spent much time at the Indiana facility since the sellout to Ogata had been announced.

"Don K. is here?" I asked.

Joe jerked a thumb toward the front of the building. "Up in the conference room."

"He wants to see me?" I repeated.

"Something wrong with your hearing?"

I shook my head.

"Well, if I were you, I wouldn't keep him waiting."

I sighed. There was no way this was going to be good news. "Right. On my way." I pushed past him and headed toward the front offices, wondering what else fate had in store for me.

"Sit down, Jill."

Don K. gestured toward one of the plush, crimson-colored leather chairs that were scattered around the cherry-topped meeting table. I noticed that they each had oversized Outlaw emblems stamped on their headrests.

"Like something cold to drink? I know it's still warm out there in some parts of the plant."

I shook my head. "No, thanks." I took a seat in one of the chairs he'd indicated.

Don K. was about as different from Joe Sykes as wealth and biology could conspire to make him. He was tastefully dressed in gray slacks and a pink shirt with creases sharp enough to slice cheese. He looked like he'd just walked in from a three-day spa weekend. I'd only met him in passing twice before, and neither occasion seemed all that memorable to me. That piqued my curiosity and heightened my trepidation. Why did he want to talk with me? And how did he even remember who I was?

"Thanks for taking the time to come and see me, Jill." He sat down in a chair beside me. I was surprised that he didn't automatically take a seat directly across the table. Strangely, it put me a little more at ease. I felt less like I had been called into the principal's office.

I nodded. "Joe said you wanted to see me."

Don K. smiled. His mouthful of perfect teeth had probably added a screened porch to the beach house of some orthodontist.

"He's right. In fact, I've wanted to talk with you for some time. But with the Ogata transition going on, everything's been in a swivel. Half the time, I don't know whether I'm coming or going."

I didn't know what response to make to that, so I just nodded.

"Look, Jill. I'll just get right to the point. I know your day is nearly over and you've got things you'd like to get to."

"Okay." My nervousness started to tic up a notch.

He sat back and crossed his long legs. "You know that this Ogata buyout is a great thing for Princeton, don't you?"

I nodded. I also knew that it was an especially great thing for the

Krylon family. They stood to walk away with more than a billion dollars in deferred compensation and stock options in the new company.

"Ogata plans to pump new life into the local economy, Jill. Ramping up this facility to produce the Mastodon will add four-hundred-and-fifty new jobs—and that's just in Princeton. The ripple effect from this will reach out and touch all of our feeder plants, too. Parts. Transportation. Dealerships. Housing. Retail establishments. We're talking the entire the tri-state area. Everyone will benefit. Ogata stands poised to revolutionize Midwest manufacturing, and it all hinges on what happens right here, inside this assembly plant."

He paused to let his words sink in. Since he hadn't asked me anything, I remained silent.

"But there's a bee in this bonnet now, Jill . . . a hiccough in the process. And if we don't manage things carefully, everything we've worked so hard to achieve for the people of Indiana might fall right by the wayside."

It was true that I hadn't attended an Ivy League, northeastern college like Don K., but I was pretty sure I knew where his diatribe was headed.

"You're talking about the UAW?" I asked.

He nodded. "See? This is precisely why we need you, Jill. You're smart."

It was clear to me that Don K. was working his way around to something, and I knew that the fastest way to get him there was to continue to hold my peace. Grammy Mann taught me that.

I was right. It didn't take him long to start talking again.

"We need smart people on our side, Jill. Smart people who can help us help Princeton benefit from all the things Ogata promises to deliver. Smart people like you." He leaned forward and laced his fingers together on top of the shiny wood table. "How long have you been with Krylon now, Jill?"

I was sure he already knew the answer, but I told him anyway.

"Twelve years." As soon as I said it, I realized how ridiculous it was. Twelve years of my life, going no place.

Don K. nodded. "Loyalty. We appreciate that. So does Ogata. It's part of what drives their entire business model. Ogata has a place for you, Jill. Ogata needs smart, savvy people to head its transition team. Ogata needs managers who can help them realize their vision for the people of Princeton."

I felt like I was listening to one of Kenny Purvis's sermons at the House of Praise. It wouldn't have surprised me to hear someone shout "amen" from the corner of the room.

"Are you one of those people, Jill? Are you prepared to stand up and help us lead this plant to the forefront of automotive and manufacturing excellence?"

I felt sweat running down the back of my shirt, which was surprising, since it was cool enough in that conference room to hang meat.

"I'm not really sure what you're talking about," I said. "What, exactly, is it you want me to do?"

Don K. smiled. Then he seemed to shift gears. "I just got off the phone with Tony Gemelli. He and his colleague have invoked their right to come inside our plant and post notices about an upcoming union information session they're hosting next week. Of course, we all know that even in the closest families, things sometimes happen that generate bad feelings. Not everyone is as loyal or dedicated to Krylon as you are, Jill. It's important for us to do all we can to prevent a few small incidents of discontent from snowballing into something that could spell disaster for everyone."

"I don't really see how I could—"

"I pay attention, Jill. And I'm not alone in that. This is a small town. I know that you've grown . . . *friendly* . . . with Ms. Rzcpczinska."

Now I was doing more than sweating. I was sure that my face was turning beet red.

"I'm not—" I began. But Don K. talked over me again.

"I'm sure you understand that we'd like to have this union matter settled before the Ogata team arrives at the end of the month. As one of our newest production managers, I feel confident that you could use your connections and influence with the rank-and-file members of our Krylon family to smooth over any rough spots that might mistakenly lead them to think hospitably about the UAW's false promises."

I wasn't sure I'd heard him correctly. Was he offering me a promotion? In exchange for what? For me to become Krylon's Mata Hari?

I pushed back my chair and got to my feet. "I think you have the wrong person, Mr. Krylon. I don't have that kind of influence."

He withdrew a fat envelope from a leather-bound folio. "Don't be so hasty." He handed me the envelope. "Take some time and think it over. You'll find the details of our offer in here." He smiled at me again. "I've enjoyed our chat, Jill. It's been too long."

I stood there in front of him, sweating and holding the fat envelope with the embossed Krylon Motors logo on it. I wanted to tell him to go to hell—that I wasn't willing to become a whore for Krylon any more than I was willing to become a whore for the UAW. The only difference was that El had never asked me to do that. Right then, that one difference seemed huge—bigger and more important than anything Don K. and the Ogata team had to offer me.

"You're still sweating," Don K. added. He shook his head. "I know it's hot out there . . . brutal. But, Jill?"

I looked at him.

"You need to know that if this union vote happens, Ogata will pull the plug on Princeton. They'll move the Mastodon and everything associated with it to their plant in Smyrna. And if there's one thing I know for sure, it's that Georgia is a state just full of people who can take the heat without complaining."

An electronic alarm went off, and Don K. looked at his Rolex.

"If you'll excuse me, I have a conference call coming up. I think you can find your own way out?"

I nodded.

"Good. You can let me know your decision by Monday."

He turned away from me and picked up the handset of the console telephone that sat on the credenza behind his chair.

I backed out of the room, clutching the fat envelope to my chest like some kind of twisted life preserver. I didn't even bother going back into the plant. I walked out the main entrance and headed straight for my truck. There was only one place where I felt like I still belonged.

"Take my advice." Aunt Jackie slapped a third bottle of cold Stella down in front of me. "Taper off or order some food. You keep this up, and I'm gonna ask for your keys."

I'd been sitting at a back table by myself, staring at the unopened envelope Don K. had pushed into my hands before he dismissed me at the end of our friendly chat.

"I'm okay," I said. She wasn't buying it.

"Honey, I been slingin' suds at Hoosier Daddy since Methuselah was just a gleam in his daddy's eye, and one thing I know is how to spot somebody who ain't okay." She reached inside her blouse and tugged at her bra strap. "You look like somebody shit in your last bowl of Cheerios."

I shrugged. "It's just something at work."

"Work?" She shook her head. "I don't suppose this would have anything to do with Luanne Keortge gettin' her ass fired today, would it?"

"You heard about that?" It always amazed me how Aunt Jackie stayed on top of things. She had a better breaking news service than CNN.

Aunt Jackie waved a bar rag toward the street door. "Hell. Everybody in three damn counties heard about that. She roared through here like a bad case of Montezuma's Revenge."

I looked around the bar. It was still early and there were only two or three other customers.

"Where'd she go?"

"Hell if I know. She pounded a pitcher, tapped, and took off outta here as fast as she showed up. I think she was outta cigs." She pushed at her left bosom again. Apparently, it still wasn't settled to suit her. "You know I don't sell 'em no more since nobody ever came by to fix that damn machine." She pursed her lips. "Nobody fixes nothin' anymore. In my opinion, that's what's wrong with this country."

I was just about to agree with her when there was a loud commotion up front. Somebody had burst into the bar and started hollering.

"Hey? Jackie? Where are you? You seen Luanne or Friday?"

It was T-Bomb. Her boisterous entrance succeeded in rousing

Lucille, who had been snoring beneath a barstool. He rolled to his feet and waddled toward her, barking and complaining.

"Well, what in tarnation?" Aunt Jackie turned around saw her. "We're over here! Can you pipe down and try to behave like a normal person? Lucille . . . stop that racket right now!"

T-Bomb barreled over to my table and dropped her massive shoulder bag onto an empty chair.

"I been lookin' all over for you. Where the hell did you get off to?" She didn't wait for me to answer. "That asshole Joe Sykes fired Luanne. She lit outta there like her hair was on fire. That whole place is going straight to heck. What are you drinkin'? That foreign crap?" She looked at Aunt Jackie. "Is it too early to get one of them five dollar pitchers? I need it after this day." She eyed my lineup of empty Stella bottles. "Better bring us an order of fries, too." She gestured at me. "This one's a lightweight." She pulled out a chair and sat down. "So what are we gonna do about Luanne?"

"Are you talking to me?" I asked. I wasn't certain that her tirade was over.

"Hello? McFly?" She shook her head. "Ain't you sittin' right here in front of me?"

Aunt Jackie sighed. "I'll be right back with the beer." She walked off.

"Look, T-Bomb . . . I've had a shitty day. I just need some peace and quiet. Okay?"

"*You've* had a shitty day? How about Luanne's shitty day? How about the shitty days all of us have had workin' in that damn sweat shop? They can't keep treatin' people this way. Somethin's gotta change. I'm tellin' you."

"I'm not the one you need to be telling this to."

She raised an eyebrow. "Ain't you the one who 'has the ear' of the management?" She made air quotes with her fingers.

I shook my head. "I don't have anybody's ear."

She sat back against her chair with a huff. "Bull crap. What the hell's the matter with you?"

"Nothing. I'm just tired."

"Tired?"

I nodded.

91

"Hell. I'm tired, too. We're all tired. Sick and tired of dealin' with them low-life assholes they call managers."

I nodded again.

She sat there glaring at me for a few seconds without saying anything. And experiencing a few seconds of silence from T-Bomb was like being stranded on an iceberg in the middle of a snowstorm. Even Eskimos didn't have a word to describe quiet like that. Finally, she leaned forward. "Listen. I get that you're frustrated and that you got a lot going on right now with El DeBarge and all. But we still have to figure out a way to fix this mess for Luanne. Jay don't make crap workin' at Champion. She needs this job—especially while Jay Jr. is in the joint and can't contribute."

I took a deep breath. "I know. I already fixed it with Joe."

She blinked. "You did?"

I nodded.

"When?"

"Right before I left for the day."

She dropped back against her chair again. "Well, I swear. Why the heck didn't you tell somebody?"

"Because I needed a break."

"Why?" She looked me over. "What happened?"

"Nothing."

"Well, hell. If this is how you look when *nothing* happens, I'd hate to see you when *something* happens."

I didn't say anything.

She sighed. "Are you gonna tell me how you fixed it with Joe?"

I had to smile at that, even though I still felt pretty miserable. "It wasn't hard. I just got him thinking about how much firing Luanne would hurt Jailissa."

T-Bomb threw back her head and about laughed herself out of her chair. "That dern horndog! I bet he had to pole vault his way back to his office."

"Yeah . . . especially after I told him about the outfit she's wearing for Pork Day on Saturday."

T-Bomb was still chuckling. "Outfit? Why? What's she wearing?" She uncapped the ketchup bottle.

I shrugged. "I have no clue. I just made something up."

Aunt Jackie showed up bearing a pitcher of Old Style and a big platter of French fries. "What are you two laughing about?"

T-Bomb liberally doused the mound of fries with the ketchup.

Aunt Jackie clucked her tongue. "You wanna at least wait until I set the damn plate down?"

"Heck no." T-Bomb shook salt all over the fries, and everything else within a three-foot radius. "I think I sweated off five pounds today standin' around in them damn fires of hell." She pushed the plate toward me. "Eat up on some of these. You need to soak up that beer before we head on over to the fish fry."

Aunt Jackie just shook her head and tugged at her bra strap before wandering off toward another table. The place was slowly starting to fill up with hot-and-thirsty autoworkers.

I had completely forgotten that the VFW fundraiser was tonight.

"I'm not going to the fish fry." I did my best to sound definite. "I don't have the energy for it."

"Oh, hell's bells. How much damn energy does it take to cram a hunk of catfish down your gullet?"

I sighed. "Don't hassle me, okay?"

"Don't you know by now it's my job to hassle you?"

"Well, you're pretty damn good at it."

"Ain't that the truth? I wish it paid benefits so I could quit watchin' my life roll right past me on a dern assembly line." She poured herself another glass of beer. "Hey? Didn't you say that Grammy was comin' this year?"

I nodded. "She's riding with Ermaline."

"Oh, lord. She'll give all them codgers somethin' to fixate on."

"Grammy?"

"Hell no. *Ermaline*." T-Bomb lowered her voice. "She don't wear no panties."

It was a good thing I had already swallowed my mouthful of beer. "*What?*"

T-Bomb was dragging a fat French fry around the edge of the plate to mop up a line of ketchup. "Last year, I got stuck sittin' at a table with that crazy old coot, Delbert Clinton, and all he did was sit there and mutter about how Ermaline kept winkin' at him. After about the tenth time, I asked him what the heck he was talkin' about, and he just pointed over toward the wall, where she was sittin' with Betty Greubel. You know? Where they line up all them straight chairs near the bathrooms? Well, I thought Delbert was just havin' one of his *Twilight Zone* episodes." She waved her finger around in tight, little circles next to her ear. "But damn if she didn't uncross her legs and show off everything god gave her." T-Bomb shook her head. "I think that's probably just something she got into after Kenny took up with them hoppers. A lot of women go downhill after they get done wrong like that."

I was amazed. I wondered if Grammy knew this about Ermaline? Probably.

Grammy seemed to know everything that went on in our world.

I was almost blinded by a flash of bright light as the street door opened. I blinked over T-Bomb's shoulder and saw Luanne Keortge fill up the door frame. She was carrying a white, plastic grocery bag. Aunt Jackie saw her, too, and jerked a thumb toward our table.

"Here comes Luanne," I said to T-Bomb.

She turned around. "Well, hell. I think we're gonna need more fries."

Luanne reached our table and yanked out a chair.

"Where the hell have you been?" T-Bomb asked.

"I ran outta smokes." Luanne pulled a carton of Viceroys out of her bag. "I had to head over to Walmart 'cause they're cheaper." She looked at me. "You have to think about things like that when you're unemployed."

"I talked with Joe—" I began.

"I know. He called Jay."

I was surprised. "He did?"

She nodded. "Well, Wynona Miles did."

Wynona was Joe's secretary.

Luanne ripped open the carton of cigarettes and dumped all ten packs out onto the table. "She said I wasn't fired, but I had to sit home for two weeks without pay."

"Two weeks?" T-Bomb was outraged. "That asshole. What gives him the right to dock you two weeks' pay?"

"I ain't complainin'." Luanne was already tearing open a pack to fire one up. "It's better than no job at all."

"I'm sorry about that, Luanne," I said. "I did the best I could with him."

"Don't you dare apologize. I know you were the one who fixed this mess for me. I'm just lucky I still have a job to not get paid for." She blew out a long column of smoke and chuckled. "Ain't this a great country?"

T-Bomb was shaking her head. "Someday somebody's gonna go postal on them jerk wads."

"You get no argument from me on that. Especially when it comes to that low-life Buzz Sheets."

"Why?" T-Bomb asked. "What'd he do?"

Luanne shook her head. "Nothin'. He's just stupid."

"Yeah, and Earl Junior makes him look like one of them Mensa babies."

They laughed.

"You know what that dimwit said to me when I was walkin' out?" Luanne asked.

"Buzz?" T-Bomb asked.

"Yeah. He said I was an *albacore* around his neck. That man's an idiot."

"Are you and Jay gonna be okay?" I was worried about how they'd manage with Luanne losing two weeks' worth of pay.

She sighed. "Oh, sure. Jailissa just needs to win that crown more than ever now."

"That scholarship money would come in handy," T-Bomb agreed.

"Don't I know it? That girl has her heart set on going to Wabash Valley College in September."

"She still wants to be a radio announcer?" I asked.

Luanne nodded. "Ever since she got that summer job over at WVJC. She either wants to study that or cosmetology." She tapped the ash off the end of her cigarette. "Young people these days have more choices than we had."

"Ain't that the truth," T-Bomb ate the last French fry and glanced at her watch. "Do you gals wanna get more fries, or head on over to the VFW?"

"Hell, we might as well go." Luanne started collecting her packs of smokes. "I already bought my tickets last week." She pushed back her chair. "You comin', Friday?"

I thought about saying no again, but I knew it was a hopeless cause. Together, they would be too much for me. It was easier just to go along and hope we could get out of there while it was still daylight. Neither of them tended to tarry long over their plates of food.

"Okay," I said with resignation. I picked up my unopened envelope. "But can I catch a ride with one of you?" I gestured toward my row of empties. "I don't think I should drive until I get something to eat."

"You can ride with me." T-Bomb was fishing a ten-dollar bill out of her bag to cover her tab. "But you'll have to sit in back between Luke and Laura's car seats."

"How come?"

She rolled her eyes. "Donnie pulled the dern passenger seat out three weeks ago because the motor quit working, and it still ain't fixed yet."

Luanne snorted. "Hell. By now, Jay would probably have it set up in the living room in front of the TV."

"Oh, lord. Don't let Donnie hear you say that. He's always complainin' that they're more comfortable than them Queen Anne chairs we bought over at Baumberger's in Evansville."

"I think these men are just a waste of our time. All they do is make messes the rest of us have to clean up."

T-Bomb laughed at Luanne. "I can think of *one* thing they mostly manage to do right."

"Speak for yourself," Luanne said. "I can get more satisfaction out of a pack of AAA batteries."

I held up a hand. "TMI, ladies."

T-Bomb slapped me on the arm. "Are we embarrassin' you, Friday?"

"No." I shook my head. "You're making me want to gouge out my mind's eye."

"Oh, like you never done it to yourself?"

"T-Bomb . . ."

"Remember that summer over at Oil Belt church camp, when you had the top bunk over Donna Steptoe?"

"Oh, god . . ."

"Every day, you ran around makin' cow eyes at her, but never said nothin'."

"T-Bomb . . ."

"But every night, them creakin' bed springs told the whole story."

I sighed. "Can we please just move along here?"

There was a long, slow hissing sound—like the noise when you blew out the spit valve on your saxophone. We all looked around. A sharp, sulfur-like smell rose up around us.

"Oh, Judas!" T-Bomb waved a hand in front of her face. "It's that damned Lucille. I wish them men would quit feeding him them eggs in beet juice." She headed toward the door. "Let's get the hell outta here."

I followed T-Bomb and Luanne, feeling strangely comforted by the fact that, finally, something seemed to stink worse than my job or relationship prospects.

Chapter 7

The VFW hall was buzzing like a beehive when we got there. T-Bomb drove around the building a third time to be sure there wasn't a vacant parking space she'd somehow managed to overlook on her first two passes through the lot.

I was starting to feel a bit queasy. Being hunched up between two car seats in the back of her minivan wasn't helping. Neither was the fact that her air conditioner was only blowing stale, lukewarm air. Apparently, the motor on the passenger seat wasn't the only thing in her van that wasn't working right.

"Can you just, please, find someplace to park? I don't think I can ride around in circles anymore."

She glared at me in the rearview mirror. "Don't you barf back there. I only just got that mess cleaned out of the carpet from Luke's chicken pox."

Luke had chicken pox? *Great.*

"When was he sick?"

She waved a hand. "About two years ago." She slammed on the brakes and threw the van into reverse. "This is ridiculous. I'm parkin' at the bowling alley."

"What?" I was having a hard time hearing her over the Def Leppard tunes she had blasting.

She didn't answer, so I decided to ask her to just let me out so I could get some fresh air and try to regain my equilibrium. Before I could get the words out, T-Bomb slammed on the brakes again and laid on the horn.

"Hey!" She rolled down her window and leaned out to holler at somebody. "You can't just stop in the middle of the dern road like that!

Move on over to the side so the rest of us can get by. Oh . . . hey, Wynona. I didn't see it was you. Why're you drivin' the church bus? Is Carleen still off on that mission trip to El Salvador?"

I couldn't hear Wynona's response, but somewhere behind us, another car horn started blowing.

"Well, *great* day." T-Bomb looked in the rearview mirror and gave whoever it was the finger. "Why is everybody in such a dang hurry?" She leaned out the window again. "I gotta get movin' so this person behind me can get on with his *important* business. I'll see you inside, Wynona." She rolled up her window, hit the gas, and careened around the church bus on two wheels. Gravel flew everyplace.

"Jeez, T-Bomb!" Since I didn't have a seat back to grab hold of, I latched onto the "oh shit" handle dangling above the sliding side door. "Are you trying to kill us?"

T-Bomb wheeled into the Gibson Lanes parking lot. She barely missed sideswiping a vintage, pea-green Electra 225 that was parked across three spaces.

"Look at how that doo wop parked." She roared into a space and screeched to a stop. "Who in the heck does he think would want to hit that ol' piece of junk?"

I was slumped down in the back seat, holding my head in my hands, waiting for the world to stop spinning.

T-Bomb was outside, hiking the strap of her massive bag up onto her shoulder and tapping on the window with her keys. "Ain't you comin'? I thought you was dyin' to get outta there." The door of the van rolled back. About two-dozen stuffed animals tumbled out onto the pavement. One of them was a Tickle-Me-Elmo, and it started giggling and writhing around as soon as it made contact with the ground.

"Lord, god." T-Bomb bent down and started scooping up the toys. "You look kinda puny. We better get you on inside." She tossed Elmo back into the van, but he was still cackling and begging her to do it again. She rolled her eyes. "That damn thing drives me to bedlam. Donnie bought it for Laura because he thought it was *funny*. Funny, my derriere. Are you comin', or not?"

"I'm coming." I twisted out of my niche between the car seats and stepped down onto the pavement. It felt better to be outside, even though it was still hot as hell. The bowling alley was hopping, too. It looked like half the teenagers in Princeton were out, enjoying their last few nights of freedom before school started. It was hard to believe that the summer was already winding down. Soon, the oppressive heat would give way to blistering cold, and the whole cycle would start all over again. It felt to me like the weather was part of the massive, general conspiracy that defined my life these days.

I reached inside the van and grabbed my backpack. "Let's get this over with."

"Well, dang. Don't sound so excited." T-Bomb closed the door and locked it.

"Sorry. I'm just not in a great mood."

"I'd like to know what in the hell else is new? You ain't been in a good mood since them agitators showed up."

We walked across the parking lot toward the VFW hall. The sun was hanging low in the sky, and it was like a bright, orange ball. Tomorrow was going to be another hot one.

"It's not that," I said.

"Well then, what in tarnation is it?"

I shrugged. "I just feel like my life is going no place."

T-Bomb laughed. "Hell. Join the damn club. Whose life *is* going anyplace? Mine? Luanne's?" She waved a hand. "Anybody's in this damn hayseed town?" She paused. "That El DeBarge just has you all tied up in knots. I don't know why you won't quit stewin' and just do somethin' about it."

"What do you mean?"

T-Bomb gave me the same look I'd seen her give her kids when they insisted they weren't the ones who dropped overcooked broccoli on the floor for the dog.

"You know exactly what I mean. You need to quit actin' like a chicken shit and take a chance."

"Are you kidding me? Take a chance on someone who's probably going to be leaving here for good in a few days? Why? That'd be about as smart as hooking up with another Misty Ann."

T-Bomb stopped walking and turned to face me. "It ain't the same thing at all."

I held out both arms in frustration. "I don't know what you want from me? It's clear that I can't do anything right."

"Well, you can quit actin' like a moron and get your head outta your butt. Who cares if it don't last forever? Nothin' in life worth havin' lasts forever. Ain't you the one who told me that? Ain't you the one who told me that it was better to have real love for a little while than never to have it at all?"

I sighed. "I was talking about that time you fostered the dog with the heart condition . . . not about getting involved with somebody who has no intention of staying around here."

"Well, that dog didn't have no intention of stayin' around here, neither. And he ended up livin' with us for nine years." She shook her head. "You got no way of knowin' what might happen or how things might work out. I seen you with El DeBarge . . . I think she trips all your triggers in just the right ways. And she's not like all them other ones . . . she's smart. And nice. I don't think she'd do you wrong. Not on purpose, anyway." She huffed. "Lord knows, you hooked up with some doozies in your time."

"Hey. It's not like you always grabbed the brass ring. Remember Andy Clodfelter?"

"Oh, hell." T-Bomb punched me on the arm. "*Randy Andy*. Eighteen hands and no brain."

"Exactly."

"Well . . . at least none of his people ever ended up in jail."

"That's true," I agreed.

"Well, I wound up okay. Donnie Jennings was a big ol' math club nerd, but he turned out to be a good catch."

"Yeah. And who pushed you to take a chance on him when you wouldn't give him a second look?"

"You did."

"Right."

"Okay . . . so now it's my turn to give you the same advice."

I really hated arguing with T-Bomb. It was like going twelve rounds with Rocky Marciano. I always ended up on the ropes.

"Can we change the subject?"

She started walking again. "Chicken shit."

"Hey? I heard you, okay?"

She looked at me. "You did?"

I nodded.

"Good." She smiled and pointed toward the side entrance to the VFW hall. "'Cause I see a fine-lookin' agitator standin' over there by that caterin' truck, talkin' to Grammy."

"Oh, god." My anxiety returned with a vengeance.

T-Bomb grabbed hold of my arm. "Come on. What don't kill you makes you stronger."

I wasn't sure I agreed with her. But at least I had one consolation: the post's famed Blue Vel-Vet Lounge was sure to be open and ready to meet all of my adult beverage needs.

సా సా సా

"Here you go, honey." Betty Greubel stacked an impressive tower of spicy chicken tenders on my plate. "You want some extra hot sauce with these?"

I shook my head. "Just some baked beans, please. And maybe some of that coleslaw?"

I wasn't really hungry, but I knew I needed to eat something. I decided to take a pass on the fish. I didn't really care for catfish, and I'd heard other people in line saying that the ocean perch wasn't as good as the walleye they had served last year. Apparently, walleye was just getting too expensive for the event organizers to make any kind of profit.

Betty plopped a big, white dinner roll atop of my mound of food. "You come back as many times as you want, honey. You look like a bit of home cookin' would do you some good."

I looked down at my plate. It had enough food on it to feed a family of five. I gave Betty a small smile. "Thanks, Mrs. Greubel. This looks like plenty."

I left the food line and noticed a couple of arms waving at me. T-Bomb, Grammy, and Luanne had commandeered some seats at a table near the stage at the back of the room. I walked over to join them.

"Why are we sitting way over here?" I asked.

Grammy gestured toward the long table on the stage that was loaded with placards advertising all the giveaway items. "Because this is where the raffle's gonna take place, and I wanna be close in case I win that spa day."

"Spa day?" I blinked at her. "You want to go to a spa?" That didn't sound like something I ever thought she'd be interested in. I picked up one of my chicken tenders and took a bite. It tasted like it had been dipped in fire. Betty must've pulled this stack from the nuclear option bin.

"Not for *me*. For Fritz." Grammy held up her wad of raffle tickets. "It's from Darleen's Pampered Pets out in Poseyville." She read the description printed on the back of the ticket. "'Treat your best friend to the ultimate spa treatment. Your winning ticket entitles the pet of your choice to a deluxe wash, clip, nail trim, and anal gland treatment by one of our I.P.G. Certified professionals. Note: ferrets or other rodents are not eligible for this prize.'"

"Anal gland?" T-Bomb looked at me. "Does Fritz still have a problem with that?"

"Lord, yes," Grammy replied before I could answer. She fanned her face with the wad of tickets. "It's righteous."

Luanne was shaking her head. "I never have known a golden retriever that didn't suffer with that affliction." She picked up her glass of iced tea.

T-Bomb chuckled. "Hey? Friday? Remember that time you tried to do it?"

I looked at her. "Do what?"

She made two fists and pushed the tips of her thumbs together. "You know . . . pop his butt gland."

"I think that's express his butt gland," Luanne corrected, "not pop."

"What-*ever*." T-Bomb cackled. "Friday watched these videos on YouTube about how to do it and then she cornered poor Fritz."

"T-Bomb . . ." I held up a hand to try and shush her. "People are trying to eat."

"You shoulda seen the look on that dog's face when she started messin' with his bung hole."

"T-Bomb . . ."

"She just kept pinchin' at it and squeezin' at it, and nothin' happened, except poor Fritz was lookin' more and more embarrassed and like she was tryin' to kill him."

Luanne chuckled. People at the next table kept turning around to stare at us.

"T-Bomb," I hissed. "Shut up with this . . . *people are trying to eat.*"

She ignored me. "Finally, she gave up and let go of him, and dern if ol' Fritz didn't decide to let it fly."

I was mortified. Even Grammy was laughing hard enough that she had to take her glasses off and dab at her eyes with a paper napkin.

But T-Bomb wasn't finished. "That mess just flew all over her. It shot outta his bum in a big ol' stream and soaked her from stem to stern." She looked at me. "I thought we were gonna have to douse you in tomato juice to get rid of that stench."

Luanne was laughing so hard she had tears running down her face. I closed my eyes. There was no way this could get any worse.

"Is this seat taken?"

The low, sexy-sounding voice came from right beside my ear.

I was wrong. It *could* get worse . . . a *lot* worse. I opened my eyes and looked at El, wondering how much of T-Bomb's story she'd overheard.

"Please tell me you didn't hear any of that," I pleaded.

"Of what? That sordid tale of animal torture?"

I sighed morosely. "Yeah. That would be the one."

"Nope." She gave me one of her cover girl smiles. "I didn't hear a thing."

T-Bomb leaned across the table toward El. "Well . . . it all started when Friday decided to watch these YouTube videos about—"

"She was *kidding*, T-Bomb," I said. "She heard you the first time." I gestured toward the rest of the hall. "I think *everybody* heard you."

El laughed.

"Why don't you pull up a chair and join us, honey?" Grammy asked El. "Jill? Quit sittin' there lookin' like you lost your last friend and get this girl a chair."

I did as I was told, and made space for El between my seat and

Luanne's. Luanne watched this interaction with interest. She had that look on her face that meant she had nothing to say, but was about to say it anyway.

I was right.

"There's one thing I can't figure out," she said, waving a half-eaten dinner roll at El.

"What's that?" El asked.

"We seem to see you two agitators almost every place, but you don't never say anything to us about signin' on to your union crusade." She shook her head. "How come? Ain't we the types you're tryin' so hard to convert?"

El thought about that. "Of course you are, Luanne. But . . ." She looked around the table at each one of us. It felt like her gaze lingered on me a moment longer than the others, but that could have just been wishful thinking. "I don't know . . . I don't have many opportunities to make friends or feel like I truly belong anyplace. I guess, for a change, I wanted a chance to see what that felt like."

Luanne didn't seem to have any response to that.

"Of course," El smiled and touched Luanne on the shoulder, "if you'd really like to hear my spiel, I've got about a dozen pamphlets and my iPad out in the car."

"No thanks, honey." Luanne held up a meaty hand. "I think I'd rather be an unenlightened friend than one of them wild-eyed converts."

El laughed. "I think I'd rather keep you that way too."

Luanne seemed satisfied with that response, which surprised me. She didn't normally take to strangers so easily.

El gestured toward Luanne's pile of raffle tickets.

"So what else are you all hoping to win?" She waved a hand toward the stage. "Personally, I've got my eye on that set of yard gnomes."

Luanne nodded. "They are pretty unusual. You don't much see the ones with guns."

"That's what I thought," El agreed. "They make quite a statement."

"I never had much use for that tacky stuff," Luanne said. "But I guess some folks take all them amendments to heart."

"Well if you ask, me, that's carrying your right to bear arms a bit too far." Grammy clucked her tongue in disapproval. "I don't want to live in a fortress."

"They ain't packin' real weapons, Grammy," T-Bomb explained.

"Does anybody have any extra napkins?" I asked. I'd already used mine up trying to wipe the residual hot sauce from the chicken tenders off my fingers.

"Well, I've got my cap set for that swimmin' pool." Luanne shoved a stack of paper napkins toward me. "It'd be nice to sit and relax out beside that water on these god-awful hot nights."

"Ain't that the truth?" T-Bomb agreed. "And this looks like a nice one, what with that redwood deck and Coral Sea vinyl liner."

Luanne nodded. "It's one of them Esther Williams pools."

I picked up another tender. But this time I held onto the edge of it with a napkin. El was giving me a curious look.

"They're hot," I explained.

"Why don't you use your fork?" she asked.

"Because you don't eat them that way."

"Oh, I didn't realize there was a chicken tender etiquette."

I nodded. "It's one of our unwritten codes of conduct. Kind of like the two-fingered wave you give everyone while driving." I demonstrated the wave. "Or our monthly tornado siren tests. Or the fact that we eat potatoes at every meal—no exceptions."

El looked down at my plate. "I don't see any potatoes."

"That's because I'm a renegade who flaunts convention."

"Oh, is that the reason?" She smiled. "I wondered."

"She's always been like that," Grammy chimed in. "Our Jill has never taken the easy path."

El seemed to consider that. "No, I don't expect she has."

"Yeah." T-Bomb nudged El. "Especially when it comes to Fritz's personal hygiene."

I rolled my eyes. "Very funny. Don't you have to go check on Donnie and the twins?"

"Hell, no." She held up her cell phone. "He just texted me to say they were still at the Otters game." She looked at El. "It's Run the Bases night, and the kids are all out on the field going bonkers."

"They'll be fast asleep two minutes after he gets 'em in the car," Luanne said.

"Yeah." T-Bomb slapped her phone back down on the table and speared another hunk of fried catfish. "Then they'll be up half the night barfin' up hot dogs." She glanced toward the next table where Betty Greubel was refilling some condiment bowls. "Hey! Betty!" She held up a nearly empty plastic bowl. "Can we get some more of that tartar sauce over here?"

Betty gave her the high sign and mouthed that she'd be right over.

Luanne studied El. "Where's that partner of yours? Don't you all usually work these events together?"

"You mean Tony?" El asked. Luanne nodded. El looked around the hall. "He's here. The last time I saw him, he was hanging around over by the bar, talking with a bunch of retired vets. He was in the Marines. They're probably swapping war stories."

T-Bomb turned around on her seat and looked toward the bar. "You mean them old codgers back there holdin' up the wall?"

El nodded.

T-Bomb started cackling, and El gave her a confused look.

"Honey, they ain't swappin' war stories," Luanne said.

El looked back and forth between the two of them. Then she glanced at me.

"Do yourself a favor and don't ask," I cautioned.

"Anybody seen Ermaline?" Luanne asked in a singsong voice.

"Hell." T-Bomb was still laughing. "I think *everybody's* seen Ermaline."

"*All* of Ermaline," Luanne added. "If there was a god, they'd all go blind."

Grammy shushed them. "There *is* a god, and he don't much like this kind of behavior."

"Well, I don't imagine he much likes *that* kind of behavior, neither." T-Bomb jerked a thumb toward the table where Ermaline sat, directly across from Tony and the group of vets.

"Ermaline can't help that," Grammy whispered. "She has a medical condition."

107

"A *medical* condition?" Luanne repeated. "No disrespect, Grammy, but refusin' to wear panties ain't due to no medical condition I ever heard of."

"What?" El looked at Luanne in bewilderment.

"She don't wear no panties," T-Bomb explained. "That's why them men are planted over there like bean poles, all fixated on her."

El looked at me.

"I told you not to ask," I reminded her.

El shook her head. "I've missed a lot living on the road."

"Yeah." I nudged her arm. "Lucky you."

She smiled. It made me feel warm all over. "Lucky me."

Betty Greubel showed up at our table, carrying a gallon-sized vat of tartar sauce. She squeezed her way along behind our chairs to reach the empty bowl and stopped between El and Luanne.

"Hold that bowl up for me," she said to Luanne. "It takes both of my hands to hold this dern thing. Them Turpin girls always fill 'em up way too full."

Luanne started to reach for the bowl, but something caught her eye.

"There she goes!" she called out. "Show time!"

We looked around startled.

"What are you yammerin' about?" T-Bomb asked.

"Over there!" Luanne threw out her arm to point toward Ermaline's table and hit Betty—knocking her completely off-balance.

Betty stumbled and danced to the side. She was putting all of her effort and concentration into keeping the vat of tartar sauce upright, and her fancy footwork reminded me of one of those competition gymnastic routines. And I had a premonition that she wasn't going to be able to stick the landing.

At the last second, I pushed El forward, clearing a path for Betty to crash into me, instead. She did, too—with a vengeance. What felt like two quarts of tartar sauce sloshed up and out of the tureen, and liberally soaked the back of my head and neck. I could feel cool globs of it running down the inside of my shirt. I didn't even bother trying to stand up. I wouldn't have been able to, anyway, with Betty sprawled across my back. The rest of the container

108

of sauce was congealing on the floor beneath our table like a lake of lumpy mayonnaise.

"Well, dang." T-Bomb was never one to allow a conversational vacuum to linger. "Talk about your curb service."

Luanne was trying not to laugh. "I guess you'll have to use ketchup on your fish, now."

El was on her feet and trying to help Betty stand up. "All you all right?"

"I'm fine," she muttered. "I shoulda worn them crepe soled shoes—these fancy ones are just too slick on these linoleum floors."

Grammy was out of her chair, too. "Let me walk you back to the kitchen, Betty. I'll get a mop to clean up this mess." She looked down at me. "You're a sight, Jill. You better get on to the restroom and try to wash that mess outta your hair." She looked at T-Bomb. "Do you have any other clothes in your car?"

T-Bomb nodded. "I got some of Donnie's dress shirts in there. We had to have new buttons sewed on at the cleaner's."

"I'm awful sorry, Betty," Luanne apologized. "I was just tryin' to tell everybody that Ermaline was fixin' to uncross her legs."

Betty huffed and picked up her empty container. "That girl just needs to have her ears pinched back. It ain't no call for nobody to be that way. She was raised better'n that." She looked at Grammy. "Ain't that true, Wilma?"

Grammy shook her head. "Judge not that ye be not judged."

"Well," Luanne drawled. "I got nothin' to say about that, so I'll just say this." She looked at me and jerked a thumb toward the bathrooms. "You better get movin' and get yourself cleaned up. There's a heap of people in here with plates full of dry catfish, and they're all lookin' at you like you're some kind of condiment Holy Grail."

I sighed and stood up. "I'm on my way."

"I'll go with you," El said.

I looked at her. She shrugged.

"Yeah," T-Bomb added. "Let El DeBarge help you out." She chuckled. "You two have experience in bathrooms."

I wiped a blob of tartar sauce off my neck and flicked it at her. Then El and I left the table and headed for the restrooms.

109

"Lean back some more."

"I *can't* lean back any more—not without becoming a quadriplegic."

"Quit being such a baby. I can't reach the back of your neck."

"Maybe that's because I'm two feet taller than you."

"Very funny. Squat down or something. All I'm doing is getting water all over your butt."

"Yeah. I noticed."

"Look, smartass. This would be a lot simpler if you'd just take your shirt off."

"I am not taking my shirt off."

"I don't see why not. You're going to have to take it off when T-Bomb brings you another one to wear."

Taking my shirt off in front of her was non-negotiable. But I did find it interesting that this was the second time in our brief history that El had tried to coerce me into doing this.

"Just do the best you can, okay?"

More water sloshed across my shoulders and ran down into the waistband of my pants.

"Oh, this is *ridiculous.*" El's exasperation was starting to show. "If you won't take your shirt off, then at least prop your butt up here on the edge of the sink so I can reach better and keep some of the water off the floor. It's not like you'll get any wetter than you are already."

I thought about that. It did make sense . . . kind of.

"Okay." I perched up on the edge of the sink.

"This has to be the smallest damn sink on the planet," El complained. "What were they thinking?"

"It's a VFW post, El. I think providing quality fixtures for the women's room was an afterthought."

"Well, that certainly would explain this wallpaper."

"Can you reach any better?"

I didn't really care, because this new position was working *great* for me. El was plastered up against me with one arm wrapped around my chest. She was scooping water up with her left hand and using it to rinse tartar sauce off my back.

110

"It's a little better," she muttered. Her voice sounded like it was coming from someplace far away.

The water running down my back was ice cold, but I didn't mind at all. The proximity to her felt luxurious—worth every one of the stares and hand claps I got walking across the hall with her to get here.

There was a nearly full-length, vanity mirror mounted on the back of the bathroom door, and I watched our reflection in it with fascination. We made a curious tableau: Maggie O'Connell meets Dana Scully, with an abundance of wet t-shirts and tartar sauce as props. Even though I had a starring role in this absurd drama, I had to admit that it was pretty hot. I could've sat there and stared at us all night.

"Do you want me to do your hair?" El asked.

My hair? I wanted her to do any part of me she could reach. My face, arms, legs, back, front, top, bottom—any of me. All of me.

I nodded.

"Was that a yes?" She straightened up and stood in front of me. That meant I couldn't see us in the mirror anymore, but it only took a moment for me to realize that I didn't really care. El at close range was a lot more mesmerizing than any fantasy reflection. She smelled like sweet, wild huckleberries—a sensory anomaly in the midst of a fish fry.

I was having a hard time finding my voice, so I just nodded again.

She bent closer. "I didn't quite hear you."

El's eyes glowed in the cool blue-and-white light. Everything about her seemed vivid and alive. When I raised my hands to touch her, they were shining, too. We were like fireflies in a jar, moving toward each other in a small swath of moonlight.

El moved her hands through my matted hair. I pulled her closer and wound my legs around her waist. I wasn't worried that she'd try to escape. I just wanted to feel every part of her. The sound of running water became one with the roar of blood surging inside me. Everything around me and within me was dissolving. I felt fluid. Formless. I needed to hold her. I needed to melt into her. I needed to know her as I now began to know myself. When at last I touched her as a lover, I knew that, finally, I had found my way out of this land of lost content.

El seemed to know it, too. She was both limp and solid in my arms. Her head was tipped back, and her beautiful face was hot and radiant with light.

Her eyes popped open like the shutter on a camera lens. Her head snapped up. Her mouth opened, but no sound came out. She had a panicked expression on her face.

"What is it?" I panted.

She pushed at my shoulders. "Hot," she gasped.

I tried to pull her closer again. "I know. I feel it, too."

"No!" El tried to move out of my grasp. "Your fingers—they're *hot!*"

Oh my god . . . the spicy chicken tenders.

"Jesus!" I yanked my hand away. "Oh, god . . . I'm *so* sorry."

In my frenzy to free her, my watchband got caught on the zipper of her pants. I kept yanking on it until it broke loose. I could hear the clatter of tiny links and pins scuttling across the floor.

El was still gasping and breathing heavily—trying to recover from the duet of raging infernos. She dropped her head back to my shoulder. Then she laughed. Soon, I could feel her body shaking against mine. She was laughing so hard that it took a minute for us to hear the groaning sound beneath us. Then the sink lurched lower.

El and I looked at each other.

"Uh oh . . ." I began.

The sink ripped completely out of the wall, and El and I tumbled with it to the floor. We were a writhing heap of tangled arms and legs, slipping around on the wet floor as we tried to get unhitched and scramble to our feet. A geyser of cold water jetted out from the broken sink pipe, soaking everything in the room.

"What the hell?" El tried to fasten her pants. It wasn't happening. Apparently, my watchband wasn't the only casualty of my hasty retreat.

I was on my knees now. "Oh, my god . . . we broke the sink."

"You think?" El gave up on her zipper and gestured wildly toward the fountain gushing behind us. "Turn off the damn water!"

I gave her a blank look.

"*Really?*" She stared back at me in abject disbelief.

She pushed past me and crawled through the ponding water until she reached the tiny cutoff valve located near the floorboard.

"I thought you grew up in the country?" she said, as she twisted the valve shut.

The stream of water lessened to a trickle. El sat back on her haunches and looked back at me. We were both soaked to the bone. The tiny restroom was in shambles. The persistent *drip drip drip* from the broken water pipe resounded from the walls like hammer blows on a coffin nail.

I sighed. "We're toast."

El gave me a crooked smile. "You look great with wet hair."

I felt myself blush, which seemed ridiculous considering the event that had precipitated our dilemma. I opened my mouth to render the same compliment back to her.

Loud pounding shook the bathroom door.

"Would you hurry the hell up and let somebody else have a chance?" a voice boomed. "I have to tap off."

It was Luanne. Of course.

I gave El a miserable look. "Any ideas?"

She looked around the room. "This bathroom has an appalling lack of transom windows."

"I know. Next time, we'll have to plan more carefully."

We smiled at each other. I got to my feet and extended a hand to her. "Come on, we might as well face the music."

El stood up and tried to pull her shirt down to cover the gaping front of her pants. Then she got an idea. "Hang on a minute."

She sloshed to where the broken sink lay. She picked it up and tested its heft. "Perfect," she said, settling it against her waist. "Let's go."

I took a deep breath and unlocked and opened the door.

Luanne and T-Bomb stood together on the other side. They looked like a pair of those raffle gnomes—without the grenade launchers. I noticed that T-Bomb was holding a folded, blue shirt.

Luanne looked us both up and down. "What in the hell happened to the two of you? You look like something the cat drug in."

"Why is there water all over the place?" T-Bomb asked.

I held up a hand. "Trust me . . . you don't want to know."

El pushed past me, carrying the sink. "Excuse us ladies, we had a minor restroom malfunction."

113

She walked off with squishing shoes. A rivulet of water trailed along behind her.

"What she said," I added.

I pushed my plastered hair back from my forehead and moved on past them.

"Malfunction?" Luanne called after me. "This looks more like the damn *Poseidon Adventure!*"

I could hear T-Bomb laughing. "I told you them two had experience in bathrooms . . ."

Their voices faded into the background. So did all the other sights and sounds inside the hall. I didn't notice the stares or comments we surely got as we made our way out. I just kept my eyes focused on El's straight back, and followed her out into the balmy summer night.

Chapter 8

"Damn."

"What is it?" El looked at me from the driver's seat of her SUV. We had just left the VFW parking lot and were headed west on Broadway.

"I left my backpack inside the hall."

"Do we need to go back, so you can get your keys?" she asked.

I shook my head. "Not unless you mind dropping me at home instead of back at Hoosier Daddy?"

"Of course I don't mind taking you home. But don't you want to get your truck?"

"No. It'll be fine there overnight. T-Bomb can give me a ride to work in the morning."

I thought about the unopened letter inside the backpack. That could wait until the morning, too. I wasn't even sure I wanted to read it then.

"House keys?" El asked.

I looked at her.

"Let me guess. You don't lock your house?"

"I lock the front door," I said, defensively.

"Is there a back door?"

"Of course."

"But you don't lock it?"

I shook my head.

She laughed. "Indiana. Main Street of the Midwest."

"Don't forget I have a dog," I reminded her.

"Fritz?"

I nodded.

"Oh. *Well*. Then I'm certain potential thieves would avoid plundering your place for fear of being licked to death."

"Very funny."

"Who takes care of him during the day?" she asked.

"You mean when he isn't out at Grammy's?"

She nodded.

"He's kind of on auto pilot. I have a screened porch, and he can get out into the yard from there."

"Don't you worry about him when it's this hot?"

"He's got a dog door into the house." I studied her with interest. "Why all this concern about Fritz?"

She shrugged. "I like dogs."

"Yeah, well it appears to be a mutual admiration society."

El gave me a confused look, and then rolled her eyes. "Oh. You mean Lucille?"

"Yeah. That seems like a love affair for the ages."

"Unrequited, I assure you."

"You don't find his attachment . . . appealing?"

"No," she replied. "I don't find his *flatulence* appealing."

I chuckled.

"Although," she continued, "Aunt Jackie has been pestering me to take one of his puppies."

"The Jack Affs?" I asked. "Seriously? Are you thinking about it?"

"Only in the throes of delusion," she said. "There's no way I can have a dog with the life I lead."

"That's too bad. You're missing out on a lot."

It took her a minute to reply. "I know."

I thought she sounded sad.

We approached the intersection at U.S. 41.

"Which way do we go?" she asked.

I was tempted to say she could take me anywhere she wanted. Instead I told her to continue on straight.

"I live in Owensville," I explained. "We go about another five miles or so, and take a left at the blinking light. It's about a fifteen minute drive to my house. Are you sure you don't mind going that far out of your way?"

116

"I don't mind a bit," El replied. "Maybe you can lend me a pair of pants."

"Sure. But you'll probably have to roll the legs up."

"That's okay. I'd rather be compared to Ellie May Clampett than Ermaline."

I stifled a laugh. "I'm really sorry about your pants."

"It's all right. I'll keep them as a memento of our night of almost passion."

"Almost?"

"Well. It did sort of end just as things got interesting."

"No kidding. That seems to be a pattern for us." I paused. "I'm . . . uh . . ."

She looked at me. "You're what?"

"I wanted to ask . . . if the burning stopped?"

El laughed. "Yes . . . it was overwhelmed pretty quickly by the onset of mortification."

"I know that always works for me."

"Oh, really?" El asked. "You have prior experience with hot sauce?"

"No," I said quickly. "That isn't what I meant . . ."

El looked at me over the rims of her glasses. I thought it was charming that she had to wear them to drive at night. They made her look downright professorial, which I now knew was not a stretch for her.

"Oh," I said. "You were teasing."

"Right."

"Sometimes I have a hard time telling the difference."

"I know. It's really sweet."

I felt shy and embarrassed by her comment. I tried to cover it up by being glib. "Sweet is always the thing I go for when I'm trying to impress a woman."

"Ah, but that's not how it works. It's *not* trying to impress that makes you sweet."

"I'm very good at my craft."

El gave me a look that could only be called sultry. "I know I have only limited experience, but I'd have to agree with you about that."

That response didn't help ease my embarrassment. Fortunately, we'd reached the turnoff for Owensville.

"Left turn up here." I pointed toward the blinking light ahead of us. I was grateful to have a reason to change the subject.

"It's a good thing they put this flashing light here. All these roads look exactly the same."

"Trust me. When you grow up out here, they kind of are. No matter which way you go, you seem to end up right back where you started."

We were rolling through another sea of cornfields. They flanked the road, and were only disrupted by an occasional fence row or lone stand of trees. At night, the gray strip of road seemed narrower. It was like driving through a leafy tunnel. The full moon was waning, but it was still bright and high on the horizon. It made the winding rows of corn look soft and deep.

"I'm always amazed by how much space there is out here," El said. "I can't get used to it."

I studied her profile. It looked blue and white—a combined trick of the moonlight and the gauges on the dashboard. Her hair was still wet, just like most of the rest of her. It was amazing how soaked we both got in such a short space of time. I thought again about the ruined, tiny sink. El had hastily tossed it into the back of her SUV before we left the parking lot.

"What are we gonna do about that sink?" I asked, jerking my thumb toward the cargo area.

"Oh, god." El waved a hand. "I don't know. Pick up a new one, I guess. Where's the nearest plumbing supply store?"

"Menards . . . back in Princeton. We can get one there."

"I suppose we should pay to have the wall fixed, too?"

"Yeah. I don't imagine they're too happy with us right now."

"You think?" El chuckled. "A hall containing about two hundred people, all swilling beer and iced tea, and we take one of the two bathrooms offline? Why would they be upset about a little thing like that?"

"I think they have other restrooms in the bar area."

El glanced at me with an amused expression. "Are you always this literal?"

I sighed. "Unfortunately, yes."

She patted my leg. "Not to worry. This is why god created expense accounts."

"For real?" I was having a hard time ignoring El's hand, which still rested on my soggy thigh.

"Of course."

"They wouldn't question an expense like this?"

She looked at me over the rims of her glasses again. I decided right then that this little head duck gesture was my new favorite thing about her. Well . . . maybe my second favorite thing. Her hand on my leg was feeling pretty good, too.

"Buying a new sink for the local VFW wouldn't even make the top ten on the UAW's list of spurious reimbursement requests."

"Really?" I was intrigued now. "What does make the list?"

"Let's see . . . if memory serves, we once paid to replace the carpet in the banquet room of a Holiday Inn outside Wentzville, Missouri."

"Why?"

"It was a food fight on an apocalyptic scale." El waved her hand and returned it to the steering wheel. The spot where it had been resting on my leg still felt warm. "We were doing a multimedia presentation and had a good-sized crowd. Things were going well until some pipe fitters got into a shouting match with the catering staff."

That wasn't hard to imagine. Most of the pipe fitters I knew were a pretty burly lot. "Were they defending their right to be there, listening to your treasonous rhetoric?"

El laughed. "Not so much. They were defending their right to raid the service area and help themselves to more fried chicken livers."

"Uh oh."

"Yeah. You haven't lived until you've tried to wash that mess out of your hair."

I laughed. "So my bout with the tartar sauce was kind of *pro forma* for you?"

"Oh, I wouldn't say that."

Her voice had taken on that sultry timbre again.

I mentally cleared my throat. "So, what else is on the list?"

"Hmmmm. Well. There was the time Tony paid for a shift foreman's girlfriend to have a boob job."

"Are you kidding me?"

She shook her head. "Nope. I think they classified that one as 'operational enhancements to the physical plant.'"

"Good god."

El looked out her driver's side window. "Hey? Tell me something."

"What?"

"What are those funky-looking, mechanical things that randomly appear in the middle of these fields?"

"What mechanical things?"

"Back there." She gestured over her shoulder. "We just passed one. They're all over the place out here. They look like little metal horses or something."

"Oh. You mean the pump jacks."

"Pump jacks?"

"Yeah. They're oil wells. Those are the pumping stations."

"Oil wells?" she asked.

I nodded.

"In Indiana?"

"Yes."

"In the middle of corn fields?"

I nodded again.

"But I saw one back in town, behind a Free Methodist church."

"Right."

"I don't get it. How much oil could there possibly be in Indiana?"

"More than you might expect," I explained. "Back in the early eighties, when oil prices were so high, a lot of people out here used the income from those wells to put their kids through college."

"Really? Does everybody out here have them?"

"Not everybody. But a lot do. Oil companies manage them for groups of owners. They pump it out, and divide any profits on a percentage basis between the various landowners. Most of the oil fields straddle property lines."

"So it's like Indiana's version of OPEC?"

"Sort of. But with fewer wars and less interesting head gear."

"Well, you certainly have the same climactic conditions."

"Not for long. Wait another month or two until this place turns into the Midwestern equivalent of Yakutia."

"Oh, do not even *try* to talk to me about winter here." She looked at me. "Ever been to Buffalo in February?"

I pretended to think about it. "No . . . but I kinda like the music."

El rolled her eyes. "And Grammy likes the spicy wings . . ."

The mention of spicy chicken caused my bravado to evaporate like drops of rain on hot asphalt. Lucky for me, we had reached the outskirts of Owensville. A few ragtag-looking buildings dotted the roadside. They gave way to clusters of small homes.

I pointed ahead. "Behold, Owensville."

The town looked better at night. It occurred to me that everything in Indiana looked better at night. Less depressed. More lush. Even graceful. Probably, that was because I was trying so hard to see it the way El saw it. And, somehow, El saw the unspoiled raw beauty of a landscape that had long since grown dull and lifeless for me—like a photograph that had slowly lost its color over the years and faded into a muted mass of gray.

"This is really charming," she said.

It sounded like she meant it. I looked out my window at the abandoned gas station on the corner. "Charming" wasn't a word I would have chosen to describe the entrance to Owensville.

"Turn right at the next intersection after the Methodist Church," I said. "Stay on 65."

"Okay."

We were in what passed for the center of town. A small strip center on the right had battered aluminum awnings and several empty storefronts. But the Dollar General was still doing a robust business.

"Turn left here," I said. "On Main Street. It's only three blocks. On the right, after the funeral home."

As we got closer to my house, I began to doubt the wisdom of letting El bring me home. It wasn't that I was embarrassed about her seeing my place, it was more that this trip was like crossing some kind of boundary—even more than the one we'd crossed when El came to Grammy Mann's for pot roast and rhubarb pie. I thought again about the letter from Don K. I was glad it wasn't in the car with us, writhing around on the back seat like the garter snake some kids once tossed into my truck at the Quik-Stop. It didn't belong there—just like I was beginning to believe that I didn't belong here. Not anymore.

"This is it," I said. "On the right."

El turned her blinker on and pulled over next to the curb.

"Oh, Friday Jill," she said. "This is your house?"

I nodded.

"It's adorable."

I could hear Fritz barking. It sounded like he was on the back porch. I was surprised he wasn't already in the side yard and investigating this potential threat. Apparently, El's canine magic continued.

El hadn't shut the engine off.

"Do you want to come inside?" I asked.

To be fair, I wasn't really sure how I wanted her to respond. I thought about that famous quote. The one about there only being two things in life to fear: not getting what you wanted, or getting what you wanted. Right then for me, it was pretty even money on either result.

El turned off the engine, and I knew right away that I did want her to come inside with me. I wanted that more than anything.

"I'd like that," she said.

Fritz stopped barking and came around the side of the house to greet us. He was prancing back and forth along the low, iron fence with his tail wagging. El and I got out of the SUV and made our way down the sidewalk toward my small front porch. She took a quick detour to walk over and greet Fritz.

"Hello there, handsome," she cooed. "Aren't you a good boy?"

Fritz was standing on his hind legs, licking El's face. I walked over to join them.

"Let's go in this way." I unhitched the gate that led into the back yard.

El was studying the outside of my small house. "I love all the roof lines. It looks so gothic. How old is this house?"

"I think it was built sometime in the early 1900s. It's one of the older homes in town. I was lucky to get it."

"How long have you lived here?"

"About six years. I've been working on it pretty much nonstop. It wasn't in the best shape."

El shook her head. "It certainly looks great now."

I led the way to the back porch. "Trust me. It's a work in progress. I still have a lot of work left to do on the interior."

"Are you doing it all yourself?"

"As much as I can. There are some things I can't do—like wiring and plumbing."

El laughed. "Right. I think you've demonstrated your lack of proficiency with plumbing."

"Hey. That wasn't just my fault. As I recall, you were present, too. Besides . . . I never said I wasn't good at demolition."

"That's true."

Fritz followed us onto the back porch. I held open the door that led inside to the tiny mudroom and the kitchen beyond. I was pretty proud of the kitchen. I had torn out the old one, which had really been more like a lean-to, and rebuilt it all from scratch. I scoured around for quite a while before finding old pine cabinet doors with unglazed glass windows at an estate auction in Fort Branch. They were narrow, tall doors that reached all the way to the ceiling. I had sanded off the rough spots but left all the various undercoats of paint showing through in places. They had, at various times, been painted yellow, blue, and white, and I decided I liked the muted patina of all three colors. The base cabinets were solid white. So were the appliances. I had refinished the pine floors, and they were now a soft gold color, speckled here and there with black dots left by the nails that had once held the old linoleum in place.

El was staring at the kitchen with an open mouth. "You did this yourself?"

I shrugged. "Mostly."

She looked at the ceiling. "Is that real bead board?"

I nodded. "I pretty much had to do that. The old ceiling had those cellulose tiles, and they were pretty stained and awful looking. The roof used to leak back here . . . there was quite a bit of water damage above the dropped ceiling when I tore it out."

El shook her head. "This is just gorgeous. How on earth did you figure out how to do all of this?"

"It wasn't all that hard. It was mostly undoing what had been done over the years. I really just took it back to the way it likely was when it was built. I mean, except for obvious things like newer appliances and better wiring."

"The countertops look like concrete."

I smiled. "Good guess. I actually thought about that, but opted for quartz instead." I ran the flat of my hand along one of the surfaces. "I didn't realize that a lot of people have concrete allergies—not something you probably want to take a chance on in your kitchen. So I picked a color that looked a lot like cement." I looked at her. "Once they were installed, I was afraid that maybe they looked too . . ." I didn't know what word to use.

"Butch?" El suggested.

I laughed. "Exactly."

"They don't at all. They look perfect."

"So I don't need to hang my tool belt in here?"

"Do you *have* a tool belt?"

"Of course. Don't you?"

She seemed to consider that. "Not the last time I looked."

I leaned against the sink. "What kind of union do you belong to, anyway?"

"Are we speaking literally or metaphorically?"

I smiled at her. "Yes."

"Okay. I guess I belong to the I'm-not-a-real-straight-woman-but-I-play-one-on-TV union."

I was intrigued. "So nobody at work knows you're gay?"

"Tony knows. A few others do. I generally don't advertise it all that much. It's a lot simpler that way."

"Forgive me for saying this, but you didn't really try to disguise it when we first met."

"You were different."

My reflexive response to comments like that was to want to change the subject, but I didn't. Maybe being on my own turf allowed me to feel braver and less tentative.

"What made me different?"

El looked amused. "Explaining that would be a longer conversation."

124

"Longer than what?"

She glanced down at her soggy ensemble. "Longer than I want to have while standing here in wet clothes."

I wasn't at all sure if she intended for that to sound provocative. But to be fair, I had to admit that El could read from the Yellow Pages, and I'd probably think it was erotic poetry.

"I can take care of that," I said. "Let me give you something else to wear."

She raised an eyebrow. "Does it involve a tool belt?"

"Not unless you want it to."

"I think I'll pass." She stared at me for a moment. "Okay, dry clothes would be great."

"Follow me."

I led her out of the kitchen and through the dining room toward the front of the house. It took me a moment to realize that she wasn't keeping up with me. I turned around. She was standing in the middle of the dining room shaking her head.

"What is it?" I asked.

She gestured toward the floor to ceiling bookcases. "I suppose you've read all of those?"

"I don't suppose you'd believe me if I told you they came with the house?"

"Really." El walked over and pulled a fat book off a shelf. "*Bondage of the Will?*"

I shrugged. "I thought it was an S&M classic."

El rolled her eyes. "Nice try." She returned the book to the shelf. "This place just gets better and better."

"I'm really glad you like it. Sometimes I think I'll never get it finished."

She gestured toward the row of oak chairs that were still missing their seat bottoms.

"What are those?"

I sighed. "I foolishly bought those, thinking I could learn how to re-cane the seats." I pointed at the one I had been working on with Grammy. "You can see that I don't have any real skill in this area."

El went to examine it. "I don't know . . . it doesn't look too bad."

She tipped it over. "You just need to tuck these longer ends in better before you clip off the shorter reeds."

I was dumbfounded. "Are you kidding me?"

"What?" She set the chair down.

"You know how to do this?"

"Of course."

I had a hard time not blurting out the words, "Marry me." How was it possible that El, a hard-nosed UAW agitator, knew how to do something this folksy and antiquated?

"How on earth did you learn to do that?" I asked.

She laughed. "When you grow up in a blue collar family with six kids, you learn how to fix things that are broken."

"I guess I missed a lot being an only child."

"I don't know." She looked me over. "You don't seem to have fared too badly."

"Now you're just flattering me."

She smiled. "Pretty much."

There was that panicked feeling again. I wanted to kick myself. Here I was, finally, in my own home with someone who was smart, funny, high functioning, and, as far as I knew, unattached. And she seemed to be telegraphing her interest in me. And as if that uncommon combination of attributes wasn't enough, she was drop-dead gorgeous, too. Things like this just didn't happen. Not a Thursday night in Owensville, Indiana, and not ever to me.

Maybe T-Bomb was right. Maybe it was time for me to get my head out of my ass and do something about it. I took a step toward her.

"El," I said.

"Friday Jill," she said.

Then the phone rang.

I closed my eyes. It rang again . . . then again. There was something annoyingly familiar about the persistence of the rings. It could only be one person.

I sighed and walked to where the phone sat on my desk in the living room.

"Hello?"

"Hey? Friday?" It was T-Bomb. "You left your backpack at the VFW. I called your cell phone seven times until I figured out it was in the dern backpack. Luanne fished it out and showed it to me. I didn't hear that stupid 'Give Me Back That Filet-O-Fish' ring tone goin' off like crazy in there."

"I know. I'll get it from you in the morning, if that's okay?"

"I was gonna ask if you needed me to pick you up. I figured El DeBarge wouldn't drop you off at Hoosier Daddy since you don't have your keys."

"No. She brought me home."

"She did?" She tried to muffle the speaker on her phone while she talked to somebody else. "El DeBarge took her home," she whispered.

I sighed. "T-Bomb?" There was no answer. "T-Bomb?"

"What?" she asked.

"I can hear you talking to somebody. Who's there with you?"

"Well, dern," she said. "It's just me and Luanne. Is El DeBarge still there with you?"

"Yes." I saw no reason to lie to her—she'd probably just drive by the house to check if I said no.

"El DeBarge is still there," I heard her whisper.

"T-Bomb?" I called out. "You don't need to whisper. I already know Luanne is there."

"Hey?" She was back on the line. "Luanne wants to know what you two are gonna do with that sink?"

"Why? Does she need one for something?"

"Yeah. She says that Jay's been wantin' one to put on the back porch for cleanin' fish."

I sighed. "Tell her she can have it."

"She says the post commander was hoppin' mad when he saw that bathroom."

"I know. We're going to pay to get it all fixed."

I heard muffled talking in the background again.

"Hey?" T-Bomb continued. "She says to tell you that your Grammy won that dern swimmin' pool."

"She did?" I was shocked. It was hard to imagine Grammy with an above ground Esther Williams pool. Although I figured Fritz would probably love it.

"Yeah," T-Bomb said. "But she don't want it. She traded with Ermaline."

"What did Ermaline win?"

"Them garden gnomes. But she said they already had a set, and she really wanted that swimmin' pool."

I was confused. "What's Grammy going to do with a set of paramilitary garden gnomes?"

T-Bomb cackled. "Nothin'. She traded them with Wynona Miles, who got the free anal gland thing from that place out in Poseyville. She don't have a dog no more since Buddy got hit by that bookmobile last year."

I'd had about enough of this conversation. "I'm hanging up now, T-Bomb."

"Hey?"

"What?"

"Tell that El DeBarge you snore!"

I could hear her laughing as she hung up her phone. I held the receiver against my chest for a moment before returning it to its cradle.

El was watching me with an amused expression. She'd been standing near my desk, looking at one of my business law textbooks.

"T-Bomb," I explained.

"I gathered as much," she replied.

"So. About those dry clothes . . ."

She nodded and put the book down. "Right behind you."

She followed me across the living room and up the stairs that led to my bedroom. Fritz trotted along behind us. I noticed that he was sticking pretty close to El's heels.

My house was really just a story and a half. The upstairs area housed only one bedroom and a small bathroom. But the space was homey and inviting with a bank of three windows that overlooked the street in front of the house. I actually had another bedroom on the main floor, but that one I kept set up as a guest room. It was important for me to have a space that might be suitable for

Grammy, if she ever got to the point that she didn't feel comfortable staying alone out in the country.

El looked around the room with interest.

"I like this," she said. "It's very spare. Almost Amish."

I laughed. "Amish? Is that code for undecorated?"

"No, smartass. I meant it as a compliment. I really like the simplicity of the colors and the furniture."

"Well, Grammy gets the credit for that. This was all her stuff." I pointed at the bed, which, mercifully, I had remembered to make up that morning before I left the house. "The quilt was made by her mother. That's partly why the colors are so faded."

"It's beautiful." El looked at me. "I like your house. It's a lot like you."

"A work in progress?" I asked.

El shook her head. "No. Open. Uncluttered. Balanced." She smiled. "Smart. Nice to look at."

I knew I was blushing. "Thanks. Although I don't know of anyone else who would say my life is uncluttered."

"I wasn't talking about relationships."

"Neither was I."

"That's good to know."

"How about you?" I asked.

She looked confused. "What about me?"

"Is your life uncluttered, too?"

"Oh." She gave me a small smile. "Yes. For some time now."

"I guess that's also good to know."

El laughed. "Why are we acting like two kids passing notes in homeroom?"

I looked around the room. "Because it's late, we're both soaking wet, and we're standing here in the middle of my bedroom without a chaperone."

El looked down at Fritz, who was sprawled out at her feet. "What about him?"

"He doesn't count."

"Are you scared?"

I nodded. "Shitless. How about you?"

129

"I'd say that shitless about covers it for me, too."

"I don't want to be scared, El."

"Neither do I."

"So where does that leave us?"

She shrugged and ran her hand along the oak footboard of my bed. "Soaking wet and standing in the middle of your bedroom without a chaperone."

"Be serious."

"I'm sorry. I don't know what else to say."

"Really?"

She nodded.

I sighed. "This is one for the record books. An agitator who doesn't know what to say."

"Well . . . we are better known for being people of action."

"At least that's something. What would a person of action do right now?"

El gave me an ironic look.

"Besides *that*," I added.

El laughed. "I think you should lend me something dry to wear and take a shower to wash that mess out of your hair."

"Agreed." I walked toward my dresser. "Will you wait for me?"

She nodded again. "Sure. Fritz can keep me company."

"He'd like that." I pulled a maroon t-shirt and a faded pair of gym shorts out of a drawer and held them out to her. "These will be too big, but I suppose you can make do."

El took them from me. She unfolded the shirt and held it up to examine it.

"Salukis?" she asked.

"My alma mater," I explained. "Very exclusive."

She smiled and draped the shirt over her arm. "Come on, Fritz." She patted a hand on her thigh. "Let's go downstairs and wait on mommy."

Fritz got to his feet and followed her toward the stairs with his tail wagging. I watched them go.

"Help yourself to anything you want to drink," I called after her. "There's beer in the icebox or wine in the rack on the counter."

"I'll figure it out," she answered. She and Fritz were already halfway down the stairs.

I stood rooted to my spot in the middle of the room, trying to make sense out of everything that had happened that day, and how it had all ended up with me about to take a shower while El reposed someplace downstairs with Fritz.

I gave up and headed for the bathroom. I knew there'd be plenty of time later for me to pour over events and get even more confused. These days, that was just about the only thing in life I could count on.

෨ ෨ ෨

Ella Fitzgerald was singing about falling leaves and sycamore trees.

I paused at the bottom of the steps. *Moonlight in . . . Owensville?*

It didn't have quite the same magic.

I walked toward the silvery sound. El and Fritz were on the back porch. El had changed, and was draped across the swing in a heartland parody of an art master's odalisque—all except for the baggy shorts and the Salukis t-shirt. It didn't matter. She still looked pretty mesmerizing. If Menards had been able to put a photo of her in their Sunday newspaper ad, they'd have sold out of porch swings five minutes after opening the store.

Fritz was splayed out on the rug at her feet, happily munching away on a rawhide bone. El was thumbing through a Renovator's Supply catalog.

I stood in the doorway and watched them. Maybe I was wrong? *Moonlight in Owensville* did seem to have some magic.

El saw me standing there staring at her.

"I hope you don't mind," she said, gesturing at her bare feet. "I made myself comfortable."

I walked over to join her. "I don't mind at all." I didn't see any kind of beverage on the table in front of her. "Didn't you want anything to drink?"

She put the catalog down. "I thought I'd wait and see what you were in the mood for."

131

The buzz I'd had earlier in the evening had long since evaporated. I thought I'd probably be safe to indulge in something else.

"Do you like wine?" I asked.

"Not as much as I like five-dollar pitchers of Old Style."

"Really?"

El rolled her eyes. "No. Not *really*. Of course I like wine, goofball."

"I guess I did it again."

"Did what again?"

I waved a hand in frustration. "That . . . *thing*. You know . . ."

El seemed to be enjoying my discomfort. "I can think of several things I'd *like* to have you do again, but I'm hoping none of them would make you this nervous."

"You think this is funny, don't you?"

"Let's see." El sat up and pivoted her legs around so she could stand up. "Yes. Pretty much." She smiled up at me. "I think I know why you're in so much distress."

I kind of doubted it. "You do?"

"Of course. It's the elephants."

Elephants? I looked around the porch. "What elephants?"

El shook her head. "Oh, lord. You really are that literal, aren't you?"

"I thought we'd already established that."

El got to her feet and took hold of my hand. "Come on. Show me your wine stash."

I still felt like I was playing catch up. El led me into the kitchen.

"What elephants?" I muttered.

"In the room, Friday Jill. The elephants *in the room*." She looked at me over her shoulder. "You know . . . the ones we haven't talked about."

"Oh. *Those* elephants."

"As opposed to which other ones?" she asked. "Or are you going to try to tell me they're indigenous to southern Indiana, too?"

I shook my head. "No. Not the last time I checked."

El perused my modest wine stash.

"You think we have elephants?" I asked.

She held a bottle of red zinfandel. "Only about as many as there were in *A Passage to India*."

That was one of my favorite books. "I only remember one elephant in that."

"It only takes one."

I pointed at the bottle she was holding. "Is that the one you want?"

"Maybe. I'm not sure yet." She slid it back into its spot and pulled out another bottle to examine. "Oh, I like this one."

It was a pinot, and one of my favorites. "I do, too."

She handed it to me. "Sold."

I took it from her. "It's not the good one."

"Are there bad ones?"

I shrugged. "More expensive ones."

"That doesn't make this one bad."

"No . . . just cheaper." I turned the bottle over and read the label. "I'd say that this one is about the third rung on the MacMurray Ranch ladder."

El crossed her arms. "Funny. I'd never have pegged you as a wine drinker."

"Why?"

"I dunno. Maybe because I've only ever seen you drink beer."

I smiled. "Have you ever looked at Aunt Jackie's wine list?"

"She has a wine list?"

"Oh, yeah. But it's only about three or four boxes long."

"Boxes?"

I nodded.

El laughed. "Okay. I see your point."

"Wanna take this back to the porch?"

"That'd be nice. We can join Fritz . . . and the elephant."

"Maybe we should take four glasses?"

"I don't think so."

I opened a drawer and pulled out my corkscrew. "Wanna grab the glasses? They're in that cabinet over there next to the icebox."

El walked to the cabinet and opened the tall door. She pulled out a glass and held it up to the light. "These are beautiful. What are they?"

"They were Grammy's."

"They look like old Tiffin glass."

133

"I think that's right. I think they were wedding gifts. Most of them came from the Montgomery Ward catalog." I smiled, remembering when Grammy gave them all to me. "Half of them were still in the gift boxes. She never used them, as far as I can remember. She always said they didn't hold enough iced tea to suit her. So she gave them to me a couple of years ago."

"There must be a dozen of them in here."

"Sixteen, actually. Isn't it strange to think that service for twelve used to be the norm?"

El laughed. "Not in my family. We bought everything by the dozen."

"I keep forgetting that you have so many siblings."

"I wish I could."

We walked back out to the porch. El sat down on the swing again, but this time, she left space for me to sit beside her. I took the hint.

"You didn't like being part of a big family?" I started to open the wine.

"It wasn't so much that. It was more the total lack of anonymity. I always felt exposed—like I was living my life through all of them. Even in school, I was viewed as a subset of my brothers and sisters." El shrugged her narrow shoulders. "I was like the human embodiment of whatever lurked beyond the ellipsis at the end of the family sentence."

"Is that why you don't live near any of them?" I asked.

"It's why I don't live any place."

"Because you want to be anonymous?"

"I used to think so."

I handed her a glass of wine. "But you don't want to be anonymous now?"

El gazed back at me for a moment. "Not right now. No."

I knew we were treading on dangerous ground, but I didn't really care. I held up my glass.

"Here's to discovering . . ." I searched for the right toast. "Happier punctuation marks?"

El laughed and clinked rims. "I'll drink to that."

We tried the wine.

El gave a little moan. The sound of it stretched across the swing and vibrated along a path that ended up someplace near my toes.

"Good?" I asked.

"Oh, god. Yes." El tipped her head back against the swing. "I am so tired."

"Long day?"

"Long life."

"You talk like you're a zillion years old."

"Sometimes it feels like it."

The music changed. Ella became someone else. It was a bluesy sound—edgier, with more overtones of swing. Like Bessie Smith on steroids.

"Who's that?" I asked.

El looked toward the table where I kept my iPod dock. "The music?"

I nodded.

"It sounds like the Red Hot Skillet Lickers."

"Excuse me?"

She laughed. "Lavay Smith. They're a San Francisco band."

I listened for a moment. "I like it."

"I can't take credit for it. It's Pandora."

"How did you manage that?" I asked.

"It was easy. I saw your dock over there and just stuck my phone on it. I hope you don't mind."

"I don't mind at all. But how'd you figure out my password?"

She smiled. "I didn't have to. I was able to connect to an open network."

"You found an open network?"

"Apparently. I think it belongs to someone named Eubanks?"

"Eubanks." I thought about that. "You mean *Uebinger?*"

"Yes. That was it."

"Really?" I shook my head in wonder. "Lurleen Uebinger has Wi-Fi?"

"Is that a surprise?"

"Yeah. I didn't even know she had indoor plumbing."

El laughed.

"You think I'm kidding, but I'm not. You'd be amazed by how a lot of people out here still live."

"No I wouldn't." El set her wine glass down. "I've worked in some areas that would make Gibson County look like Manhattan's gold coast."

"America's auto workers," I mused. "Overpaid, but still underprivileged."

"Ain't that the truth?" she quipped.

"It sounds depressing."

"It is," she agreed.

"So why do you keep doing it?"

She gave me an amused look. "Doing what?"

"You know . . . agitating."

She sighed. "I honestly don't know."

We sat quietly for minute or so, just listening to the music. The Skillet Lickers were racing toward a rollicking finish. At our feet, an oblivious Fritz continued munching on his chew bone. This one still looked mostly intact. Grammy must have hooked him up with it when she dropped him off earlier on her way to the fish fry.

"Why'd you leave Ithaca?"

El looked at me in surprise. I hadn't meant to just blurt the question out like that.

"I'm sorry if that's too personal," I added quickly.

"It's fine." She touched my knee. "You can ask me anything."

I could tell by her expression that she was being sincere.

"Okay," I said.

"Why did I leave Ithaca?" She picked up her drink but didn't sip from it. Instead, she gently twirled it, causing the purple-red liquid to swirl and coat the sides of the glass. She held it up in front of her face and looked at me through the lines of receding color. "Nice legs for a third rung."

Of course, it was impossible for me not to drop my gaze from her glass to her other set of legs—the set that would inhabit the top rung on any scale.

She caught me staring. I looked up at her with what I was certain was a guilty expression. But her gray eyes were anything but accusing. They were translucent. Open.

"The short answer would be to say I left after the divorce. End of story."

Divorce? El had been married?

"What would the long answer be?" I asked.

El looked dubious. "You really want to hear it?"

I nodded.

She sighed and slumped a bit lower into the swing. "It was an old story. He was a professor of mine—one of my dissertation advisers, actually. It was wholly inappropriate. But then, so was I. I was running pretty hard and fast in those days—away from everything and toward nothing . . . except what I thought everyone wanted me to do."

"What was that?"

"Get married and make babies, of course. Catholic family. Remember?"

"I remember."

"Well," she sighed, "I got it half right."

"What do you mean?"

"I managed to snag a man, but he was more than twenty-five years my senior. That kind of took the whole let's get pregnant thing off the table." She smiled. "That part actually worked very well for me. In retrospect, I realized that I chose him very carefully. Besides, Ivor already had kids who were nearly my age. It wasn't something he was interested in, either."

"Ivor?"

"Oh. Yes." She laughed. "Ivor Halvorsen. A luminary in international labor relations. He was a visiting professor at Cornell."

I was still trying to wrap myself around the revelation that El had been married. To a man. To *Ivor*.

"Are you all right?" El touched my leg again. I wasn't aware that I had been staring off into space.

"I'm sorry. I'm fine. I was just . . ."

"Trying to imagine me married?" she asked.

I nodded.

"You never thought about it?"

"For myself?" I pointed a finger at my chest. "God, no. I have a hard time even committing to buy a dozen eggs."

El laughed.

"You find that humorous?"

"And profound. Believe me . . . there are a lot of similarities."

"Such as?"

"Both are extremely fragile. A lack of moderation with either can ruin your health. They each begin to stink without proper care."

I was incredulous. "You're awfully good at making lists."

"I'm a Leo. It's what we do."

I shook my head. "I'm a Libra."

"Ah. See? That explains everything."

"It does?"

She waved a hand. It was easy to imagine her in front of a classroom. "Of course. Libras are indecisive and incapable of commitment."

"That's not true. We're people who crave balance."

"Oh, horse hockey. Libras are wimps who won't go left or right because they're terrified of making the wrong decision."

"See? *Balance.*"

"See? *Paralysis.*"

I huffed. "Leos are bullies."

"No. Leos are leaders."

"And bullies."

"We're not bullies. We just have the ability to present compelling arguments for whatever we want to do."

I laughed. "Must be nice."

"Sometimes it is," she agreed.

"Well, clearly, as a person incapable of decisiveness, I wouldn't know."

"Don't worry." El bumped my shoulder. "You're trainable."

"I hope so." I drained my wine glass and picked up the bottle. "My track record hasn't been the greatest."

El held out her glass. I topped it off, then refilled my own.

"Are we talking about relationships again?" she asked.

"Do you have to ask?"

"Apparently. You still haven't told me who Misty Ann is."

"She's no one." I felt bad about the words as soon as they left my mouth. "That's not true. She's . . . fine. I just made a bad decision and got involved with someone I shouldn't have."

"We've all done that."

"Yeah? Well, I've sort of elevated it to an art form."

"Why?"

I shrugged. "I don't know. I guess I'm afraid of getting hurt."

"Don't these bad decisions ever end up hurting you?"

I looked at her. "They all do."

El chewed the inside of her cheek. "Then it sounds like your strategy isn't working very well."

"You might say that."

"Maybe it's time to try a different approach?"

I thought about a variety of different approaches I could try right then, but opted to sip my wine instead. El was right. Libras are wimps.

"What approach?" I asked. "I don't think marriage would work out for me."

"I wasn't thinking about marriage," she replied. "And by the way, marriage didn't work out so well for me, either."

"What happened?"

"With Ivor?"

I nodded.

"We lasted about two years. Barely. Turns out he was gay, and so was I. The difference was that he knew it and I didn't."

I was confused by her explanation, and it must have showed on my face.

"Ivor wasn't looking for a wife, he was looking for a companion. He knew I was gay long before I did. I suppose he thought it was an arrangement that would work well for each of us." She shrugged. "Our relationship was never sexual . . . that should've been a clue for me. But frankly," she looked at me, "I was just relieved that it wasn't something he seemed to be interested in."

"How did you . . . ?"

"Figure it out?" El asked.

I nodded.

She sighed. "We were friends with another couple—both professors. They had an open relationship . . . not uncommon at Cornell. She was only too happy to help me find my way." She raised an eyebrow. "See? I told you that you weren't the only one who made bad decisions."

"Wow."

"Yeah. Believe me . . . I couldn't get out of Ithaca fast enough. And to be fair, I really wasn't cut out for life in the classroom. I needed more real world experience. I wanted to do more than just *talk* about labor relations. I wanted to make a difference—not just spend my days deconstructing failed case histories on a white board for a roomful of bored twenty-somethings."

"So you became an agitator."

She held up her finger. "A divorced agitator."

"Who likes girls?" I asked.

"Who likes a certain girl," she added. "A lot."

There we were again. Right back where we started. It was the same place El and I always ended up: the center point of our circle.

I looked down at my lap. I knew El was waiting for me to say something, but I was too afraid of saying the wrong thing . . . or the right thing.

Libras. Wimps.

"Does that scare you?" El asked in a soft voice. I barely heard it above the music. It was Bobby Darin now . . . searching for happiness beyond the sea.

Things didn't work out so well for him, either . . .

"Friday Jill?" El asked.

I looked up at her. "Yes. It scares the piss out of me."

"Why?" She touched my hand.

"Because you're leaving."

"I can come back," she said.

"You won't."

She looked confused. "Why do you say that?"

"Oh, come on." I waved a hand in frustration. "Who comes back to Indiana? This is a place people leave. Not a place people stay."

"You stayed."

"I don't count."

El squeezed my hand. "To me, you do."

I sighed, knowing it sounded every bit as morose as I felt. "It's a losing proposition."

"Why do you say that? We wouldn't be the first two people to deal with distance as a relationship factor."

"It's not just the distance. I work in a truck factory, El. You're a labor organizer." I paused. "Anything about those two facts seem at all irreconcilable to you?"

"Not really. You forget. I live in a world where irreconcilable differences are a starting point for negotiation."

I had to laugh at that one, even though I knew I was sinking deeper into the mire of hopelessness.

"There's no arguing with you."

El smiled. "That's the first sensible thing you've said."

I shook my head. "What makes you so sure this can work?"

"What makes you so sure it can't?"

"Because things like this don't happen to me."

El looked confused. "Things like what?"

"Things like you."

El sat there quietly for a moment, then pulled out the gaping neck of my Salukis t-shirt. She tucked her chin back and took a long look inside.

"Nope. It's me, all right. Nobody else in here." She released the shirt. "Sorry. Looks like things like me *can* happen to you."

"El . . ."

"No." She held up a hand. "Stop trying to end this before it even gets started. You've been like someone on a seesaw—one minute you're up, the next you're down. It's making me crazy." She set her wine glass down and moved closer. "And it's a colossal waste of time."

Her proximity was causing all kinds of signal flares to ignite. Sparks were flying off in all directions. But what were they warning against? And instead of running for cover, why did I suddenly have a desire to join in, fire up a few more, and sit back to watch the show? Already the patterns of light were spectacular.

El kissed my neck. I closed my eyes and watched as an endless cascade of blue-and-white flowers blazed and exploded against the night sky inside my head.

I remembered the very first time I saw fireworks at the Princeton fairgrounds. T-Bomb and I were lying on an old army surplus blanket that Grammy had spread out over the wiry grass. It was the fourth of July, and everything around us was alive with color and flashes of light.

The loud booms went on and on. The hot summer sky was transformed into an electric canvas, painted by a thousand different brushes. It glowed and vibrated. We were positive that the ground beneath our backs would be changed forever—that so much color and light falling to earth would have to transform the monotonous miles of cornfields into something magical. Something extraordinary.

The fireworks emanating from El were just as sensational. Just as new and exotic. They held just as much mystery and promise. I turned my head and began my own exploration. This time, it was slower and more deliberate. Not fast or frenzied. There was no threat of discovery, no insistent interruption looming on the other side of the door, and no gauntlet of staring eyes to frame a path of retreat. And, remarkably, we weren't soaking wet—at least, not on the outside.

The slow river of lost hope and longing that moved through my darkest places was overflowing its banks. I was in the midst of a millennial flood, and I knew it. It had never been like this for me. I didn't recognize the sensations because they'd never been part of my canon of experience. I couldn't call them by name or understand how they fit together. But what I could see and understand was that all of my empty places were filling up with something warm and solid. Shadowy images that had always been incomplete were gaining contours—coalescing into things I recognized. I could see people walking, and they no longer looked like trees.

That was the moment when everything changed for me. I drew back and held El's face between my hands.

"I can see you," I said.

It was that simple.

She smiled at me. It was that small smile of hers—the one you might miss if you weren't looking for it. But I was looking. And finally, I was seeing.

She pressed her face into my hands. "Thank god."

I kissed her forehead. "Stay with me."

I realized after I said the words that I meant them in every sense. I wanted her to stay. Tonight. Tomorrow. A thousand tomorrows.

She didn't reply. But I felt the subtle movement of her head as she nodded.

Fritz chose that moment to decide that his night was at its end. He climbed to his feet and rested his chin on El's knee.

"He wants his bedtime walk," I explained.

El patted his head as he panted against her leg. "Okay."

"Want to join us?" I asked.

She nodded.

We untangled ourselves and stood up. Fritz was already dancing beneath the hook where I kept his leash. El slipped her shoes back on and joined me at the door. I took hold of her hand, and we followed Fritz out into the balmy, blue-and-white night.

Chapter 9

T-Bomb was running late when she picked me up on Friday morning, so we didn't have time to stop at Huck's for coffee. I ducked into the break room before clocking in, just to grab a fast cup. That's when I saw it, big as life, tacked to the message board over the trash can . . . right where it belonged. It was a leaflet. Typed up on somebody's PC and printed on bright orange paper.

WILL THIS PLANT CLOSE IF THE UNION GETS IN?
<u>Here are the facts:</u>

FACT: Unions never did anything to help American workers.
FACT: Unions make plants close, and jobs go overseas.
FACT: Unions make the cost of living get higher and push people onto welfare.
FACT: Unions want to control your time and your money.
FACT: Unions make you play by THEIR rules, whether you agree with them or not.
FACT: Union bosses are your judge and jury.
FACT: Unions can take away your seniority.
FACT: Unions can force companies to cut wages and benefits.
FACT: Unions will use any lies or tactics to get you to sign up.

<u>Who wants to pay dues for that?</u>

SAVE OUR JOBS! GET THE FACTS!!

It was clear to me that this hadn't come from Buzz or Joe. For one thing, it wasn't full of spelling errors, and it actually had punctuation that made sense. This one had Don K.'s fingerprints all over it. He must really be running scared if he was stooping to scare tactics like this flier, and the promotion he'd dangled in front of me the day before. I wondered if El and Tony were wrong about their dwindling prospects for getting a vote at OTI?

I looked at the orange leaflet again. I also wondered if it would be treasonous for me to tell them about this. There was no way propaganda like this could be legal. But little details like that never stopped guys like Don K. It was clear that he wasn't going to let anything get between him and his Japanese-made golden parachute. I was just about to pull the thing off the board and stick it into my pocket when I heard the break room door open.

"I should've known you'd be all over *that*," a brittle-sounding voice behind me declared.

I turned around. Misty Ann Marks. *Great. Just what I needed.*

I wasn't sure I cared to understand what her remark meant, so I didn't say anything.

She waved a hand at the bulletin board. I noticed that her nail extensions were bright pink and dotted with glitter. Grammy would say she was puttin' on the Ritz. One thing was true about Misty Ann—whatever she was puttin' on, she managed to make it look fast and cheap.

"I heard you were all lathered up over that union agitator." She snorted. "She's right up your alley, too. Classy. Maybe you two should start a book club? But then, she won't be around long enough to finish anything, will she?"

"Misty Ann . . . the only thing around here that's finished is this conversation."

I tried to walk by her, but she stepped in front of me.

"Not so fast," she said. "You sure had time for me when you didn't have anyone better to play around with."

I sighed. "That's not true, and you know it. You never had any intention of breaking up with your husband."

"Oh, *now* that bothers you?" She sneered. "Funny . . . I don't remember you being all concerned about the state of my marriage any of those times we played tonsil hockey in the back seat of his car."

"Misty Ann . . ."

"Save it." Her hand flew across the front of her throat in a mock, slashing gesture. "I'm tired of being used by turncoats like you. You're no better than the rest of those deadbeats out there who think a damn union is the answer to all their problems. Donny thinks you're on his side, but I know better. You'll choose a pretty piece of ass over loyalty to this company any day."

Donny? Don K. and Misty Ann? Good god . . .

"You're not in his head, Friday."

Thank god, I wasn't in his pants, either.

"I don't have time for this." I pushed past her and headed for the door.

"That's right," she called after me. "You run along and make your little report. I'm sure your girlfriend and the rest of her union trash are waiting to hear from you."

I stormed out of the break room and headed for the line. I was halfway there before I calmed down enough to realize that not only had I forgotten to pick up my cup of coffee, I'd forgotten to punch the damn time clock. My little interlude with Misty Ann was going to cost me an hour's pay. Krylon didn't believe in splitting hairs. If you were ten minutes late, you got docked for an hour. Oh . . . and you got a nice butt-chewing from Buzz Sheets, too. For a day that started out so great, this one was sure going to hell in a hand basket at light speed.

There were several guys standing around near the time clock when I reached it. I didn't recognize two of them, but the third was a flunky who worked up front with Don K. I nodded and said hello, but they just stared back at me without speaking. It gave me a creepy feeling, but I shrugged it off. I didn't want my encounter with Misty Ann to make me paranoid.

I could tell there was something different about my time card as soon as I started to pull it out of its slot. It felt . . . heavier . . . more rigid. Then I noticed that something was attached to it. I turned it over. Part of a union authorization card was taped to the back.

Someone had written my name on it, and the words "UAW Whore" were scrawled beneath it on the job title line.

One of the men I didn't know started snickering.

I turned to them. "You guys know anything about this?" I held up the card.

They shook their heads in unison.

The front office flunky managed to pull a straight face. "You never know who your friends are, do you?"

I rolled my eyes. "You guys must be a real hoot on Halloween." I tore their little love note off my time card. I was going to drop it into the trash, but thought better of it and stuck it into my back pocket instead. I could still hear them laughing as I walked away.

Morons.

I felt like every pair of eyes in the plant were burning holes into my back as I made my way to my section. What the hell was going on? Did Nancy and Udean pilot one of their Christian Tour busses past my house? I wondered if the entire plant knew that El and I had spent the night together.

It wasn't T-Bomb who'd spread the word. I was certain of that. As much as she loved to gossip, she had a code where her own were concerned.

Hell. Why was I surprised by this behavior? Half the population of Princeton watched us leave the VFW hall together last night. I remembered how I followed along at El's heels like a dazed rodent being led out of town by the pied piper.

I actually had to smile at that. The rat reference wasn't too far off the mark. I congratulated myself for the metaphor.

Luanne Keortge was waiting for me when I reached the chassis assembly line. She did not look happy.

"Where the hell have you been? Buzz Sheets has been up my ass for the last half hour." She looked at her watch, then at my face. "Never mind. I guess I know the answer to that."

"Hey? Don't blame me for being late. I rode in with T-Bomb."

Luanne was giving me a good once over. "Well, you look like you been up half the night."

I felt myself blush.

She held up a hand. "Oh, lord. Spare me any of them details about what you all do between the sheets."

I looked around. "Would you mind not broadcasting that?"

"Hell. Nobody in this place could hear an atom bomb going off. Besides. You two weren't what I'd call discreet leavin' the fish fry last night."

I ran a hand over my face. This was going nowhere fast.

"You talk with your Grammy yet?"

Grammy. Shit. I hadn't even thought about that yet.

"No." I was afraid to ask. "Was she okay?"

Luanne chuffed. "You're just lucky she was more concerned with trading out them damn combat gnomes for that dog spa thing. She didn't even notice you were gone until after the raffle was over."

"Did Ermaline give her a ride home?"

Luanne nodded. "She and Doc have already invited everybody out to their place for a pool party." She shook her head. "If that don't beat all. Those two need a damn swimmin' pool about as much as a parakeet needs a can opener." She looked over my shoulder. "Shit. Here comes that dipstick Buzz Sheets again." She glared at me. "Hope you're locked and loaded. I'm gettin' back to work. See you later at Hoosier Daddy?"

I nodded. "I still have to pick up my truck."

She nodded and turned away.

"Wait a minute," I said. "What are you doing here? You're supposed to be on furlough."

"Furlough my ass. Joe is so damn worried about the parade tomorrow, he told me to come on into work."

"The parade?" I was confused. "Why is Joe worried about the parade?"

"He wants Jailissa to ride in his pickup, and he knew that I was madder'n snot at him. So we worked out a deal." She waved and waddled off down the line. "I gotta go. One ass-ripping a day is enough for me."

Buzz was fuming when he reached me. I held up a hand to halt his tirade before he had a chance to spool up.

"I know I'm late, okay? But I'm here now, and it won't happen again."

Buzz was already sweating, and it was barely seven-thirty. He must've been raising hell over in the section of the plant where the AC was still out. His cheap plaid shirt was showing dark, underarm stains that were about the size of radial tires. He mopped at his forehead with a yellowed handkerchief.

"You and that loudmouth Jennings have about pushed me to my last stand. When you don't show up on time, I have to find somebody to cover your station, and that costs me money."

"It's not your money, Buzz."

"See? That's exactly the problem with troublemakers like you." He fumbled around in his shirt pocket. It was stuffed so full of papers, pens, and notepads that it sagged forward. Half the stitching on one side had already started to give way. The distended square of fabric hanging off the front of his chest was like a plaid fishing net. Finally, he found what he was looking for. He held out a folded square of bright orange paper.

"You need to read this. It talks all about people just like you."

I glanced down at the flier like I'd never seen it before. "What is it?"

He shook it back and forth. "Just take it. Maybe you'll learn something. They told us to pass these out to people like you."

People like me?

"You mean line supervisors?" I took the paper from him. I knew that the best way to keep him talking was to act like the dimwit he thought I was.

"No. Not line supervisors." He scoffed. "Jesus, Fryman. You need to get with a program."

I started to unfold the paper, but Buzz stopped me.

"Read that on your own goddamn time."

I looked up at him. "Do you need it back?"

"Nope." He patted his sagging shirt pocket. "Got plenty more of 'em to pass out. Now just get to work. And be glad you're only getting docked for one hour."

One hour's pay for being ten minutes late. It was ridiculous. "Buzz . . ." I began.

"Stow it, Fryman. That bus has sailed."

He walked off.

Idiot.

I shoved the orange square of paper into the back pocket of my pants and put on my safety goggles. It was going to be a long day.

ა ა ა

T-Bomb and I pulled into the parking lot at Hoosier Daddy, and we noticed a couple of people milling around beside my truck. They all seemed to be looking at something.

"Well that can't be good news." T-Bomb roared into a space and jerked to a stop, causing the mound of stuffed animals behind me to slide across the cargo area. Somewhere at the bottom of the heap, Elmo started cackling. I sighed and reached for the door handle so I could climb out of the back seat.

The cluster of people who had been blocking our view evaporated as soon as they saw us approaching. I could see why. The words "RIGHT TO WORK" were spray-painted across the side of my truck in fluorescent, blaze orange. I actually had a fleeting thought that Don K.'s minions were doing a pretty good job with their union-busting campaign . . . orange was clearly their signature color. In this application, it stood out very well against the navy blue backdrop of my Outlaw 250.

I felt my shoulders droop.

"I really can't take much more of this."

"Them assholes!" T-Bomb was loaded for bear. "They can think whatever they want, but they don't have the right to damage personal property this way." She walked around the truck. "Well, dang. It's on this side, too."

Of course it was. I sagged against the bed of my truck. Maybe Grammy would let me borrow her ancient Ram 1500 while I got this thing painted? Whoever did the defacing was a master. They made sure they hit every panel on the vehicle. There was even some kind of impressionistic flourish on top of the cab. To my untrained eye, it looked like a lame attempt at recreating a part of the female anatomy.

"Maybe I'll keep that," I said.

"What the hell are you talkin' about?" T-Bomb demanded. "This just makes me madder'n a hornet's nest."

I pointed to the top of the truck. "That's got kind of a Georgia O'Keefe flair, don't you think?"

T-Bomb looked at me like she expected me to start drooling at any second.

"Pornographic is what it is." She stood back and clucked her tongue. "You ain't gonna get this mess fixed at Earl Scheib. You're gonna have to have this whole dern thing professionally repainted."

"I guess I asked for it, leaving the thing parked here unattended all night."

"Are you nuts? Nobody asks for this." She waved a hand over the truck in disgust. "It's just hooliganism. Downright hooliganism."

I sighed. "I'm not driving this any place. Will you give me a ride out to Grammy's, so I can borrow her truck? I'll have somebody from Quick Stop come over and pick this up. Mike Scoggins does a good job on paint and detail work."

She nodded. "Okay. But first we're going inside for a drink. I'm about parched from workin' in that dern sweat shop all day."

"Can we make it a quick one?"

She eyed me suspiciously. "Why? You got a hot date or somethin'?"

"No. I'm just on overload from all of this crap. I'd like to know what in the hell happened? I feel like I'm walking around with a target on my back."

"Well, hell. If you don't think dosey doe'in your way across that VFW hall with El DeBarge last night was enough to land you right smack in the middle of about two hundred sets of crosshairs, then you ain't half as smart as I thought you were."

"Don't start, okay?"

"Don't *start*? You're telling *me* not to start? That's rich."

"T-Bomb . . ."

"Come on." She started walking toward the bar. "We can argue about this inside. I promised Luanne we'd meet up with her here. She's about off her rocker over that damn competition tomorrow."

Shit. Pork Day. "I forgot about that."

"You forgot about Pork Day? What the hell is the matter with you?"

"Nothing is the matter with me. I'm just tired."

"Tired?"

I nodded.

She burst into laughter. "I don't doubt it. That El DeBarge looks like she's got some stamina."

"That isn't what I—"

"Don't even go there, missy. Even with all this dern union mess heatin' up, you've been runnin' around all day with a shit-eatin' grin on your face. It don't take no scientist to figure out what put it there."

I had a hard time denying that one, so I didn't even try.

My cell phone vibrated. I pulled it out of my pocket and looked at the display. It was a text message ... from El.

"Do you mind if I answer this?" I held up the phone. "I'll meet you inside in just a minute."

"Oh, so now you're not in so much of a hurry? I get it." She strode off toward the entrance to the bar. "Tell that El DeBarge I said to keep her powder dry. It looks like huntin' season is comin' early this year."

I watched her go inside. Then I sat down on the running board of my truck to read my first-ever text message from El.

Hi there, F-J. So sorry I haven't been in touch before now. Tony and I are in Evansville at the NLRB satellite office. We should be heading out before long. Will you be around? Would it be okay if I called when we get back to Princeton? I know it's un-seemly, but I miss you. Last night was lovely. Perfect. Really.

It was crazy. I'd had what was arguably the worst day of my entire work life, but staring at that tiny screen with its short, tidy rows of vowels and consonants was nearly as intoxicating as staring at El. Her mention of last night sent small shivers up and down my limbs. Lovely? It was beyond lovely. It was beyond anything I'd ever experienced. I didn't have a vocabulary to describe what last night had been like for me.

Lovely? Perfect?

Maybe she was right. Waking up before dawn with a naked El draped halfway across me beneath Grammy's old quilt was both lovely *and* perfect. I decided to give her that one. With her customary dispatch, she'd pretty much nailed it.

I wrote back.

> Hello yourself. Let's agree to be unseemly. I miss you, too. Call anytime.

I paused in my typing. Did I want to hint at any of what had happened today? I thought about the orange flier, still folded up in my back pocket. What was that old Bible verse? "Sufficient unto the day is the evil thereof." No. It could all wait until later. It was likely that with all her contacts inside the plant, she'd find out about everything before I had to tell her, anyway.

> I'm at Hoosier Daddy with T-Bomb, but I'll be going home soon.

I hesitated again. Then I decided I had nothing more to lose. I was already in it with both feet.

> P.S. Lovely and perfect about sum it up for me, too. Really.

I sent the message and stood up to head inside. I was halfway across the parking lot when my phone vibrated again.

> You just made this agitator very happy.

I smiled and stuck my phone into my pocket.
A cold Stella was starting to sound pretty good, after all.

ᔕ ᔕ ᔕ

"I'm tellin' you, them juries is all fixed." Luanne was warming to her topic, and her second pitcher of Old Style. "There's no way in hell them Horton girls can walk away with that crown year after year. Between the three of them, they only have one full set of teeth."

T-Bomb choked on a French fry.

Luanne smacked her between the shoulder blades. "You need to ease off that ketchup, girl. You gotta be rottin' your insides with all that acid."

"It's not *that.*" T-Bomb cleared her throat. "I was thinkin' about how many times they've sashayed across that stage in blousy dresses, tryin' to cover up that they had buns in the oven." She held her hands out in front of her belly.

"You mean like pigs in the poke?" Luanne asked.

They collapsed into laughter.

I rolled my eyes and stole a glance at my watch. At this rate, I'd be lucky to get home by nine. I looked around the bar to see if I saw anybody else who I might coerce into giving me a ride out to Grammy's.

I felt more than heard the soft buzzing of my cell phone. I fished it out of my pocket and read the message.

Just dropped Tony off at the hotel. Is this an okay time to call?

I looked up at T-Bomb and Luanne. They appeared to be settling in for the evening. It was Friday night, after all, and tomorrow was Pork Day USA—the second most sacred day of the year in these parts. Half the plant was working extra shifts tomorrow—we'd all lucked out, and none of our areas were affected by the mandatory weekend hours. Don K. was obviously determined to push productivity to a record level in advance of the arrival of the Ogata transition team.

Hoosier Daddy was hopping with revelers who wanted to jump-start the celebration. They deserved to be able to kick back and join in the fun without having to worry about carting me around.

I wrote back to El.

Got another suggestion. Would you be willing to pick me up at Hoosier Daddy and give me a ride out to Grammy's? I need to borrow her truck for a few days.

A minute later, she wrote back.

Of course! I'd be happy to. But is something wrong with your truck?

I quickly replied.

It's a long story.

El seemed to take my word for it.

Be there in five minutes. Pick you up out front.

Perfect. Now I just needed to make my escape.

T-Bomb was asking Luanne something about Jailissa riding in Joe's truck tomorrow. Luanne told her it was pretty hard to refuse his offer since the two of them had started dating.

Dating? I thought my brain was on tilt. Joe Sykes and Jailissa? Maybe I needed to rethink my idea about leaving early . . .

My phone buzzed again.

Make that ETA three minutes.

I smiled. Nope. I was outta there.

"Hey." I held up my phone. "I just got a ride out to Grammy's, so I'm heading out. You two stay on and have fun. I'll see you both tomorrow in Albion."

I stood up to go but T-Bomb reached out a hand to stop me.

"Not so fast." She nodded toward my cell phone. "Who's picking you up?"

I chewed the inside of my cheek.

"El DeBarge?" She shook her head. "You two are worse than a couple of them dime store rabbits."

Luanne drained her glass. "You might wanna think about pacing yourselves. All that pounding can wear them things down to nubs if you ain't careful."

T-Bomb socked Luanne on the shoulder. "They only *have* nubs, you dimwit. That's the problem when two girls start hittin' it. There ain't nothin' to wear off."

I stood there looking back and forth between the two of them. "You don't really need me for this conversation. You know that . . . right?"

T-Bomb actually smiled at me. "Get on outta here. I ain't seen you this happy since you busted your toe in the ninth grade and got to skip gym for a whole month."

I smiled back at her. There was a reason she was my best friend. Even when she knew something was probably going to end up kicking my ass, she still stayed right in my corner.

"I'll call you tomorrow."

"You better." She waved her hand. "Now git . . . your girlfriend's waitin'."

As I walked out and headed for the parking lot, I couldn't help thinking about Joe and Jailissa. And I marveled that even in the throes of real of happiness, the absurd could still find a way to insinuate itself into the middle of my consciousness.

ᔓ ᔓ ᔓ

El's face was a picture of shock and disbelief when she saw my truck.

I opened the passenger door of her SUV and climbed in. "I know. Don't even ask."

"Who the hell did that?" She was fuming.

I snapped my seat belt into place. "Take your pick. One of Don K.'s lackeys, probably."

"That's reprehensible." She looked at me. "I'm so sorry about this, Friday Jill."

Her expression was so earnest that I was tempted to tell her I was thinking about keeping the new paint job. It did exude a certain urban art quality, and it lent a kind of dignity to my misfortune. But I realized that joking about it was probably not the right way to go. Not yet, anyway. Besides, El didn't know about the rest of Don K.'s little campaign and my starring role in it. I continued to debate about whether or not to tell her.

She was aware that I was not saying something.

"What is it?" she asked.

"What is what?" I replied.

"What is it that you're not telling me?"

"You can tell I'm not telling you something?"

"Of course." She gestured toward my foot. It was bouncing up and down like the floorboard was on fire. "You have a tell." She met my eyes. "You'd be a pushover in a poker game."

I nearly told her that I'd be a pushover in any game she chose to play. But I figured she probably already knew that. I'd done a pretty good job demonstrating it last night.

"Let's get out of here," I said. "I'll tell you about it all on the way to Grammy's."

"Okay."

She pulled out of the parking lot, and we headed out of town.

"So here's the deal," I began.

El looked at me with a raised eyebrow. "There's a deal?"

I nodded.

"You might want to rethink this revelation . . . I *am* a professional negotiator, you know."

I couldn't help smiling at that. "I know. I remember."

It was easy to imagine her as a precocious five-year-old bargaining with her mother to stay up ten minutes past bedtime. Given my recent tenure being on the receiving end of something she wanted, I was pretty certain she won every round.

"I wasn't talking about *that*," she said.

"Too bad. I can't stop thinking about *that*."

"Really?" She sounded almost shy—a bold departure from her normal style.

I rested my hand on her thigh. "Really."

She slowly shook her dark head. "Some hardcore agitator I turned out to be."

I laughed. "I don't know. You were pretty successful at getting your way."

"Not entirely. If memory serves, you were unwilling to try that Double Kangaroo Scissor-Kick maneuver."

"Hey." I held up a palm. "I told you . . . I draw the line at anything that could potentially put me in traction."

"Wimp."

"Pervert."

She laughed merrily. "As long as we understand each other."

"I think we've made a pretty good start."

She sighed.

"What is it?" I asked.

"You know I adore your Grammy . . . but . . ."

"But?"

She looked at me. "Do we really have to go out there? Couldn't we just . . ?

"Go to my house?"

She nodded.

I was certain that Nancy and Udean had my street on their tour roster again for tonight. But given the events of the day, it was hard to imagine that things could get any worse for me.

"I'd like that, too. But, unfortunately, I need some transportation. I can't be late for work again, and I'm having a body shop pick up my truck to repaint it."

"I don't mean to be selfish," she explained.

"No," I said. "Please. Be selfish."

She smiled.

"Maybe you could follow me home after we pick up Grammy's truck?"

She nodded. "I'd like that."

"Have you had dinner yet?"

"No."

"Well, if I know Grammy, she'll load us up with a vat of something." We reached the turnoff for the back road. "Left at this stoplight."

El put her blinker on. "I know. I remember."

"Are you and Tony going to Albion tomorrow?"

"You're kidding, right? You think I'd miss out on seeing Luanne's daughter get crowned?"

"It's not for certain she will, you know. Those Hortons have quite a lock on that pageant."

El laughed. "I think the odds are in her favor this time. Luanne showed me some photos of her dress . . . it leaves little to the imagination."

"Really?" That surprised me. Luanne must've really gotten past her reservations about El if she was sharing cell phone pictures of Jailissa with her.

"Yeah. As long as Ermaline isn't around to distract the judges, I think Jailissa's got a real shot at that crown."

Of course, the mention of Jailissa made me think again about the prospect of her with Joe. An involuntary shiver caused my shoulders to twitch. El noticed.

"What's wrong? Is the AC too cold?" She reached out to adjust the temperature.

"No." I intercepted her hand. "I was just thinking about Jailissa and Joe."

"Joe?" she asked.

"Sykes."

"The plant manager?"

"You know him?"

"*Of* him . . . yes. Tony's had a couple of run-ins with him about getting access to the plant to review where they have our information session notices posted." She laughed bitterly. "I mean, *if* they have our notices posted."

"That sounds about right."

"What about Joe and Jailissa?"

I shook my head. "It's pretty creepy. Joe has lusted after Jailissa since she's been in pedal pushers. But tonight, I heard T-Bomb ask Luanne if it was true that they were dating."

"You're kidding?" El sounded as surprised as I felt. "Isn't there a huge age difference between them?"

"You might say that. Joe is in his forties. Jailissa is barely seventeen."

"Oh my god. This place is close to Hazard County in more ways than one, isn't it?"

"If you think that's bad, wait'll tomorrow when you get a load of Kenny Purvis and the hoppers."

El looked confused. "Is that a local band?"

I burst out laughing.

"Let me guess . . . that's not a band?"

"Not so much. Kenny is Ermaline's estranged husband—and a charismatic preacher. He runs The House of Praise, and at last count, he had an entourage of about a dozen doe-eyed followers, all with babies under the age of two."

"Oh, no. So he's kind of like Princeton's version of Warren Jeffs?"

I nodded. "Exactly."

"Poor Ermaline."

"Hey, if you ask me, she's well rid of him. Doc Baker might not look like much of a catch, but he's a good man, and I think he really loves her."

"In the last analysis, that's all that really matters . . . isn't it?"

"I've always thought so."

El took hold of my hand. "Me, too."

We rode along in silence for a minute or two. It was just starting to get dark, and the last rays of sunlight were casting long shadows across the county road.

"We seem to spend a lot of time together in the dark," I remarked.

"That's true," El replied. "Do you regret that?"

I squeezed her hand. "Not at all. We seem to do pretty well in reduced light."

"Also true. But you know, tomorrow might give us a chance to see how we do in broad daylight."

I thought about that. Why not? It wasn't like I could be any more tarred with the guilt-by-association brush than I already had been. It was clear that my career at OTI was going down the tubes with or without any complicity on my part, so why not go ahead and embrace the small amount of time El and I had left to spend together?

"Are you asking me out?"

El nodded. "I can't think of a better or more public venue than the most celebrated swine-eating festival in the Western hemisphere."

"Our appearance in broad daylight would probably turn some heads."

"You mean more than we managed to turn last night?" She glanced at me. "But if you'd rather not risk it, I certainly would understand."

I thought for the zillionth time about Don K.'s unopened letter. "I want to share something with you,"

El gave me an amused look. "I thought you'd already done that . . . several times, if memory serves."

I felt myself blush. "Something else."

She frowned. "This sounds serious."

"It is."

"Okay . . . I think."

I gave her fingers another small squeeze. "Don't worry. It's something about work."

"Oh." She sounded surprised. "Are you sure that's a good idea?"

I nodded. "I think I can trust you."

"Well, I *know* you can. But it matters a lot to me to hear you say that."

"It matters a lot to me to believe it."

El sighed. "We're pretty strange bedfellows, aren't we?"

I thought about my encounter that morning with Misty Ann Marks, and how it reminded me of all the wrong turns I'd taken. El was about as different from Misty Ann as Paris was from Princeton. "No," I said to her beautiful profile. "I don't think we're strange at all."

El smiled as she slowed the SUV down to make the turn onto Grammy's road.

"Will you follow me home?" I asked.

"If you don't know by now that I'd follow you just about any place, I must be doing something wrong."

Her words made me shiver again. But this time, the chills were caused by excitement, not trepidation.

Before I could respond, we were pulling into Grammy's driveway, and Fritz bounded off the porch and flew across the yard to greet us.

An hour later, we were standing in my kitchen, heating up a casserole that contained our combined body weights in some savory new chicken stew recipe that Grammy said she clipped from the back of the Bisquick box. She said it tasted like heaven on a drop biscuit. I knew better than to argue with her about taking it. She'd already embarrassed the stuffing out of me by observing that El and I both looked tired. My blushing at that remark didn't help. El just started laughing, and Grammy observed that she wasn't as old or as oblivious as everyone seemed to think she was.

We offered to pick her up and give her a ride to Albion tomorrow, but she said she had already accepted a ride with Doc and Ermaline. So we agreed to meet up with her in front of the lemon shake-up stand at noon. That would give us all plenty of time to eat and stroll around before the parade and the start of the day's marquis event: the Miss Pork Day USA competition.

El opened a bottle of wine, and we took our glasses into the living room to sit and relax while we waited for our dinner to finish heating up. Fritz had already inhaled his bowl of kibble and lay sprawled out on the floor at El's feet, happily chewing on a tennis ball. We were listening to Pandora again. It was Rosemary Clooney this time. I was giddy that El seemed to share my fondness for retro music. Most of my friends just thought I was a nerd with geriatric tastes.

"So." El angled her body around on the sofa to face me. "You wanna tell me about whatever it is that's going on at work?"

I sighed. This was as good a time as any. I got up, walked over to my desk chair, and pulled the fat envelope from Don K. out of my backpack. I thumped it against my palm a few times before walking back to the sofa to join El. I handed it to her.

"What's this?" She took the envelope from me.

"I think it's what you'd call a bribe."

She raised an eyebrow and turned it over. "It's unopened."

I nodded.

She lowered the letter to her lap. "You haven't looked at this?"

"Nope."

"When did you get it?"

"Yesterday."

"Yesterday? You mean, before the fish fry?"

I nodded.

"Why haven't you opened it?"

I shrugged.

"You aren't curious about what's inside?"

"Not really. I think I know what it contains."

"And that is?"

I sighed. "Don K.'s flimsy attempt to buy my loyalty, and entice me to enlist in his union-busting army."

"You talked to him?"

I nodded. "He summoned me to his lair near the end of my shift yesterday."

"Really?" El sounded impressed. "He must think you hold some sway with the rank and file in his company."

"I guess."

"In a perverse way, this is pretty flattering for you," she observed.

"Flattering? I don't know . . . it kind of makes me feel cheap."

"Cheap? Why?"

I waved a hand. "Oh, come on, El. He can't hold me in very high regard if he thinks he can buy me off with some sleight of hand and a token promotion."

She seemed to think about that. "Do you care about his regard?"

"Of course not."

"Then why are you offended?"

I knew my frustration was starting to show, but I was having a hard time controlling it. "Maybe because, against all reason, I wanted to believe that things would change when OTI took over."

"Maybe they will."

I looked at her. "Whose side are you on?"

"Yours. Of course."

"God." I raised a hand to my forehead. "I don't know what to make of any of this. It all used to be so simple. Now it's just . . . complicated. I don't know which end is up any more."

"That's easy, Friday Jill. What's up is the same end that's always been up. You just need to regain your equilibrium so you can recognize it again."

"What does that mean?"

"It means you need to consider this offer and make the best decision you can—for you."

"I used to think I knew what that looked like. Now, I'm not so sure."

El sighed. "One thing I'm fairly sure of is that most people who get to work for Japanese owned and managed companies end up with few regrets."

"What about the union?"

"What about it?"

I shook my head. "Wouldn't you say that getting a union at OTI is what's best for me?"

"For you? Not necessarily. For people like T-Bomb and Luanne—definitely."

"I don't follow your reasoning."

She sighed. "Unions can do a lot of good for people who need help and protection—for people who don't have a voice. Or for people who have a voice, but don't know the best ways to make use of it. Collective bargaining can be the only hope many workers have to gain living wages and better access to things like health care and the protections of family leave. And I'm talking about large classes of people who, through twists of fate or the predilections of biology and geography, have narrower paths and fewer options open to them than college graduates like you. You *choose* to work at OTI, but you have other alternatives and better choices available if ever you decide to walk away. Therefore, you don't necessarily need or stand to benefit from the things a union has to offer. So it's possible that a union can solve problems for many, and create them for others. Does that make sense?"

I sat staring at her for so long she finally snapped her fingers in front of my face.

"Hello? Did I lose you?" she asked.

I shook my head. "No. I'm just mesmerized by what you must have been like in front of a classroom."

El laughed. "Don't be. It's not rocket science."

"I'm not sure I agree with that." I pointed at the letter. "Wanna open it?"

She held it up. "You want me to do the honors?"

I nodded.

"Okay." She turned it over and broke the seal. "Let's see what Mephistopheles has prepared for you."

She pulled out two sheets of paper. One was noticeably shorter than the other. She held it up and examined it. Her eyes grew wide.

"This is a personal check from Don Krylon for ten thousand dollars," she explained. "Made out to you."

I took it from her. "You're kidding?"

"Not so much," she said.

I poured over the check while El quickly read through the letter.

"Well. It's pretty textbook. There are no direct references to any agreement that you will support their efforts to keep the UAW out, but it's clear that the promised promotion to management and the enclosed signing bonus are rewards for your demonstrations of company loyalty." She read on. "He's offering to make you a production manager at an annual salary of eighty thousand dollars, with generous 401K contributions." She passed the letter to me. "That's not exactly chump change."

I didn't reply. I was still staring at the check.

"Friday Jill?" El asked. "Are you considering his offer?"

I looked up at her. "Not really. But I *am* considering how many paint jobs ten thousand dollars would pay for."

El laughed. "I think those might be mutually exclusive."

I handed the check and the letter back to her. "I think you're right."

She took them from me, refolded them, and placed them back inside the envelope. "You really need to put your revulsion for Don K.'s tactics aside and think carefully about this offer. Remember that it's OTI you'll end up working for, not Krylon."

"I know. Right now, that feels like a difference with little distinction."

"It won't always."

I shrugged.

"So what now?" she asked.

The oven timer dinged.

I smiled at her. "Now we eat Grammy's Bisquick creation, then try to find new ways to keep each other awake all night."

She smiled back at me. "Is that an invitation?"

"Nope." I took hold of her hand and tugged her forward for a kiss. "It's a promise."

Chapter 10

Downtown Albion was swarming with people.

"This is ridiculous," El declared. We'd just made our fifth circuit around the courthouse square, looking for a place to park. "It's like Walmart on the damn Friday after Thanksgiving."

"Welcome to Pork Day," I explained.

"I've never seen so many pickup trucks in my entire life. I see now why you wanted to ride in this thing instead of my rental."

"Welcome to Southern Illinois."

She was still staring out the passenger window. "What's a Catholic girl from Buffalo doing in the middle of this madness?"

"Welcome to Fantasy Island."

"Is it always this hot on Fantasy Island?"

Grammy's old Ram didn't have air conditioning.

I opened my mouth to respond.

"If you say welcome to anything one more time, I'm going to clock you with one of those ham shanks people out there appear to be munching on."

"Those aren't ham shanks. They're pork chops. Bone in."

"Pork chops?"

"Yep."

"From *what?* Pigs that are raised near nuclear retention ponds?"

I laughed. "We take our pork products seriously in these parts."

"Apparently."

"Word to the wise: be careful when you bite into your pork chop sandwich."

El's eyes grew wide. "They have *bones* in them?"

I nodded.

"I think I just became a vegan."

"Oh, cool!" I exclaimed. "Here's a space. Right next to Doc and Ermaline." I pulled off onto a patch of grass about the width of a Smart Car. We were shoehorned in between Doc Baker's El Camino and the town water tower. I turned off the engine and unclipped my seat belt. "Let's go. We have ten minutes to find Grammy."

El sat there staring at me. "Seriously? How do you suggest we get *out* of this thing? Crawl through the back window and hop out of the bed?"

"Oh, come on. It's not that tight." I tried to open my door. It swung out about five inches before it bumped up against one of the metal support legs on the tower. "Um." I closed my door. "How's your side looking?"

El glanced out her window.

"Doc and Ermaline appear to smoke a lot of Camels. Judging by their floorboards, they've saved the wrappers from every pack they've purchased since Joe Camel was in short pants." She looked back at me. "It ain't happening."

I sighed. "We'll never find another space."

"Then I guess we'll have to enjoy the festivities from here."

I looked over my shoulder at the sliding window on Grammy's Ram.

"For-get it," El cautioned. "I am *not* climbing out the back window of this truck."

"Come on, El."

"No. Not happening."

"Please?"

She shook her head.

I tapped my fingers on the steering wheel. Then I got an idea. I started the truck.

"What are you doing?" El asked.

I put the truck into reverse. "I'm backing up so you can hop out."

"Then what?"

"Then I'll pull back in and climb out the window."

El shook her head. "You are one bossy woman."

"Talk about the pot calling the kettle black." I moved the truck back far enough to clear the El Camino and stopped. "Okay, hop on out."

"Before I do," she said, "I want to make sure you're aware that the bed of this truck is full of something that smells vaguely like manure."

"That's not manure, it's peat moss. Not the same thing at all."

"Riiiight." El opened her door. "One thing before I hop out."

"What?"

"This." She took a quick look around, then leaned forward and kissed me. The sensation shot from my lips to every other part of me in about zero-point-four seconds. I reached out to pull her closer, but she was already backing away. "Who knows when we'll get another chance?" She hopped out and stood on the ground next to the truck. Before she closed the door, she glanced again at the bed full of whatever it was. "Don't say I didn't warn you."

When she was clear, I pulled forward into the space again and shut off the engine. Then I rotated around and pushed open the sliding window behind the bench seat.

An unpleasant odor hit me like a brick wall.

Uh oh. Maybe that's not peat moss in the truck bed . . .

I kicked off my shoes and tossed them out so they'd have a shot at staying clean. I could see El standing by the rear bumper and watching me with an amused expression.

'Well?" she said. "What are you waiting for? Make your great escape, Houdini."

I took a deep breath and pushed my head and shoulders through the opening. El was right. The smell was ripe, and it was starting to make my eyes smart. There was no place on the floor of the truck bed that wasn't covered with the redolent muck, so I just tried to edge myself along the liner toward the side rail until I could get a leg through the window. Then I'd be able to stand up, and vault over the side. It seemed like a good plan, too . . . until I sneezed.

You have to understand. I don't have a diminutive sneeze. When I sneeze, it's a full-body, full-throttle, full-contact sport. When I sneeze, it trips seismographs along the New Madrid Fault. When I sneeze, antelope on the Serengeti make frenzied runs for cover. When I sneeze, my body bucks and recoils like a sawed-off shotgun.

Therefore, sneezing in such a manner, when your body is precariously balanced halfway through the center of a pickup truck's sliding rear window, is pretty much a guarantee that things aren't gonna end well.

They didn't.

Down I went, twisting into a sea of something that was not quite manure, but not quite peat moss, either. In two seconds, I was covered in muck from the back of my knees to my shoulders. The only part of me that emerged unscathed was my head.

"God *fucking* damn it!" I sputtered as I tried to clamber to my feet.

El seemed to be trying hard not to laugh, but wasn't really succeeding. "I think you'll lose points for not sticking the dismount. In fact, the dismount seems to be sticking to you."

I was shaking the tarry, black mixture off my hands. "Very funny."

"Are you okay?" she asked.

I glared at her. "Do I *look* okay?"

"I'm not talking about your bovine couture. I want to know if you hurt yourself."

I sighed. "Only my dignity."

She walked over and reached up a hand to help me climb out. "Well, thankfully, that's a renewable resource."

"God. What *is* this stuff? It smells like kimchi . . . and peat moss."

"You said it was your Grammy's farm truck." El wrinkled up her nose. "It smells very . . . farmy."

I hopped over the side. A trail of muck followed me and plopped to the ground near my feet.

El jumped back. "Is that stuff alive?"

I picked up my shoes. "It could be . . . I thought I saw something moving back there."

"Gross." El flicked a bit of muck off my chin. "What now? Home for clean clothes?"

I shook my head. "And lose this primo parking space?"

"You're joking."

I stared at her.

"You're *not* joking?"

I waved a hand to encompass the sea of chrome that surrounded us. "El. It's Pork Day USA. In Albion. Southern Illinois. That means half the population of the tri-state area will all be out cruising the byways, looking for *this* very space. There's no way I'm moving this truck."

She laughed. "Okay, Einstein. What do you intend to do about your . . . ensemble?"

I looked around. "Find a garden hose and some clean clothes. All the stores will be open."

"I won't pretend to understand your logic."

"There's a Dollar General across from McDonald's."

She sighed. "Lead on. At least when people stare at us, we'll have a pretty good idea why."

The streets were humming and were choked with crowds of people. Bluegrass music was blasting from someplace near the court-house. All the sidewalks were lined with booths and vendors hawking everything from beaded bags to custom face painting designs. And, of course . . . there was pork. Lots and lots of it. Cooked every way you could imagine. The event's barbecue competition was second only to the Miss Pork Day contest in popularity.

The sun was already high in the sky and heating things up. A dull haze was settling in. The crowds across the street looked like they were moving around behind one of those transparent plastic shower curtains. The heat index today was supposed to be one for the record books, with the high temperature topping out someplace in the triple digits. That probably meant afternoon thunderstorms, which also were pretty typical for Pork Day. It was hard to remember a year when you didn't have to run for cover during at least part of the festivities.

El noticed that people seemed to be giving us a wide berth as we pushed our way through the throngs.

"I think they're afraid your condition is contagious."

"Which condition would that be? The muck on my clothes, or my partiality for a certain union agitator?"

El was scanning the crowds. "I don't think many of these people would think there's a difference."

"I don't know." I sniffed at her. "You smell a whole lot better."

She bumped into me as we slowly made our way along the street. "Nut job."

We were just about to cross Main Street and head for Dollar General when El tugged me to a halt.

"What about one of those?" She pointed at a display of brightly colored t-shirts.

"*You Are My Sunswine,*" I quoted. I looked at El. "I don't think so."

"Oh, come on. It's cute."

"Cute?"

"You have to admit, it does exude a certain . . . porkiness."

"It's neon blue. I hate neon blue."

El stared at me. "Neon blue? This is your objection?"

I nodded.

El snapped one up. "I'm buying it."

I shook my head. "It's your money."

"And you're wearing it," she continued.

"El . . ."

"No arguments." She walked over to the vendor to pay for the shirt.

I looked at my watch. We were going to be late meeting Grammy. With luck, the Dollar General folks would let me clean up in their restroom. Fortunately for me, most of the damage was confined to my shirt and my pants. I'd also have to prevail upon them to give me a couple of bags to tie up my soiled clothes. I wondered if T-Bomb's cousin, Mellonee, would be working today. She'd be likely to take pity on me—mostly because she'd revel in the opportunity to tell everyone about my mishap.

I wished for the zillionth time that I lived in a bigger place, where nobody knew anything about me.

El returned with the shirt. "Okay. Let's go find you some pants."

"I am not wearing that."

"Yes you are." She ignored my protest and strode off toward the Dollar General. I meekly followed along behind her. I realized that this was becoming a pattern for us.

We entered the store, and immediately a voice bellowed out, "Hey? Friday? What in tarnation happened to you?"

Mellonee . . . of course.

I looked toward the checkout counter where she was restocking candy bars.

"Hi, Mellonee. I fell into a pile of . . . something . . . and need to get cleaned up. Can I get some new pants and use your bathroom?"

"Sure." She walked toward us. I noticed that she was staring as much at El as she was taking in my dirty clothes. "Those Capri pants on aisle seven are buy one, get one free."

"Mellonee, this is Eleanor Rzcpczinska."

"Hi there." El extended her hand. "Call me El."

"El?" Mellonee looked confused. "Wait . . . aren't you one of them union agitators?"

"Guilty," El said.

Mellonee shook her hand. "My cousin told me about you. She said you sang real good at karaoke night."

El and I exchanged glances. That wasn't the claim to fame we expected.

"It's true," I said. "She really impressed me with her talent."

Mellonee laughed and slapped me on the arm. "Yeah. My cousin told me about that, too." She was still chuckling as she led us toward the display of Capri pants. They were pretty hideous . . . a spectrum of day-glow colors that were guaranteed to make me visible from outer space.

El held out the t-shirt. "Which pair goes best with this?"

Mellonee turned away to start sifting through the rack of pants, and I gave El an "are you nuts?" look. Mellonee was wearing an ensemble that would make a pair of transition-lensed eyeglasses go black . . . indoors. She pulled out a pair of the cheap cotton pants and held them up against the bright blue t-shirt.

"I think these would look real nice."

Real nice? They were lime green with fuchsia and white polka dots on the cuffs.

I took an involuntary step backwards. "I can't wear those."

El was looking them over. "Why not? They look like your size." She took them from Mellonee. "Where's your fitting room?"

Mellonee looked confused. "Fitting room?"

"A place to change clothes?" El clarified.

"Oh." Mellonee pointed toward the back wall of the store. "You can use the bathroom. It's at the end of aisle nine, beside the fuel injector cleaner."

"Thanks, Mellonee." El smiled at her and took off toward the back of the store. I sighed and followed her. We were halfway there when Mellonee called out to us.

"You two take it easy on the plumbing back there. That new sink only just got put in a week ago."

I could hear titters of laughter coming from some other shoppers.

When I reached the bathroom, El was standing in the open doorway. She held out the components of my new outfit.

"T-Bomb is so dead to me," I said.

"No she isn't. Take these and get in there."

I was surprised. "You aren't coming in?"

El rolled her eyes.

"Right. Okay." I looked down at the collision of colors. "This stuff looks like it's vibrating."

"It'll be fine. You'll blend right in."

I met her eyes. "Therein lies the problem."

"Resistance is futile." She raised the garments up a higher, like she was presenting them at an altar. "You will be assimilated."

I stood there tapping my foot.

She stared back at me.

I gave up. I needed clean clothes, and we were already fifteen minutes late. Grammy would be out wandering around, looking for us. There was no way I was going to win this battle.

I yanked the clothes out of her hands.

"Paybacks," I muttered as I went into the bathroom.

"I'm counting on it," El said.

Five minutes later, when I still hadn't emerged, El tapped on the outside of the door.

"What's taking you so long?"

"I am *not* coming out."

"Why not?"

"Because I look ridiculous."

"You looked ridiculous before, when you were covered with . . . whatever that stuff was."

I sighed and opened the door.

El's eyes grew wide when she saw me.

"See?" I started to retreat back into the safety of the bathroom. "I told you. I look ridiculous."

El grabbed me by the arm and pulled me out into the store. "You look adorable."

"Are you nuts? I look like a pack of Fruit Stripe gum."

"Stop it. It's not that bad. It's . . . cute."

"Cute?"

She nodded.

"El." I reached out to a nearby end cap and plucked a Hello Kitty air freshener off a hook. "*This* is cute. *I*, on the other hand, look like a sidewalk sale at a Chinese sweat shop." I tugged at the front of the t-shirt. "Besides, this thing is about three sizes too small."

El was staring at my chest. "I know. It's *perfect*."

"Are you for real?"

She met my eyes. "I'd like to think so."

I shook my head. "Maybe Mellonee will lend me some scissors."

"What for?"

"So I can cut the neck on this thing. It's obviously cutting off the blood flow to my brain."

"Why do you say that?"

"Because I'm actually standing here, wearing this absurd getup."

El laughed. "Grab your dirty clothes and let's get out of here. We need to go find Grammy."

When we reached the checkout counter, Mellonee was waiting for us.

"Those fit great," she cooed. She held up a bag. "I went ahead and picked you out a second pair." I could see some hot pink fabric poking out of the yellow bag. "You lucked out on this great sale today."

Lucked out?

I was about to disagree with her when I caught El staring at my chest again.

I handed Mellonee a twenty.

Grammy was pacing in front of the lemon shake-up stand, scanning the crowd. She was juggling a tower of paper plates topped with thick, spicy pork chop sandwiches. She must've had six or eight of them, because the stack was nearly as tall as she was.

"Grammy!" I called out to her. "Here we are."

Grammy looked toward my voice, but did a double take when she saw me. "Jill?" she asked.

We reached where she stood, and I took the stack of sandwiches from her. Cutting the neckband of my t-shirt had helped a little bit, but I still thought I looked like a floozy walking around in it. I was happy to have something to carry that would conceal how tight it was. Grammy was giving me a good once over.

"It's a long story," I began.

Grammy shook her head. "I don't begin to understand what motivates you young people when it comes to fashion." She shifted her gaze to El. "It's nice to have you here with us, Eleanor."

"Thanks, Grammy." El smiled at her. "I'm so sorry we're late. Friday Jill had a little mishap and fell into the bed of your pickup. We had to get her some clean clothes to wear."

Grammy looked at me. "What in thunder were you doing up in my compost heap?"

"Is that what it is?" I asked.

"Of course. I got it from Doc. It's for my Garden Peaches."

El looked confused.

"She means her fall tomatoes," I explained.

"Let's get our drinks and head on over to the Pagoda," Grammy said. "Doc and Ermaline have our chairs all set up. Luanne and Terri are already there."

"Okay."

"Do you want a lemon shake up, honey?" Grammy asked El.

"I don't know what that is," El replied, "but if it's cold, I'll take two of them."

"It's cold, all right. And refreshing." Grammy walked over to the vendor and ordered the drinks.

Ten minutes later, all the introductions had been made, and we were seated in our long line of webbed lawn chairs near the town Pagoda, balancing our lunches on our laps and listening to the rumble of approaching marching bands. The parade was starting.

I leaned forward to Doc. "How'd you score this great location?"

He shrugged his narrow shoulders and bit into his sandwich.

"We got here at seven o'clock this morning," Ermaline explained.

I looked at Grammy. "You've been here since seven o'clock?"

She nodded.

"You pretty much have to do that if you want to stake out a good location," Ermaline continued.

"Jay and I set up our chairs and roped 'em off while it was still dark." Luanne pointed to the stage in front of the Pagoda. "We wanted to be sure we had good seats for the competition."

"Well, it'd be hard to get any better than this," T-Bomb chimed in. "Luke! Quit playin' with that bone . . . you're gonna put Laura's eye out. Donnie? Take that dern bone off his sandwich before he puts his sister's eye out."

Donnie Jennings pulled the bone away from Luke's pork chop. He was a smallish man—short, with hair so blond it was almost white in the sun. The twins were like mini versions of him. They were all dressed alike in crisp blue shirts with matching blue-and-white striped shorts.

"I told you this was a mistake," he complained. "They're gonna have this mess all over their new clothes."

"So what? They don't get to do this but once a year," T-Bomb replied. "Besides, if either of 'em get too dirty, we can borrow Friday's extra pair of new pants." She laughed merrily.

I glared at her. "By the way . . . thanks for telling your cousin about the sink."

"Hey. I didn't tell her nothin'," T-Bomb declared.

"Honey," Ermaline cut in. "Everybody in the whole tri-state area knows about you two and that dern sink. Ain't that right, Doc?"

Doc grunted.

"What sink?" Grammy asked.

"It's nothing," I said. "Just another urban myth."

"Urban myth? Is that what you're calling it now?" Luanne shook her head. Her hair was especially big today and finished off with a bunch of tight-looking curls that swept down over both ears. I figured she must've put in some extra effort since the spotlight was going to be on Jailissa all day. "I don't think that post commander thought it was much of an urban myth when he had to tell two hundred people that one of his bathrooms was out of order."

El started chuckling.

"What bathroom?" Grammy asked.

I pointed up the street. "Look, Grammy. Isn't that the Soul Stompers?"

"Where?" she asked, scanning the scene with eagerness.

"I heard they were gonna be here today," Ermaline said. "Doc said they were making the parade circuit. Last week, they were over at Owensboro. Ain't that right, Doc?"

Doc shrugged.

"I just love them fancy marchin' routines they do," T-Bomb added. "I hope Luke joins up when he gets old enough."

Donnie rolled his eyes. "It's Job Corps, Terri. You don't join up, you get sent there by the authorities."

T-Bomb glared at him. "He's *your* son. I expect he'll grow up to be an accountant soon enough. Let me have my dreams while I can."

Donnie huffed and picked a piece of lint off his shirt sleeve.

A red Cadillac convertible was gliding by with the grace of a shark in shallow water. Larry "Golden Throat" Dennis was sitting up on the white leather back seat, waving at the crowds.

"How in tarnation did the county coroner get to be Grand Marshall?" T-Bomb asked.

"It's an honorary title," Grammy explained.

"Larry helped Jailissa a lot with her diction," Luanne explained to El. "He used to be a famous radio announcer."

"The Dennises have always been good public servants," Grammy agreed.

I nudged El. "Welcome to *Long Day's Journey Into Night*."

"Stop it," she hissed. "I love this."

I felt a surge of affection for her. "You mean that, don't you?"

She nodded and bumped my shoulder.

Close behind Larry's Cadillac was a mix-n-match brigade from Cisne's Coon Creek Ridge Riders. Some of the horses were loudly decorated and tricked out with full western riding gear. Others were being ridden bareback. They clip-clopped along the brick street to a chorus of whoops and hollers.

A trail of fresh road apples marked their progress up 5th Street.

The eighteen members of the West Salem Grade School Marching Band had the unfortunate task of following along behind the horses. They did their best to stay focused on their up-tempo rendition of "Suicide is Painless" while they sidestepped the worst of the road hazards.

"Oh, Lord," T-Bomb declared. "That poor little guy with the clarinet just stepped right in a pile of horse hockey."

"That's just disgraceful." Luanne shook her head. "Why don't they make them horses wear those things they put on 'em in the big cities?"

"You mean bun bags?" El asked.

"Is that what they're called?"

"I think so. At least, that's what they called them back in Buffalo, on the Lincoln Parkway horses."

"Hey? Friday?" T-Bomb yelled across our line of chairs. "You should get on out there and show them Stompers some of your fancy footwork. I mean . . . they already got the manure and all." She cackled at her own humor.

"Very funny." I wondered how in the world Mellonee got the word out that fast.

The Soul Stompers snapped to attention right in front of us.

"Drill team!" the commander shouted. "Sound off!"

The unit of two-dozen cadets launched into a complex, synchronized step routine that was half disco and half hip hop. They chanted and slid across the worn bricks in time with their rhythmic gyrations.

> I don't know what you been told.
> Soul Stompers got lots of soul.
> Work your body to the beat.
> Soul Stompers gonna move your feet.

It was a spectacular performance, and the crowd loved every second of it.

Luanne clapped in time to their movements. "They're famous," she told El. "They performed for Jimmy Carter, and that Collins girl, when she was governor."

"Here comes the first float." Grammy was excited. She loved seeing what kinds of designs the area 4H Clubs created to honor the agricultural heritage of the region.

Luanne sat forward and scanned the street. "That means the Pork Queen contestants are coming on."

The top of the white float was shaped like a giant football helmet. It was decorated with an oversized 4H shamrock, made with hundreds of green carnations. "Take the Pledge Never to Text & Drive" was painted in bold type on long placards that ran the length of the float. Kids riding on the float waved signs that read, "TEXT 4H4ICW to 50555."

"What in the world does that have to do with farming?" Grammy asked.

"Well, all that texting and driving *is* becoming an epidemic," Ermaline explained. "I don't know how people manage. I got my hands full just shifting gears and puttin' on my eye makeup."

"Don't forget wranglin' your smokes," T-Bomb added.

"Hell. You don't need hands for that. It's why god gave you a mouth."

"Here comes that Destinee Knackmuhs." Luanne was all business now.

The first contender for Miss Pork Day USA rolled toward us. Destinee was a pretty girl, buxom with long red hair and a mouthful of large teeth—all Knackmuhs trademarks. Her lawn chair sat atop a slowly rotating dais on the back of a flatbed truck. Bales of hay and a menagerie of live farm animals surrounded her. It was pretty impressive—like a Midwestern-themed crèche. A curved banner that read "Heartland's Destinee" arched over her chair. She waved and smiled at the crowds, who oohed and awed at her display.

Luanne clucked her tongue and pointed at the passing display with her pork chop bone. "That right there is our only real competition this year."

"How'd she draw first dibs in the parade?" Ermaline asked.

"It was more like gettin' the short straw. In this game, you want to be *last*—not first."

"Where's Jailissa, then?"

Luanne smiled. "Last."

I leaned over to El. "Do you wanna go stroll around for a bit?"

I was Jonesing for the chance to be alone with her. Or, at least as alone as we could get, stuck in the middle of half the population of Gibson, Wabash, and Edwards counties.

She looked at me with wonder. "And miss seeing Jailissa?"

I smiled at her. "You really are enjoying this, aren't you?"

"Are you kidding? It beats season three of *Downton Abbey*, and it has better special effects."

"I don't think I'd go quite that far."

"Oh, come on." El gestured toward the succession of floats rolling past us. "When was the last time you saw a . . . genetically modified . . . *soybean* . . . that resembled a Volkswagen?"

I followed her gaze. "El, that *is* a Volkswagen."

"Oh." She looked back at me. "We don't do much work in German-owned plants."

"Apparently."

"Here come them Hortons!" T-Bomb was on her feet, chasing after Laura, who had dashed out into the street in hot pursuit of some Tootsie Roll Midgees that had just been flung off a float.

"Well if that don't beat all." Luanne sounded surprised. "It looks like all three of 'em are ridin' on the same dern truck."

Ermaline snorted. "It ain't hard to see why . . . two of 'em appear to be pretty far along."

"That's just wrong." Luanne shook her head full of tight curls. "They shouldn't be allowed to compete in that condition."

"Well, you'd have a hard time comin' up with a full field of contestants if you started rulin' girls out just for fallin' prey to them unavoidable indiscretions."

Luanne stared at her. "Comments like that make me wonder why you never ended up over at that House of Praise before Kenny took up with them hoppers."

"He that is without sin among you, let him first cast a stone at her," Ermaline quoted. "Ain't that right, Doc?"

Doc grunted.

"Well who in tarnation is that boy up there with them?" T-Bomb had wrangled Laura back into her seat. "He looks like he lost his last friend."

"That's not a boy, that's Casey Horton . . . the youngest girl."

"Girl?" T-Bomb asked. "I think you need to get your eyes checked."

"Nope," Luanne insisted. "It's Casey, all right. I think they pushed her in at the last minute—just as a placeholder in case one of the older girls came early. Like two years ago, when Jennica's water broke during the evening gown competition."

"Honey." T-Bomb was staring at Casey Horton, who was riding along with her sisters, staring grimly down at the floor of the truck bed, and clearly wishing herself anywhere but there. "If that's the best they got, then I think Jailissa's got this one in the bag."

"Well," Grammy said. "I think she's a fine looking young woman. Lots of girls wear their hair that short these days. And I do think her armband is . . . interesting. What kind of design is that?"

I squinted. "I think that's a tattoo, Grammy. It looks like concertina."

T-Bomb cackled again. "I think this one plays for your team, Friday."

"What team?" Grammy asked.

T-Bomb leaned forward and winked at her. "You know . . . them friends of Dorothy's."

"Dorothy's?" Grammy was confused. "You mean Dorothy Hames, from over in New Harmony?"

"I have a question," El interrupted. "Can someone explain to me how it's possible for three women from one family to compete in the same contest?"

I gave her a grateful smile.

Two more floats, a VFW drill team, and another marching band drifted by while Luanne and Ermaline took turns explaining to El the sordid history of how the Horton family had pretty much commandeered ownership of the Miss Pork Day USA crown for the last decade. Then, we heard a distant, sonorous blast—like a train whistle. All conversation stopped.

"She's coming," Luanne whispered.

"What in the world was that?" Grammy asked.

"It's Jailissa."

"Jailissa?" I asked. "Is she coming by train?"

Luanne shook her head. She was eagerly looking down the street. "It's Joe's truck." She looked at El to clarify. "She's riding in an Outlaw 650—one of the biggest and best custom-built trucks to ever roll off the Krylon assembly line. It was a special anniversary edition we built for the auto show, and Joe won it in a company lottery."

"And he's driving it in the parade?"

"Nope, Jay's driving it. Joe lent it to us for the day. He said a queen needed a real chariot."

Ermaline sighed. "That's just beautiful." She nudged her companion. "Ain't it, Doc?"

Doc shrugged.

The train whistle sounded again. Two short blasts, then a longer report.

"Oh. My. God." El was staring with an open mouth as the massive truck rolled toward us. It dwarfed everything around it—including the percussion line of the Edwards County High School Marching Band, which lost its hold on their up-tempo rendition of the *Rocky* theme song, "Gonna Fly Now," every time Jay blew the horn.

Luanne got to her feet as the truck approached. Out of respect, we all followed suit.

"That right there is poetry on wheels." T-Bomb's voice was dreamy.

The truck was a cherry red, 360 horsepower, quad cab with a 6.7 liter Cummins ISB diesel engine, 22.5 inch Duelers, an extended bed, running boards, Smittybilt XRC light bar, eight-inch chrome Peterbilt exhaust stacks, a bull bar, and a Wolo Siberian Express air horn.

To summarize all of that in plain-speak, assembly plant vernacular—it was doped.

A printed placard on the side of the truck proudly proclaimed, *Jailissa Keortge, America's Sweetheart.*

"That thing could qualify for its own zip code," El whispered.

"It's the pride of the heartland, El." I leaned toward her. "It was made with love."

She met my gaze. "I think I'm finally beginning to understand that."

We smiled at each other. As discreetly as I could, I reached out so I could squeeze her fingers. It was hard to be this close to her and not be touching.

"There she is." Luanne's voice was reverential.

There she was, indeed. Jailissa was a sight to behold. She was standing up, perfectly proportioned and perfectly poised, wearing an elegant, emerald green, banded waist jacquard cocktail dress with an asymmetric neckline and pleating at the bodice and shoulders. She made an alluring silhouette against the chrome rear window louvers as she stood tall and proud without fuss or excessive ornament.

Unless, of course, you counted her ninety-five-thousand-dollar undercarriage as a bauble . . .

Jailissa's head of thick blond hair was upswept in a netted fascinator, with loose hairs curling at the back of her neck. Everything about her hinted at class and style. She held a single, white rose in her hand. She was stunning. She smiled her perfect smile and waved at her admiring fans with an inherent grace that couldn't be taught. She made gliding up 5th Street in the back of a pickup truck look every bit as impressive as Miss America's inaugural walk down the famed runway in Atlantic City. Jailissa was a queen—in every sense of the word.

"She's gorgeous," El said to Luanne. "Her dress is beautiful."

"Jay Jr. designed it for her." Luanne wiped at a stray tear rolling down her cheek. "They teach them boys new trades in the joint. He wasn't much for food service work or carpentry, but it turns out he's a regular whiz with fabrics and colors. That there," she pointed at Jailissa, "is his modification of a Vera Wang creation he saw in one of them high fashion magazines. He said dark green would be a good color for her, and she could wear it in the parade since it's before five o'clock."

Jailissa was directly in front of us. She smiled brilliantly at us, then gently and perfectly tossed her long-stemmed rose to her mother.

"Well, dern . . ." T-Bomb's voice was shaky. "I'm about to well up over here."

The truck rolled past us. A man in a tight-fitting, dark blue suit trotted along behind it, taking pictures.

"Is that Joe Sykes?" El asked.

Luanne nodded. "He's so proud of her. He begged and pleaded with Jay and me to have Jailissa ride in his truck."

"Hell," T-Bomb quipped. "It ain't hard to figure out why you didn't have to sit at home for two weeks after you set off all them alarms at the plant."

"I thought that at first, too. But Joe explained that management forced him to exact that punishment. I only got to come back because they're runnin' all them extra shifts, and he didn't have nobody to cover for me."

El was staring at the back of the truck. "What's that purple thing swaying under the bumper?"

I peered more closely at it. "It looks like a Crown Royal bag."

"Joe covered up his truck balls out of respect for Jailissa," Luanne explained. "At first, Jay and I had a problem with his obsession with her, but we've come to understand that it's a pure love, and when you have that, age differences don't matter."

"I don't know many men who would do a thing like that," Ermaline agreed. "He might turn out to be her sheep in wolf's clothing—just like my Doc, here."

Doc grunted.

I'd had about enough local color for one day.

I glanced down at my outfit. Especially when I'm wearing the majority of it.

It was clear that the parade was winding down, so it seemed like a good time to make a getaway.

"Okay." I got to my feet. "I need to stretch my legs a bit." I looked down at El. "Wanna walk with me? We can browse the booths and see the classic cars."

"I'd like that." She stood up, too.

"Hey? Friday?" T-Bomb asked. "Maybe you can find some other good deals on new clothes?"

"I don't think so."

"Why not? I think that Whistle Stop gun store has some camouflage pants on sale." She laughed. "They'd go great with your truck."

I rolled my eyes. "I'll be sure to check it out."

"Oh, *man*." Donnie sounded exasperated. "Terri? Luke just tripped over a pile of dirty plates. He's covered in barbecue sauce."

"Is he hurt?" she asked.

"No, but he's a total mess."

"Great." T-Bomb sighed. "Findin' a place to wash him up out here is gonna be about as easy as findin' a Horton who ain't packin' more than a pretty smile." She looked back at us. "Hey? You two didn't happen to bring that sink along, did you?"

Luanne and Ermaline started to chuckle.

I scowled at her and took El by the arm.

"What sink?" I heard Grammy ask as we walked away.

☙ ☙ ☙

"Two points!"

"That's not two points. It's zero."

"It's not *zero*. It's halfway on the board."

"Yeah, but the other half is touching the ground."

"So?"

"So it doesn't count."

"Who says?"

"The rules."

"What rules? That's a complete fabrication."

"No, it's not." I waved a hand toward the board. "The only two-point option is a bag that is halfway through the hole."

She glared at me. "You're totally making that up."

I held out both hands. "Why would I make that up?"

She lowered her head and looked at me over the top of her sunglasses. "Seriously?"

"You have a dirty mind . . . anyone ever tell you that?"

"Hey. I'm not the one standing here, making crude, sophomoric puns."

"El. That was *not* a pun. It's a rule. A *real* one."

We were playing a cutthroat game of Baggo Cornhole, and it was clear that I was pretty much kicking El's ass. It was also clear that she was unhappy with this outcome.

"Fine." She sighed. "My score is zero. You win another round. Color me so surprised."

I shook my head. "I had no idea you were this competitive."

"You're kidding me, right? This is a news flash for you?"

"Well. Yeah."

"Friday Jill. I have five siblings—all of them older than me. I had to fight to survive."

"You make it sound like you grew up on the Island of Dr. Moreau."

"It wasn't that dissimilar."

"Who's making stuff up now?"

She rolled her eyes. "Let's just get the bags and play another round. I want to at least break even."

"I could give you a handicap?" I suggested.

El drummed her fingers against her thigh.

"Feeling antsy?" I asked.

She socked me on the arm. "I'm so gratified you're enjoying this."

"I am, actually."

"You know," she said with exaggerated patience. "I can think of all kinds of things that might *never* end up halfway through any holes."

I stared at her with an open mouth.

"Hah. That took the wind out of your sails, didn't it?"

She strode off across the grassy median to retrieve our throwing bags of corn. I was still pretty much speechless when she returned. She handed me my pile of bags.

"Okay, smartass. Give it your best shot."

I was staring at her. "Do I know you?"

She looked at me with a raised eyebrow. "Of course you do. In *every* sense." She smirked. "Including the biblical."

I had no argument with that last one. Of all the senses, it was my current favorite.

"Right. Okay." I hefted my corn bag. "Here goes."

I made a few practice heaves, and then let it fly. It hit the board and slid toward the hole.

"Cow pie!" I exclaimed.

"Shit," El mumbled.

I gave her a brilliant smile. "Exactly."

"Move over." She shoved me out of the way.

She took careful aim, wound up like she was throwing the last pitch at the bottom of an extra inning, and hurled her bag high into the air. It flew right over the board, and smashed into the back of a rather portly man standing in line at the Moose Lodge Pork Chop Hut. He turned around and stared at us, before bending over to pick up the bag and toss it back.

"Sorry for the Screaming Eagle," I called out to him.

El frowned at me. "Do I even want to know what that is?"

"Use your imagination."

"I think I should get a do-over . . . there was a cross wind."

I lifted my chin into the air to check. There wasn't even the tiniest hint of a breeze. "Nope. Not feeling it. It's still dry as a bone and a hundred degrees in the shade."

El mumbled something and moved to the side.

I cocked an ear toward her. "I didn't quite get that."

She glowered at me. "I said that man was holding about twelve plates of food."

I shrugged. "He's probably heading home to catch the Cheez-It 355."

"The what?"

"From the Glen?" I added.

El was looking at me like I had two heads. "I have no idea what language you're speaking."

"*Watkins* Glen," I explained. "Up in your stomping ground. Ever heard of it?"

She gave me a withering gaze. "Of course I've heard of it. I just have no idea what a Cheesy 350 is supposed to be."

I laughed. "It's the Cheez-It 355, El. A NASCAR race."

"Oh."

"You do own a television, right?"

She rolled her eyes. "Keep it up, Einstein. Paybacks are hell."

"Oh, really?" I took my place at the throwing line. "What are you gonna do? Bludgeon me with authorization cards?"

"I thought I'd already done that."

"True."

"Okay." I held up my burlap bag full of corn kernels and took careful aim. "Let's take this home."

I gave it a good heave. The bag landed near the base of the board and slid forward to stop just below the base of the hole.

"Blocker!" I cried. I now had two bags near the high scoring position.

El stared at me with her hands on her hips. "Don't get cocky. Close only counts with hand grenades and nuclear weapons."

I held up a finger. "And Baggo Cornhole."

"What-*ever*." She took her place at the line.

Her toss slid around both of my bags and dropped halfway into the hole.

"Ha!" El faced me with a triumphant expression. "What do you call *that* one?"

I shook my head. "Dumb luck?"

"Hey . . ." She tagged me on the arm again. "Be as liberal with your praise as you are with your censure."

"Okay, okay." I rubbed my arm. "But quit socking me. It's going to leave a mark."

"Oh, please. I barely touched you."

I pouted.

She gave an exasperated sigh. "What if I promise to rub it later."

That got my attention. "Rub it?"

"I seem to recall that you're partial to rubbing."

It was hard to argue with that. I was lost in the land of happy recollection for a few moments.

"So?" she asked.

I looked at her. "So?"

She waved a hand toward the board. "So, what do you call that snazzy maneuver I just pulled off?"

"Um . . . that's called a hooker."

She smiled smugly. "I just had a hooker."

"I hear there's always a first time . . ."

She made a fist, but I danced out of her way. "My turn. Prepare to be upstaged."

"Give it your best shot."

I hefted the bag a few times and swung it back and forth in several, practice throwing motions.

"Any time in this life would be good," El commented.

I looked at her. "Could we have silence in the peanut gallery, please?"

"Oh, I'm sorry." She pointed a finger at her chest. "Am I causing you to have performance anxiety?"

I lowered my bag. "I don't know. Are you talking about this game, or do you mean in more general terms?"

She stared back at me. "Yes."

"*Very* helpful."

I turned back toward the board and took careful aim. My throw was a good one. The bag landed smack dab on top of El's.

"Yes!" I started to celebrate but then noticed that neither bag had dropped into the hole. They both teetered there, half in and half out. I stared at the board in disbelief. We now had a cluster of four bags near scoring position—all of them in front of, behind, or halfway through the hole.

I was flummoxed. "This *never* happens."

"What never happens?" El walked over to stand beside me.

"That." I waved a hand toward the board.

"It does look rather congested near the opening."

I looked at her with incredulity. "You sound like you're reading the six o'clock news."

"Really?" She shrugged. "Maybe I could give that Golden Throat whosis a run for his money?"

"I still don't believe this."

"Who cares? It's my turn again."

I moved so she could make her toss. It landed woefully shy of the board."

"Sally!" I called out.

She glared at me. "Who?"

"Your wimpy throw . . . it's called a Sally."

"It wasn't *wimpy*. I wasn't ready yet, and it slipped out of my hand."

I shook my head. "Sorry. Those are the breaks."

"I'm not sure I like this game." She pouted.

"Yeah, well . . . stand aside and console yourself elsewhere. It's my turn again."

I prepared to make my last throw of the round. If I could manage to land my bag on top of the others teetering across the opening, I should be able to knock them all through. I started my wind up.

"Are you going to try to knock them all through?" El asked, just before I let it fly. Her voice was close to my ear.

I sighed and lowered my throwing arm.

"Will you stop that?" I turned to her. I noticed that she had taken off her sunglasses.

She was giving me the whole "who me?" treatment with her smoky gray eyes.

"Stop what, Friday Jill?"

"That thing you do with your eyes. It's distracting."

She fluttered her eyelashes. "It is?"

"Oh, like you don't know it."

"Oh, I know it all right. I'm just gratified it's working."

If we hadn't been standing in the middle of a median on Main Street, surrounded by half-a-dozen pork chop vendors, face painters, and Hadi Shriners zooming around on those ridiculous little muscle cars, I would've grabbed her and showed her how well it was working. Instead, I took a deep breath and a step back. It was better not to tempt fate.

"Let's just see if we can get this game over with in this life." I glanced down at my watch. "I don't want us to miss the talent portion of the pageant."

El's eyes grew wide. "There's a *talent* competition?"

I nodded.

"Well, what are you waiting for? Toss that damn thing and set us free."

"That's the plan."

I took careful aim again and let my last bag fly. Incredibly, amazingly, impossibly, it landed with the grace of a falling autumn leaf right on top of the other four bags. But none of them budged a single centimeter. I dropped my arm to my side and stared at the sagging pyramid of bags with an open mouth. The hole was now completely covered.

It was impossible not to see the metaphor at work in this one.

I faced El. "Do you think this game is trying to tell us something?"

She laughed. "What? That we're mutually incapable of follow through?"

I nodded. "Or completion?"

"Or chutzpah?"

"Or determination?"

"Or commitment?"

That one stopped me cold.

"You think we're incapable of commitment?"

She shrugged. "I think it's possible."

I didn't have a ready response for that one. It certainly wasn't an outcome I wanted—not for this damn game, and not for anything else, either. I glanced back at the board. El had one bag left to throw. I looked at her.

"Here's your chance to change all of that."

"I'm not sure I like these odds."

"Does that mean you don't want to play anymore?"

"Oh, no." She took her place at the throwing line. "I want to play."

She took a deep breath and closed her eyes.

I touched her arm. "Don't you want to see what you're doing?"

She shook her dark head. "Nope. Sometimes, it's best just to go with your gut."

She tossed the bag. It seemed to leave her open hand and fly away from us in slow motion—like time had decided to conspire with it and was dragging its foot along through the dirt to slow the spinning of our cosmic carousel.

I watched El's bag of corn soar across the sky and coalesce into a unified tapestry with everything else around us. It became one with the group of musicians on a makeshift bandstand who were tuning their stringed instruments. One with the large man in a tiny red car who made lazy figure eights around a group of giggling children with faces painted like circus animals. One with some hoppers from the House of Praise, who were passing out leaflets and singing an a cappella rendition of "Falling in Love with Jesus." And it became one with every hope and fear I'd ever known growing up as part of this quirky and curious world, where I fit and didn't fit all at the same time.

But gravity won the momentary tug of war, and El's bag changed course and drifted back toward earth. I followed its graceful descent with anxious excitement. I wanted to close my eyes, too. But I couldn't. I needed to see it. I needed to know if the colors of my world were about to change.

It landed with a resounding thud—directly on top of our precarious pyramid. I held my breath. The pile of bags didn't budge. They hung on, stubbornly refusing to slip through the opening.

I gave El a morose look. I thought she seemed equally demoralized.

"What do you call that one?" she asked, in a quiet voice.

"They don't have a name for that one," I answered.

She exhaled and looked past me toward the board. Her eyes widen. She grabbed my arm. "Look!"

"What is it?" I followed her gaze.

All four of the bags had disappeared.

"You gotta be *kidding* me?"

"They fell through!" El was giddy with excitement.

"Yeah." I bumped her shoulder. "Double Deuce, baby."

"I guess we both win."

I smiled at her.

"I can live with that." She linked arms with me. "Now let's go watch Jailissa win this damn pageant."

I knew better than to argue with her. For once, it seemed like all the omens were looking good.

"What the hell kind of instrument is that?" T-Bomb leaned forward between El and me and pointed up at the stage in front of us.

"Shhhh." I held a finger up to my lips. "Hold it down."

"It's a euphonium," El whispered.

"A phony-what?" T-Bomb asked.

"A *eu-phon-i-um*," El said again. "Like a trombone—only with valves instead of a slide."

"That don't look like no trombone I ever seen." T-Bomb dropped back against her seat with a huff.

On stage, an oblivious Casey Horton was hammering out a somewhat lackluster arrangement of "I'm Every Woman."

"Well," Luanne hissed. "I think her musical selection is in pretty poor taste."

"I think it's supposed to be ironic," I offered.

El chuckled.

"I bet that Chaka Khan is rollin' over in her grave," T-Bomb mumbled.

"Chaka Khan ain't dead," Luanne said. "But this performance would probably make her wish she was."

"Well it still ain't as bad as that poem . . . why in tarnation would Destinee Knackmuhs quote that dern Eskimo thing on the hottest day of the year?" T-Bomb fanned herself with a paper plate.

She had a point, there. For some reason, Destinee had chosen to recite the Robert Service epic, "The Cremation of Sam McGee." It was an eclectic choice, to say the least, but the crowd seemed to love it. And that was probably because most of the people in attendance had had to memorize the same piece in eighth grade English class, too.

"Would everyone please be respectful and stop yammering?" Grammy was giving us the evil eye.

We all managed to remain silent until Casey finished blowing her way through the R&B classic. There was a lukewarm smattering of applause. Casey gave a short head nod, pushed her horn-rimmed Buddy Holly glasses up her nose, and strode off the stage.

That concluded the talent portion of the competition.

"Well, I think Jailissa cleaned up in this part of the contest," Luanne proclaimed.

"What contest?" T-Bomb asked. "Neither of them other two finalists came close to Jailissa's twirling routine."

Luanne nodded. "It's true. Jay Jr. said she should add that flaming baton at the end. It was a showstopper at the Edwards County Fair last year."

"I thought the sparks from that thing might catch some of them judges' hairdos on fire." T-Bomb laughed. "Now that would've been a real showstopper."

"What happens next?" El asked.

"Well," Luanne explained. "The three finalists come out on stage and answer questions from the emcee. They'll all be wearing their evening gowns, too. They kinda combined those two events for this year."

"You mean to tell me that Horton boy is gonna come out in an evening gown?" T-Bomb asked.

"I keep telling you he's not a *boy*—he's a *girl*." Luanne's exasperation was starting to show. "It's *Casey* . . . the youngest one. She's always been . . . different."

"Hell. Different is sure one way to describe it." Ermaline stood up and brushed off her shorts. "She looks like she'd rather have a root canal than participate in this pageant." She turned around and scanned the crowd. "I need a smoke. Anybody seen which way Doc went?"

T-Bomb pointed across the square. "Him and Donnie took the twins over to look at those stupid little Shriner cars."

Jay Keortge walked up with Joe Sykes in tow.

"We've got the truck all ready in case she wins," he told us.

It was customary for the new Miss Pork Queen to take a victory lap around the courthouse square.

I could see Joe eyeing El. She noticed it, too. Before I could introduce them, she stepped forward and extended her hand.

"Hi there," she said. "I'm El . . . one of the agitators."

Joe actually smiled . . . sort of. "Joe Sykes." He briefly shook hands with her. "I've heard of you."

"Likewise," El replied.

Jay was fidgeting. "What's taking so long?"

"Will you just calm down?" Luanne looked at her watch. "They need time to change."

"Why ain't you helping her?" he asked.

"Because Violet Fewkes is back there with her."

He looked confused. "The florist?"

Luanne nodded. "She's putting all them little flower doodads in her hair for this final round."

Ermaline coughed. "Well I wonder if she brought any smokes along . . . I'm about ready to succumb."

"I told you to have one of mine," Luanne replied.

Ermaline shook her head. "I hate them damn Viceroys . . . they taste like floor scrapings."

Luanne rolled her eyes.

Joe fished around in his jacket pocket and pulled out a hard pack of Camels. "Want one of mine?" He held out the pack.

Ermaline's hand was a blur as she snapped the cigarettes away from him. "Well, praise the Lord."

Joe was staring at my outfit.

"What?" I asked.

He shrugged. "I'm not used to seein' you look so . . . girlie."

El stifled a laugh.

"Friday had one of them wardrobe malfunctions gettin' outta her truck," T-Bomb explained. "Didn't you, Friday?"

I sighed.

"Well," Joe was still looking me over, "I think you look . . . nice."

Nice? I looked like a refugee from the bargain bin at Dollar General.

El gave Joe one of her blinding, million-dollar smiles. "I agree, Joe."

He gave her a respectful nod and nervously shifted his weight from one foot to the other.

I looked back and forth between the two of them. If this kept up, they'd soon be joining hands and singing, "We Are the World." I continued to marvel at how well El could work a crowd. No wonder she was so damn good at her job.

"Here comes Larry!" Luanne exclaimed.

We all turned toward the stage.

"Oh," Grammy gushed. "I do love to see a man in a tuxedo."

"Maybe he can lend it to that Horton girl," T-Bomb quipped. We all took our seats.

"I don't think he'll have to," Ermaline whispered. "It looks like she brought her own."

The three finalists followed Larry "Golden Throat" Dennis out onto the stage. They were a sight to behold.

Destinee Knackmuhs wore a canary yellow, one shoulder taffeta creation with a sweetheart neckline and big ball gown skirt. The shoulder strap was topped with a huge ruffle, and the waistband was beaded with dozens of handmade flowers. She looked like every bridesmaid's worst nightmare.

Casey Horton took a more . . . eclectic . . . approach. She wore a western cut leisure suit in pale blue, finished off with a bolo tie and bull hide cowboy boots.

Jailissa was last to take the stage. She wore another stunner: a form-fitting, cobalt blue bustier gown with a flowing skirt. Her only jewelry was a simple necklace, ornamented with three white pearls, and matching pearl earrings. For a moment, it felt like we were in the front row at the Golden Globes—not sitting on metal lawn chairs in front of the downtown Pagoda in Albion, Illinois.

El shook her head. "She looks like Kate Winslet."

"Without the airbrush," I whispered.

Larry "Golden Throat" stepped up to the microphone.

"Welcome to the final round of the Miss Pork Queen competition."

There was a robust round of applause and a bevy of wolf whistles.

Larry let it go on for a moment, then held up a hand to quiet the crowd. "Our three finalists will now answer a series of four questions before the judges submit their ballots and tell us who the next winner will be. Remember that we will have a Miss Congeniality, a First Runner-Up, and, of course, a new Miss Pork Queen." He turned to the contestants. "So really, all three of you young ladies are already winners." There was another smattering of applause. "Now, back stage, you three lovely young women drew straws to determine the order for the questions. What I'm going to ask each of you to do is step forward to that microphone stand when I call your name and answer your question. Then step back and let the next contestant come forward. You'll all take turns answering one question at a time, until this round is through. Are we all clear on that?"

The girls nodded.

"Okay, then. Let's get started." Larry lifted his thin stack of index cards. "Our first contestant is Miss Casey Horton."

Obviously, Casey drew the short straw backstage. She sighed and took two steps forward to stand just behind the microphone. She seemed to be eyeing Larry with suspicion—like she expected him to ask her something insidious, instead of simply inane.

Larry held up his first little white card. "Casey, our judges would like to know what quality you like most about yourself, and why?"

Casey rubbed two fingers along the side of her nose.

"I don't know, Larry," she answered in a voice that sounded remarkably like her euphonium. "Avarice, sloth, envy, lust . . . I think there's a couple more, too." She looked at the judges' table. "Do I have to name just one?"

Larry stared at her with a blank expression, and then consulted his card again. A few people in the crowd tittered, and finally, someone began a round of polite applause. Casey nodded, and stepped back to reclaim her place in line.

Larry cleared his golden throat. "Our next contestant is Miss Destinee Knackmuhs."

Destinee surged forward with all the grace of a street sweeper. She stopped moving, and her dress kept right on going. It flounced and surged around the base of the microphone stand in a tidal wave of bright yellow. It looked like Mountain Dew sloshing around in the base of a mason jar. She ignored Larry—and the audience—entirely, and turned to the card table where the judges were seated.

Larry rolled with it. "Destinee, what quality do you like most about yourself, and why?"

"Well, Larry," Destinee flashed the judges a brilliant smile, full of big, white teeth, "I really like that I'm a super nice person, and people really like me. A lot. I'm really popular, and that means people want to be my friend . . . including the kids that no one really likes."

Destinee's sizeable claque in the audience leapt to its collective feet and whooped and hollered. Larry patiently waved his little stack of index cards. Finally, the applause tapered off.

Luanne huffed and fidgeted in her seat. "Them Knackmuhses shouldn't be allowed to carry on like that—it ain't fair to the other contestants."

Jay patted her puffy hand. "It's okay. Jailissa won't let it rattle her."

T-Bomb snorted. "And that Casey Horton is too occupied with starin' at Destinee's derriere to even notice."

"Well," Luanne remained agitated, "I'm still worried. We didn't prepare any answers for trick questions like this."

Trick questions?

"What kind of questions were you expecting?" I leaned across El and asked.

"Ones about doing that GMO stuff to crops, neutering pets, or creating world peace." She waved a hand. "The usual things."

El chuckled.

"I think Jailissa can handle it," I said.

"And now let's hear from our last contestant, Miss Jailissa Keortge," Larry said.

Jailissa glided forward like she was riding on a conveyor. She smiled shyly at Larry.

"She's really extraordinary," El whispered to me.

"Jailissa," Larry said, "tell us what quality you like most about yourself, and why?"

"Well, Mr. Dennis," Jailissa replied in her soft, soprano voice. "I like to think that I'm a glass half full kind of person. By that I mean that when I see something like puppies covered in ticks, or read in a magazine about how some elderly people have to eat cat food, I remind myself about how soft puppy bellies are when you rub them, or how lots of older people drive really nice Buicks."

The crowd erupted into another bout of raucous applause.

I glanced at El, who was staring at Jailissa with a confused expression. She turned to me. "And yet . . . maybe not so much."

I bumped her shoulder.

Jailissa smiled at the crowd and demurely stepped back to reclaim her place in line with the other contestants. I prayed that maybe her abundant poise would carry more weight than her . . . depth of expression.

Larry was ready for round two. He gave a nod to Casey, who sauntered forward again.

"Casey," Larry said. "Here is your second question. If you could change just one thing about the world, what would it be?"

Casey cleared her throat and bent toward the microphone. "Well, Larry," she said with confidence, "I'm glad you asked me that. I'd abolish telemarketers. Then surely, world peace would ensue, or at least, world peace of mind."

A few seconds of dead silence ensued.

Casey gave the audience a shrug. "Am I right?"

A few people responded with tentative claps, and then the entire square erupted into thunderous applause. Casey nodded smugly and took her place back in line with the other two contestants.

A confused Larry looked out across the crowd. "Well. I guess we can all agree with that."

He turned back to the remaining contenders, and Destinee had already claimed her spot behind the microphone.

"Destinee?" he asked. "If you could change just one thing about the world, what would it be?"

She gave the judges another blinding smile.

"I think the world would be a better place if young men today would take more responsibility for things like mowing yards for their grandparents, emptying the dishwasher, and buying condoms." She paused. "And I mean those really good ones that don't break after just one time."

Larry's lips moved, but no sound came out.

"Well, dang," T-Bomb whispered. "They oughta just call her Destinee *Knocked-up*."

"She could give them Horton girls a run for their money," Ermaline said.

"All except that boy one up there," T-Bomb replied, pointing at Casey. "He don't need 'em."

"I wouldn't be too sure about that," someone mumbled.

El and I looked at each other.

"Was that Doc?" she asked.

I shook my head. "I honestly have no idea. I've never heard him say anything before."

"Would you all hush up?" Luanne glared at us. "It's Jailissa's turn."

Jailissa stood at the mike, ready to answer her next question.

A somewhat exasperated looking Larry faced her. "Alrighty, then. Jailissa? If you could change just one thing about the world, what would it be?"

"Well, Mr. Dennis . . ." Jailissa looked out over the audience with a dreamy expression. "Even though some folks don't believe in it, I'd like to fix global warming." There was a collective gasp from the crowd, but Jailissa soldiered on. "That would make people's crops better and give them higher yields. Then they could afford to buy newer and more efficient farm equipment and do things to improve their property, like build garages and maybe quit parking in their yards."

There was a restrained round of applause. Jailissa took her place back in line.

"That don't bode well." Luanne shook a Viceroy out of her pack. "I kept telling her to leave her political views out of her answers." She fired up a smoke. "I hope these last two questions go more her way."

"All right. We're down to our last two questions, so we're going to kick it up a notch." Larry pulled the microphone off its stand. "I'm going to ask each of you to answer your question, then pass the mike on to the next contestant. When Jailissa finishes with her answer to the first question, she'll pass the mike back to Casey for the second, and final, question of our speed round. Are you ready?"

They all nodded. He handed the mike to Casey.

"Casey. If you could be on the cover of any magazine, which would you chose and why?"

Casey smirked. "*Garden & Gun*, because they have something for everyone."

Casey passed the mike to Destinee.

"*People Magazine*," she said. "Because they have professionals who do your makeup and hair, and I'd be, like famous, and look really super good."

She continued to hold on to the mike. Jailissa held her hand out for it. Destinee seemed to let go of it with reluctance.

"*Martha Stewart Living,*" Jailissa said. "Because she has really good recipes, craft projects, party planning tips, and all kinds of things that you can do at home with stuff you already have."

Jailissa passed the mike back to Casey.

"Okay. Now we're down to our final question. Ladies? It's time to leave it all on the table." Larry consulted his last index card.

"Well, dang," T-Bomb hissed. "That's kinda creepy coming from a coroner."

There was a titter of laughter.

Grammy glared at her.

El had my knee in a death grip. I was positive it would leave a mark.

"Here is your fourth and final question," Larry said with great ceremony. "Good luck, ladies. In a few minutes, one of you will be crowned the new Miss Pork Queen." He paused for effect. "Are you ready?"

The three contestants looked at each other, then nodded at Larry.

"Casey Horton. Here is your final question. What bothers you most about America today?"

Luanne dropped her head into her hands. "It's another political question," she whispered.

Jay ran his hand in small, consoling circles over her back.

Casey, however, seemed undaunted.

"Bad spelling," she said, before calmly handing the mike to Destinee.

Destinee stared at Casey for a moment before facing the audience and flipping her red hair back behind her shoulder.

"Well, Larry. I think we need to do more to protect our school children from vicious attacks by lawless troublemakers. As Americans, we should make our schools safer by arming our teachers, cooks, and bus drivers." Destinee faced the judges. "This is our sacred duty, and our second amendment right."

"Oh, lord." Luanne still had her head buried in her hand.

I was pretty sure I was going to need a knee transplant before this "speed round" ended.

Somehow, Jailissa managed to wrangle the microphone away from Destinee. She squared her shoulders and faced the audience.

"While I agree that there are a lot of things that America could do better to help its people. I really believe that our biggest threat comes from the endless cycle of ignorance to poverty that occurs every day in our own back yard." Jailissa seemed to look each of us in the eye. "I know that if we try, we can do more to help each other, and our community, be stronger and better prepared to face the challenges that will continue to come our way in the future." She smiled. "Thank you all for taking the time to come here and listen to our views on these important issues."

Larry gave Jailissa a grateful-looking smile. He stood back and extended his arm to encompass all three women.

"Ladies and gentlemen . . . your Miss Pork Day finalists."

The square erupted into enthusiastic applause.

Luanne blew out a nervous breath. "Now we wait."

"Hell," T-Bomb was still clapping. "You ain't got nothin' to worry about. She just locked that one right up."

I found it hard to disagree with her.

El was looking down at her cell phone.

"Something wrong?" I asked.

She shook her head. "Just Tony. He's in the crowd someplace and needs to talk with me."

"Can it wait until after the competition?"

She nodded. "He said he'd come and find us in a few minutes."

Luanne eyes were glued to the judges' table. "Look! They're signaling for Larry to come over . . . I think this is it."

It was true. Larry walked over to confer with the three judges. One of them handed him a sealed envelope.

He walked back to the center of the stage where the three contestants waited.

"Ladies," he said. "The judges have reached their verdicts and have made their selections. It's now time to crown our new Miss Pork Queen."

The three contestants joined hands.

Larry opened the envelope.

"Third Runner-Up and winner of the Miss Congeniality Award, and the recipient of a two-hundred-and-fifty-dollar gift card from the Southern Illinois Lumber Company is . . . *Miss Casey Horton!*"

The crowd broke into a chorus of wild cheers and applause. Casey was plainly thrilled with this outcome. She repeatedly pumped the air with a fist before grabbing Destinee Knackmuhs and kissing her square on the mouth.

"Well, dang," T-Bomb was on her feet, clapping, "I hope she brung along some of them good kind of condoms."

A nonplussed Larry continued. "Second Runner-Up and winner of a five-hundred-dollar scholarship from Ingram's Funeral Home is . . . *Miss Destinee Knackmuhs!*"

There was a loud gasp—as if the entire audience inhaled at the same time.

"This means that our new Miss Pork Queen," Larry shouted above the thunderous applause, "and the recipient of a fifteen-hundred-dollar scholarship from the Herschel Johnson Implement Company is . . . *Miss . . . Jailissa . . . Keortge!*"

Jailissa stood with both hands pressed against her mouth. Casey made a congratulatory move toward her. Larry intervened and took Jailissa by the elbow to move her forward on the stage.

The reigning Miss Pork Queen, Amanda Horton, waddled out onto the stage, bearing the crown and sash for the winner. She had to be at least eight months pregnant.

Luanne and Jay had tears running down their faces.

Joe Sykes looked like he was about ready to break down, too. "I'll go get the truck started."

He took a last, wistful look up at Jailissa, then beat a hasty retreat, wiping at his eyes before disappearing into the crowd.

The audience was still going wild. The applause and the cheers went on and on. It was clear that Jailissa was this year's popular choice. People were crowding the stage, taking pictures with cell phones and cameras. I thought I saw some bigger flashes of light, too. Distinct, telltale rumblings rose above the noise and the cheering. I looked up at the sky. It wouldn't be Pork Day without at least one gully washer. I just hoped the storms would hold off long enough for Jailissa to take her victory ride around the courthouse square.

El and I were on our feet, too, clapping and hollering. Jailissa stood, regally, at the front of the stage, smiling and waving at the crowd. Camera flashes were still going off. Above the din, we could hear music . . . sort of. Over at the edge of the platform, Casey Horton was playing her euphonium.

I leaned closer to El, and gestured toward Casey. "What's she playing?"

El cocked an ear toward the sound. "It sounds like 'Isn't She Lovely?'"

I laughed. "That Casey Horton is a class act."

El nodded and leaned into me.

We were still smiling and clapping when I saw Tony making his way toward us.

I nudged El. "Here comes Tony."

When he reached us, he nodded at me in greeting before taking El by the arm and leading her to stand near the edge of the Pagoda. He seemed to be showing her something on his cell phone.

El's face looked stricken. She glanced at me, then closed her eyes and slowly shook her head before giving her full attention back to Tony, who was still talking and gesturing. He pointed at something off in the direction of the high school. Then he glanced at his watch. El nodded and touched him on the arm. She said something to him, and then headed back to where we all stood.

I could tell by her expression that something was wrong—very wrong. She was moving like an inmate walking The Green Mile in one of those Stephen King novels.

I decided to meet her halfway.

"What is it?" I asked when I reached her. "You're white as a sheet."

She let out a deep breath and looked at me. Really looked at me. I don't think I'd ever been looked at in quite that way before. Not even by old Dr. Guttmann, who did my first GYN exam when I was sixteen.

"Something horrible has happened." She touched my arm. "I mean at the plant."

"My, god. What is it?"

Judging by the expression on her face, I knew it had to be bad.

"A woman working in the warehouse—I think Tony said her name is Ruthie Miles—had what appears to be a heart attack, likely brought on by heatstroke." She slowly shook her head. "The EMTs weren't called in time . . . she died on the way to the hospital."

Ruthie Miles? Wynona's sister-in-law was dead? From the heat? While working in the warehouse?

I closed my eyes. "Oh my god."

"Apparently, she went to her supervisor to tell him she was feeling sick and having chest pains, but he told her to go sit down in a front office for a while, until she felt better and could return to work."

Her supervisor? Oh, god . . . Earl Junior.

"They didn't call for help?"

El shook her head. "Not for more than three hours."

I was incredulous. "She sat there for three hours?"

El nodded again. "I think Buzz Sheets finally called the EMTs—after she lost consciousness."

"Buzz knew about this?" I was feeling sick . . . and furious.

"I'm so sorry."

El did look sorry, too. She looked as sick and miserable as I was starting to feel.

"Those bastards. Those stupid, fucking bastards . . ."

El squeezed my arm. "I know."

"The air conditioning wasn't even *broken* in that part of the plant. They just never fucking turned it on to save money."

El dropped her hand. "I think we need to stop talking about this now, Friday Jill."

We stood there, staring at each other like gunfighters facing off in a spaghetti western. More thunder rolled in the distance.

I blinked first. "What do you mean?"

"I mean, you shouldn't talk any more about this—or the plant—to me."

"Why not?" I started to feel sick for an entirely different reason.

She sighed. "I think you know why not."

"No I don't," I lied. "What does this have to do with us?"

I knew it wasn't a fair question, but I couldn't stop myself from asking her. I needed to hear her answer.

"It seems likely that Ruthie Miles died because of a sad and regrettable combination of extreme heat and Krylon's pattern of neglect and contempt for workplace safety." El sounded as frustrated as I felt. "You know that as well as I do."

I couldn't disagree with her, so I simply nodded.

"I have a job to do. You know that, too."

I knew it, but I didn't *want* to know it—not any more than I wanted to know about things like global warming or the fact that all the fracking going on around here was probably poisoning our ground water and giving all the women in Gibson County breast cancer.

"Okay, I get it," I said. Even though I couldn't begin to process it all right then. "But where does this leave us?"

El took a moment to answer. "Right now, there is no us. There can't be until this is over."

"Until *what* is over?"

"Getting a vote."

I was confused. "What vote?"

"The vote that brought me here." She was starting to sound exasperated. "The union vote."

"I thought you said that wasn't going to happen—that you were ready to pull up stakes and leave?"

"Not any more. This is a game changer."

A game changer?

I was shocked. "That's what Ruthie's death is to you? A game changer?"

For a moment, I thought she might slap me. But she didn't. El had too much poise for that.

"I need to go now," she said. "Tony is waiting for me." Her voice was toneless. Flat.

My head was spinning. "Can I call you later?"

"It's probably better if you don't."

She turned to walk away, but I grabbed her arm.

"El?"

She stopped and looked back at me.

"Is this really it?"

"No, Jill. This isn't it. But right now, this is the only it we have." She gently removed my hand from her arm. "I can't make this situation better or different for you. You're going to have to find your own way through it." She hesitated. "Just like me."

"I don't know what that means."

"I know you don't," she said sadly. "Maybe when you do, we can talk about the future." She looked at her watch. "I have to go now."

I stood rooted to my spot like a sapling and watched her walk away. It was only after she disappeared behind the Pagoda, that I realized it had started to rain.

Chapter 11

It rained all night. I was sure of it because I spent most of the night sitting up watching it come down. Fritz finally got tired of watching me watch the rain and wandered off to his bed. I kept thinking El would call, but she didn't. I kept thinking I might call her, but I didn't. It was plain that we were at what Grammy called sixes and sevens.

I still wasn't sure what that expression meant. But I remembered the line about it from a college Shakespeare course. Was it *Richard III*?

"But time will not permit: all is uneven, And every thing is left at six and seven."

Yeah. Well if memory served, things didn't pan out so well for him, either . . .

I was fidgeting. "Antsy." My mind was skating.

Six and seven. Stuck in the middle of . . . what?

Maybe it was just a bad throw in dice?

Or Baggo Cornhole?

Shit. Thinking about that sure wasn't helping.

This was ridiculous. Pathetic. As bad as I felt, I wasn't the one who'd lost a family member. Ruthie Miles was dead. Dead because of circumstances that should have been one hundred percent preventable. I knew the Krylon method well enough to guess that they would blame it all on a preexisting heart condition. It wouldn't matter to them that Ruthie sat on a straight chair in a front office for more than three hours, feeling nauseated, dizzy, and short of breath. It wouldn't matter to them that no one called the EMTs until she finally passed out. It wouldn't matter to them that they knowingly put a moron with no sense or training in charge of an entire functional area of the plant. And it wouldn't matter to them that the shift supervisor—a man with training and better sense—knew what was happening and still did *nothing* to intervene.

The only thing that would matter to the Krylon family was how they could manipulate the OSHA investigation and prevent the union from making hay out of Ruthie's misfortune.

In my opinion, it was too late for that one. As Buzz would say, that bus had sailed.

Idiots. They were all idiots. Soulless idiots.

Ruthie was dead.

I didn't know her well, but I knew who she was. Ruthie was about forty-five years old. She'd worked at Krylon for ten years or so. She was short and always wore pink. She had a pronounced dimple in one cheek that always made her look like she was smiling. She played the piano at the Moravian church, just like Wynona. She had three kids.

I could imagine how this news was spreading through the company rank and file like wild fire.

"It's probably better if you don't," El said, when I asked her if I could call.

I tried a thousand different ways to take the sting out of that simple phrase, but none of them worked. Even though I knew in my gut what she really meant and, against my will, I understood all the reasons why her declaration made sense.

Everything had changed. Everything.

Ruthie was dead.

And El was no longer an agitator. She was an *organizer*. Now, there was something to organize around.

A game changer.

Out of the same mouth proceed blessing and curse. Isn't that what the Bible said?

It was perverse to think that I wasn't feeling morose and preoccupied because El would be leaving. I was feeling morose and preoccupied because El would be *staying*, but she'd be staying in a way that meant there no longer was an "us."

That's what she said to me. There *is* no us.

My cell phone vibrated again. Then the house phone rang. I ignored them both. I knew it was T-Bomb. She'd been trying to reach me off and on all night—probably ever since she found out about Ruthie.

I'd left Albion right after El told me about what had happened at the plant. I didn't really have the emotional stamina to stay around and face the fallout from the news. I knew it was probably pretty shabby for me just to disappear like I did. But since everyone was off celebrating with the Keortges, I thought I could make my exit quietly, without the fuss I knew would ensue once the others heard about Ruthie.

It was impossible to imagine what it would be like at the plant tomorrow. Frankly, I didn't care if I ever set foot in that place again.

I thought for the thousandth time about the letter from Don K. I knew now what my answer was going to be. Don K. could blow his thirty pieces of silver right out his tastefully clad ass. I had no idea what I'd do next. I didn't really care. I knew my parents would let me work at the Fast Mart until I figured something else out. And I had enough savings to be okay for a while.

Maybe I'd move to St. Louis and try to get back on at Boeing, or head to Louisville to finish my MBA? I could rent my house for a year . . . it wouldn't be hard. Grammy would keep Fritz.

He had reappeared shortly after sunrise, wanting a pee break and breakfast. Now he sat at my feet, with his chin resting on my leg. I scratched the top of his head.

Maybe I wouldn't leave him behind? He was my best friend . . . the only real constant in my life, besides Grammy.

My cell phone vibrated again. I stared at it.

And T-Bomb. I still had T-Bomb.

Fitz jerked his head up and looked toward the kitchen. Then he took off barking. I heard the porch door open and close. Then the barking stopped.

"Hey? Friday?" an angry voice called out. "Where the hell are you?"

I sighed. It was inevitable that she would show up. And it was my own fault that I never locked the back door.

"I'm up here in the living room."

T-Bomb barreled into the room like the thunderstorms that still raged outside.

"What the hell is the matter with you? I been callin' you all night."

"I know. I'm sorry . . . I needed some space."

She took off her rain jacket and hung it on a hook by the front door. "*Space?* What the hell does that mean? Everybody's in a swivet about Ruthie Miles."

"I know."

"You know? How'd you find out?"

"El told me before she left."

"Left?" She glared at me. "Where'd she go?"

I shrugged. "I have no idea. Off with Tony."

"She left with that other agitator?"

I nodded.

She sat down on a chair that faced where I lay sprawled across the sofa. "Is that why you took off without telling anybody?"

I nodded again.

"You two have a fight?"

I was tempted to tell her to mind her own damn business, but I knew that would be a lost cause.

"Why would you ask me that?" I said, instead.

"Because you look like death warmed over, that's why."

I didn't reply.

"You been up all night?"

I sighed and nodded again.

She sat there for a few moments without saying anything. Then she got to her feet.

"Where are you going?" I asked. I realized that I didn't really want to be alone any more.

"I'm gonna go make us some coffee." She headed for the kitchen. "It won't do us any good to both sit here like zombies."

I decided to get up and follow her.

She was right, after all. Wallowing in my own self-pity could wait. I had all the time in the world to indulge myself with that. Today, we needed to talk about Ruthie and what the fallout at work was likely to mean for all us all.

T-Bomb filled the coffee pot with water. I got a bag of beans out of the pantry and pulled out the grinder.

"Why don't you just buy Folger's like everybody else?"

"I hate that kind of coffee. It tastes like hot water." I dumped a hefty mound of beans into the grinder.

"Well, I'd rather drink hot water than that sludge you make."

I sighed and scooped some of the beans back out and returned them to the bag.

"You're a wuss," I said.

"I'm a wuss?" She huffed. "People who live in glass houses shouldn't throw beer cans."

"What's that supposed to mean?"

She poured the water into the coffeemaker. "It means that every time you get your heart broke, you crawl off into a hole and hide from everybody."

I chose to let the earsplitting noise of the burr grinding be my response. Besides, I couldn't argue with her about the broken heart. The truth was, I'd never felt this hurt or despondent. And I knew it was going to linger for a good long time. Probably forever.

I dumped the ground coffee into the filter and handed it to T-Bomb.

"How did people find out about Ruthie?" I asked.

"Joe Sykes got a call during Jailissa's victory lap. That pretty much brought everything to a halt. It was starting to rain by then, anyway, so we all packed up and left."

"Has anybody been to see the family yet?"

She nodded. "It's pretty terrible. Them kids is all to pieces. You know, their daddy lives up in Terre Haute with his new wife?" She shook her head. "I sure hope she's ready to take on an instant family."

"God. I just can't believe this happened."

"I know." T-Bomb leaned against the counter while we waited on the coffee. "But as hot as it was yesterday, it's amazing that they didn't cart more than just one person outta that sweat shop."

I stared at her. "You know what this probably means, right?"

"Hell, I can think of all kinds of things it probably means. Which one did you have in mind?"

"The union."

"Yeah. The parking lot at Hoosier Daddy was overflowin' with cars

212

last night when we rode past it on the way home. I never seen it like that. People were parking along the road and over in the NAPA lot."

"You think El and Tony were there?"

"You don't?"

I shrugged.

"Of course they were there. It's where they do business. I bet they filled up the rest of them union cards last night. People are hoppin' mad at them Krylons. I even heard some mumbling about a sickout tomorrow, but you know nobody'll do that. People care too much about their paychecks to let being pissed off get in the way."

That was true. "What about a slowdown?"

T-Bomb raised an eyebrow.

"What?" I asked.

"Are you sure you know which side of this nightmare you're on?"

I was offended by that inference. "I'm on *our* side."

"Our side?" She scoffed. "Do you even know what that means?"

"Hey, look." I was losing my patience. "I'm not the enemy here."

"That's my point, Friday. There ain't no enemies here, except maybe them Krylons and the dern knuckle-draggers they put in charge."

"Well I'm not on their side."

"So are you gonna sign one of them authorization cards?"

I shook my head.

"Why not?"

"Because if I do, everyone will think it's because of El."

She gave a bitter-sounding laugh. "Hell, that don't make you unique. Half the men in that plant would sign up if it meant they could get close enough to her to cop a feel. Most of 'em ain't smart enough to figure out that she don't play for their team."

The coffeepot beeped. We filled our mugs and headed back to the living room. Fritz trotted along behind us.

T-Bomb reclaimed her seat on the chair. I walked to the desk and retrieved the offer from Don K.

"I want to show you something."

She took the envelope from me. "What is it?"

"Don K. called me in for a little chat last Thursday." I nodded toward the letter. "I think that's what you call a bribe."

T-Bomb looked confused. She pulled letter and check and looked them over. Her eyes grow wide as she read. When she finished, she dropped the pages to her lap and glared at me.

"Are you gonna do this?"

I shook my head.

"You're not?"

"No."

"Why not? Are you crazy?"

"Oh, come on, Bomber. How could I work for them after what happened to Ruthie?"

"Don't be stupid." She held up the sheets of paper and shook them at me like a rattle. "A job like this one would allow you to fix some of the things that killed Ruthie."

"I'm not going to be a puppet for the Krylons."

"The Krylons ain't gonna be runnin' things there in another month. They'll all be off on a beach some place, countin' their money."

I was stunned by her reaction to the offer from Don K. "You seriously think I should do this?"

"Why not?"

"Because I'd be letting them buy me off. And because I'd have to promise not to have anything more to do with El."

She huffed. "I think that part already took care of itself, don't you?"

I shrugged.

"Besides," she continued, "once this dern vote thing is over with, it won't matter who you're carryin' on with. The UAW will move on to the next place, and you and El DeBarge can pretty much do whatever you want."

I didn't reply.

"Look, Friday." She leaned forward on her chair. "When this buy-out first got announced, we all celebrated, and not just because it meant we'd all keep our jobs. Weren't you the one that told us that them Japanese companies had better benefits and better workplace conditions than a lot of the plants that had unions?"

I nodded.

"So why wouldn't you want to be a part of that?" She glanced down at the papers again. "And get a damn big raise in the process?"

I was amazed that her reaction to Don K.'s offer was nearly identical to El's.

"I just can't do it. Not anymore. Not after Ruthie. It'd be like taking blood money."

"So you're gonna just run away and let assholes like Buzz Sheets keep raisin' up a whole new crop of Ruthies? Is that it?"

"No, that's not it." I was getting angry, and I was tired of trying to disguise it. "I have no fucking life here." I waved a hand in frustration. "It's like living in a goddamn fishbowl, and I've had enough of it. I finally meet the right person, and she ends up being the *wrong* person . . . all over again. I'm sick of this twisted pattern of hope and disappointment, where I'm only as good as my last fucking failure. I want out. Enough is enough."

My tirade hung in the air between us like a passing storm cloud. T-Bomb didn't say anything. She folded the letter and slid it back into its envelope. Then she took a sip of her coffee.

I sat watching her while I waited for my heart rate to settle down. I took a deep breath. "Don't you have anything to say?"

"Yeah," she said. "You need to suck it up, cupcake."

"*I* need to suck it up?" I pointed a finger at my chest.

"Yeah. You." She slammed her mug down on the table beside her chair. "You think you have it so rough? You got no clue how hard life really is for me and the other five-thousand rednecks that are chained to those damn assembly lines. We ain't got no options, and we ain't sittin' on any offers for a better tomorrow. That truck plant in that damn rusted-out town is all there is for us. We can't give Don K. the finger and walk off to some greener pasture just because we're offended by his . . . methods. There ain't any greener pastures for us. The only choice we ever have is to just keep takin' whatever him and his candy ass flunkies keep shovelin' at us until the Japanese take over, and hope we're lucky enough not to end up like Ruthie before they get a chance to make things right." She huffed and dropped back against her chair. "So you just keep right on sittin' here, weepin' and wailin' all you want about how none of your precious relationships ever work out, and blame whoever you want. Cause you and I both know that the only thing they all have in common is you."

There was a reason T-Bomb was my best friend. As painful as her words were, the truth they conveyed was impossible to deny. She knew it, and she knew that I knew it, too.

I didn't want to cry, but I was having a hard time avoiding it. I wiped at my eyes. "I'm a mess."

"You ain't a mess," she said. Her voice had come down out of the rafters. "You're just scared. Hell. Everybody who pays attention is scared. But it's time for you to stop being a prisoner of your fears. If you don't, you'll just end up in the same dang place, no matter where you go to hide."

I nodded. "I know."

"So. Are you gonna talk with El DeBarge?"

I shook my head. "Not anytime soon."

"Why not?"

"Because she's got a job to do, and she said that meant there was no more us."

"Did she mean right now, or never?"

I shrugged.

"You didn't ask her?"

"Of course not."

"Don't be stupid. She's the best thing to happen to you in . . . hell . . . probably forever."

"Do you really think that?" I felt like I was five years old, wondering if it was really safe for me to try to cross the street by myself.

"Would I tell you that if I didn't? Would Grammy . . . or Luanne? Or Ermaline? Hell. Even Joe Sykes seemed to like her."

I actually smiled at that. "He did, didn't he?"

T-Bomb nodded. "Though I don't know if I'd take that as a good reason to keep seeing her. He ain't exactly got the best instincts, if you know what I mean."

"Except for Jailissa."

T-Bomb rolled her eyes. "That's just creepy, is what that is."

"Luanne said she believed it was a pure love."

"Yeah? Well, Luanne also believes them green olives that have the little red pimentos inside 'em *grow* that way." She slowly shook her head. "The human mind can be a terrifying thing."

"You'll get no argument from me on that one."

"You know what I think?" she asked.

"No. But I'm sure you're going to tell me."

"Smart ass. I should just let you die wonderin'."

"But you won't."

"You're right." She sighed. "I think you need to just cool your jets and see how this all plays out. You don't know enough now to make any big decisions—about the job or about where this thing with El DeBarge goes or doesn't go once this union mess is over with."

"I'm tired of waiting around for things just to happen."

"Then do something about it."

I was confused. "Didn't you just tell me to wait and see how things play out?"

"I meant that you shouldn't run away. There ain't a thing wrong with fighting for what you want."

"But I'm not sure I know what that is."

"I think you know exactly what that is. It's just easier to pretend you don't. Then it ain't your fault if it don't work out."

I stared at her. "You should be a shrink, you know that?"

She smirked. "Hell. Maybe I was wrong about them greener pastures." She extended her hand, palm up. "That'll be eighty-five dollars."

Nothing was settled or changed for me. I still had no idea what I would do tomorrow when I walked into work. I still thought that any shot I'd had at a future with El had flown right out the window on a stack of union authorization cards. And Ruthie Miles was still dead.

But somehow, for just a moment, I felt better.

I guess the Bible was right. Knowing the truth really does make you free.

∾ ∾ ∾

When I got to work at a quarter to seven on Monday morning, I noticed a ragtag group of people milling around just outside the gates that led to the Krylon parking lot. They were leaning into car windows and chatting up anyone who stopped on their way into the lot. I had a sneaking suspicion that I knew what they were up to, but I was wrong. Instead of being handed a union card when I pulled forward and stopped, a man I didn't know gave me a small, postcard-sized photo of Ruthie Miles. Pinned to the back of it was a pink heart cut out of felt. The message on the card read, "Wear this today to honor Ruthie—one of our own."

I swallowed hard, thanked him, and drove on.

I had my answer ready for Don K. I'd stayed up half the night crafting it and re-crafting it. After working through a dozen drafts that were as varied in tone and complexity as *The Gettysburg Address* and Hirohito's surrender to the allies, I decided upon a single sentence.

I was quitting.

It wasn't that I didn't consider all the things T-Bomb—and El—had pointed out about what might change and improve once the Krylons were gone. I thought about all of that. Even though it strained credibility, I tried hard to believe that it *might* be possible to implement a better, safer, and more worker-centered operational model in a manufacturing facility that was firmly planted in the middle of a right-to-work state.

I wanted to believe it, but I didn't. Deep down, I knew it was a lost cause. Just like my odds at having any kind of a future with El. I was giving up on that fantasy, too.

It was time for me to move on. After I delivered my response and worked out my notice, I was going to collect what was left of my savings and my self-esteem, and I was going to find temporary housing in Louisville so I could finish my MBA as quickly as possible. Then? I wasn't sure about what I'd do after that. But I was pretty certain that whatever it was, it wouldn't involve staying on in Princeton.

Not in this factory, anyway. I was sure that I had value to add some place, but it wasn't going to be here . . . not at a place where aspirations to be the best we could be were sacrificed on the altar of the least we could get away with. I was tired of living my life like a lemming, with no better sense or prospects for a brighter tomorrow. Enough was enough.

I was getting out, and that's all there was to it.

As soon as I stepped inside the door, I realized that something was different. For one thing, it was quieter. There was still a mild cacophony of machine noise, but it was nowhere near as deafening as usual. And there were sizeable groups of people standing around in random locations.

I walked to the time clock to punch in and noticed something attached to my card.

You gotta be kidding me . . . not again?

I pulled my card out of its slot and read the folded paper clipped to it.

ATTENTION
ALL LINE SUPERVISORS AND PROCESS MANAGERS

Please be present in the company cafeteria at 7:15 a.m. for a mandatory meeting with Mr. Tam Shigeta, Director of Operations, Ogata Torakku USA. He will share important information about the future of this manufacturing facility. Your prompt attention is appreciated.

Oh shit. This couldn't be good news.

I looked around. Judging by the expressions I was seeing on most of the faces around me, everybody else shared the same opinion.

What the hell had happened? And when did Tam Shigeta get here?

This had to be about Ruthie.

Along with their somber expressions, most people inside the plant seemed to be wearing the pink, felt hearts that had been passed out in the parking lot. It was like a curious double entendre: a memorial for Ruthie and a talisman for whatever was about to befall us all.

I didn't see Buzz or Joe, but I did see Luanne. I walked over to where she stood holding up a section of wall near the canteen entrance. I thought she looked a little pale. No doubt Ruthie's death, and whatever was happening here this morning, had taken some of the shine off Jailissa's victory on Saturday.

I held up the notice. "Do you know anything more about this?"

She shook her head. "Only that a crew of big dogs from Tokyo came roarin' in here like samurai warriors yesterday." She lowered her voice. "I heard that Buzz Sheets got canned . . . and Earl Junior."

I was surprised. "Really?"

She nodded. "I took a casserole by the house last night, and Wynona told me that this Shigeta fella *personally* walked Don K. out to his car."

"Don K. is gone?" I was incredulous.

Luanne scoffed. "Him and his golden damn parachute. Good riddance, if you ask me."

I didn't know what to say. Don K. was gone? Buzz and Earl Junior, too? And now this mandatory meeting about the future of our plant?

And why was it so damn quiet in here?

"Are they shutting us down?" I asked.

"You tell me." She clucked her tongue. "It don't look good. Half the lines ain't runnin.' They started a phased work stop last shift."

A work stop at seven-thousand dollars a minute was a big deal. A *very* big deal.

"Where's Joe?" I asked.

She made an oblique gesture. "He came stormin' back here after he heard about what happened to Ruthie. Him and Don K. had words, and Don K. fired him." She slowly shook her head. "Jailissa is all to pieces about it . . . we ain't heard nothin' from Joe since last night."

"Good god. Don K. fired Joe?"

She nodded. "Joe never wanted Earl Junior to get that ware-house job, but nobody in the front office would listen to him. You know, he's worked with them Miles girls for nearly ten years."

Maybe I wouldn't have to worry about handing in my letter of resignation. Maybe there wouldn't be anyone left to receive it.

I glanced at my watch. It was seven-ten. "I guess we need to get in there and find out what's happening."

Luanne sighed. "I wish I had time for a smoke."

I didn't tell her that I had a feeling she'd soon have all the time she wanted.

We followed a somber and morose-looking group of men and women toward the meeting location. As our group narrowed to file through the doors that led into the cafeteria, it occurred to me that we probably looked like sheep being led to the slaughter.

Once inside, I saw three people wearing khakis and dark blue Ogata polo shirts standing together on a low riser near the steam tables. Tam Shigeta was easy to pick out. He was tall and handsome, and looked exactly like every photo of him I'd ever seen in *Bloomberg Business Week*. I had no idea who the other two were. They were not Japanese. Something about the woman reminded me of El . . . she looked small, but powerful. They all appeared calm and composed, which put them all miles ahead of us.

Once we had all found a place to sit or stand, Tam stepped forward.

"Good morning, everyone," he said in perfect, unaccented English. "My name is Tam Shigeta, and I am Director of Operations for Ogata Torakku, USA. I can appreciate that these circumstances seem unusual. But I hope we can clarify things in short order, and allay any fears that you or your direct reports might be experiencing due to current conditions in the plant. I'm going to read a short statement, and then we'll do our best to answer any questions you have. Copies of this," he held up a document, "will be made available to each of you as you leave here this morning. Please share it with employees who work in your respective areas. Additionally, a new web site, *ogataUSA.com/princeton*, and a toll-free information line will be up and running by this afternoon. For the near term, any notices or communications related to plant operations during this transitional period will be posted there." He looked over the room. "Is everyone clear about that?"

He waited for a majority of heads to nod.

"Good. The web address and info line number are printed on the bottom of the statements we'll be handing out. Encourage all of your direct reports to use it. Now, I'd like to introduce you to two people who will be helping to lead the Ogata transition team. Janice Baker." He turned and indicated the dark-haired woman standing beside him. "Janice is a fifteen-year veteran of the automotive manufacturing business. She has a Ph.D. in industrial engineering from the Georgia Institute of Technology, and has been Ogata's Chief Operations Analyst for the past five years. Steven Haley." Tam indicated the other man on the riser. "Steve heads up Ogata USA's Human Resource Development Division. He's been with us since 1997, when we opened our first North American plant in Marysville. You'll be seeing a lot of both of them." He turned back to us. "Now I'd like to ask for your indulgence while I read this short, formal statement."

He paused a moment. The only sound in the cafeteria came from frozen cubes dropping into the storage bin of the ice machine in the corner.

"Prior to the formal acquisition of the Krylon Motors Princeton Plant and its Outlaw brand several weeks ago, Ogata Torakku performed careful due diligence of all processes, equipment, and human factors related to the sale. We soon became aware of a series of disturbances across numerous processes that were causing plant operations to deviate from accepted and safe operating states. We also discovered that a post-acquisition/pre-transition reallocation of crucial operations and maintenance funds had occurred. Ogata intended for those funds to immediately address crucial training, process improvement, and deferred maintenance issues that were deemed likely to endanger human life or result in catastrophic consequences. That did not occur.

"We are all part of the Ogata Torakku family. The foundation of our great company is 'Success by Purpose.' As a corporation and as a family, Ogata Torakku is deeply saddened by the tragic loss of Ms. Ruthie Miles, and we will honor her by ensuring that no other Ogata Torakku employee is ever placed in a dangerous or inappropriate workplace situation.

"As you will soon learn, the Krylon family and many members of their senior management team are no longer associated, in any capacity, with this transition process, the Outlaw product line, or operations in the Princeton plant.

"Effective immediately, this entire facility will be put into safe state, and a team of internal and external evaluators will perform an assessment of the compliance status and associated vulnerabilities of all plant process, equipment, and personnel resources. They will work in tandem with OSHA investigators, who we expect to arrive within the next few days. This team will also consider root causes and determine immediate, near-term, and long-term response actions. The first stage of this assessment is beginning as we speak, and it will address the most critical concerns for worker and workplace safety. We anticipate, based on our initial evaluation, that we will be able to return the plant to full operation in several days.

"Until we have restored safety to the plant floor here in Princeton, Yutaka Ikeda, our esteemed CEO, has personally granted that all employees not essential for basic plant operations or those participating in our assessment, will be placed on paid leave, effective immediately.

"Unless you are contacted by Steven Haley, Ogata's Director of Human Resource Development, you are free to leave and should plan on returning to your workstations within the next few days. Please check the web site or the toll-free information line referenced at the bottom of this memo for updates about the resumption of normal operations. Thank you."

He lowered the paper and looked out over the room. "Does anyone have any questions?"

At the front of the room, Big Otis Fishel, a manager in the transportation unit, took off his Outlaw ball cap and scratched his head. "So, you're really gonna pay us to sit home for a few days?"

Tam Shigeta nodded. "Yes, sir. We will."

Big Otis still seemed dubious. "And, we'll still have a job when we come back?"

"Yes, you will."

"And benefits, too?" Big Otis asked. His question was like an accusation.

"Yes, sir," Tam replied. "We will be transitioning each of you to the Ogata Torakku benefits plan during the next few weeks. You will have no loss of coverage. Once it's implemented, we think you'll like the new package, and the lower premium costs, much better."

Big Otis looked around at the rest of us. "That's all I got."

Tam smiled at him and looked around the room. "Any other questions?"

There were no takers. After a few nervous glances at each other, we all looked back at Tam or stared at the floor.

A few more seconds ticked by. More ice cubes dropped into the stainless steel bin.

"Okay." Tam nodded at us. "Please, enjoy this unplanned time off. We look forward to seeing you all in a few days. Remember to check the web site or the toll-free info line for updates about your schedules. Janice will meet you at the doors to hand out copies of the memo for you to share with your teams. Thank you."

We all waited while Janice Baker made her way to the back of the room.

I looked at Luanne. "I guess we need to go and get this done."

Her face was a study of mixed emotions. "I don't care what time it is. I'm gonna need a cold one after this."

From the riser, Steve Haley raised a hand. "Is Jill Fryman here?"

Luanne and I exchanged nervous glances.

"Here," I answered.

When he saw me, he gestured toward the riser where he stood with Tam. "Would you mind staying behind for a few minutes? We'd like to speak with you."

Great. With my luck, I'd get fired before I had a chance to resign. I nodded at him.

"Janice will talk with your team," he said.

I gave Luanne a forlorn look, and she squeezed my arm.

I took a deep breath and made my way toward the front of the room.

ဢ ဢ ဢ

"Please sit down, Jill."

Tam Shigeta indicated one of the plastic chairs that stood next to a round, Formica-topped lunch table. He and Steve Haley waited for me to be seated before they followed suit.

The cafeteria had emptied out. As anxious as I was feeling, it was hard not to wonder about the conversations that were going on out in the plant.

Steve Haley set a small stack of the leftover prepared statements on the table. A manila folder sat on top of them. FRYMAN, JILLIAN A. was neatly typed on a tiny label stuck to its tab.

He didn't open the folder or pass it to Tam. I guessed they both were already familiar with its contents. I just wished I shared their understanding of what it contained. Knowing Don K. and his flunkies, it probably made for interesting reading.

Tam saw me looking at the folder. "I'm sure this feels awkward to you, Jill. But I want to assure you that this conversation doesn't portend anything ominous."

I raised an eyebrow at that.

Tam smiled. "Okay . . . nothing any more ominous than the announcements we've already made."

I nodded. "That's a relief." I looked at Steve Haley. "I think."

"What do you know about Tiger Teams?" Tam asked.

"A little," I said. When he didn't reply, I realized that he was waiting to hear my definition. I cleared my throat. "Well, it's a catch phrase used to describe a group of people who are tasked to conduct oversight assessments of operations and processes. They identify vulnerabilities and recommend corrective actions. I think they're more common to the IT and aerospace industries than they are to auto manufacturing."

Tam and Steve looked at each other.

My nervousness inched back up a few notches.

"That's true," Tam said. "But we're about to change that dynamic."

I didn't reply.

"I was surprised to learn that you did your undergraduate Co-Op training at Boeing in St. Louis," Tam continued. "What kind of work did you do there?"

I was pretty sure he already knew the answer, but I told him anyway. "The program emphasis was on process improvement—Six Sigma and lean manufacturing. Most everything related to that."

"You went through the industrial technology program at Southern Illinois?" he asked.

I nodded.

"And now you're working on your MBA at Louisville?"

I nodded again.

"How is that progressing?" he asked.

"Slowly."

Steve Haley chuckled. "I got my MBA at Howard while working full time, too. It's brutal."

"That's why I chose Louisville. It's a quicker and easier drive than IU in Bloomington, but still two hours each way."

"How much more work do you have to do to finish?" he asked.

"Two terms, or four classes." I shrugged. "Two electives and two Capstone projects."

Steve gave me a sympathetic nod and smiled. I guessed he was about my age, or maybe a few years older. He had a kind face and an easy demeanor. I guessed that he was pretty good at his job.

"Are you at all familiar with kaizen?" Tam asked.

"I've heard of it. Isn't it a Japanese term for improvement?"

He nodded. "We call it change for the best. Know anything about how it relates to business practices?"

"Only what I read about it on the Ogata web site after the buyout was announced."

Tam laughed. "You do your homework."

"I never realized there'd be a quiz," I said, in an undertone.

"I'm sorry, Jill," Tam said it like he meant it. "That's not what this is."

I took a deep breath. "Okay. What is it?"

"When we received word about the circumstances surrounding the death of Ruthie Miles, we realized that we needed to expedite the transition process," Steve Haley said. "We're assembling a Tiger Team to address the hazards, risks, and vulnerabilities that must be corrected immediately before we return workers to the production lines."

Tam nodded in agreement. "After that phase is completed, they'll stay on to help us address near-term fixes and, ultimately, long-term fixes."

The door to the cafeteria opened.

Janice Baker poked her head inside. "I'm sorry to interrupt. But could you join me for a few minutes, Steve?"

He nodded and pushed back his chair. "Sorry for the disruption." He looked at me. "I'm sure I'll see you later, Jill."

I noticed that he took the pile of memos, but left my personnel folder behind.

I began to wonder if Janice's interruption had been planned. Now I was alone in the empty cafeteria with Tam Shigeta, an icon among *Fortune* 500 companies.

He seemed perfectly at ease.

I think he sensed my discomfort.

"I'm sure you're wondering why we asked to speak with you," he said.

"To be truthful," I replied, "I really have no idea."

He laid his hand on top of the file folder. "I'm not going to pretend that we're unfamiliar with your tenure here. And it's apparent to us that you've been grossly underemployed at Krylon. Your education and background experience are exemplary. You're a Six Sigma black belt with Lean Silver Certification, yet you're still punching a time clock. Why?"

I sighed. "Frankly, I've been asking myself that same question."

"And?"

"Until recently, I'd have had a good answer for you. Now?" I shook my head. "Now, I just don't know why."

"I'm aware of the . . . offer . . . Don Krylon extended to you before his departure."

I didn't say anything.

"I'm also aware that you haven't made any response as yet."

I was prepared to tell him that I came into work today, intending to do just that. Instead, I decided to indulge my curiosity. "Did he explain why he made the offer?"

Tam nodded. "He characterized it in slightly more sanitized terms than I would have used."

"Meaning?"

"I don't find extortion to be an effective, or acceptable, form of negotiation."

"That's good to know."

"You'll find that our methods have very little in common with the Krylon business model."

"So, I guess that means you'd like to rescind the offer?"

Tam leaned forward. "On the contrary. We'd like to amplify and expand it, for an entirely different set of reasons."

I was surprised. "You're not interested in enlisting me as an internal ally to thwart the UAW's attempts to organize the plant?"

He smiled. "No."

"So you're not worried about that?"

"I don't find it productive to worry about things I can't control. The tragic death of Ruthie Miles has made the likelihood of a union vote a near certainty. I'd be surprised if Mr. Gemelli and Dr. Rzcpczinska didn't already have the requisite number of signatures they need to file with the National Labor Relations Board."

I was surprised that he mentioned Tony and El by name. I wondered what else he knew about them.

"What if they do have the signatures?"

"If they do, then we enter the customary thirty-day campaign period that precedes a vote. Hopefully, that would give us enough time to show the employees of this plant that our standard business practices and compensation models are competitive with, and sometimes superior to, what they could expect to achieve under union auspices."

"You wouldn't close the plant?" I asked.

"Is that what Don Krylon told you?"

I nodded.

He took a slow, deep breath and stared up at the ceiling. It was clear that he was making an effort to remain composed.

I studied him. He was a good-looking man—probably in his midforties. He seemed unusually tall for a Japanese man, but then, I had to admit that I hadn't known many Japanese men. He had a beautiful head of thick, black hair that looked like it had just been cut. There was a thin, white scar, about a half-inch long, above the corner of his upper lip. It was odd how that one thing changed his appearance. It made him look approachable . . . almost ordinary. Not at all like what you'd expect from last year's Automotive Executive of the Year. I noticed his hands. They were smooth and unmarked. He had long fingers. I wondered if he played the piano. It looked like he could reach an entire octave with no problem. He wore a gold class ring . . . I didn't recognize the seal, but I was pretty sure it was from one of the Ivies.

Tam lowered his chin and looked back at me.

"I take it that was a misrepresentation?" I asked.

"You *might* say that." He shook his head. "Although I won't deny that Ogata would prefer to commence its Princeton operation without that particular variable at play, we certainly would not abandon our plans to transform this campus into the flagship of our North American manufacturing centers."

"So, you'd still bring the Mastodon to Princeton—even if the plant organizes?"

"I didn't say that," he clarified. "We're looking at several options for diversifying product lines here. And that was the case even before the UAW became a player in the transition. But we would never consider closing this facility. The Outlaw brand is a tremendous asset, and it's just beginning to hit its stride as a mainstay of the international automotive market. We think Ogata and Princeton have a bright future. And we'd like you to be a part of that."

There wasn't any ready response I could make to that. In fact, my head was reeling from these revelations. Don K. had done his level best to intimidate me, and countless others, by wrongly asserting that a pro-union vote would drive Ogata away from Princeton, putting all of our jobs in jeopardy and destabilizing the economic health of the region.

In fact, the only economic health he cared about protecting was the one tied to his own net worth.

I dropped my gaze and stared at the letters of my name, printed on the index tab of the manila folder. They were a tidy combination of straight lines and curved lines. Symbols that, when taken together, identified me, summarized me, differentiated me from everyone else.

I was FRYMAN, JILLIAN A.

I was also Jill.

And Friday.

And now I was some hybrid name, Friday Jill, too.

But most of all, I was me.

And somehow, I'd allowed the Don K.'s in my life to lead me to lose sight of that. And just when I'd decided that "me" was lost for good, there I was, neatly typed up and slotted into place exactly where I was supposed to be. Right here, in the middle of this godforsaken assembly plant, located in one of the most conservative, right-to-work states in the nation.

Oh. And there was one other tiny detail, too. I knew that I was more than ninety-nine percent in love with a labor organizer. That unique characteristic now defined me as neatly as the pattern of straight and curved lines that combined to spell the letters of my name.

I felt a strange sensation, sitting there on that hard plastic chair in the quiet of the company cafeteria. It was palpable—like a tingling that started from some place deep inside me and spread outward along my arms and legs. All the positive and negative atoms that had swirled around me for weeks finally came together in one, explosive charge.

To say that I knew who I was would be inaccurate. I'd always known that. But the curious, mini-epiphany I was experiencing was reminding me of things I thought I'd lost touch with—like why I stayed at Krylon in a dead end job. And why, against all reason, I clung to the life I lived in this big, sprawling, backward space that seemed so small.

I didn't have fewer choices. I had the same number of choices I'd always had.

And I was beginning to understand what I needed to do.

Tam was watching me. Probably in the same way I had been watching him a few moments ago.

"You were going to quit, weren't you?" he asked. His voice was quiet, almost like he was afraid someone would overhear this part of our conversation—even though we were the only two people in the cavernous space.

I looked back at him without saying anything. I didn't really have to. I nodded, but it was so slight a gesture that it would have been easy to miss if he hadn't been paying attention.

He saw it.

He pushed my folder away and sat back against his chair.

"I grew up in a small town, too—Rikuzentakata, in the Iwate region. My father was an oyster farmer, like his father before him. I never had any aspirations to leave or to have a different kind of life than the one that had defined my family for generations. I certainly never imagined that I'd end up manufacturing monster trucks halfway around the globe."

"But here you are," I said.

He nodded. "Here I am. And my journey wasn't that dissimilar from yours."

I found that hard to believe. "How so?"

"Education. My parents were simple people, but they embraced the country's cultural belief in the value of post-secondary study. I was enrolled in a vocational program with Kanto—part of the Toyota Group. From there, it was an easy transition to our local public university—the only affordable option for my family. Ironically, it was because of my years working the assembly line at Kanto that I landed the scholarship to attend TTI at the University of Chicago. The rest . . ." He waved a hand. "The rest is the rest."

"How does your family feel about your success?"

He looked down at the table. "Rikuzentakata was wiped off the map by the tsunami that followed the Great East Japan Earthquake. When the town seawall failed, the waters swept away everything in sight. The waves were more than forty-two feet high. None of my family survived."

I felt sick and horrified. I didn't know what to say. I'd never read about this in any of Tam's official, company biographies.

"I'm so sorry." I knew it sounded inadequate, but I couldn't find better words.

"It takes time," he said. "But you learn to live with it. I only shared this with you so you'd know that I understand part of your . . . *dichotomy*."

"My dichotomy?"

He nodded. "What it's like to be part, but not part, of the place that made you. Only in my case, I never got to choose to leave it behind. It left me. So in a real way, my job—my mission—is to help make this place be the best it can be for all the people who do choose to make their lives here. Does that make sense?"

Kaizen. Change for the better.

Yes. It made sense. But there was something else we needed to discuss. I wanted everything on the table. Tam had been honest with me, and I felt I owed him the same courtesy.

"I feel confident that Mr. Krylon informed you about my personal relationship with one of the UAW organizers," I said.

He nodded.

"Are there aspects of this that cause you concern?"

"Not really," he replied. "You're a professional, and I have every reason to expect that you would conduct yourself accordingly. Besides," he smiled, "I've known El for years, and I know she'd never behave unethically."

Tam Shigeta knew El?

I'm sure I must've looked like a deer in the headlights. He took pity on me.

"We were classmates for a semester at the ILR School in New York. She's a pro . . . they don't come much sharper. Or tougher." He folded his arms. "Any other concerns?"

I shook my head.

"Good. When Steve comes back, he's going to talk with you about becoming one of the plant reps on our assessment team. At the end of that process, we'd like to move you into a role that more appropriately fits with your specialized skill sets."

"Okay . . ." I wasn't sure exactly what that meant.

"We're going to be creating a new operational excellence unit at this campus, and we'll need to staff it with analysts, managers, and a director. I see you as a key player in that process, particularly related to the application of Six Sigma and lean manufacturing principles. You have real value to add, Jill. And I want you to be a part of this process."

Value to add. I was amazed that Tam used the same phrase I'd bounced around earlier, when I was certain that my tenure at Krylon was over.

But this wasn't Krylon. Not any more.

And I had a choice to make.

The door to the plant opened, and Steve Haley appeared.

"Are you ready for me?" he asked Tam.

Tam looked at me. "Are we?"

I nodded.

"Yes," he said to Steve. "We're ready."

Chapter 12

I wasn't sure what to expect when I pulled into the lot at Hoosier Daddy that night.

I'd been at the plant for a solid ten hours, and had next to no contact with anyone who normally worked my shift. I sent a quick text message to T-Bomb on my way out, asking if she could meet me for a drink.

I received five messages back from her in rapid succession.

Hey? What the HELL is going on?

Me and Luanne are already here. This place is hopping like Buehler's on double coupon day.

Aunt Jackie started selling $5 pitchers at noon.

You won't even believe the stories that are coming out. When will you get here?

Hey? Luanne wants to know if you'll pick her up some cigs?

I told her that I'd get the cigarettes and meet them there in about fifteen minutes.

She hadn't been kidding about the crowds. The place was jammed. Music was blasting from the jukebox, and the mood inside was anything but somber. Of course, if Aunt Jackie had been pouring five-dollar pitchers of Old Style since noon, that part wasn't too hard to understand. For all practical purposes, everyone who worked at OTI was on a paid holiday.

I spotted Tony Gemelli right away. He was holding forth with a large group set up near the pool table. It was pretty clear that enthusiasm for the UAW had surged. It looked like half the chairs in the bar had been dragged over to that area. He saw me and winked as I walked by. I didn't see El. I was half relieved and half sick about that. I figured she must be off working another event some place. I wondered how much they were hearing about the Ogata Tiger Team. I wondered if El knew that Tam Shigeta was here. And I wondered if she knew that I was working as part of the assessment unit now.

Mostly, I wondered if she was feeling as miserable as I was about our lapsed and murky status.

I saw T-Bomb standing up and waving at me from their table near the back of the bar. I waved back and started to head that way when something cut across the floor in front of me and nearly knocked me off my feet. What the hell?

I looked down.

Puppies?

Yep. Puppies. And they were profoundly . . . *ugly* . . . puppies, too.

There had to be half a dozen of them zooming around in crazy, random patterns like water bugs on a summer pond. They looked like canine tinker toys, cobbled together from parts that simply did not match. Their fat bottoms slid and skidded across the floor behind their sleeker front ends as if the motor neurons carrying the message to "run really fast" got waylaid in transit.

I heard a staccato sequence of ear-splitting barks wind up and project from the dark corner behind T-Bomb's table. An exasperated-looking Lucille waddled out into the half-light, wheezing and raising Cain. Magically, the puppies all reversed course and headed toward the table, piling into an ungainly heap at Lucille's feet. He growled and snapped at each of them, before turning around and retreating back to his dark corner. The puppies sat looking forlornly at each other before meekly following Lucille and settling down next to him on the pile of old hunting jackets that served as his bar bed.

I reached the table and pulled out a chair. "What's with the puppies?"

Luanne waved a hand in disgust. "Did you remember to get my smokes?"

I nodded and pulled the pack of Viceroys out of my backpack.

"Honey, Aunt Jackie is about to go postal over these dern ugly dogs," T-Bomb explained.

Luanne was ripping the cellophane off the pack of cigarettes. "That lowlife Jerry Sneddin came by here last night and just left them dogs outside in a big box." She smacked the pack against the palm of her hand to dislodge a cigarette. "I got no time for any human being who would do such a thing. That man is like ten pounds of shit in a five pound bag."

I was looking at Lucille and his . . . brood . . . and tallying up the number of dogs. Seven.

"Didn't Aunt Jackie say there were nine of these?"

T-Bomb cackled.

I looked at her. "What?"

"Two of 'em have already been adopted out."

I looked down at the motley pile of creatures again.

"Who in the world would take *one* of these—much less, *two?*" I asked.

T-Bomb slapped me on the arm. "Congratulations! Fritz just got himself two new playmates."

My jaw dropped. "What the hell are you talking about?" I looked down at the little shop of horrors now snoring in a heap behind our table. "I'm *not* taking two of these dogs . . ."

"Not you," T-Bomb clarified. "Grammy."

"Grammy?"

Grammy took two of Lucille's spawn? It was impossible.

"That's not possible."

"Well, apparently it is." T-Bomb drained her glass. "She picked 'em up today. Two little females."

"Oh my god. What the hell is she going to do with two of these dogs? She's eighty years old."

"So what? That don't mean she can't take care of 'em. Hell. She keeps Fritz more than you do."

Her comment bothered me, mostly because it was true. "Fritz is different."

Luanne picked up a folded sheet of paper and fanned the air in front of her face. "Not *very* different—if you get my drift." She laughed. "Maybe them females will have better digestive tracts."

I sniffed the air. "Oh, *god* . . ."

Acquiring two more dogs with righteous flatulence was *not* what I needed.

I put my head in my hands. "I need a drink."

"Well, buck up, Betty Lou." T-Bomb gestured toward something behind me. "I think your prayers are about to be answered."

I swiveled around in my seat to see Tony Gemelli approaching. He was carrying a pilsner glass and a frosty bottle of Stella Artois. When he reached our table, he set them both down in front of me.

"You look like you could use this," he said.

"Thanks." I picked up the bottle and took a sip. I didn't bother with the glass. "It looks like business is good over on your side of the bar."

He shrugged. "I can't complain." He nodded in acknowledgement to T-Bomb and Luanne. "I wish the surge in enthusiasm wasn't tied to such a tragedy." He slowly shook his head. "Nobody wants a victory at a price like that."

"Well, dern," T-Bomb chimed in. "That don't sound like somethin' an agitator would say."

He looked at her. "Agitators have hearts, too."

"I got nothin' to say about that, so I'll just say this. Ruthie's misfortune might end up bein' the wake-up call everybody at that place needed." Luanne pointed a finger at Tony. "And that don't necessarily mean that folks woke up on your side of the bed, neither."

Tony rubbed a hand across his chin. He looked like he needed a shave. "I know that too well. I've been doing this work a long time."

"You mean this ain't your first rodeo?" T-Bomb asked.

"Exactly. Although my butt sure feels like it. Aunt Jackie needs to invest in some better chairs."

T-Bomb laughed. "You wanna sit down with us for a spell? It might be fun to make all them converts over there think we're signin' up, too."

He shook his head. "I don't want to tar you ladies with that brush."

He looked at me. "I think there's already been enough guilt by association going on around here."

"Oh, hell," T-Bomb replied. "Don't you worry none about Friday's bad luck with transportation . . . one thing we all got around here is access to an endless supply of trucks." She laughed merrily.

"You know, I did notice that." Tony smiled at her.

"Where's El?" I asked. I tried to make it sound casual, but I knew I wasn't fooling anyone.

Tony dropped a hand to my shoulder and gave it a warm squeeze. "She had some meetings this evening. I expect her to show up a bit later on."

I nodded but didn't say anything.

Tony glanced toward his raucous contingent of followers. "I'd better get back . . . I don't want to lose my captive audience." He looked down at me. "I just wanted to say congratulations to you. From what I hear, it's long overdue."

I wondered how he knew about what had happened.

Who was I kidding? Everybody in Princeton probably knew about it . . . including El.

"Thanks," I said. "I guess we'll see how it goes."

He nodded. "That we will." He gave a small salute to Luanne and T-Bomb. "Ladies? Enjoy the rest of your evening."

He left our table and wandered back toward his group.

"Them Italian men sure do have the nicest derrieres," T-Bomb said in a dreamy voice.

I looked at her like she had two heads.

"What?" She pointed at Tony's retreating backside. "I know he don't play for your team, but you ain't *dead*, neither. That's some fine raw material there."

Luanne poured herself another glass of Old Style. "He's too short."

"Who cares?" T-Bomb waved a hand. "He could always use a stepladder." She warmed to her theme. "Or make two trips . . ."

"You just ain't right." Luanne fired up another Viceroy.

T-Bomb ignored her. "Hey? Friday? Are you ever gonna tell us what the heck happened today? What are you doin' on that Japanese Cougar Crew?"

Cougar Crew?

"That's a Tiger Team, you idiot," Luanne said before I had a chance to reply.

"I guess that means you already heard about what's happening?" I asked.

"No details," Luanne replied. "Just a lot of speculation."

"I stayed behind to talk with Tam Shigeta and Steve Haley," I reminded her.

She nodded. "We waited around for you, but it was obvious that you weren't gonna be comin' out any time soon, and they wanted everybody to clear out, pronto."

"How did your team react to the memo?"

"Most of 'em were just relieved to be gettin' a few days off with pay . . . everybody thought the work stop meant the plant was gonna be closin' for good."

"Same here," T-Bomb added. "And that Janice Baker told us that the air conditioning was gonna be fixed real soon."

Luanne shook her head. "Too late for Ruthie."

"Ain't that the truth?" T-Bomb sighed. "I just hate this for those children." She looked at me. "You know, that Shigeta fella went by there and spent more than an hour with her family."

I was surprised. "He did?"

Luanne nodded. "Wynona told Joe about it."

"You heard from Joe?" I asked.

"Jailissa did," she replied. "It turns out Joe was the one who called Ogata and told them the truth about what happened to Ruthie. Then when that Shigeta fella got here and started cleanin' house, he contacted Joe and told him he wasn't fired."

I hadn't heard that. "So Joe is keeping his job?"

"I don't know nothin' more about that," Luanne said. "All I know is he ain't fired."

"That Jerry Sneddin is gone, too," T-Bomb added. "That's why he dropped off them Jack-Aff puppies. Aunt Jackie said she tried to find him, but he'd already cleared outta town. You know, he never did put down any roots after he came here from that PPG plant over in Evansville. I heard he was *encouraged* to leave there, too."

"Good riddance to bad news, if you ask me." Luanne looked at me. "I wonder if Misty Ann will follow him."

I hadn't thought about that possibility. "Maybe if we're all lucky. Although, recently, I think she was a bit more interested in Don K."

"Oh, good lord." Luanne huffed. "Somebody needs to turn a garden hose on that girl."

"Don't remind me," I said.

"Oh, hell. That lapse in judgment wasn't your fault. It ain't like there were any fertile fields around there for good pickings. And that woman is a first-class Jezebel."

"Thanks, but I still feel horrible about letting that happen."

"Well, I still feel horrible about the day I ate that first bag of fried pork rinds, too. But this here body is the result I got from all them transgressions that followed, and I just need to accept it and get on with my business." She pointed a chubby finger at me. "Sometimes you just gotta pull up your queen-sized panties and keep on keepin' on."

"Unless you're Ermaline," T-Bomb quipped.

I looked fondly at both of them. They truly were my best friends. "I love you guys."

They raised their glasses in a toast. I lifted my bottle.

"Here's to Ruthie Miles," I said. "And to a better tomorrow for everyone."

We clinked rims, and drank to the future I knew we always would share.

৩ ৩ ৩

An hour later, I was making a much-needed visit to the restroom before heading out for home.

T-Bomb had already left to meet Donnie and the twins at Pizza Hut. She said it was his night to cook, so that meant they'd be eating out.

Luanne was right behind her. Jailissa was scheduled for an early-evening photo shoot at Hogg Heaven, the restaurant that took top honors at Saturday's barbecue throw down. It was her first official duty as Miss Pork Queen, and Luanne was taking the errand very seriously.

I was physically and mentally exhausted, and I knew that today was just the beginning. Tam had prepared us all for a grueling couple of weeks. Our first priority was to resolve all critical safety issues and return the plant to full operation as quickly as practical. With the problem areas we'd been able to identify today, it seemed that we'd be able to accomplish the lion's share of this work in another forty-eight to seventy-two hours. Amazingly, Ogata technicians had already managed to arrange delivery of replacement HVAC components, and their teams were working around the clock to repair the malfunctioning units.

I stared at my reflection in the mirror while I washed my hands. I looked tired, but I thought I looked less anxious than I had when I left home that morning. It was true that my eyes still resembled road maps, but they didn't look as . . . sad.

Not that I wasn't still feeling sad. I was. But it was a different kind of sadness—duller and less acute. It was more like the cold snap that shows up after Christmas and promises to hang around until the spring thaw. The kind of sadness you learn to live with and know how to dress for.

I stared at my face in the dim light and realized that the expression it wore was one I'd seen a lot of lately. In fact, I was beginning to realize that the world was full of faces that looked just like mine did right then. It led me to wonder how many other people were doing what I was now cosigned to do: grind out their days, putting one foot in front of the other until their disappointed hopes faded into vague memories.

My thoughts were about as bleak as the ancient wallpaper in that damn bathroom. I shook the excess water off my hands and grabbed a paper towel to dry them. I was at the door when it swung open and bumped into my foot.

"I'm sorry," an anxious voice called out. "Are you okay?"

I stepped back to allow the woman to enter. It was El.

We stared at each other in disbelief. Then we started talking at the same time.

"I didn't know you were here," she began.

"I'm just leaving," I said.

We stopped and stared at each other some more. An awkward silence ensued.

"How are you?" she finally asked. Her voice was soft and low.

"Okay," I lied.

She continued to stare at me.

I folded. "All right . . . not great."

"Me either." She sounded almost relieved.

We gave each other shy smiles.

"What kind of losers are we?" I asked. "We each feel better knowing that the other is miserable."

"I don't know," El said. "I think that kind of makes us winners."

"You do?"

She nodded.

"I guess I need to change my point of view."

"That's always been the case, hasn't it?"

I wanted to be sure I understood her. "Are we talking about business or pleasure?"

"Yes."

I rolled my eyes. "You really drive me crazy, you know that?"

"Isn't that supposed to be my job?"

"Which job would that be?"

She shrugged. "Take your pick. Lately, I've kind of sucked at both of them."

I was confused. "What do you mean?"

"I don't know." She lowered her gaze to the floor. "I don't think I have the heart for this work anymore."

I was surprised. "Why do you say that?"

She looked up at me. "Lots of reasons."

"That's ironic," I said.

"Why?"

"I seem to have rediscovered mine."

"You have?" She sounded intrigued.

I nodded.

"Tam Shigeta is pretty persuasive, isn't he?"

"He said he knew you."

She smiled. "We logged some hours together in Ithaca."

"So he said. He thinks you have integrity."

She raised an eyebrow. "That seems like a curious observation."

I felt mildly embarrassed. "I may have mentioned something to him about our . . . well . . . you know."

El folded her arms and regarded me with that professorial look of hers. "No. I don't think I do. Would you like to clarify what 'you know' means?"

I glanced around the bathroom like I expected someone to crawl out from under the stall.

"What's the matter?" El asked.

"Maybe we could find a better place to talk?" I suggested.

"Why? Are you afraid this bathroom isn't secure?"

"No." I sighed. "It was just a lame attempt to buy some time."

She laughed. "Sorry, Charlie. I just got here, and I can't leave yet. Tony would kill me."

"Bummer."

"So," she leaned back against the door, "you were saying?"

I scratched my ear. "I may have mentioned something . . . vaguely and in passing . . . about the fact that you and I might be . . . sort of . . . something . . . slightly more than . . . business . . . acquaintances . . . maybe."

"Maybe?"

I nodded.

She rolled her eyes. "And he kept talking with you?"

"Of course."

She shook her head in apparent disbelief.

"That surprises you?" I asked.

"No . . . if that's truly how you expressed yourself, it *astonishes* me."

"Very funny."

"I'm curious," she said.

"About what?"

"About what motivated you to tell Tam that you and I were more than business associates."

"Well, that's hardly rocket science. He already knew about Don

242

K.'s little offer. I figured it was safe to assume he also knew about what precipitated it."

"Did he?"

"I think so."

"But he still made you an offer."

It was my turn to raise an eyebrow. "How did you know he made me an offer?"

"He'd be an idiot not to—and Tam's not an idiot."

I sighed. "Well . . . I sure hope he's not an idiot, because I accepted."

El's eyes widened. "You did?"

"Yeah."

She was staring at me with an unreadable expression, but it didn't look unhappy.

"What is it?" I asked.

"I'm just . . . surprised. And gratified," she added.

"You are?"

"*Of course.* This is a wonderful outcome for you, and for Ogata."

I could think of a few other outcomes that would be even more wonderful for me than signing on to work with Tam Shigeta, but I didn't feel confident enough right then to mention any of them.

El gave me that measured look of hers—the one that made you feel like you'd just been caught cheating on an exam.

"I wish we had more time," I said. The words came out sounding so earnest, that they surprised both of us.

"I know. I'm sorry I have to work tonight. It's . . . critical right now."

I didn't reply.

El kept looking at me. "Friday Jill?"

"What?"

"You do know that our present circumstances won't stay the same?"

I nodded. "I know."

"But," she continued. "With very good luck, you and I will."

I felt a flutter of optimism. I wanted to ask her to explain what she meant, but I was afraid to do so. And that knee-jerk reaction of mine was frustrating the hell out of me.

El noticed.

"You're doing it."

"What?"

"That thing you do . . . finding ways to talk yourself out of something before you have a chance to get into it."

"I don't always do that."

El raised an eyebrow.

"I didn't do it today," I said defensively. Then I smiled. "I didn't do it with Tam or his Cougar Crew."

"His *what?*" El looked completely perplexed.

I waved a hand. "It's a long story . . . the industrial world according to T-Bomb."

"Oh . . . *thank god.* I was beginning to think I'd been out of the workplace for too long."

I laughed. "You see . . . I'm not always a chicken shit."

"For my sake, I hope not."

I took a step closer to her. She noticed.

"Is Indiana one of those states that offers refunds to people who stockpile good intentions?"

I thought about that. "Not if they're tossed into a box with glass bottles."

"Damn."

"That doesn't mean you shouldn't save them," I added.

El unfolded her arms. "I need a minute to sort through all those double negatives."

"How about I offer to take something on deposit anyway?"

"What assurance can you offer that you'll always be good for it?"

Her words seemed vaguely provocative. I decided to test them out.

I bent toward her, but stopped just short of her mouth. I hovered there, feeling the faint puff of her breath against my face. Then she closed the remaining distance between us, and I didn't feel anything except the overwhelming rush of everything I always felt when I was this close to El.

We held on to each other like shipwreck victims clutching at flotsam. El was whispering against my ear. I couldn't quite make it out.

"What are you saying?" I muttered against her neck.

"Time. I just need time."

I was going to ask what for, but I never got the chance. Someone started pounding on the outside of the door.

"El?" More pounding. "Are you still in there?"

It was Tony. El grabbed hold of my arms and squeezed them tightly before she pushed me back.

"I'm sorry," she whispered. "I have to go."

My fear and insecurity returned like a bad penny. I gave her a hopeless look.

She saw it.

"Please," she said. "I need you to trust me . . . can you do that?"

"Yes" was such a simple word. It should've been easy for me to say it. I opened my mouth to try, but before I could get it out, Tony rapped on the door again. I closed my eyes.

El dropped her hands. "I'll be right there," she called out to Tony. She gazed back at me with profound sadness. Then she composed herself and turned away.

"What the hell took you so long?" Tony asked, when she opened the door. "We've got a situation out here."

"All right, all right," El said. "Let's get it taken care of."

The door closed behind them, and I continued to stand there, alone, in the middle of the dim room.

෴ ෴ ෴

Grammy was in my kitchen when I got home. I could smell the sweet evidence of her presence before I actually saw her.

Fritz met me on the back porch, dancing around me in circles and wagging his tail. I ruffled his ears and kissed him on the head.

"Is that you, Jill?" Grammy called out.

"Yes, ma'am," I answered. I walked inside to join her. She was sliding something into the oven. "What are you cooking, and how'd I get so lucky?"

She closed the oven door and turned to me. "I heard about what happened at the plant today when I went by to see Wynona and the family. I took them one of those chicken bruschetta casseroles you like so much—that one from the Stove Top Stuffing box? And I thought you might like one, too."

I walked over and hugged her. "You always know exactly the right thing to do."

"Not always." She patted my back. "Sometimes I just get lucky."

"Will you stay and eat with me?" I hadn't even realized how hungry I was until I walked into the world of wonderful smells now swirling around my kitchen. Garlic. Fresh basil. Tomatoes. Roasted chicken. Mozzarella. And, of course, stuffing—lots and lots of stuffing.

I could hardly wait until it was ready.

"I might sit and have a bite or two with you." Grammy looked at the wall clock. "But it's not really good to eat this late—it gives you bad dreams."

"It's barely seven o'clock," I said. I didn't tell her that my dreams were likely to be bad, whether I had them on a full stomach or not.

I dropped down onto a stool. Something caught my eye. Grammy had brought one of my project chairs into the kitchen. I pulled it over to where I sat.

"Were you going to work on this?" I asked.

"No," she said. "I just wanted to check on your progress."

"You mean lack of progress, don't you?" I flicked at a stray piece of reed that projected from one of the holes. My untouched basket of caning supplies sat on a small table next to my stool. "I haven't had much opportunity lately to work on these."

"That's because you spend too much time gallivanting around."

I looked up at her. She was chopping carrots . . . probably for a salad.

"I don't gallivant." I understood what she meant, but I was pretty certain I hadn't been doing much of it.

She tsked.

"I don't," I said again.

I kept fiddling with the reed. It really needed to be removed.

Grammy walked over and handed me a shallow bowl of water that contained several lengths of damp cane.

"What's this?" I asked.

"I thought this would give you something to do while we waited for dinner to bake," she explained. She resumed chopping vegetables.

I pulled one of the damp lengths of cane from the bowl. "I don't think this is likely to relax me."

"You never know until you try," she said. "Wynona told me there were some big changes going on at the plant today."

"Yeah, you might say that." I fished my mallet and some wooden pegs out of the basket. "The Ogata transition team showed up yesterday. All the lines are shut down while they address all of the workplace safety concerns."

"Wynona said the Krylons are gone."

I nodded. "They are . . . and a lot of their senior management along with them."

"How was it that you ended up working today when they shut everything else down?" Grammy asked.

I tapped wooden pegs into the holes around the opening of the chair seat to hold down the loose pieces of damp cane.

"Tam Shigeta, the man heading up the transition team, asked me if I'd like to work with them during this period while they're changing things over."

Grammy nodded. "That's good. They should want your help with that."

"I hope so." I cut some lengths of cane and started weaving them together across the opening. "It's kind of strange to see where this day ended up. This morning, I thought I might be quitting."

Grammy paused mid-chop. "Well that wouldn't have made any sense . . . why would you want to think about doing something like that?"

I shrugged. "It just seemed easier."

"Easier than what?" she asked.

I knew that I should never have started down this road with her.

"Easier than staying on and dealing with another set of failures," I muttered.

Grammy didn't much care for that answer. She set her knife down and glared at me. I tried to concentrate on my weaving and pretend I didn't notice.

"Jillian Fryman, do not even pretend that you didn't just say that. I might be an old woman, but my hearing is just *fine*."

"I know, Grammy."

"I honestly do not know what's gotten into you lately . . . you keep burnin' your bridges before you even get to 'em." She huffed. "What in the world has you running so scared?"

"I'm not running," I protested.

"Well if this behavior of yours isn't running, I don't know what it is."

"I'm trying to *change* that, Grammy. I took the job they offered me."

"Well," she picked up her knife, "I suppose that's something." She resumed chopping.

I was relieved that I seemed to have dodged the worst of that bullet.

For a minute or two, she chopped, and I wove in relative silence.

"What about Eleanor?" she asked.

I ran the end of one of the cane strands up under my fingernail.

"Damn it!"

So much for that bullet-dodging fantasy . . .

I sucked on the end of my finger and looked at her.

"Well?" she asked.

"Well, what?" I mumbled.

"Take your finger out of your mouth."

I complied.

"Now," Grammy continued. "What are you going to do to make sure that girl stays around?"

I was dumbfounded by her question. "Grammy . . . I can't do *any-thing* to make her stay around."

"Of course you can."

"No, I can't." I fanned my sore finger. "She's a labor organizer . . . she goes where her work takes her. She'd never want to settle down in a place like this."

"Have you asked her that?"

"Of course not."

"Why not?"

I was so frustrated I was practically sputtering at her. "Because she'd never do it."

Grammy put her knife down again and faced me with her hands on her hips. "Is mind reading part of that fancy MBA program you're always workin' on? Cause if it isn't, I don't know how you can be so sure you know anything about what she'd say."

"Grammy . . ."

"I think that girl is the best thing that's ever happened to you, and I don't understand why you won't just admit it."

"I *do* admit it."

"Have you told her that?"

"Of course not."

Grammy sighed. "Didn't you just tell me that those new owners hired you to help straighten out the mess at that truck plant?"

I nodded.

"And how, exactly, do you all plan to do that?"

I sighed. "We'll study all of the processes and procedures and fix or replace the ones that don't work, or that compromise safety and productivity."

"And I suppose you'll do that by guess work?"

"Well . . . no . . ."

"You mean you won't just *assume* you know what's wrong or what's likely to happen?"

I rolled my eyes. "No, Grammy."

"Really? Even though that method seems to work just fine in the rest of your life?"

"Okay, Judge Judy . . . I get it. You've made your point."

"Are you sure about that? I'd hate for you to have to assume you know what I'm thinking."

I opened my mouth to say something else, but thought better of it. I'd already given her way too much raw material for one night.

Something else occurred to me. I grasped at it as a way to get her off this topic and get myself off the ropes in the process.

"There is *one* thing about your *thinking* I'd like to ask you about," I said.

She looked suspicious. "What's that?"

"Oh . . . let's see . . . it might involve two mongrel puppies?"

Her face softened. "Oh . . . those sweet babies. Don't you *dare* say anything mean about them."

Sweet babies?

"Grammy . . . what on earth possessed you to adopt two of the ug—" she glared at me, and I searched for another word, "*oddest* puppies in the world?"

"I had my reasons," she explained. "Besides . . . Fritz just loves them. They ran and played together all day today. When I left to come over here, little Jimmie and Eddie were curled up in a ball, sleeping on your grandpa's chair."

"Jimmie and Eddie?" I was pretty sure that T-Bomb said the puppies Grammy adopted were females.

Grammy nodded. "At first, I thought it was strange to give girl dogs boy names, but Aunt Jackie explained that it made sense, since Lucille was their daddy."

I didn't even bother to comment.

The oven timer dinged.

"Dinner's ready." Grammy walked my way. "How much progress did you make?"

I set the chair down and pushed it toward her.

Grammy took her time, checking it out from top to bottom. Then she straightened up and looked me square in the eye.

"How bad is it?" I asked.

I was prepared for her to let me down gently. Maybe pat me on the hand before showing me all the places where I needed to go back and rework my weaving. It was clear that I was just never going to get the hang of this.

Grammy continued to stand there for a few moments without speaking. Then she smiled.

"Jill, this is *perfect*."

I was shocked. I hadn't even really been paying attention to what I was doing.

"It is?" I looked down at it like I was seeing it for the first time. In fact, it did look pretty tidy.

"See what happens when you don't think things to death?"

I shook my head in amazement. Maybe she was right about some other things, too?

But not about those puppies . . .

Chapter 13

The rest of the week was a blur. I pretty much rolled out of bed at sunrise and dropped back to the mattress at sunset like a falling rock. Working with Tam's transition team was exhausting but exhilarating all at the same time. By the end of the third day, we were able to fire up the production lines and return all of Ogata's 4,485 workers to their jobs in a safer—and cooler—environment. Our FTE numbers had decreased slightly due to the early departure of many of the Krylon loyalists and hangers on. Some of them left by escort, others by attrition, and a few more at their own behest.

Two notables among the volunteers who vacated were Pauline Grubb and Misty Ann Marks. No one made much of a fuss about Misty Ann's departure, but Pauline's seemed to do more to lighten and improve the mood of employees than the unexpected boon of getting thirty minutes during their shifts to have time to eat a prepared meal. Steve Haley was able to engage an independent contractor to manage the cafeteria, but all of its employees continued to work for Ogata. Creamed corn was slated to become nothing but an unhappy memory.

I expected an immediate surge in the colon health of southern Indiana.

Other improvements were longer reaching in their effects, and would take more time to implement. But the early release of information about Ogata benefit plans, profit-sharing programs, and retirement options made for lively discussion around the vending machines, and around butt buckets in the designated outdoor smoking areas.

Even with the bevy of sweeping improvements taking shape, the mood among the rank and file remained somewhat somber. Many people continued to be more motivated by suspicion than elation. Tam even quipped that this transition was about as easy as trying to turn an ocean liner around in a swimming pool. I promised myself that I'd never mention that concept to Doc and Ermaline. At this point, an ocean liner was about the only motorized piece of equipment they were missing at their compound. And with the addition of the Esther Williams "natatorium" over there (Doc rigged an awning for their new pool from a couple of cast-off tents from Colvin's funeral home), anything was possible.

I didn't see El again after our encounter at Hoosier Daddy on Monday night. I figured that she and Tony were as busy busting their humps as we were. It was strange to think that we were both working around the clock on opposing sides, aiming for the same set of outcomes—with one important difference. And sometimes, I thought even that difference was so slight it was barely perceptible.

I wasn't exactly feeling more optimistic about our relationship odds, but I was beginning to think that maybe Grammy was right, and I should take a chance and tell El how I was feeling. I just hoped I'd get the opportunity.

On Monday night, after Grammy left, I sat for a while and stared at the chair seat I'd finally gotten right. It was incredible. When I relaxed and forgot about making mistakes, the strands of cane passed through their tiny holes in exactly the right ways . . . just like Grammy said they would. I realized that maybe I did tend to over-think things. So I decided to give in to an impulse and send El a text message. It was simple and direct. I hoped she'd understand it in the way I meant it.

I can wait.

As much as I hoped I'd hear back from her, I didn't really expect a reply. So I was stunned when, a minute later, my cell phone beeped.

You couldn't have said this at a better time.

That was it. I didn't write back, and neither did she. Now, most of a week had passed, and I still had no idea where we were.

But I knew where I was right now—at least with regard to the pile of reports I had to plow through before the stand-up team meeting we had every morning at seven o'clock.

At least I was lucky enough not to be assigned to the OSHA unit. For the last few days, I'd been looking at processes and workflow in the paint and plastics area, and my personal learning curve was pretty steep. Janice Baker was bringing me along, and she'd told me on more than one occasion that I had a real aptitude for the work.

I wanted to believe her. It was incredible how much more personally gratifying it was to be able to use some of the skill sets I'd worked so hard to acquire. This was a perk from the buyout that I never thought I'd have. I hoped that my fellow toilers would realize some of the same benefits, but only time would tell where that was concerned. It was clear that union fervor was still riding high in the aftermath of Ruthie's death, and many people plainly believed that the UAW was going to be their new path to salvation.

The pop-up meeting reminder dinged on my laptop. I had fifteen minutes until I needed to head for Tam's office—just enough time to grab another cup of coffee in the cafeteria. One of the best things about the new food service was the better coffee. They now carried Darrin's, a local micro-roaster up in Zionsville. It was wonderful, and one of the things I looked forward to every morning. To be honest, getting coffee in the cafeteria also gave me a chance to connect with my friends, who all would be heading in to begin their shifts.

I left the front offices and made my way toward the cafeteria. Luanne was heading in the same direction. I hurried to catch up with her.

"Hey there, stranger." I touched her on the back of the arm.

She jumped about two feet into the air, which, for Luanne, was a miracle of physics.

"Lord, God!" she cried out. "You scared the bejesus out of me."

"Sorry," I apologized. "Are you getting coffee?"

"Hell, no. I can't drink that stuff they serve in here now . . . it tastes like tar."

I didn't bother to disagree with her. Anyone who thought the sun rose and set in a pitcher of Old Style probably did have different standards about what passed for acceptable in a breakfast drink.

"How're things going?"

"Well, I can't say it's not a relief to have things get back to normal—even though them three days off was a nice bonus."

I nodded. We walked into the cafeteria together. It was buzzing with activity. People were loading up on caffeine and pastries before starting their shifts. Luanne ambled over to a kiosk and snagged a bear claw off a tray. I filled my travel mug with Indy Brew Espresso and joined her near the checkout line.

I thought Luanne was looking at me strangely, and I wondered what was on her mind.

"Did I spill something on my shirt?" I asked.

"No. I just thought you seemed pretty upbeat, considering the news."

"What news?" I was confused. Did something else happen in the plant that we hadn't heard about yet?

"About them agitators," she said.

We reached the register. Luanne started to fish in her front pocket for money, but I stopped her and handed the cashier a five.

"My treat," I said. "What about the agitators?"

She gave me a worried look. "They're gone. Pulled up stakes and left town."

I felt the floor beneath my feet give way. I swayed, and Luanne grabbed hold of my arm. She hauled me over to a table.

"You need to sit down," she demanded. "I shouldn't have just told you like that."

I still wasn't quite hearing her. Gone? El and Tony were gone? Just like that . . . and without saying goodbye?

How had I not heard about this?

I looked at her. "When did they leave?"

She shrugged. "Yesterday or maybe the day before? I'm not sure. Aunt Jackie told me last night."

"That's not *possible*." I sank down onto a chair. It shouldn't have been possible. "What about the vote?" I was grasping at straws. Surely the UAW wouldn't abandon its crusade just like that—without preamble or warning?

"Well, that's just it," Luanne explained. "They got enough names on them authorization cards to make the vote happen, so their work here was finished."

I was shocked. "They got to thirty percent?"

She nodded. "Maybe even more."

My heart was hammering. I set my cup down on the small table so I wouldn't drop it.

"You want to eat a bit of this?" Luanne shoved her pastry toward me. "You're lookin' a bit peaked."

"Oh, god, no." Her chocolate-covered confection was the last thing I needed. My head was swimming and my stomach was about to follow suit.

So the vote was going to happen. I wondered vaguely if Tam already knew?

But why did El and Tony leave? Somebody had to run things during their campaign phase.

"I don't get it." I looked at Luanne through a haze of hurt and confusion. "Who's going to run things for the UAW until the vote happens?"

"Honey, I don't know nothin' about how them agitators work," she said. "That Italian feller told Aunt Jackie that the Detroit folks would likely send down a different team to handle the run up to the election."

"Where did they go?"

"Who?"

"Tony and El."

"Lord if I know. I think maybe some place in Texas?" She sighed and shook her head. "Aunt Jackie said they had another hot prospect down there . . . some Mazda plant or somethin'? Hell . . . *anything* in Texas is gonna be hot this time of year. I suppose it's another one of these transplant operations."

Texas? El was in Texas? *She might as well be in Timbuktu.*

So much for my brief sojourn through the land of hope and optimism . . .

Janice Baker hurried past us, carrying her own supersized cup of coffee. She noticed me seated there and backtracked.

"Jill? Are you coming to the meeting?" She smiled and nodded at Luanne. "Hi there."

Luanne dropped a protective hand to my shoulder. "She was feelin' a bit woozy, so I told her to sit down."

I swallowed hard and nodded up at Janice, who was looking at me with concern. "I'm okay." I got to my feet. "Maybe I can catch up with you after work?" I asked Luanne.

"You know where to find me." She squeezed my arm and lowered her voice. "It ain't nothin' we can't handle, girl."

I tried to smile at her, but didn't quite succeed.

I picked up my coffee mug and headed for the front offices with Janice.

ട ട ട

Tam's stand up meeting morphed into a longer, sit-down session in the boardroom. Janice told me on our walk back to the offices that there had been some developments related to the union campaign, and that Tam needed to brief us all about what to expect. I didn't mention that I already knew what those developments were. I didn't mention, either, that my heart was fractured into more pieces than a pre-assembled Outlaw Super Duty King Cab. It was all I could do to hold myself together.

I took my seat at the table and tried to compose myself. All fourteen members of the Tiger Team were there. Seven came in with Ogata, and the rest of us had been Krylon employees. Even with my complete level of distraction, it was impossible not to think about the conversation I'd had with Don K. in this very room. Right then, it felt like that exchange had happened in another lifetime.

"Good morning, everyone." Tam entered the room and took a seat near the door. Even through my haze of misery, I noticed that he seemed pretty calm—especially considering the announcement he was about to make. But I was learning that composure was something Ogata's senior management team had in abundance. "I apologize for co-opting more of your time this morning than our scheduled ten minutes. But we have some important news to share, and some specifics related to a new initiative to discuss. I'll try to summarize where we are as quickly as possible, before we shift into a broader conversation about strategies. At that time, I'll introduce you to a couple of new additions to our corporate response team. You'll all have the opportunity to ask any questions you have, but be aware that much of this is developing in real time, so we may not be able to answer every query right out of the starting gate." He looked at each of us in turn. "All good with that?"

Everyone nodded.

"Great. Let's get started." He opened a manila folder that sat on the table in front of him. "Many of you may have heard by now that the UAW was successful in garnering authorization signatures from more than thirty percent of Krylon—now Ogata—employees."

There was a chorus of groans.

Tam held up a sheet of paper. "This is a copy of an email I received late yesterday from the NLRB Region 25 office in Indianapolis, informing me that the United Auto Workers have filed for the right to hold an election in this plant. Barring the discovery of any complications or irregularities during their investigation—which we do not expect—that election will be scheduled to take place sometime within the next thirty days."

"So what impact is that likely to have on the work we're doing now?" Janice asked.

"For all process and systems evaluations—no impact," Tam replied. "All of your work continues as planned. With regard to certain human resource initiatives, we'll want to refocus our near-term objectives and jump-start some new strategies that address immediate shortfalls in worker engagement. I'm sure that most of you are already familiar with the 'Who's On First?' routine now playing out at the Volkswagen plant in Chattanooga. People engaged in that debate are changing sides so fast it's hard to keep up with who's on what side of which issue. To put it all simply, the UAW is claiming that it has a mandate to hold union elections in the plant, and, oddly enough, Volkswagen is not opposed to that. However, a contingent of employees backed by a national Right to Work organization has filed a counter petition to stop the vote, alleging that Volkswagen has unlawfully conspired with the union."

There were some titters of laughter around the table.

Tam smiled. "To put it in the vernacular, it's a Class A clusterfuck. But there are some important takeaways for us. Volkswagen, because of its roots in the EU, is comfortable with the practice of giving workers a direct forum to discuss job-related issues—although wage and benefit discussions remain off the table. They would like to institute domestic models for these European-style works councils. But some legal experts allege that those councils are tantamount to employer-managed unions, which are a violation of U.S. Labor law. So the debates, and the battles, continue. Now, the governor of Tennessee and a U.S. Senator have upped the ante by wading into the middle of the dispute. In an effort to resolve the debacle, Volkswagen has reached out to some high-powered consultants who have expertise in bringing all warring factions to the table to find common ground."

"I'd pay big money to see Bob Corker split a Wiener Schnitzel with Bernd Osterloh," Steve Haley quipped.

"Are you kidding?" Janice added. "He'd probably ask for separate checks."

Even I had to smile at that one. I didn't know Janice had a sense of humor.

"You might get to test the truth of that, Janice. Because we've engaged the same firm to help us avoid some of the pitfalls our friends in Tennessee are having to navigate now." Tam sat back and folded his arms. "Look. Let's be blunt here. We would prefer that OTI remains a non-union shop. And, hopefully, the plans and initiatives we're putting into place will lead our workers to give us that vote of confidence when the election takes place. But we can't rest on our laurels and assume we're doing everything just right, and that our employees will give us the benefit of the doubt. We can have the best-laid plans in the world, but if they're not managed and communicated to our workers in the right ways, or if our workers are excluded from these conversations, or if we don't roll them out in a timely enough fashion, we're going to end up on the same kind of slippery slope, and our carefully crafted business model will be blown to smithereens."

No one could dispute the truth of that. We all understood that in most cases, workers who voted for unions were really voting against bad management. Once Ogata employees had a chance to compare apples to apples, they'd probably realize that their new wage and benefit packages would outstrip those offered at comparable Big Three plants.

"What happens if the union vote goes the other way?" I asked.

Tam looked at me. "Then we pay really smart people a lot of money to develop ways for us to meet their goals, while maintaining the integrity of our business operations. Ogata is committed to this endeavor." He looked around the table. "Are there any other questions before I ask our consultants to join us?"

We all exchanged glances, but remained silent.

"Okay." Tam signaled his admin. "Kevin, would you go to my office and ask our guests to join us?"

Kevin nodded and left the room.

"I'll save formal introductions until they get here," Tam said. "But while we wait, let me tell you a little bit about the two people who will lead us through this process." He referenced another document in his file folder. "One of them was deputy undersecretary of labor during the Clinton administration. During his tenure, he dealt specifically with employer-union relations, including employee participation programs and the TEAM act, the appointment of the Commission on the Future of Worker-Management Relations, and numerous other issues regarding the National Labor Relations Act. Since 1998, he has gained a solid reputation as a labor relations consultant, and has worked extensively with both organized labor and industrial clients. In the last several years, his firm has focused on issues related to foreign-owned transplants in North America, with special emphasis on automotive manufacturing. He now heads one of the most highly respected consulting firms in the United States."

Tam flipped to a second sheet of paper. "The other member of this dynamic duo may surprise you. She is an acknowledged expert in the field of U.S. labor law and industrial labor relations and comes equipped with a thorough, first-hand understanding of the policies and practices of the UAW."

UAW? What the hell . . . ?

I took an anxious look around the room.

"She has written and lectured extensively on issues of U.S. labor law, worker rights, and trends in international labor relations. She is a laureate of the prestigious New York State School of Industrial and Labor Relations, and a former associate professor at Cornell."

Jesus Christ. This can't be happening . . .

My heart was hammering, and I was sure everyone in the room could hear it.

"She comes to us highly recommended by the Chairman of Volkswagen's General and Group Works Council, who recently engaged her to consult with his company on the impasse in their Chattanooga plant."

I could hear the words he was saying, but I was having a hard time taking in their meaning. It was like he had stopped speaking English and decided to finish his introduction in Japanese.

My eyes were glued to the door. Finally, Kevin and the two consultants walked in. The innocuous-looking, white-haired man with him was a complete stranger to me. The woman wasn't.

El was dressed to the nines in a tailored, black Armani suit.

Holy shit . . .

Tam was talking again. I made an effort to pick my jaw up off the table. I couldn't take my eyes off her.

"Please welcome Arnie Erdmann and Dr. Eleanor Rzcpczinska." Tam glanced down at the sheet of paper he was still holding. "I realize that you're all meeting Arnie for the first time. But several of you may already know the good doctor here by another name."

El was wearing her glasses, but I could see the smile in her eyes after her gaze swept the room and landed on me.

"Some called her the agitator," Tam was still talking, but his voice was fading, like it was coming from a million miles away, "but I'm told that certain others among us know her better as El DeBarge."

ᥒ ᥒ ᥒ

That night after work, I sat on the front steps at Grammy's house and watched Fritz being chased around the yard by the puppies. Even though I was reluctant to admit it, Jimmie and Eddie *were* kind of

261

cute . . . in a Yoda-meets-the-Hunchback-of-Notre-Dame kind of way.

Still, I had to wonder about Grammy's sense, or lapse of sense.

But she was right about Fritz. He seemed invigorated by the energy of the two youngsters.

I was still reeling from the revelation about El. The rest of the meeting flew by in a blurry confluence of words and images. I stared at El and worked not to stare at El with equal energy. It was all too incredible to take in. It was as if I'd been given a reprieve from a terminal diagnosis. Like I'd walked into my doctor's office and heard him say, "We're so sorry, Miss Fryman. The lab mislabeled the test results. You're not going to die a horrible death, all alone in a barren land."

El wasn't gone. El was *staying*. And, for now, El was staying in Princeton . . . at Ogata.

With me.

But was she with me? That last part was the one thing I was uncertain about.

We didn't get to talk after the meeting. Tam whisked El and Arnie off to his office for a conference call with the leadership in Tokyo. I did my best to remain calm. I resisted every impulse I had to call her, to text her, to follow her, or to invent a reason to loiter around outside Tam's office until she reappeared.

I managed not to do any of those things. Barely. And she didn't do any of them, either.

So now, here I sat, ten hours later, at Grammy's house, wondering what was next.

T-Bomb and Luanne both found ways to seek me out once the news about El filtered out into the plant. It didn't take long. News at that place always did travel faster than the speed of light. No revolution in leadership or corporate culture would ever change that dynamic.

I was irrationally pleased that they both seemed happy about the news.

"I always knew things would work out," T-Bomb declared. "All it took was for you to get your thumb outta your derriere and quit actin' like a doofus."

I wasn't too sure what she meant by that doofus part, but I did have to admit that life was better when my thumb wasn't planted in my . . . derriere.

Still. There was more unsettled than settled between us. And as happy and exhilarated as I was feeling, it was hard not to be miffed at El for keeping me so in the dark. The days since Ruthie's death had been grueling for me . . . nearly torturous. I had to make a Herculean effort not to be angry at El for not reaching out to me or finding some way to let me know what was in the works.

But then . . . if I were fair, I had to admit that she *did* try. When I thought back through our earlier conversations and recalled exactly what words she said—and not the meaning my pain and disappointment grafted onto her comments—she actually *had* tried to calm my fears, without breaching any confidentiality constraints that surely prevented her from being more open about her plans.

I heard the grind of a car starter. Across the road at Doc's, Ermaline was trying to fire up the Buick. It wasn't cooperating. After five or six nagging attempts, she got out of the big car and slammed its door in disgust. She looked around the yard for some other conveyance that might accommodate her. Apparently, Doc was off somewhere in the El Camino. She took a long drag off her cigarette, and then ground the butt out on the sole of her shoe. She glanced at her watch.

Ermaline had some place to be.

Next up was an old Pontiac Catalina. The car was a shiny, sea foam green color, and had been pretty spiffy before Doc sideswiped the Lyles's Station Bridge one night on his way home from the Elks Lodge. Now the entire driver's side looked concave—like the car was trying to suck in its breath so it would fit better through narrow spaces.

Ermaline climbed in and retrieved the key from above the visor. She gave it a shot. The thing roared to life on the first crank. It shuddered and rumbled, and belched blue-black smoke into the sky. Before she pulled out, Ermaline cracked open her door and liberated three or four cats. They did not appear to be happy with the disruption or the ruckus. They fled the scene like rats deserting a sinking ship.

I was worried that Fritz and the puppies might decide to chase after the cats, but, amazingly, they sat down in a nearly perfect straight row and watched with rapt attention until Ermaline pulled out of the yard and disappeared around the bend. As soon as she was out of sight, they resumed their raucous game of tag as if nothing unusual had happened. It was clear that dogs had some inbred code of conduct that defied human understanding. Or maybe they just liked Pontiacs?

It was a toss-up.

Grammy was inside making dinner. I told her not to bother, but she insisted. When I shared the news about El with her, her reaction seemed restrained. It's not that she wasn't happy with the outcome— it was clear that she was. It was more that she was withholding comment until we had more information. And that seemed unlike her to me.

I kept checking my cell phone every few minutes in the hopes that I'd have a message from El. But as the minutes ticked by and piled up into quarter hours, half hours, and hours, I knew it wasn't looking very likely.

Grammy was cooking a pork loin with sauerkraut, and it smelled wonderful. I caught whiffs of it whenever the wind shifted and pushed the early evening air through the open doors and windows of the house. I lifted my head into the breeze and basked in the wonderful medley of smells surrounding me on the porch. They were like warm hugs.

I hoped she'd make mashed potatoes, too.

It was amazing how my appetite was returning. For weeks, I'd had little interest in anything related to food. Now I found myself thinking about things like eggplant bisque and wondering if Grammy could spare a few quarts of the German Johnson tomatoes she'd been canning.

The dogs all snapped to attention again. They heard the approaching car before I did. I figured it was probably Ermaline, coming back to retrieve something she'd forgotten. There generally wasn't much traffic out here on these county roads after six o'clock—unless it was Wednesday night, and people were headed for prayer meeting.

It wasn't Ermaline. I saw the sun glinting off something . . . purple. Bright purple. It was an odd-looking car. Small—like a motorized roller skate. A flaming *purple* roller skate. It slowed down and turned off into Grammy's driveway.

All three of the dogs went nuts and roared out to greet it. The puppies did their best to keep up with Fritz, but they had their customary difficulty getting their back ends pointed in the same direction as their front ends. Watching them was like watching one of those demolition derbies, where the cars all ran at breakneck speeds in reverse.

When the car came to a halt and its door opened, I recognized the fantastic pair of legs that appeared before the driver climbed out.

El was still wearing her power suit, and she didn't seem the least bit bothered that Fritz and the puppies were climbing all over her. I could hear her cooing and talking to each of them in her silky, low voice.

My heart was racing, and I was torn between wanting to rush out there and join in the frenzied bout of licking, or staying put on the top step and pretending to remain calm until El made her way to the house.

Forget remaining calm. I lasted about two seconds before I was off the porch and running toward the driveway.

El met me halfway.

We stood in the middle of the yard, with the dogs dancing in their ageless, wild patterns around our feet and clung to each other like beggar ticks on a wool sweater. Neither of us said anything. We just held on.

Finally, El pushed back and looked at me. Her gray eyes were shiny. "I hoped you'd be here."

I nodded. My throat was thick. "I came for dinner." I knew it sounded stupid . . . obvious. I had a hard time finding my words. They were tumbling all over themselves inside me. I couldn't latch onto the ones I really wanted because I wanted them all, in every possible combination.

El smiled, and I felt my insides melt. It was so palpable that I was tempted to look down at the ground beneath us, just to see if all of my pent up hope and longing was seeping out between my toes. This was it. This was my moment. And I knew that I would never get another one. I knew that I needed to tell her, and I knew that I needed to tell her now, while I still had the chance.

I dropped my head to her shoulder. El rested her hand on the back of my neck. Her palm felt warm and strong.

"I love you," I said.

She hugged me closer. She muttered something indistinct. It sounded like "thank god."

It didn't really matter. None of it mattered.

For once in my life, I was fully, completely, and one hundred percent present. I no longer saw my world through a glass darkly. I saw it face-to-face—in bold, brilliant, and breathtaking color. And I understood that the fullness of life that spread out before me in that single explosive moment would be enough to light my path for the rest of my days.

૭ ૭ ૭

After dinner, El and I walked together through the waning light. It was a warm evening, but cooler breezes continued to blow in from the north, and that made it feel almost fall-like. The dogs raced off ahead of us, but occasionally, they would stop and look back, just to be sure we were still following along. We didn't have any particular route in mind, although El said she wanted to visit the rhubarb patch again. I thought it was likely that Grammy's garden would always serve as our self-styled Mecca. Somehow I knew that this would be a pilgrimage we would make often, and always together.

I had been shocked to learn that Grammy knew all about El's career transition. I had no idea that all through the days leading up to Tam's big announcement, El had been spending a good deal of time with Grammy, trying to sort through the tangled web of her feelings for me, and her uncertainty about her future with the UAW. I was equally stunned to learn that El had actually been staying at Grammy's since her resignation from the union. I made that discovery when she reemerged after a so-called trip to the bathroom, dressed in shorts and one of my old, faded Salukis t-shirts. When I looked at her new ensemble in confusion, she just shrugged and smiled.

"She's staying in your room," Grammy explained. "I told her to help herself to any of those old work clothes you keep here."

On our walk, El explained that Arnie Erdmann's firm had been pursuing her for some time. She had already concluded that for the American labor movement to survive, it would have to embrace innovative approaches. That meant thinking outside the UAW box, especially with regard to the new paradigms presented by transplant manufacturers.

Nearly as surprising was my discovery that the puppies weren't Grammy's, they were El's. She said that adopting them was the first thing she did when she made her decision to leave the UAW.

"I wanted to put down roots, and they seemed like the best way for me to start," she said.

As we meandered along the path that led to the garden, and I watched her "girls" lope ahead of us in their curious, non-linear patterns, I asked her about their names.

"I get the whole giving them boy's names as an homage to Lucille thing," I said. "But why Jimmie and Eddie?"

She had her arm linked through mine, and she tugged me closer as we continued along the path beside the garage.

"My father's name was James Edward. His memory is very important to me—it still drives everything I do in my work life. I guess I wanted him to have a connection to my personal life, too." She looked up at me and smiled. "That's a new thing for me . . . a personal life. I know now that I deserve to have one."

Her simple explanation filled me with happiness.

"We both do."

"I need to figure out a way to get my car and the rest of my things here from Buffalo."

"Oh," I teased. "That purple, side-loading dish washer you rolled up in isn't your car?"

She bumped my side. "Nice try. It was the only thing they had at Enterprise when I turned in the SUV." She looked at me. "Beggars can't be choosers."

"You know I'll help you move," I said. Then I grinned at her. "We can use Grammy's pickup."

"Great idea," she replied. "You can ride in the back . . . you already have the outfit for it."

"As charming as I'd look, those aren't exactly moving clothes."

"True," she said. We walked on for a bit. "I also need to find a place to live."

I was tempted to tell her she could just stay with me. I nearly said it, too. I think El realized that I was biting something back.

"I can't move in with you," she said.

Even though I knew she was right, I still felt disappointed. "Why not?"

"Because we're not teenagers," she replied. "I want us to take our time and do this right."

"I want that, too."

"Besides," she said, "I'm pretty sure we're both aware that we'll be spending all of our time together when I'm not in Tennessee. It's better for us to at least have the illusion of maturity."

I smiled. But the mention of her travel schedule made me think about something else.

"You don't seriously expect me to take care of those two spawns of Cerberus, do you?"

She looked offended. "Of course I do."

"It'll cost you."

She raised an eyebrow. "Oh, really?"

I nodded.

"What did you have in mind?"

I shrugged. "I'm not sure yet . . . but I think you'll probably enjoy it."

"Well, that sounds like a win-win proposition to me." She gave me one of her professorial looks. "Maybe we have this whole thing backwards?"

"What do you mean?"

"Maybe you should be the high-powered negotiator and I should be the one who gets paid to play with Legos?"

"Legos?"

She looked up at me. "Isn't that what you do all day now? Make little models of toy assembly lines?"

I rolled my eyes. "Yes. Exactly. That's precisely what I do all day."

We rounded a corner and entered Grammy's garden. The midsummer heat had taken its toll on the plants, but they were still loaded with fruit. Cucumbers, tomatoes, and bright yellow peppers glowed in the fading, blue and white light. Thick vines loaded with butternut squash sagged toward the ground.

"The green ones are my favorites," I added.

El gave me a confused look. "Excuse me?"

"Legos," I said. "I'm partial to the green ones."

She socked me on the arm. "Nut job."

Fritz and the puppies came crashing through a row of pole beans.

"Do they ever settle down?" I asked.

"Not really."

"Great."

El leaned into me. We stopped and watched the dogs disappear behind a cluster of maple trees. The sun was nearly down now, and the lightning bugs were starting to flit about in search of . . . whatever it was lightning bugs did.

I gestured toward a row of sunflowers, where we could see them beginning to light up the night sky.

"What do you suppose they're doing?" I asked.

"The lightning bugs?"

I nodded.

"They're searching for their mates," she said.

I gazed at them for a minute, aware that El was watching me. I met her eyes and bent toward her, she met me halfway.

We were getting pretty good at that maneuver.

After we separated, I took hold of her hand and we walked on, into the soft Hoosier night.

About the Authors

ANN McMAN is the author of seven novels and two short story collections. She is a recipient of the Alice B. Lavender Certificate for Outstanding Debut Novel, and a four-time winner of the Golden Crown Literary Award. An award-winning graphic designer, she resides in Winston-Salem, North Carolina.

SALEM WEST is the publisher of Bywater Books and a Trustee of Lambda Literary. Previously, she was the voice of The Rainbow Reader, a highly regarded review blog that combined original essays with insightful analyses of all genres of LGBT literature. She lives in Winston-Salem, North Carolina with her wife, Ann McMan.

Acknowledgments

The exercise of producing this book presents a better example of collective bargaining than the story it purports to tell. And that's one point of view we can all agree upon.

We extend special thanks to the 6,721 residents of Edwards County, Illinois, who informed the telling of this story, which also is their story. We borrowed liberally from an endless supply of anecdotes and a rich lexicon of family names. To all of the unsung heroes now going about their quiet lives in the lower Midwest, this Old Style's for you.

Thanks also are due to the real life "agitators" we have known and loved. We each are mindful of the formative experiences we had logging countless hours on production lines in manufacturing plants—and are grateful for the important lessons we learned. Fond recollections of the people we knew and worked with found a home on nearly every page of this book.

We tip our hats to the real life T-Bomb, Terri Smith. Thanks for your many years of friendship, truth-telling, and unwavering support. You're a one in a lifetime pal. Now read this damn book.

We are insanely proud of Barrett, Sandra, Bev, Baxter, and the rest of our extended family at BInk, and the synergy of talent, verve, and psychosis we exude—especially at IHOP, when we're trying to split a check. TOTS.

Warm hugs, special thanks, and a top-secret handshake go to our FOWH Lodge Sister, Barista. You do honor to the headgear.

Maddie, Gracie, and Lucy? The public works project you undertook to excavate two-thirds of the back yard while our attentions were diverted stands as a testament to canine engineering. Thank you for finding so many creative ways to amuse yourselves during the months it took for us to write this book. We also extend special thanks to Cooper, the late, obese Jack Russell terrier who provided the inspiration for Aunt Jackie's dog, Lucille.

To Marianne K. Martin and Kelly Smith, thank you for giving our little heartland romance a brand new home that is warm and loving.

Last, but never least, is the sincere debt of gratitude we owe to our wonderful community of readers. Your unflagging warmth, support, and encouragement give value and meaning to everything we do.

—Ann McMan and Salem West

Backcast

"*Backcast* is a memorable story about the unbreakable strength and resilience of women. Skillfully executed, the story is easy to become emotionally invested in, with characters that are guaranteed to entertain and enthrall." —*Lambda Literary Review*

"I love Ann McMan."
—Dorothy Allison, author of *Bastard Out of Carolina*

Backcast by Ann McMan
Print 978-1-61294-063-2
Ebook 978-1-61294-064-9

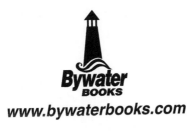

www.bywaterbooks.com

Bywater
BOOKS

At Bywater Books we love good books about lesbians just like you do, and we're committed to bringing the best of contemporary lesbian writing to our avid readers. Our editorial team is dedicated to finding and developing outstanding writers who create books you won't want to put down.

We sponsor the Bywater Prize for Fiction to help with this quest. Each prize winner receives $1,000 and publication of their novel. We have already discovered amazing writers like Jill Malone, Sally Bellerose, and Hilary Sloin through the Bywater Prize. Which exciting new writer will we find next?

For more information about Bywater Books and the annual Bywater Prize for Fiction, please visit our website.

www.bywaterbooks.com

CPSIA information can be obtained
at www.ICGtesting.com
Printed in the USA
LVHW092357300519
619666LV00005BA/6/P